Chloe's Song

LESLIE THOMAS

Chloe's Song

ARROW

Published in the United Kingdom in 1998 by Arrow Books

1 3 5 7 9 10 8 6 4 2

The extracts from 'You Make Me Feel Brand New' by Thom Bell and Linda Creed are quoted by permission from International Music Publications Ltd.

Copyright © Leslie Thomas 1997

First published in the United Kingdom in 1997 by William Heinemann

Arrow Books Limited
Random House UK Limited
20 Vauxhall Bridge Road, London, SW1V 2SA

Random House Australia (Pty) Limited
20 Alfred Street, Milsons Point, Sydney,
New South Wales 2061, Australia

Random House New Zealand Limited
18 Poland Road, Glenfield
Auckland 10, New Zealand

Random House South Africa (Pty) Limited
Endulini, 5a Jubilee Road,
Parktown 2193, South Africa

Random House UK Limited Reg. No. 954009

A CIP catalogue record for this book is available from the British Library

Papers used by Random House UK Limited are natural, recyclable products made from wood grown in sustainable forests. The manufacturing processes conform to the environmental regulations of the country of origin.

Typeset by Deltatype Limited, Birkenhead, Merseyside
Printed and bound in Great Britain by
Mackay's of Chatham plc, Chatham, Kent

ISBN 0 7493 2274 8

For Denis and Liz Riley
With my thanks for their generosity – again

You ... You make me feel brand new ...

The Stylistics (1974)

1

Early spring, Saturday, Salisbury market day and, as it happened, Grand National Day too: they drove me from the overnight police station cell to the magistrates' court. For some reason it was not until they slammed the doors of the van, leaving me like a dog in a cage, that the seriousness of my position really dawned on me. It was not every day they had a decent housekeeper of forty-four on a murder charge.

The young policemen who slammed the door on me was genuinely apologetic. 'You *can't* shut these doors softly, love,' he said. 'They're only meant for slamming.'

'Why is that?'

Apparently no one had asked before. 'Something to do with authority, I suppose,' he said. 'Showing the prisoner who's boss.' I had plenty of time to get used to resounding doors.

As we travelled they told me cheerfully that the van was different from the normal transport I would be using to and from prison. 'When you come up, when you're on remand,' said the boyish constable (he was younger than my son Donny would be now, if only I knew where he was), 'when you go backwards and forwards to court they use prison vans. They're privatised.'

He was sitting in one of four rows of upright seats in the front, a cage of thick wire between us so that we had to peer at each other through the metal squares. Although the others were empty I could imagine them full of rather comic Gilbert-and-Sullivan-type policemen sitting straight with their truncheons held vertically and singing in chorus. 'All prison transfers are done by a security company,' contributed the driver, a woman constable with a round, shiny face. 'We don't get the time, do we, Phil.'

Phil said, no, Patty, they didn't. I not only felt apprehensive now, I felt foolish. They normally used the van, they said, for picking up drunks and druggies around the town. The inner cage surrounded me, squares of toughened wire and beyond this a smoked window so that I could see out but the people in the streets and the market could not see in. I was grateful it was not the other way around.

'Funny time to have a court,' chatted Phil.

'Very rare, Saturday afternoon,' called back Patty cheerily. 'They'd only do it for a murder.'

Phil looked pained. 'Something important,' he amended. 'We might have to wait until they can rustle up some magistrates.'

Through the smoked glass window I saw that we were outside Cooper's cake shop where I had once worked on Saturdays when I was still young. A boy was putting a tray of pastries in the window and I thought it might have been one of the sons. And to think I could have been his mother. Then I saw two women I had known when they were girls, gossiping and tugging their children towards Woolworth's while I was on my way to prison.

We went alongside the market. It was a bright day and all the colours of the stalls and the goods they sold seemed lit up even through the smoked glass. My heart was full because I had killed the one man in my life I had loved dearly.

The police van turned in to the old Guildhall, parking alongside the market clutter. When I realised I looked nervously through the special window. I did not want anyone I knew to see me like this. My life was bad enough as it was.

'What d'you fancy for the National?' asked Phil as he opened the clanging rear door. I felt sure people would hear it and turn to look. It seemed important for Phil to keep up a conversation, perhaps he needed assurance.

The driver came around to the back of the vehicle. 'I've got Tearaway in the sweep,' she said.

'I didn't get a horse,' said Phil. 'Fifty pence down the drain.'

He regarded me crouched in the cage. There was only just height enough to sit.

'Do you want a blanket, Chloe?' he asked with that strange and immediate familiarity policemen seem to have with their prisoners.

I thought he had seen me shivering. 'I'm not cold,' I said. I was just nervous.

'I mean for over your head,' he said. 'Stop people gawping at you.'

'Will they?'

'If you get a move on, they won't,' he said. The driver had gone through a door at the side of the Guildhall and come out again with a big, genial-looking man. 'They haven't rumbled yet,' continued Phil giving a quick, almost guilty glance around. 'But once they do they'll all be trotting over to take a look at you, nosey sods.'

'I'm the court officer,' said the friendly-looking man. 'Let's get you inside.'

We made the few yards to the side door swiftly with

3

the three of them shielding me but even then I was conscious of a rush of onlookers apparently trying to race us to the entrance. Some of them were dragging children, urging them forward.

I held my face in my hands as we dashed inside and the door was closed firmly behind us. 'Nosey,' repeated Phil. 'Can't understand it myself.' He took a moment to study me. 'You're only a person,' he said. 'After all.'

The court officer now introduced himself with a touch of formality. His name was Mr Victor. He knew who I was but I told him my name anyway. 'We'll have to wait for the magistrates,' he said. 'It's a bit unusual. Saturday is difficult, people have to be got from home.'

'Next time I kill anyone I'll make sure it's Monday,' I said.

I could feel tears on my cheeks although I had not realised I was crying. Mr Victor patted my arm. 'It won't be so bad,' he said. 'I'll take you up to the prisoners' room and get you a cup of tea.'

Phil was going to stay with me, to make sure I did not make a run for it, I suppose. They said Patty could stay with me if I preferred, although she was due to go off-duty. I said it did not matter and Patty said she would be going back to sign off. As she went she fumbled in her pocket and took out a slip of paper. She glanced unsurely at Mr Victor and said: 'I hope this is in order.'

Mr Victor asked her what it was.

'My Grand National sweepstake ticket. Hundred quid for first,' she said. She held it towards me adding: 'Tearaway,' and looked at the clock on the wall. 'They'll be off in half an hour.' Again she glanced at Mr Victor. 'It's just for the coppers and the court staff.'

Mr Victor said he knew. Patty held the ticket towards me and repeated: 'Tearaway.' I did not know what to say

4

to her. Slowly my hand went out and I took the slip. Mr Victor said: 'Second favourite.'

He held the inner door open. When the policewoman went out of the street exit I caught the frightening sight of the pressing people outside. Their voices rose. 'Is she in there?' some women shouted. A man who sounded drunk called: 'Murderer.'

Mr Victor led me through the inner door and up some echoing steps. There was a leaded window and the sounds of the crowd outside came through the glass. Phil followed me saying: 'I don't understand people.'

We went into a cheerless room with a scratched table and three chairs. Phil and I sat down and Mr Victor went out and came back with a cup of tea for me. 'I can only find one cup,' he said to Phil. 'It's Saturday. They've locked the cupboards.'

'You have to these days,' said Phil. 'Even in here.'

There came a polite knock on the door and Mr Victor opened it. 'Ah, Mr Spelling,' he said. 'You made it.'

'I had to nip over to the golf club on my way and cancel this afternoon's game,' said the man who walked in. He was spare, bespectacled and studious-looking; my solicitor. I had liked him the first moment we had met, when I was charged at the police station that morning.

He smiled at me as though I had won a prize instead of being under arrest. Mr Victor and Phil left the room together. 'In time for the off,' said Phil. He turned back and gave me a small wave. 'See you later, Chloe.'

'Everybody's so nice,' I said.

'They are when you're in trouble,' said Mr Spelling. 'And I'm in trouble.'

'I'm afraid so. How much, we shall have to see.'

'Sorry about your golf.'

He grinned and patted my arm as Mr Victor had

5

done. 'Major Tully was all set to watch the National. He's the chairman of the magistrates. He told me as we came in. He's just waiting for Mrs Rose now.'

'He won't be pleased with me.'

'It doesn't matter if he isn't, it's only a remand.' He frowned over his glasses. 'There won't be any question of bail, I'm afraid.'

'I didn't think there would be,' I said. I regarded him hopelessly. 'I'll have to go into prison.'

'It will be in the special wing. The remand wing. It's not too uncomfortable there.'

'How long will it be?'

'A few weeks, I'm afraid. In the meantime, we'll have to discuss how you intend to plead.'

'It wasn't murder.'

'Right. We'll have a lot of long chats about it in the future. But while we're waiting for Mrs Rose would you mind repeating your story – just tell me again what happened.'

Mrs Rose was carrying a shopping basket full of fruit and vegetables from the market when she arrived in the court. She put the basket down beside her as she sat on the high wooden stage alongside a miffed-looking man who I took to be Major Tully. They sat high, almost perched, in the corner of the room. Everywhere was dark wood; there was only a handful of people in there when I stood in the dock. It still seemed unreal. There was a clerk, a young woman, sitting at the desk below the magistrates. Mr Spelling sat with his back to me and along from him there was a young man looking uncomfortable in a stiff suit. A policeman in uniform who I could not remember clearly but had apparently arrested me was talking to a sad-faced man, Detective Sergeant Ron Brown.

Mr Victor suddenly appeared alongside me.

'There are members of the public outside, your Worships,' he said to the magistrates. 'We do not have our normal ushers today.'

'We'll have to let them in though, won't we?' said Major Tully looking disgruntled.

'Yes, sir.'

'Let them in then. Only as many as you can handle. Any noise and disturbance and they're out.'

'Yes, sir, I understand.'

He went to the back of the court and the door squeaked. Even though he closed it behind him I could hear his sternly raised voice. 'It's only a remand,' grumbled Major Tully. He looked at his watch irritably. 'I don't understand them.'

'They want to gawp,' said Mrs Rose.

I stood motionless with my back to the door as I heard them come in. They were mostly women, straight from the market by the sound of the shopping bags. Mrs Rose said something quickly to the other magistrate and he glared at the back of the room. 'Take that dog out!' he demanded. 'This isn't Crufts.' Mrs Rose motioned me to sit down. I did so gladly. It meant there was less of me for them to see.

'I want complete silence,' said the chairman threateningly. 'Or I'll clear the public seats. Understand?'

Scattered women's meek voices said: 'Yes.'

'Stand, please,' said the clerk to me. Several people behind me, apparently misunderstanding, stood too. 'Not you,' snarled Major Tully. 'Sit down.'

The clerk read out my name and address and asked me if they were correct. I said they were although I knew that I would never live in that house again. Then the charge against me was read out. It was like someone

7

reciting in a dream. I felt I wanted to cover my ears. I *knew* what had happened; I did not need to hear it again.

The man in the awkward-looking suit stood and said that the prosecution was asking for a remand in custody. Mr Spelling tried his best but it was no good applying for bail even if I promised not to run away to the Bahamas. I no longer had a fixed abode. I was remanded in custody for seven days. Detective Ron Brown looked at me and nodded as if to acknowledge that he would see me again. Without looking at the spectators I followed Mr Victor from the court.

'Tearaway came second,' he whispered. 'You still win fifty quid.'

2

My life was once more in fragments when on that rainy day two years before I went down on the train to meet Sir Benedict and Lady Annabel for the first time. Fragments, and what is more I knew exactly the *number*, for they were in the plastic holdall which was my only luggage. Never was a holdall more aptly named because in it was everything I had left of my forty-two years of life.

It contained a single decent change of underwear, a pair of tights, more ladders than tights and a Mickey Mouse hairbrush which was, in the absence of anything else, my most prized belonging and certainly my oldest; there was also a toothbrush, a pack of playing cards and an address book recording the names of people I hoped I would never see again – a catalogue of catastrophe. There was also a collection of small pebbles in a linen bag to remind me of my son Donny who had vanished when he was eighteen. They were wordless messages from remote places. I could tell only by the smudgy postmarks because there was never a word nor an address. The latest had been sent from Cox's Bazar which, if you look it up as I did the same day in the public library, is in the Bay of Bengal. Each pebble is about the same size and shape, like a Smartie, and the colours and tints are only varied a little. I suppose he started sending pebbles because you can find them anywhere; they arrived from

Australia, New Guinea, Russia, a change of seashore every time, just to tell me he was still alive, always supposing I was also still alive.

That was about it as far as the contents of my bag, the contents of my life so far, were concerned. My finances were down to a few coins. If I did not get the job, if they turned me away, then I would have no money even to *go* away. It was a risk I had to take.

I have always tried to do things for the best – if not always the wisest – reasons, but how I came to be in this state on that April morning is a story which I can scarcely believe myself. One more slap in the face, another half a step down, another stumble, and I doubt I could have got up again. Half of my problem was trying to do things for the best, which is a proven poor policy. Men, naturally, were the villains of most of it, a whole rogues' gallery of them. After my latest débâcle in London (which I shall not even bother to describe) I never wanted to look at, let alone speak to, another man in my life. At Waterloo station I even dodged from perspex window to perspex window to buy my ticket until I found one that framed a female face, a face I could trust.

Then, of all things, a young clergyman got on the train and sat on the opposite side of the aisle, thin and with his neck poking from his vicar's collar like a snake coming out of a basket. He struggled with a heavy, old suitcase, almost wrestling with it. I found myself moving to help him but then realised what I was doing and drew back. Once he had got his luggage aboard he puffed: 'This *is* the Salisbury train, isn't it?' And I briskly answered: 'It might be for all I know,' before getting up and moving to a more distant seat. Behind my back I felt his upset face. 'So sorry,' he said.

Once the train started off through the greying rain I

began to feel safer and better. I could not afford, for a number of reasons, to stay in London any longer than could be avoided, and every sway and clatter took me further away. With my finger I began tracing the splashes of rain sliding down the window and feeling it was good that I was returning to a part of the country I knew so well. My father had shot himself on Salisbury Plain and I had lots of early memories of Wiltshire.

Certain that the position advertised in the paper would have been filled a hundred times, I had telephoned Canon's House, reversing the charges and lying about not being able to change a twenty-pound note. 'Housekeeper required: county couple,' it had said. 'References essential.' The references, as I was rehearsed to tell them, had been left on the train and I might even ring up to see if they had been found. I had to become that housekeeper to this county couple. There was nowhere else.

By the time we reached Hampshire the rain had drawn away like a gauze curtain and the April sun really dazzled on the fields, new and so green they hurt the eyes. I heard the young clergyman begin to sing softly a few seats away (there were few other passengers on the train) and I felt ashamed I had been so brusque with him.

He stopped, then started again. It was a hymn of sorts that he sang as though very privately, to himself, like a musical mumble. I stood up, just as softly, and tottered the few steps down the centre until I reached where he was sitting. His neck was so thin and the rim of his clergy collar so wide that I found I was looking right down into it, like a hole. 'I'm sorry I was so rude,' I said. 'I get fed up with people sometimes.'

He had been so engrossed in his secret song that he had not heard my approach. His neck straightened. 'Oh,' was all he said, half-rising and then standing up entirely.

He was extremely tall: long and narrow as a post, but with a nice smile which curled around his thin face. 'Don't apologise. Do sit down.' Primly as I could I sat opposite him. He continued to smile as he took me in, then he sighed. 'I'm afraid I feel the same for much of the time,' he said. 'Mankind is far from kind.'

'Not even to you?'

'Especially not to me.' He seemed relieved to unburden himself; perhaps he had been waiting for someone he could tell. 'I'm afraid I'm fleeing from London.'

'Me too.'

'I could not stand another moment of humiliation.' He ignored the possibility of my sad story, *my* need to tell it, so anxious was he to relate his own. 'I have been used, thoroughly *used*,' he said. 'I was acting curate in a difficult parish. And difficult it most certainly was. Laughed at me openly they did, even the children who occasionally attended at Sunday school. Because I am on the slim side. Laughed.'

'That's not nice.'

'And they used me like a drudge. You know, part of the clergy's work these days is to go around like some social services nanny and try to sort out some of the horrendous problems these people have. And believe me, they have.'

'I know.'

'But the swines would wait for me to call and get me to do the washing-up, or weeding or hoovering or seeing to their gran. I was like some sort of religious serf.' He leaned forward, his chin blue and pink. 'Do you know, they would send for me and I would go hoping to impart some sort of spiritual help and I would end up changing the nappy on some wet and weeping baby while they went off to the damned pub. I simply couldn't take any more.' His anguish abated a little. 'I'm going to Salisbury where, presumably, some of the people believe in God.'

'I expect they do,' I was glad to contribute at last. 'The bishop must.'

'You know the cathedral then.'

'Oh, yes. Of course. I've been inside a few times. I had a terrible accident there once with a duck.'

It was true and I told him. When my father's regiment – well, *not* my father's *regiment* as the normal expression is, because he was not in command or anything, indeed there were times when he was scarcely in command of himself – when they were being sent overseas there was a showy parade and a service in Salisbury Cathedral. Everybody had to go, wives, children, everyone. I was about twelve and I was standing there singing and chanting when a brown duck appeared from behind the altar and tore through the air right up the middle of the cathedral, up the nave. It zoomed above the congregation, twenty feet up, neck out, flapping and flying like mad, and then turned and came back again. And on the return run it let go, shitting right on my head. It was like a blob of warm paint. There was a commotion because security was tight and they thought something had happened. They had to get me out to clean me up. Duck crap reeks. I did not know whether to laugh or cry but my father laughed all the way home and my mother said it ought to bring me good luck.

'And did it?' asked the young priest.

'Not a lot,' I said.

I was born into the army. My earliest recollections are the blaring of the bugle; I learned to count by marching boots. Until I was three or four years of age I believed that all men wore khaki and often I was frightened by sergeants shouting on the parade-ground because I wondered why they were so angry. I still have a fear of shouting men.

My father, William Smith, had struggled to the rank of captain. He was, by his own sad admission, an undistinguished and, for much of his life, reluctant soldier. When he had started his heavier drinking he would weep and say: 'My only claim to fame is that I've got an illustrious name.' He would look around for anyone who dared to doubt him, then sob: 'William Smith founded the Boys' Brigade.'

When I grew older and thoughtfully looked at photographs of him, he reminded me of one of those dusty, dead-eyed officers in the First World War who had spent weeks in the trenches – except he had never been near a trench. 'His disappointment,' my mother Rosa used to say to people as she stored the photographs carefully away, 'was that he never got established in the band. He got in it but he was soon out again. His heart was set on being a drum major.'

By the time of the incident with the duck in the cathedral he had settled, beaten, into the life of a desk soldier; the Royal Army Pay Corps had claimed him for its own. He became a drunk, a thief and eventually a suicide, but he was a lovely father: crumpled, defeated, but able to play the piano with considerable style. His talent he left to me and it has often stood me in good stead. Somewhere there is always a piano waiting for a player.

My mother loved him as I did, with an understanding sorrow and forgiveness; she even forgave his end. 'In the band,' she would say to those who might not already have heard it, and quite a few who had, 'he was a fine bombardon player, the finest. That's a tuba you know.

The Director of Music had earmarked him.' Her eyes would mist. 'But he sometimes needed a drink for his confidence.'

He had one too many before the Sovereign's Birthday parade. The companies and battalions were drawn up, the fine day reflected in the vividly polished instruments and there was swanky drill. Even now I can hear my mother croaking a warning as she saw her husband veering off from his band, still pumping away at his tuba, his eyes closed, unaware that he was capering across a parade-ground lined with spectators, some quite important. He staggered a long, indirect course, a zigzag, and ended in a heap on the distant hardness of the parade-ground with his tuba held to his stomach, flashing in the sun like a signal for help. There was even a picture in one of the newspapers showing the whole procession in the foreground, and all the important people on their platforms peering out from under their caps and bonnets at the crumpled pile on the distant side of the square.

At his court martial (his *first* court martial, that is) he conjured up what my mother thought was a brilliant defence: that the sun shining and moving in the brass of his instrument as he marched had at first blinded and then mesmerised him. An army doctor admitted, although doubtfully, that this was possible and my father was acquitted. But he never played in the band again and all his dreams died that day. Eventually he was posted and commissioned in the Pay Corps because the fingers that had been so adept on the valves of the tuba took easily to the adding machines he despised.

Rosa loved him hopelessly and he loved her; I remember the blushing pleasure of witnessing their domestic embraces. While he remained thin and angular, although an office stoop crept in later (he blamed it on

15

low ceilings), she grew more round and pink every year. He did not appear to notice. Even when she went to visit him in the military prison, after his major attempt at defrauding the army, the pair of them used to laugh in the visitors' room, one each side of the grille. The men in charge said hardly anyone ever laughed like that in there.

It was in Folkestone that they first met, when he was playing in a military band at a dance. She sat, slim and shy by all accounts, and he saw her and somehow contrived to get off the bandstand and take her for a dance. They often recalled that coastal summer night, with all the drill hall windows open and people foxtrotting or doing the palais glide. They had danced to a tune called 'Chloe' (sometimes they still play it on the radio: 'Through the hush of night, I gotta know where you are' or something like that) and that's how I got my name. I was more fortunate than my younger brother, whose first name was Mortimer, after a famous trumpeter, his second Kneller, after the Royal Military School of Music at Kneller Hall, outside London. He was always called Kneller in the family and at school (although he later became known as Nelly).

When they were newly married in the early 1950s our parents lived in army married quarters – more like an iron hutch – and over the years they rarely had anywhere decent to call their home. Hers was the lot of the army wife, setting up house, getting things together, replacing curtains, bits of furniture and ornaments and then being ordered to move on, selling various possessions including some of my early toys and Kneller's bicycle. It was the disposing of my brother's bike that, I still believe, had a deep effect on his later sexuality. He often said how he hated my father after that, although it may just have been a convenient excuse. He never told us.

When I was growing up we moved every eighteen months or so. My father would come home and say: 'We've been posted.' My mother would sit like a big, nice mouse, then sigh and get out the boxes and tea chests and they would begin to sort out the belongings which would have to be sold. Around army towns there are always second-hand shops loaded with lamps and settees and stools and kitchen stuff, junk from abroad, old records and scruffy paperbacks. Once we returned to a second posting at Aldershot after being away for two years and found some of our household things still in the shop, so we bought them back; it was as if our home had been waiting for us.

The foremost thing my father did every time we found ourselves in a new place was to get a piano. We had a succession of pianos, once even a grand, scratched and tinny though it was, which took up most of the living space of our quarters in Singapore, one leg propped up by a biscuit tin full of earth. It had been left behind by a naval family and my father bargained with them up until the very moment they were leaving for home. He was very proud of it and he was a fine player, dashing sometimes, dainty at others, picking out an old melody or some little classic with great delicacy even though three of the keys only clunked. The quarters in Singapore were more expansive than usual (we even had an Indian amah). Even so the piano was half in, half out of the main room, jutting onto a verandah. There was a leak in the verandah roof and the water dripped onto middle C sometimes making it sound in the night like a one-fingered ghost. The army always took a long time to get around to maintenance and in the end my father used to cover the piano with his gas cape.

Wherever we were serving we used to have some

grand times around whichever piano we had at the time – the instrument in residence, as my mother called it. My father taught me to play and I took my lessons seriously. Kneller liked to pluck the harp and he had a sure and gentle touch. My mother trilled rather than sang and was clever with the castanets. Sometimes I would come home from the army school with the other children, keeping in the cool places below the trees as we walked up the humid hill, and hear the nearing sound of our piano. I knew then that my father had managed to escape his stifling office and had come home early. I would run up the white road, jump the monsoon ditches and hurry in to sit beside him and join him in a duet. Sometimes, even now, when I think of him, my second-hand Chopin, it makes me want to cry.

3

The thin young priest on the train had listened atten-
tively. Now a certain hesitancy overcame him. 'I suppose
we should introduce ourselves,' he mumbled peering
down at his knees pointing sharp and shiny through his
trousers. A narrow arm slithered from his sleeve, a
veined, pinkish hand on its end. 'My name is Ivor
Popple.' His sigh creaked again. 'You can imagine what
those London people made of that, can't you. *Popple.* My
mother lives in Salisbury, in the cathedral close. I am
going there.'

'I am Chloe Smith,' I said. His despondency engulfed
him again and it seemed he had almost forgotten what
we were doing. 'I am so sorry. How do you do.'

His eyes went to the travelling fields and then returned:
'I don't know what I shall do.'

'Aren't you going to be a vicar?'

When he smiled, even sadly, he looked surprisingly
nice. Fattened up, he could have been presentable. 'It's
not as easy as that.' The bones in his shoulders shrugged.
'I've no prospects in that direction. No, I'm going to
write. I have made the decision. Write. Providing I can
live on pennies my mother will provide a roof. She never
thought I was tough enough – rough enough, as she used
to put it – for the Church. Maybe I can get something to

keep body and soul together, guiding people in the cathedral perhaps.'

'I'm going for a job,' I told him. It was my turn now. 'I haven't got anything. I'm hoping to get a job as housekeeper to a couple, Sir Benedict and Lady Bowling. They live in Canon's House.'

'Yes, yes, I know them,' he replied in his mild way. 'At least my mother knows them. I've met them a few times. He seems quite nice but batty, but she's a nasty old piece. Even when I was a small boy and we were invited to their house she used to *shout* at me. Imagine *that*. In front of my parents, too, and other people. She accused me of kicking her rabbits.'

I said doggedly: 'Whatever happens I've got to get this position – I have nowhere else to go.' He shook his head as if he had heard enough misfortunes and did not want to hear any more. We sat there saying nothing, looking at the shiny wet fields and damp cattle. 'Well,' I said. 'I'll leave you in peace. I was just sorry I was rude, that's all.'

'Thank you,' he said. 'Bless you for speaking to me.'

A little embarrassed, I held out my hand and we limply shook hands again. He rose with me. He was very tall, almost to the luggage rack. 'Best of luck,' I said. 'Ivor.'

'And to you, Chloe.'

Retreating to my original seat I sat viewing the dull passing scene. Some allotments went by the window, and then some more, ordered oblongs, almost black earth with rows of string and bits of fluttering paper to keep the birds off the seeds. There were straight lines of plants and the plots had perfect edges. Each allotment had its little shed, like a small dwelling. I had always dreamed of being married to a proper man who had an allotment, who cared about carrots and cabbages, and about me. A man who would look after me. Oh, what I would have given for it right then.

I remained there in the seat until the train was almost at Salisbury. Ivor and I stood near each other waiting for it to reach the station. As the cathedral spire came into view, he began to recite softly and suprisingly:

> 'Some day we shall see beckoning
> A spire over the hill.'

'Did you write that?' I said.

'John Meade Falkner,' he mumbled. 'I wish I had.'

We left the train and walked out of the station almost side by side. He could only drag his heavy case. It scraped on the station stones. 'Are you going to pull that all the way?' I asked.

He looked at me. 'We could get a taxi. How much have you got?'

'One pound and eighteen pence.'

'I've got one pound fifty-four,' he almost boasted. 'That should be enough.'

'Where's your mother's house?'

'It's not much further after you. My mother might be at home and she would not lose face with a taxi-driver.' He dragged his case towards the rank and I followed.

The driver helped him to put his luggage in the boot saying: 'It looks like it'll burst, reverend.' I sat inside wondering, as I often have done, what was going to happen to me next. When Ivor got in he said: 'It's old but perfectly good, my case.' He gave me a telephone number which I added to the numbers in my address book, of men I never wanted to talk to again. 'Perhaps we will meet,' he said awkwardly and added: 'I am thinking of writing a life of John Meade Falkner. He wrote *Moonfleet*, you know, about smugglers.'

That was all he said until we drove through the ancient arch and into the close. What a sight it was on that April day, the trees and grass new with spring, beautiful old houses and the point of the cathedral almost touching the large moving clouds. Ivor and I shook hands as I got out of the taxi. Somehow meeting that sad young man had made me feel happier. I suspected that my life might change. The taxi-man obligingly waited for a minute while I looked in his wing mirror to brush my hair with my Mickey Mouse brush. Then with a wave from each of them, they drove off. Ivor stared white-faced at me as though suddenly he missed me, he did not want to be alone. I watched them go, two kindly men in one day, something of a record. I looked up at the house. It almost reared before me, wide, tall, brick, with ranks of windows and a squared roof, a Georgian beauty. Resolutely, I opened the iron gate, crunched through the gravel and stepped bravely to the big door. There was I with my plastic holdall and no foreseeable future. I rang and stood as the bell resounded through the interior.

It was answered, although after some interval, by a frightened-looking bald man in a patchy butler's coat. He wore white gloves, one of which he held up as a sort of warning. 'Any chance of you coming back?' He eyed me warningly. 'Her ladyship's in one of her furies.' His face turned away as the sound of crashing came from deep in the house. 'Shit,' he said to himself and to my surprise. He returned to me. 'Maybe tomorrow? Or the next day? It takes time.'

'I can't,' I said firmly. There was another bang, which could have been the report of a gun. I tried to look around him and beyond the dark cave of the hall. 'I have other offers,' I lied.

'If I was you I'd take one of them,' he confided his cheeks shaking. 'I'm at the point of no return.'

'The interview was today,' I said even more decidedly. 'Two o'clock.' As if in support a clock deep in the house boomed two.

'All right,' he surrendered. 'You'll have to see her ladyship. He's in the cupboard.'

'Sir Benedict?' I asked.

He seemed oddly surprised that I knew the name but then said: 'Yes, him.' He held the door a little more open. 'Step this way, will you. You are . . .?'

'Miss Smith,' I told him. 'Chloe Smith.' I lowered my voice. 'Have there been a lot of applicants?'

'A lot,' he muttered. He edged around me as I entered and he closed the door. 'But no acceptances.'

'Her ladyship is particular?'

'No.' He was down to a whisper now. 'The applicants.' He straightened himself and rearranged his white gloves. 'Just wait here, will you. She seems to have eased a bit. It may be all right.' He left, still fussing with his gloves. Standing in the hall I looked around. There was a powerful smell of floor polish. A fine, carved staircase curled up the wall. Below it was a grandfather clock ticking threateningly. There were some heavily rich pictures on the dim walls, ancestors and scenery, and a long, fine table upon which stood a dull brass pot containing some flagging flowers. The butler returned through the shadows. 'Her ladyship will see you now,' he said with a sort of controlled satisfaction. 'She has rallied. I will announce you.' He went before me whispering: 'Shit, shit, shit,' so low it was scarcely audible. I learned that he often said it as he walked, as though he were in some sort of pain.

I cannot pretend that I went through the house and

23

into the room without trepidation, but I had experienced too many fierce people and unpleasant encounters in my life to be unduly worried by a violent old lady. 'Miss Chloe Smith,' announced the butler and then quickly went out.

She sat in a high-backed chair against the pale spring light from a grubby window. Her face and her eyes and everything about her was narrow, although it could be, as I discovered, even narrower. If the window had been clean, and the curtains fully apart, there would have been a good view of the garden.

'What did Urchfont say your name was?' Her hand came forward in a little accusing poke; her eyes were stiff with suspicion and already, it seemed, dislike.

I was not going to be bullied. 'He said it was Chloe Smith,' I said.

She took an old red book from behind her, examined it and, pushing her eyes close, checked down it, her nose pointing like a stick. 'Ah yes,' she said. She sniffed, then snorted, then slapped the book shut. 'And *you* want the job?'

'Yes. That's why I have come.'

'How old?'

'How old is what?'

'You,' she said but not so querulously. 'Your age.'

'I am forty-two.'

'And you are an experienced housekeeper? I can't train anyone.'

'Yes,' I said. After all I had kept house, any number of them – although not for long in most cases.

'We're elderly. I'm angry and he's mad.'

'I could manage.'

'Money is not plentiful. How much will you want?'

'What salary is offered?'

24

'Fifty pounds a week and your room and keep.'

'That will be all right.'

She looked surprised and then got up from the chair with apparent difficulty. (I soon discovered this was one of her ploys for, apart from getting out of the bath she was as lithe as an old tiger.) Sighing, she went to the window and peered into the garden. 'Damned spring,' she said. 'I hate the spring.' She returned towards her chair and seemed to be taken aback to see me still there. 'References? I must have references.'

Manufacturing a blush, I mumbled: 'Unfortunately I left them on the train.'

'References, I must have.' In a moment of unconscious prophecy she added: 'I could be murdered. Is there no one you know who could give you one?'

She was getting tired of the game, I could tell that. She needed someone and it might as well be me. But she gathered herself: 'I have several other applicants. You had better come back at the end of the week. Or telephone.'

I heard myself saying: 'I *do* know someone. The Reverend Ivor Popple. He lives here in the cathedral close.'

'Popple, Popple,' she repeated with two jabs of her chin. 'I know the Popples but ... oh, it's that nincompoop of a son. The one who wants to serve God, if God will have him. I thought he'd gone abroad where God is not so particular.'

'No. Ivor is here in Salisbury,' I said with deliberate familiarity. 'He is staying with his mother. He wrote to me the other day.'

She sniffed. 'Better than nothing, I suppose.' Her chin rose. 'You don't speak any Arabic dialects, do you?'

'No,' I admitted. 'Would you like me to contact the Reverend Popple?'

'How? On the telephone?'

'Yes. I have his number.' I took my red address book from my holdall.

'I really need someone who speaks Arabic,' she argued but with not much conviction. 'My first husband was in the Empty Quarter.' She gave up. 'All right. Call him from that telephone.' She pointed at a gruesome black instrument, uncleaned for years.

With the address book open in one hand and with the phone in the other, I dialled the number I had been given only half an hour before. He picked it up. 'Ivor?' I said.

He was unsure who could possibly be wanting him. 'Yes . . . this is he.'

'Wonderful,' I said. 'How have you been keeping?'

'Get on with it,' snarled the old lady.

Ivor sounded astonished. 'Who . . . who is this?'

'It's Chloe. How nice to speak to you again so soon.'

'Oh . . . who? . . . Oh, yes. Chloe.'

'Yes, Ivor. I am with Lady Bowling. At Canon's House. I came down today. I'm seeking a position as housekeeper, but I stupidly left my references on the train. Unlike me, you'd agree. I wondered if you would be very sweet and just tell Lady Bowling something about me.' His gasp was audible and I hoped she did not hear it, but he answered weakly: 'Er . . . yes . . . all right. Of course . . . be pleased . . .'

The old lady stuck out an arm like a pole and grasped the phone. 'Yes, Popple,' she said. 'I thought you were off converting savages. You're obviously not. What about this young woman? You know her?'

Later I thanked him with a kiss because he did put on an act. I could hear him making it up, lying like fury. She nodded and grunted and eventually, with no word of goodbye or thanks, heavily replaced the phone. 'Buffoon,' she said. She went back to her chair. 'When can you start?'

'Now,' I said. 'I'm here.'

'Right. Then the first thing you can do is to get that wretched fool Benedict out of the cupboard.'

'What's he doing in the cupboard?'

'He retreats there to escape the tongue-lashing he so richly deserves. And it's difficult to get him out. *You* try. He spends his life dealing cards. Playing patience.'

I followed her from the room. My heart was grateful. Once more I was saved. I had a roof, a bed and food. She went to a cloakroom off the main hall. In the corner was a cupboard. She pointed. 'Benedict, come out!' she shouted.

'No.' The refusal was faint but brave.

'We have a new servant.'

'Oh, really. Well, I'm staying in here.'

'He's keen on cards you said?' I enquired.

'Patience. He has no one to play with otherwise.'

I had carried my holdall with me into the cloakroom. She wore an unconvinced expression as I opened it and took out my pack of cards. Swiftly I took the cards and dealing myself in, one by one pushed seven under the door. 'Sir Benedict,' I called confidently through the crack. 'This is Chloe Smith. Do you play knock-out whist?'

Two of the cards remained poking out on my side of the door. Abruptly they disappeared within. There was a pause of half a minute and then the door creaked slowly open. An ancient hand holding the fanned-out cards, backs towards me, emerged. And a voice from the concealing darkness asked: 'What's trumps?'

4

When I had first been shown to my bedroom and the door had shut leaving me alone, it was all I could do to prevent myself bouncing on the bed. Instead I took my shoes off and lay quietly down feeling for once relieved and quiet and safe. Everything was going to be all right.

I had looked after myself despite all the various adventures and disasters that had overtaken me. When sometimes I stood naked in that room high under the roof of the house I could look down between my breasts and see my feet. I had always looked after my dark and plentiful hair and now I had a room with a basin, I could wash and brush it as I liked. My face filled out after a few weeks because there was plenty of food. Sir Benedict and her ladyship, although they ate in separate rooms, hardly accounted for a meal between them, but Urchfont and Mrs Trebet, the help and cook, always made sure there was plenty for us three staff.

When I had filled out, my brown eyes looked nearly young again. My neck was firm and shoulders not saucered or bony. My stomach was flat as a frying pan and my legs had kept their slimness and their shape. My breasts had never become tired or loopy. I studied them in a hand mirror, one at a time.

But it was at times like these that I felt most alone; I sat in my high room, hearing the afternoon sounds of the cathedral close outside. Sometimes a car would come by, slowly, almost reverently, and I would hear some children from the school or the tapping of an old person's walking stick or chatting voices.

Afternoon would come into the room; it crept through the curtains. When the cathedral clock stopped sounding a bicycle bell tinged below the window as though adding a couple of tinny notes of its own. I felt quite settled. All the unhappiness had been squeezed out of me by then; I knew I had exchanged my uncertain life for a safe loneliness.

Lady Bowling was always asking me to take up Arabic, even one of the lesser dialects. Her first husband had vanished, never to be found, in the Arabian desert – what she referred to as the Empty Quarter – and she had some vague plan to go and search for him, although many years had gone by. In the meantime, however, she occupied herself by sitting in her room every day, shadowed even in the sun of summer, writing letter after letter. It was my early afternoon job to take them to the post office.

They were not normal letters written to friends or relatives or even to Arabs, but complaints. Some were addressed to the Queen – one was a criticism about Prince Philip's bald patch. There were dozens of others over the course of a month, letters to the Zoo (about the smell of the camels), letters to banks who she claimed were diddling her, letters to the National Rivers Authority over the flotsam from the supermarket that floated down the River Avon which ran beyond the garden (she even complained about noisy geese), and there were letters to clergymen written in appalling language. She never deigned to lick the envelopes; as this was part of my job I was able to read the contents. Sometimes a letter would be so abusive (one, I recall, to the Pope) that I would appoint myself a sort of censor and just throw it away.

Mrs Trebet left shortly after I arrived. 'I have to or I'll go mad,' she said. 'But I just wanted to leave them in safe hands.' I took over the cooking and a girl came in to do the cleaning each day, a sniffy girl who wafted a duster around the legs of the chairs until I showed her how to plug in the hoover and wash the windows.

I enjoyed doing the daily shopping. Salisbury, the little leaning city, was not all that much changed from when I lived there as a girl. One afternoon I went to what had once been my grandmother's house, in a terrace at the back of the town. All the houses were alike and I was unsure which was which. Then a door opened and a fat, untidy woman came out and tottered, eyes down, towards the market. I recognised her as the girl who had lived next door. She had always walked like that, as if she were looking for something on the pavement.

One afternoon when I was coming out of the butcher's I almost collided with a slight man in a long coat who was hurrying past like a spy. In swerving to avoid me he almost tumbled into the road. 'Chloe!' he said. 'It's me, Ivor Popple.'

He made me laugh. 'Of course it is,' I said. 'I wouldn't forget you.' He blushed and fingered his clerical collar. He looked better fed. 'I wondered, that's all,' he said. He seemed silenced by shyness. I asked: 'How is John Meade Falkner?'

His face lit. 'Fancy you remembering that.' He patted my arm shyly. 'I'm still engaged in the research,' he said looking both ways like somebody imparting a secret. 'Gathering information.'

He regarded me uncertainly. 'Would you like a cup of tea?' I said I would. He was already fumbling in his trouser pockets. 'Not that I've brought any money with me,' he groaned. 'Not enough for two.'

I bought the tea. We sat in the Wiltshire Home Café at a wooden table. I found it strangely thrilling. 'You were very kind,' I said, 'giving that reference to Lady Bowling. What a wonderful liar you would have made.'

His laugh did not halve his broader face now. 'I'm not sure that's a compliment to someone wearing one of these.' He fingered his collar again. 'Nor am I sure that I was doing you much of a favour. She's a terrible old scold.'

'I don't have all that much trouble with her,' I said. 'Although she keeps on about me learning Arabic. And the old man's a love. We play cards.'

An anxious look came over him. 'One day . . .' He hesitated. '. . . would you like to come to Meade Falkner's chapel with me? It's in Dorset, near Chesil Bank. We could go on the bus.'

I accepted and we arranged to go there as soon as I had a full day off and he had saved enough money for lunch.

I really began to like my life there. For the first time in years, it seemed, I knew where I was, what I had to do to complete the day. Each morning, at nine o'clock, I would take tea to her ladyship and help her remove her ear muffs. She wore them, she said, to eliminate the noise of winds and possible burglars. In her room were huge, bulky curtains and I used to heave them open. The first time I did this an avalanche of dust fell out, leaving me and the old lady choking. With Urchfont's help I had taken them down. They came back from the cleaners revealing a rich pattern. When I pulled them apart each morning her ladyship would moan: 'That damnable sunshine. Look at it all over the bed.'

She really was in a terrible mess. I helped her to undress at night and to dress in the morning; if I had not been there she would never have bothered with clean clothes and would have put everything on in the wrong order. Urchfont told me that her ladyship had once received a visitor wearing her drawers over her skirt.

Sir Benedict, on the other hand, was spotless. He even had me clip the hairs from his ears with a sewing scissors. His ancient tweedy clothes were without fault and he wore a different tie for each day of the week, ties decorated with badges, stripes and medallions, although he had long forgotten what they signified. 'Chloe,' he would sigh, 'I am suffering from something called oldness.'

Oh, but he was a fine, grand man, old but strong, tall and kind with one wild, blind eye and the other filled with understanding and tenderness. Her ladyship was cruel to him. Once, in the winter, she locked him out of doors in the snow and I found him piled up like a snowman against the door. She said she had only meant to keep him out there half an hour but had forgotten him as she was writing letters. He and I used to have some good games of cards, not speaking, just playing in the warmth and quiet of his study for up to an hour. I had never felt so settled.

Early every evening, even during the summertime, Sir Benedict would have a fire lit in his study. I would light it about seven o'clock and the daily girl would clear the ashes next morning. After his solitary dinner (until they came to their pact to kill each other, they always ate in different rooms) he loved to play cards with me. We played double dummy whist, with two spare hands. 'It's also called honeymoon whilst, you know,' he smiled. We would sit in the glowing room, with just a table lamp; with a cagey smile he would shuffle the cards, and one of us would deal. It was so wonderfully peaceful; hardly a word, just the sound of the fire grinding away and night noises shuffling or squeaking outside the window. (It had to be open in the summer because the heat of the room became unbearable.) Quite often he said things, just dropped them in as though suddenly remembering them from long ago; often it was only a sentence, a memory, a person's name. 'Barty Johnson,' he would mumble. 'Ruined, you know. In Knebworth.' It was no good asking him what he meant or even to tell me more because it would be gone, forgotten in a moment. We would just go on playing.

One evening about eleven – when we habitually dealt the last hand and I prepared his bedtime drink, cocoa laced with Demerara rum – he remembered something important. You could tell because of the way he raised his handsome, grey head with his eyebrows rising separately and his good eye gleaming. 'Chloe,' he said. 'I have a tandem, you know.'

He laid the cards with a soft plop on the table. 'I even remember where it is,' he said in a pleased way. 'It's been there for years.'

'Where?'

'It's in the barn. I know it is.'

'Perhaps we could find it some day.'

'But we must go and look *now*.'

I rose as deliberately as he did. 'Now?' I said. 'Tonight?'

'It won't wait,' he said darkly. 'If she – her ladyship –

finds it I'm sure she'll get rid of it, sell it probably. They're very valuable now, fetch a lot of money.'

'But it's so late.'

He rolled his eye: 'There's a moon.'

He began shambling towards the French windows at the far end of the room. I helped him on with his corduroy sports jacket. He attempted to open the window but he was making so much noise that I did it for him. We went out into the flat night.

I had a sense of excitement, even daring, as if we were going out on an adventure together, a raid. He seemed to feel the same because he paused on the grass. An owl sounded like a warning. Sir Benedict put his finger to his lips and said: 'Hush.'

We stepped through the moonlight, across the grass and the paved courtyard and reached the barn door. It was a double door, massive, and as it had not been used for so long, almost impossible to move. But there was a small door set in the stone wall alongside. 'I'll be to the fore,' he decided. 'You open the latch. It's rusty.'

I did so and it scraped. Again he made a shushing noise and I said: 'We should come back tomorrow.'

'Nonsense. Some things are best done by night.'

I pushed the door and it opened without further scraping. 'There's a whiff,' he said. Now we were inside, in the dark and the closeness and a strong smell of mildew. To my surprise he remembered a light switch on the wall. A solitary bulb flickered, through its coat of cobwebs. 'Well done,' he said.

He advanced through the shadows. I was looking around for rats. There was a mass of junk lying against the opposite wall and he went towards it. It was just like the debris from a disaster, old beds and mattresses, garden stuff, piles and pieces of furniture, a wrecked pram. I wondered who that had belonged to. Amazingly, he found the tandem without great difficulty. 'It used to be here, somewhere,' he said pulling some small items clear. 'There.' He straightened. 'I can see the front handlebars.' He began moving stuff which was burying the machine, and after the middle part was exposed, up to the rear set of handlebars, we both pulled, and the old tandem came clear quite easily. It was broken and covered with dust, the saddles mouldy, the chains tight with rust, but the wheels on their perished tyres still turned creakily. He spun them reflectively. I let go, so he could stand and hold it upright. A private silence had come over him, something I could not interrupt. 'There she is,' he said with satisfaction. 'Just as she was.'

'Did you and Lady Annabel ride it much?'

Even in the dim light I could see he was distressed. 'Not Lady Annabel,' he mumbled. 'My first wife, *Lucy*, the first Lady Bowling.'

I simply said: 'Oh, I see.'

'She was pushed over a cliff, a precipice,' he said sadly. 'By the present Lady Bowling.'

I felt my mouth fall open in the lamplight.

He sniffed and patted the tandem. 'Her own sister.'

5

The army officers' married quarters in Singapore were the best I could remember in all our travels, built in a long arch across a hill facing west so that when one of the fierce sunsets occurred after an afternoon rainstorm, the light would transform the houses into a rainbow. Each house had a verandah under an arch with a little square of scruffy garden at the back. Sometimes a Tamil would turn up to hack at the weeds but they soon grew again. My mother would sit in the middle as they sprouted and flowered, sprawled in a striped deck-chair. She used to laugh and say: 'Look, I'm the queen of the jungle!' The rooms of the quarters were small because they had been built for Japanese officers during the war, although apparently they had hardly moved in before they lost. There was a rumour that the Japanese commander had disembowelled himself in one of the houses and that his ghost still appeared. No one knew which house.

Every day was hot – and often rain-soaked. The rain came down in tropical torrents some afternoons and the water gushed along the deep, open monsoon drains. Going home from school we used to have races with paper boats. A half-Chinese, half-Welsh boy once had to be rescued when he got lodged in one of the drains. We had to keep his head above the rushing water while someone ran for the nearest help who turned out to be the tipsy wife of the adjutant, who just waved her hands and shouted nonsense. Before poor Chan Humphries was rescued, the rising water was going up his nose.

From our front door we could see down the hill to the barrack blocks, where the other ranks lived, set around the parade-ground. The mornings were often clear as a mirror, and the square glistened with the sun. The garrison would fall in on parade and you could hear the orders echoing and the stamp of the boots like explosions delayed by distance. My father, who by that time was a desk soldier and did not often have to go on parade, used to get on his bike and wobble away down the hill. He was the only officer who rode a bike and he was very funny on it at times. Even when he was on the way to the office he despised so much, he would do a quick wobble and wave and fling his legs out, just to amuse us. My brother Kneller said thoughtfully one morning as he watched him go: 'He'll fall off one day. Off something.'

The army school was not far from the Chinese village. Our headmaster, Mr Puddley, sometimes told us what it had been like when he first arrived there many years before as a young conscript. My mother said that some of the Chinese girls who were there in his soldiering days were ancient women by now. She wondered if they recognised each other. He was in charge of a school for about sixty army children with three other teachers, including Mr Gul, an Indian.

I was almost fourteen and I could feel myself growing. Looking at the old school photographs now, I can see my breasts pointing through my dress. 'Don't outgrow your strength,' Rosa said.

In my face, too, I looked a bit older than the others, not pretty in a childish way but with clouds of dark hair and a grown-up smile. The climate did not help to preserve a girl's childhood either, so heavy and hot and deep that it seemed to seep into my body everywhere. I was a bit frightened of what was happening. If I had told my mother she would have laughed and hugged me and we would have ended up singing at the piano. It was not a singsong that I needed.

Then one hot night the cat from next door came in through my bedroom window.

I had been standing in my pyjama top looking out at the sky. Millions of cicadas sounded. Even the moon seemed to sag. I slunk back to bed and was lying awake – well, hardly *lying*, because it was beyond me to be still in that room, directly under the roof. The sweat oozed from me. The window was wide in the hope of catching some absent-minded breeze but all that came in was Persimmon the cat.

The family in the next-door quarters had inherited the cat from the previous occupants. Persimmon was midnight black with a white shirt-front. People regularly remarked what a huge animal he was. Much of his time he spent lurking among the weeds along the sides of the monsoon drains watching for frogs. The frogs, big bullfrogs, were agile but so was Persimmon. He would pounce, fling the frog in the air and catch it as it came down. We used to gather to watch him dismember them.

That night Persimmon came through my window like a leopard. I was lying there oozing in the dark, the bottom half of me naked. I had taken off the pants of the short cotton pyjamas I wore, throwing myself to one side and then the other in the clammy bed. My pillow was damp, my hair stuck to my head. I was aching to sleep but I was nowhere near it and the next day we had a scripture exam.

Persimmon sat on the narrow sill, his big silhouette against the glowing sky. He shut his eyes, only his shirt-front showed, but then he opened them, just half at first, a pair of split peas, but deep, deep lovely green. I slid from the bed and putting out my warm hand I stroked him; he wriggled his head into my palm. I felt he had come on purpose.

A brief waft of air came in from outside and I lifted my top to let it cool my front. Persimmon's eyes rolled up to my breasts, and he stared at me so intently that I let the top fall again. 'You bad cat,' I scolded quietly. I felt ashamed and excited and turned away from him, saying: 'Go on home.' He remained where he was, sitting, watching, letting his pointed red tongue come out and lick the tip of a paw. Backwards towards my bed I went, never taking my eyes off him. The illuminated green hands on my alarm clock were pointing to three thirty. The scripture exam was only six hours away. Climbing on the crumpled, damp sheets, I stretched out, fanned open my legs for some air, and resolutely closed my eyes. I tried taking deep breaths, my chest rising and falling. I knew he was still there. Then I heard the padded, firm drop as he came from the window.

With a mixture of fear and fancy I allowed myself another peep. He was sitting confidently on the coconut rug. 'Go on home,' I said primly. 'Go on.'

Instead he jumped onto my bed, smooth and heavy, and just stood, kneading with all four large and silent paws, his eyes closed. Then he opened them, those wicked ocean-coloured boats, and they settled on me. 'You really ought to go home,' I said.

How many times have I said that since.

Upright as an ornament he sat. My voice seemed to move him as an invitation might because, after another lick of one paw, he blinked into my stare and then casually climbed onto me. He languidly rolled himself out full length across my glowing legs and naked belly. His tail flopped between my thighs, the fur quivering, his great face flat against my cotton-clothed chest, the chin resting between the mounds of my breasts. He moved towards me as if to make himself more comfortable; his great head now filled my entire horizon. The green eyes locked onto mine. His claws were unsheathed but blunt, unhurting, against my skin, his weight and his fur overwhelming in the heat. His breath had a faint froggy smell.

I lay there, Persimmon lay on top of me. *And then he began to purr.*

He purred very strongly, deeply, as though warming up his engine. It was so thrilling. It went right through his big, lovely, soft body, and into mine. If only men could learn to purr. *Grnnnn, grnnnn, grnnnn*, he went. Every vibration from his belly trembled into mine. The pleasure overwhelmed me. Then he began to flick his tail.

I was in my very first ecstasy, brimming with it. It all happened down in my body and I had to bite the wet sheet to stop myself crying out. It was as though some part of me had broken away and was flapping around loose inside me.

As I thrashed about, the cat sulkily left the bed. He loped off like a leopard and, briefly pausing, easily jumped to the open window. He stood on the sill, formed against the moonlight, his tail, that wonderful tail, swishing. Carefully, he turned his face towards me and our eyes met for the last time. Then he left.

My door opened and my mother's head appeared. 'You were shouting, Chloe,' she said. She had her

Egyptian tablecloth wrapped around her. 'Were you dreaming?'

'Yes,' I said. 'Dreaming, mum.'

It was the end of Persimmon and me. He never came back and when I saw him in the garden or waiting for frogs alongside the monsoon drain, his only response to my inciting words was a catty stare. For him I was just somewhere to sleep.

6

Rosa, my mother, could hear marching soldiers from her Aldershot bed; she was still apt to cry when a military band played. For years as a widow she lived in a little coop of a flat in what has always been an army town, her front window looking over the road to the parade-ground. The squaddies drilled and she liked to see them marching up and down and to hear the echoes: 'H'eft, roit, h'eft, roit.' Often she would join in herself as she moved about her home: 'H'eft, roit, h'eft, roit.' It was like a song. She enjoyed overhearing squaddie talk in the streets when she went shopping. She did not know any officers or their wives.

It was strange when she decided to go back there. Again, she recognised in the second-hand shop some bits and pieces we had sold to them long before, a vase and a Chinese lamp and a picture of cows, and she bought them back and put them gladly in her rooms. She was Rosa to everybody and she helped out in a troops canteen, going home sometimes to play old records and to dance alone in her sitting-room. I saw her once from the street doing a tango all by herself, going jerkily to and fro across the window, hair down, head back, face set as though still at the camp dance with him holding her in his arms.

One area of the wall had a small exhibition of pictures

of my father and she had a bedside photograph of him which she kissed each night. She had done this for so long and so deeply that the glass around his lower face had become worn and discoloured giving him a sort of beard.

He smiled beguilingly, engagingly, from the wall, with more confidence than he had really had. One pose showed him in scarlet uniform, hugging his tuba; it was taken on the very day he ruined his life by staggering from the marching band at the Sovereign's Parade and ending in a crashed heap.

There was an earlier photograph taken on the day he was commissioned, stiff with hope and alertness, and another after he had shaved off his slender moustache for the first time because he felt it made him appear a touch shady. Significantly, he shaved it off a second time just before he began defrauding queen and country although this, as it was said at his court martial, was one of the factors that actually drew attention to him. There were pictures of the family at the Singapore seaside, a bit of beach and some English-type bathing huts; Rosa laughing, her face framed by a huge sunhat, Dad, athletic in black woolly swimming shorts and Kneller posing with a parasol. I am in my scratchy bathing suit and like Dad I am expanding my chest. There were others, grown fawn with age and Aldershot sun. Dad posing with a field gun (probably the nearest he ever got to one), so upright his back was concave and with the fateful service pistol high on his hip; another in which he was attempting to look like a leader of men with the other ranks in his office section, standing on the balcony in Singapore. All except him are holding tin tea mugs; he holds his china mug with the crest of his former regiment on it and this he displays to the camera like a reminder that he had once known days of pomp.

One afternoon when I went to see Rosa, which I tried always to do when I could disengage myself from whatever my current troubles were, she surprised me by producing a file stuffed with letters, more photographs and a few newspaper cuttings which she said she wanted me to have. She had not been feeling well.

As a rule, she did not dwell too long on past things when I visited her. We merely had a cup of tea, sometimes there at the flat, sometimes in the nearby Happy Gunner Café – the proprietor had been discharged as deaf from the Royal Artillery. She had little to relate even when we had not seen each other for some time. This time we talked a bit about Kneller who was now playing the glockenspiel. Abruptly, she got up, went to the bedroom and returned holding the box file. 'You should have this, dear,' she said, half-opening the lid as though afraid something might jump out. 'It's only bits and pieces. But I want you to keep it.'

When I got back that night I poured myself a glass of wine and sat on the bed to open the file. I found myself doing it with a nervous slowness. There was a newspaper cutting about their wedding with a faded photograph which I had not seen in years. It was a jolly picture of the bride and groom with some guests and time had given it a tender softness. I looked at it for a long time and I still look at it now. There were two reports from the *Straits Times* regarding his second court martial and another a few years later from the *Salisbury Journal* about the inquest. He always said that he wanted to achieve something that was worth being written up in the international press. There was also a folded piece of ruled foolscap headed 'Future Plans' but with the word 'Future' crossed through in pencil. I remember him doing that, pointing out that all plans had to be future so the word was not needed. We all thought how clever he was.

The proposals in this document, so pathetic now, which had been agreed around the table in our quarters in Singapore, were written in my father's flamboyant hand, each step given a separate space on the paper and treated to a lot of underlining. I can see us now in the cosy lamplight, the bullfrogs and the cicadas grunting and clicking like machines in the dark beyond the screened window, Kneller and I eagerly leaning forward to see what he was planning. How different the reality would be.

The first line of the document is very definite: 'Leave Service' heavily underlined. Below are the details we knew by heart, of how he could seek his discharge at the end of his ten-year engagement which was to be completed eighteen months from then. The next line was headed 'Quarters' and detailed his strategy for buying a rosy cottage in the country, on a frequent bus route. The bus was important because of the third provision, 'Occupation'. He intended to give music lessons from this idyllic but remote house and the bus was to bring his pupils from some supposedly wealthy neighbouring town. It would also carry my mother and, presumably in time, Kneller and me, off to some gainful employment in the same place.

Laying my fingers on the paper, I found myself smiling at it as you would do remembering a foolish, but generally happy dream. No mention of finances to fund the dream was made. There was a gratuity from the army and some sort of pension but how to obtain solid money must already have been cooking in his mind.

Putting the other newspaper cuttings aside (I had read them long before and I was sure their pain would not be made less by the years) I rummaged among the old mess bills, invitations and sports programmes (he was quite a good hurdler) at the bottom of the file and eventually brought out what must have been one of the earliest outlines of his conspiracy.

It was a list of Gurkha names, strange-sounding, and written across the top was '24th. Coy. Gurkhas'.

One stifling afternoon he was sitting under the grinding fan in the pay office, staring at an accounts page for some distant Gurkhas and thinking how odd and alike the names were. Just for fun he began to concoct some names himself and from there it was only a few stages to creating a fictitious army unit, giving it a name, number and posting and, eventually, *paying* it.

What began as an idle game crystallised into a scheme. He needed accomplices and his section sergeant in the pay office was only too glad to join in. This sergeant made duty visits to various army units in remote areas and there he recruited a local pay sergeant to tie up the other end of the plot. And it worked. It worked for months. The Singapore office was slack and my father and his accomplices were easily able to manipulate the figures. But he began to go to his desk in the evenings, to catch up with his work so he said, and it was this uncharacteristic enthusiasm that finally undid them. The colonel, returning home from some military dinner, spotted a light in the office and stopped to ask the sergeant of the guard about it. He was told that Captain Smith was busy in there and went home wondering. Nobody worked voluntary overtime in the army. Two nights later he went to the office and glanced over my father's unknowing shoulder. Although the colonel went home quietly, apparently satisfied, my father knew the game was up.

Once he knew he was caught a strange freedom came over Dad. He was under open arrest so that he stayed at home all day and was allowed to wander about the garrison, provided he did not go near the pay office and was in his quarters by sunset. He even went and had some golf lessons which he somehow believed might help with his defence because you met influential people at the golf club.

Quite often when Kneller and I returned from school he would be at the piano, playing with a sort of serene melancholy as though he knew only too well what was in store. In the evenings he would cheer up immensely and we would gather for a singsong, me playing duets with him, Rosa quivering to notes she could never reach and rattling the tambourine or castanets, and Kneller with his little harp. There was a song from the South African War which my father had discovered in an old music book. It was called 'The Boers Have Got My Daddy' but he, and then we, laughingly sang it as 'The Bores Have Got My Daddy'. They had, too.

He and his sergeant and the other conspirator were court-martialled and the trial hardly extended to a couple of days. My father was sentenced to five years' imprisonment; the sergeant got less because he told all. He was a creepy sort of a man, the lenses kept falling out of his glasses which got him some sympathy in the court. In a year he was back in the pay office and, as my imprisoned father said, it served him right. The third man got an even lighter sentence but when he came out he wandered off into the jungle and, so the story went, was eaten by ants.

*

It was just before these events that Mr Gul, the Indian

teacher at school, began to take an interest in me. I was clever in class and eager, too, because my father told us that education was the beginning of everything, even happiness, especially if you developed an active imagination – although it did not do much for him.

There was an upright piano at the school and I was often asked to play it at assembly, always concluding with the national anthem. Mr Gul made a little, silly joke once coming up behind me in his friendly way when everyone else was going off to the classrooms, and lifting me by the waist as I was sorting out the music for the next day's hymns. 'Chloe,' he said so close to my ear that his nose was almost in my hair, 'you should try standing for the "God Save Our Queen" *yourself.*'

'While I'm playing it, Mr Gul?'

'*While* you're playing it!' he said and started to laugh. His laugh, like his voice, was low and shy. His eyes were like nuts, his face small.

I knew he had always liked me. Sometimes he patted my bottom under my dress. In those days it was only counted as fondness. He would be seen walking at the edge of the jungle listening to the birds and monkeys and humming aimlessly to himself. He was lonely.

There was a scrubby undergrowth around the barracks. A road came up from the village, past the guard post and the lifting barrier, and into the garrison. But it ended there, just petered out into red earth and a sort of jungle. There were bumpy hills and groups of palm trees. About a mile away were some reservoirs and, on cooler days, we children would walk up there. Some officers had boats and used to sail them and you could have a picnic on the bank. Towards the reservoirs were some deep pits where, just after we arrived in Singapore, they found some skeletons from the war. There were skulls and legs and other bones. It was all roped off but the army children stood transfixed in groups waiting to see what would be brought up next. One of the men digging found a skull and dropped it as he was coming out of the pit. I was not afraid and I picked it up and handed it back.

My adventure with Mr Gul happened on a Sunday. There had been a church parade earlier, for which I had worn my best blue and white dress. I looked very pretty in this dress. Sometimes I would stand in front of my mother's long mirror and pose and whirl to make the short skirt fly out, and push out my chest and cock up one leg saucily behind me. After church Mr Gul, who must have been a Christian, told me how nice I looked in the dress.

In the afternoon I changed into a top and shorts. I had arranged to walk up to the reservoir with Helen Hotchkiss. There were rumours that jewellery was hidden in the pits where the bones were found and we planned to look. But Helen did not arrive outside the cookhouse where we had planned to meet. Sometimes she had to stay at home to help her mother when her father was on weekend duty. Mrs Hotchkiss was a nervous woman, terrified of the Chinese who, she said, were always looking at her.

For a while I hung around listening to the clanking of the cookhouse washing-up squad, banging the tins and shouting and swearing on the hot Sunday afternoon, and rubbing spaces in the steamy windows so they could look out at me. When Helen did not come I went on the walk by myself.

When I was out of sight of the camp I saw Mr Gul standing alone on the path ahead looking down a slope into a small tangled valley. He was very thin and he was wearing his best bush jacket. He turned as though we had arranged to meet and offered his hand. I shook it. 'You looked very nice in your blue dress this morning,' he said again. We stood there, more or less facing each other, not saying anything more. He was not frightening because he was so mild and not much taller than me. Then he said: 'Would you like to have a wrestle?'

I laughed. But he said: 'Come on, Chloe, what a lovely day for a bit of a wrestle.' His eyes were shining happily. He looked clean and smart in his bush jacket, his black hair was neatly parted and his skin was level and brown.

'All right, Mr Gul,' I said.

He did not seem to know how to go about it, how to start, and nor did I. Blinking nervously, and with an expression of smiling doubt, he flapped his arms impotently at his side. 'What do we have to do?' I asked. We began to circle each other.

'Get a hold,' he said eventually in his musical voice. 'We must get a hold.'

We stopped circling and I held out my arms as if I were carrying a big basket of flowers in front of me and he struck a pose opposite me before saying: 'Just one moment.' I backed off although I kept my arms in position. He studiedly rolled up the sleeves of his bush jacket and smiled more firmly: 'That is more like it.'

There was a flat area around us, mostly grass (indeed thinking about it now, it was strange that it was so levelled, trodden down by the look of it; perhaps he had planned it, after all) and once more we began circling each other. At our feet was the descending slope. The sun seemed very hot and I could feel my heart was sounding. I was excited.

'Now!' he said abruptly. 'Let us engage!' His eyes were bright and his breath was slightly scented. He came to me and clutched me in his arms. I was strong and well-developed, but his body though small was hard as wire.

Not that he hurt me. It was more like an embrace than a wrestling lock. He rocked me to and fro. He was getting warmer. My head was alongside his, I could see inside his ear. He instructed quietly: 'Now you, Chloe. Get me.'

Obediently I put my arms about his body and tried to push him over but I could not shift him and he hugged me again while we performed a sort of dance in the sunlight. It must have looked very strange, a neatly dressed Indian man and an English schoolgirl in shorts shuffling around like that. I managed to get my head against his chest and I butted him ineffectually. He giggled happily. What girls were supposed to do, even in those days, was to jab a knee in the groin. But I did not want to hurt him. He had done me no harm. He grunted a few more times and then, very carefully, put me on my back on the grass. Without fear, I looked up to see him peering down at me with his warm dark eyes. 'Jolly well done, Chloe,' he said.

'Don't fall on me.'

'I would never do that.' He lowered himself very lightly to the ground, half on top of me but with no pressure; he was keeping his weight on his elbows (always the sign of a gentleman). Then he rolled me over so that I was above him. We were both sweating. I was laughing and he began to make a hooting sound as we bounced lightly against each other.

We clutched and rolled, huggered and muggered, first me on top and then him. I felt myself brimming with excitement in the same way as I had been with Persimmon. What a start to a sexual life.

Mr Gul seemed to be getting stronger, but he was still not rough, not hurting me, although his face was crammed up, and his shirt wet. We rocked a bit more and then, in a moment, we overbalanced and started rolling down the slope.

It was not far to the bottom but it seemed as if we rolled and rolled. I was laughing hysterically and he was still hooting in his strange way, his perfumed breath in my face. We clung onto each other and went down in a bundle, like two clowns. I was above, I was below, I was above. He kept his weight off me and when we reached the bottom it was I who was on top. Red-faced and puffing I laughed at him and pushed down with my hands onto his shoulders. Suddenly he was looking worried. The sweat was trickling down my face, I could feel my chest was soaking. Then he eased himself over and I lay back on the grass. He was astride and above me. 'I've got to be off,' he said as if he had just remembered. His eyes went briefly towards the garrison. 'I have a lot I must do.'

I could feel and see he was trembling as he eased himself away from me. He got to his knees and unsteadily to his feet as if he had been in a real fight. 'Thank you so much for such fun,' he said gravely. Then leaving me lying there on my back, he ambled up the bank and went from my view.

After several minutes spent trying to understand what had happened I stood up, brushed myself down, and climbed slowly up the bank. I felt very foolish and lonely.

Of course I would never have told anybody. But Mr Gul did. On the Monday he confessed to Mr Puddley, and I was called into the headmaster's room where I denied everything. Mr Gul stood there trembling with his head bowed and I managed to look at him as if he were crazy (which he probably was). I said he must have imagined it. Mr Puddley was only too eager to agree with me because he did not need trouble. He only said: 'Are you sure, Chloe?'

'Of course I'm sure,' I said. 'He's making it up.' He dismissed me and I treated Mr Gul to another odd look as I went. He left the school that afternoon carrying a small bag and it was many years before he turned up again.

Even so I thought the matter had taken a turn for the worse when the military police turned up at home. There were three big puffed-looking men, their pink thighs bulging in shorts, with another who was some sort of army detective. He had a moustache which twitched like a rat and he asked questions from his nose. My first thought was that Mr Gul had confessed again and that this time someone had believed him. Had they arrived to arrest me? Could I be charged?

But instead they asked for my father. It was the moment when his game with the fantasy Gurkhas was up. He did not seem the least bit worried. 'It's all an army cock-up,' he boasted to my mother. She said: 'What have you done with the money?' All he did was wink.

Once, during this time before the court martial, he sauntered up in the early evening towards the pay office, probably with some thought of disposing of evidence, and was halted nervously by the sentry, a young lad who liked him (he was something of a hero to the other ranks) but who would not let him enter. Rifle in hand, the squaddie burst into tears and said how sorry he was. My father came slowly home.

Facing the music had, of course, always been his ambition; he had wanted so much to be a drum major. He made a joke of it during those few weeks before the trial. Although under arrest, he had never been so unconstrained. Unless they were interrogating him, he was at liberty within the garrison, having been suspended from duties, and he took on a new freedom. Apart from his golf lessons he helped Rosa with the shopping, cooked curries and took the washing to the Chinese woman who used to trundle a cart to the main gate. Or he would sit at home and play the blues on the trumpet or sing in a hushed sort of way at the piano, acting out the part. In the afternoons he came to the school to walk home with Kneller and me and with the other soldiers' wives and children. People enjoyed talking and strolling with him; he was an object of curiosity.

But we knew it was not real. As the time lessened, I heard them both having a cry in their bed and I went in to them, to cry too, and found them sitting up clutching each other like two ghosts under the sheet. We were like those Japanese ivory figures that all fit around each other so tightly. My father was sobbing: 'With luck, I might get off.'

That sort of luck was beyond him. On the first day of the court martial he was up at dawn to spruce himself (as though that made any difference) and we could see that if it had not been for the looming consequences, he might well have enjoyed the limelight of the thing. In the afternoon I went straight from school and climbed up the rough bank behind the garrison offices. There was a guard outside the front door but not at the back and I was able to stand on tiptoe and get a view through the window into the room where the court was sitting. Everyone was laughing. And right in the middle was my father making some explanation, telling some yarn, putting off the inevitable. The president of the court, a rosy-looking colonel, was wiping his eyes. Everyone said afterwards that it was one of the most enjoyable courts martial ever. It lasted two days. He got five years in a military prison in England. The next day my mother, with her deep and silent patience, began to pack, and Kneller and I said goodbye to our friends. A week later we were on the plane away from the eastern colours, the warm rain and the oriental sun and landing in pale old England.

7

I have spent half my life in what you might call the
armyland, bounded by Aldershot in the north, Winchester to the east, Blandford and Dorchester to the southwest, with Salisbury and the surrounding camps and
military villages, Tidworth, Devizes and Warminster in
between. When I was very young I thought Warminster
was named after war.

It was in this region that we stayed while my father
served three and a half years of his sentence at Barton
Stacey in what they called the Glasshouse. The army had
to keep us housed because he was still a serving officer
even though all he was serving was time.

Prison did not suit him much but he made the best of
it, forming a band and playing at dances. They played
rock and roll and waltzes and quicksteps although the
prisoners had no one to dance with but each other.

Rosa soon adapted to being single-handed. We were
billeted in a place surrounded by security wire on the
fringe of Salisbury Plain. They used to joke that the wire
was not to keep intruders out but to keep us in. Nobody
asked us about our father because everybody knew. He
was not the only father who was serving time, in fact the
army had reserved the whole street for the likes of us.
One family's father was doing life for murdering a
sergeant who had shouted too loudly at him. Our

immediate neighbours did not expect to see their father for at least seven years. They pretended he was on a secret mission. There were also quarters occupied by dependants left behind, either by circumstances or by choice, when the soldier had been posted abroad. It was like a village of women and children. My mother formed a club and the members shared a bus to visit their husbands who were locked away at Barton Stacey.

They were days in limbo for us, waiting for him to come home. Every night my mother said her prayers for him and putting my ear to the wall I could hear her and I too would whisper the prayers. She had made herself a special calendar from which she privately crossed off the months. Kneller went off to an army school where they taught music and both my mother and I were relieved to see him go. He had been found experimenting with her make-up and wearing her clothes. 'It will get him out of the habit,' she said. 'Make a man of him.'

Our billet was not a bad place, high up so you could see for miles across the patterns of Salisbury Plain: hills like domes, the moving shadows of windy clouds, the colours of the fields always altering. From my bedroom window I could see tanks moving across the country, throwing up clouds of dust and exhaust smoke, and on some early mornings we were almost shaken from bed by artillery practice. Salisbury Plain was like the backcloth of my young life. When I was fifteen I lost my virginity, or some of it, at Stonehenge, to a thick-witted boy whose father was in the signals.

We went up there with our bicycles, a long trudge after school in August and we were hot when we arrived. In those days you could just wander among the big stones. It was about seven o'clock and their long shades were spread over the ground. We stood next to them and our shadows looked like giants. There was a massive sunset. It seemed like the right time. Even at that age I was romantic. His bike fell over in the middle of what we were clumsily doing and he got up from me, half-tugged up his jeans and straightened the bike against one of the stones. I never knew whether or not we had done it properly. In the dusk he stretched out on one of the flat stones in a sort of triumph. I sat on the edge. I was trying to cry, from disappointment or whatever.

He did not notice. His eyes wandered past me to his bicycle. 'That bike's got to last me,' he said, 'till my old man comes back.'

When my father was released from military prison we had to leave our army quarters and we went to live with my grandmother at the back of Salisbury. We had never told her that he was in Barton Stacey. We pretended that we had all been posted to Germany. One day, when she believed we were in Gütersloh, I saw her in Salisbury market and had to hide behind a vegetable barrow. My father even coached us to speak some phrases in German and when she was present we sometimes reminisced about places that we had never seen.

My mother and my grandmother had never been close, although our absences, real and imaginary, had kept them from having to be with each other; but when we moved in to share her terraced house after my father's release, it soon became crowded. She had a worn old one-toothed dog which had the best chair. It would sniff at my father, then growl and try to bite him with its gums.

My father told us that he had enjoyed more room in his cell than in this house, and promised Rosa that we would soon be able to move. Late at night they conversed in whispers for fear of waking the dog. My grandmother slept deeply. As usual he had plenty of plans, ambitious and extravagant, but the more he expounded them the more they faded into the distance.

He played the piano in pubs; he played for his supper and drinks. From my bed I listened to hear him coming along the night-time street, knocking on the wrong doors and loudly apologising in his officer's voice. 'Most terribly, terribly sorry . . . My mistake, I'm afraid.' Once he started drinking he could not stop. It was as though it had been lying in wait for him for years. As soon as my grandmother went shopping in the morning he would start to cry. Rosa would stand, hopeless and silent, by the kitchen table while he sat, head in hands.

He tried to find real work, ever more pathetically, even scheming to rejoin the army under an assumed name. One evening he came home covered in blood and horror after his solitary day as a slaughterhouse assistant. He would have never made a fighting soldier.

All this my mother suffered with loving stoicism. So did I, for that matter, although there were taunts at school: 'Whose old man fell down the steps at the Bell last night?' We prayed for the day when he would arrive beaming on the doorstep and announce that he had at last obtained a position worthy of him. 'I need some pride,' he would moan. 'I've swallowed it too long.'

One day he vanished. We thought that he had set out on some adventure (which I suppose he had in a way) but there was no dramatic note, which was unlike him. If he had gone to join the Foreign Legion, or to work in a circus, or to become a diver, he would have let us know. But there was nothing.

My grandmother pretended not to notice his absence but on the fourth day she mentioned to Rosa that the service revolver, which she had previously spotted hidden in the roof space, had vanished also. My mother went to the police station where they knew my father by sight and two nights later she had a dream that he was somewhere on Salisbury Plain.

In the street lived a kind man called Mr Jobb, who had been a policeman and owned a car. He drove us out over the plain, taking the narrow roads. It was May, a cold, blue evening, and you could see for miles. We stopped on the rises and climbed onto gates trying to spot him in the countryside, staggering across the landscape with a lost memory perhaps. Mr Jobb had a pair of field-glasses and scanned the horizon like a scout. But we could not see my father.

We tried again the following evening, taking some of the roads alongside the army areas, tank-testing grounds, ranges, places used for manoeuvres, land shut off with barbed wire fences and warning notices. It was while we were driving over some raised ground, alongside one of the barriers, that my mother said quietly: 'It's strange how those sheep all stick together in that one place, isn't it. When they've got the whole big field.'

The flock was packed as though penned into an oblong in the middle distance. 'Stupid things, sheep,' said Mr Jobb. He stopped the car and we looked towards them. 'That's a restricted area, it's probably full of mines or unexploded stuff, but they've got in there because the grass is thicker. They must have broken the fence down.'

'Or somebody broke it down,' I said to myself. We went as far as Amesbury and then turned back. It was dusk now but looking across the same hillside we saw that there were two camouflaged vehicles and some soldiers standing alongside the place where the sheep were gathered. One vehicle was an army ambulance.

'The army doesn't send ambulances for sheep,' observed Rosa. Mr Jobb braked and we all got out. After telling us to stay on the road he climbed over a gate on which was a warning notice with a skull and crossbones. By the time he had got halfway across the side of the hill the sheep were being shooed away by the soldiers.

Mr Jobb reached the army vehicles and we could see him talking to the men. My mother knew. With a small sob she climbed the gate and I went with her. We ran, staggering across the sloping ground. The sheep scattered. Mr Jobb saw us coming. He started forward with his arms spread out, trying to forestall us. We stood still and he came forward. 'It's him,' he said. 'He's dead.'

'Why did he go in there?' muttered my mother.

'I don't know.'

'Perhaps he planned to blow himself up,' she said in a matter-of-fact way. I began to weep, holding her around the waist.

'He broke down the fence and that's how the sheep got in,' said Mr Jobb. 'Don't go and see him. He shot himself.'

We stood in the distance, isolated in the middle of the dim field, and watched the medical orderlies carry away the stretcher.

'There's no explosives, it's been cleared,' said Mr Jobb. 'They told me.'

A sergeant came over to us. We could see that there was a sheep lying stiff on its back in the compound. 'Must have missed with the first shot,' he said with a sort of cheeriness. Perhaps he did not realise who we were. 'He shot the sheep.'

8

Sir Benedict soon had the tandem in working order. Although he was often bewildered by even the most familiar surroundings, although he could sometimes only just recall his last sentence, and although he had on occasion failed to recognise his own reflection in a mirror, he was quite lucid about some things, perhaps from years before.

On the day following his unearthing of it in the midnight barn we took the tandem creakily down to the cycle shop in town. I did the wheeling and he fussed alongside like someone encouraging a pony on a leading rein. It was not really a shop but a cottage by the river. The single word 'Deakin', painted years before, was over the door. The front room was full of wheels and spokes and frames and had bunches of bicycle pumps hanging like strange fruit from the ceiling. We went in and Sir Benedict bent his tall body low under the door. 'You caught your napper on that at one time, sir,' remembered a man sitting inside. He was blowing up an inner tube with his mouth, his cheeks like a trumpeter's. 'Practice,' he smiled when he saw that I was admiring him. 'Years of it.' He screwed on the valve and stood up.

He took in the tandem which I was supporting in the doorway. 'Now look at that,' he said, almost whispering. 'I never thought I'd see that again.'

'It's been a while,' conceded Sir Benedict. They both studied the machine.

'What happened to the saddle-bag?' asked the man.

Sir Benedict shrugged. 'Vanished,' he said eventually as though it were one of the great mysteries of the world. 'As things do.'

'I might be able to get one.'

'Please try.'

I realised I was watching a ritual, a careful game, played by two old men. I just held the tandem.

'Remember how much a machine like this cost?' Deakin patted the forward handlebars. 'Fifteen pounds ten shillings.' He answered his own question as though it would have been impertinent to expect Sir Benedict to do so.

'Without the pump,' put in Sir Benedict in a polite but pleased way. 'The pump was seven and sixpence.'

The bicycle man ran his finger along the crossbar in front of the first saddle, touching it surely at intervals like a piano tuner.

'I haven't been out on it for some time,' said Sir Benedict. 'Not since Lady Lucy died. She went over a cliff, you know. Not on the tandem.'

'I know,' nodded Deakin as if he had read about it yesterday. 'Very sad.'

'But I think I'll get more use from it now. Young Chloe here ...' He placed a pleasantly proprietorial hand lightly on my shoulder. '... is an enthusiastic tandemist.'

'Couldn't get better,' said Deakin. For a moment I wondered whether he meant me or the machine but then, running his finger over the frame, he said: 'You'll cause a sensation when you get this on the road.'

'Can you get the parts these days?' I asked.

'I can get them,' said Deakin with a minor sniff. He

frowned. 'The chain might be a problem. Finding one.' He lifted it with his engrained finger. 'But it'll probably be all right. I know somebody.'

'It's always the chains that go,' said Sir Benedict.

'Nearly always,' said Deakin. He repeated his small sniff. 'Just give me till next week, sir.'

We had some wonderful times on that tandem. It was ready by Thursday of the following week, as promised, and Sir Benedict and I went around to the low, oily house–shop by the river to collect it. Deakin spotted us coming along the waterside path and stood poised just inside the shadows of the door with the machine.

It was a lovely pale green, like a pea pod, and it looked complete and strong, as though it had just come from the manufacturers. 'A beauty,' confirmed the bike man. He patted the front saddle and touched the forward wheel with his knee. 'Good as new. You'll have some fine riding on that, sir.'

On the first morning, the day after we had reclaimed the bike (curiously we had walked it home, as though hesitant to mount it), he appeared in his cycling knickerbockers, stockings to the knee and a gingery jacket, with his brown shoes gleaming and ready for anything. Everything fitted him neatly. I was glad I had not worn shorts as I had thought at first, but a pair of jeans, a denim top to go with them and short socks and flat shoes. He approved. 'You look the part, Chloe,' he nodded. 'Born to it.'

Well, I was not born to it. It was far more intricate than it looked. We wobbled around the narrow roads of the cathedral close on a trial run, wriggling through a clutch of clergy, skirting a crocodile of children who laughed and called after us and more dramatically scattering a long double line of docile Japanese tourists who were threading into the cathedral. Sir Benedict shouted like a cavalry officer. They flew in all directions on their short legs, crying out and holding their arms over their heads. Somehow they all escaped except the tour guide who we pinned to a tree. Astonished, I saw that it was Ivor Popple. He was too shaken to recognise me. Fixed against the tree-trunk he began to blather apologies. We backed the tandem away while he, pink-cheeked, stumbled back to his charges.

We straightened the bike and made sure that the front wheel was undamaged and the handlebars aligned. Behind us Ivor Popple waved a pennant, blew a whistle and the Japanese visitors obediently formed up again.

We rode out again later, on the same evening, while there was still a summery light and few people about. Lady Annabel, if she had even noticed the tandem, said nothing. We had carried it in and out of the side gate, however, in case she heard the crunching on the gravel. 'Perhaps she'll think it is the ghost,' commented Sir Benedict glancing towards her window. 'You've heard about Lady Lucy?'

'Yes, you've mentioned her.' I wanted him to tell me more but I knew that I would have to wait.

We ventured out in the twilight. There was hardly any traffic in the town and we began going around the one-way system in the reverse direction. I tried to warn him but I was bent double. 'Braking now!' he called over his shoulder. He braked and we skidded, but halted more or less upright in front of a signpost. 'Devizes,' he breathed as if it pointed to Shangri La. 'On to Devizes, Chloe!'

Even his enthusiasm was not enough to attempt the whole journey. But we went out onto the country roads and then the lanes. A man with a gypsy caravan waved to us as though we were fellow survivors from a lost age. His dog chased us and Sir Benedict, bent low across the handlebars, shouted a challenge at it.

My original worry had been that Sir Benedict would not have the strength to pedal very far but he was amazingly robust and he soon got into the way of it. When he did wilt we would switch places and I would take the front seat while he rested behind. It was heavy going but he only changed over when we were on flat roads or when there were descending hills such as those coming down towards Salisbury from the plain. He was a gentleman.

It was lovely out there, peaceful with the horse chestnut trees massive over our heads and the evening air in our faces, cows staring at us and people looking up and sometimes greeting us from their gardens. We stopped at a thatched pub and leaned the tandem against a bench outside. The landlord saw us through the window and came out to see what we would like to drink. He said his mother and father had ridden a tandem. He still had their bicycle clips. We each had half a pint of cider. Rising and falling around us was Salisbury Plain, dimming now, with a solitary piping bird, and the distant grind of a late army tank going home. We could not see it but I knew the sound well enough. I knew that over the next rise was where my father had shot the sheep and then himself. The man brought the drinks and left us sitting there. Eventually Sir Benedict rose from the bench and went over to the tandem to make sure that the lights worked. They did. The sharp beam cut through the darkening evening.

'Well done, Deakin,' said Sir Benedict as though to himself.

He sat down by me again. I don't think I have ever felt

more at home, more serene, with anyone as I did with that old man. 'I'll tell you how Lady Lucy came to go over the cliff,' he said.

9

When I was on remand in prison, awaiting trial, Detective Sergeant Ron Brown came to see me. I was playing table tennis with Madonna, a young inmate who I was teaching to read and write. Table tennis and car theft were her skills. She had been in so many institutions, remand homes and prisons and they all had a table-tennis table.

'Watch 'im,' she warned flicking the ball from five feet beyond the other end, 'Like an 'awk, Chloe.' The ball clipped the edge at my end and flew out of reach. 'Seventeen, four,' she said.

She put the bat down and, while the woman warder who had come for me waited, she said: 'Just 'member what I told you.'

She had told me a lot of things since we had become friends. 'They got my bruvver Rento for nearly nuffink. . . . My uvver bruvver Kilroy 'ad done much more crimes than 'im and 'e's out in no fucking time.' 'Fucking' was one of the few words she could write. She had seen it on walls.

Detective Sergeant Ron Brown had been waiting by the door. 'What's she called?' he asked the woman who had come for me. 'The black girl.'

'Makepeace,' said the warder. 'Madonna Makepeace.'

'I know them.' He gave a sort of 'Huh' and then said: 'Hello, Chloe,' as though we had been friends for years, and shook my hand, reaching down to get hold of it. He glanced at the warder. 'Is the little office free?'

She went to look. I said to him: 'I'm trying to teach Madonna to read.' He looked unconvinced. 'They're what they call a dysfunctional family,' I said.

'Well, I know they don't work,' he said mildly.

He looked around the association room. In the distance Madonna was playing the table-tennis ball against the green wall. 'What's it like?' he asked. 'It's not often I get into a women's prison. I did go down to one in Sussex. They have to make yoghurt. All day they mix yoghurt. I can't stand yoghurt.'

We hung around until the warder returned and said the little office was free. Ron went first and I followed and the warder followed me. It was just another miserable room with a window jammed high against the ceiling. I could see it was bright outside. 'Nice day,' I said.

He looked surprised and then glanced over his shoulder. 'Didn't notice, to tell the truth,' he said with a shrug. 'With this job you don't get a lot of time to notice things.'

'I thought that *was* the job,' I said. 'Noticing things.'

'Ah,' he smiled and studied me. 'Oh, like that, you mean. Yes, you have to notice some things, naturally. You wouldn't be any good as a copper if you didn't. But not necessarily the weather.'

'What did you want?' I asked. There was a table with two chairs; he sat in one and motioned me to sit opposite. 'I've made umpteen statements.'

'I know,' he nodded. 'It's a funny old business, murder. There's murders and there's murders.'

Thinking it was some sort of police trap, I said nothing.

'The fact is,' he continued, 'I'm not really supposed to be here at all, seeing as you've already been charged, but

69

there's something that I'm curious about. In an unofficial capacity, if you get my meaning.'

I nodded. 'It's all right by me. I don't get many visitors – in fact, I don't get any.'

He was tugging something from his jacket. It was a shabby sports coat with patches on the elbows and he leaned on these as he bent forward after taking a single sheet of paper from the pocket. It was folded in quarters. He spread it on the table. I recognised Sir Benedict's handwriting with a touch of shock as though it might be some spirit message.

'This turned up among the old man's papers,' said Ron Brown. 'In his solicitor's office.'

'What is it?'

'It's dated ten years ago.' He turned the single sheet around so that I could see the date but before I could read further he turned it back. 'It's about his first wife, Lady Lucinda ... going over a cliff.' With a serious expression he looked up and pointed his finger towards the floor.

'Yes,' I said carefully. 'She did. He told me.' My hand went towards the rim of the paper. 'Can I see?'

'Don't see why not,' he said as though he were trying to think of a reason. He pushed it around on the table again and then said: 'It happened a long time ago.'

I felt I was going to cry as I began to read. I could see the old man, and in my imagination he looked just as I knew him, sitting solitary at his desk, late at night, writing down what he believed had happened, reading it carefully, folding it in an envelope and sending it to Spriggs & Spriggs. I read it:

My first wife Lady Lucinda Bowling – known to us all as Lucy – died aged forty on May 21st, 1956, after going over a cliff at St Bride's Head, Dorset. We were staying at the Cliff Edge Hotel the night before my mother's eightieth birthday celebration. Also staying there was Lucy's sister, Annabel, who later became my second wife.

At about six thirty in the evening Lady Lucy, who was dressed for dinner, announced that she was going for a walk. I offered to go with her but I was not ready and Annabel said that she would go. They left and I last saw my dear wife from our window walking with her sister up the sloping lawn of the hotel. They reached the ridge at the end and disappeared from view. Fifteen minutes later (I was still tying my tie) I saw Annabel's head appear above the ridge. She was hurrying and very agitated. I raised the sash window.

As she neared she stumbled and called something like: 'Oh Benedict, oh Benedict, a terrible thing! Lucy has gone over the cliff!'

Naturally I was very alarmed. I hurried downstairs and rushed up the lawn with Annabel following me, weeping and moaning. I did not really believe what she was saying because she was always a lying and dramatic woman. At the time I thought that perhaps Lucy had slipped and was lying hurt on the path which was just below the lip of the cliff, but when I got there I was shocked and dismayed to see she was floating in the sea far below. She was wearing a blue dress. The rescue services were telephoned. I kept calling to her, calling her name, but she only moved with the sea.

The inquest recorded an open verdict. Annabel told the coroner that she had been looking in the other direction, had heard a cry and had turned to see Lucy go over the cliff. Years later, long after we married, I began to suspect Annabel's story. She changed it whenever she retold it and she seemed to take an unseemly delight in doing so, especially for visitors. She began to suggest that she had seen Lucy take a long run and jump over the cliff. This was wicked and I never *believed it. She never said it to my face although I challenged her to do so. There was no reason for Lucy to have done anything like that.*

This remained the situation until one month before the date of this document. At that time I received a letter from a Mr Tom Goodbody, a former coastguard who lived in a cottage to the west of St Bride's Head. I attach a copy of this letter. It will be seen that, although he was half a mile from the place where Lucy plummeted, he had a powerful telescope and was in the habit of scanning the sea and coastline. According to his story, he saw, through his telescope, two women apparently struggling on the cliff top and one of them go over into the sea.

Naturally I was very concerned about these revelations and went, as soon as I could, to St Bride's Head to talk to Mr Goodbody only to find that he had recently died. His wife said that the fact that he had not long to live had made him write the letter and she had promised to post it after his death. It had been on his conscience for years, she said, but he had thought, and she had helped to persuade him, that he was mistaken, that one lady had only been trying to grasp the other as she stumbled on the edge of the cliff. Besides which he did not wish to make trouble and the telescope was not officially his. He was worried he might be questioned about it and his pension might suffer. But in his heart he knew what he had seen. Whatever the reason, he had not come forward with the information either at the inquest or since.

Slowly I handed the piece of paper back across the table. Poor Sir Benedict. 'Why didn't he tell the police?' asked the detective. 'This was written ten years ago. But he only filed it at his solicitors. Why didn't he tell us?'

'Don't ask me,' I said. 'Maybe because he was married to Lady Annabel by then. Maybe he didn't want to upset her.'

I knew he would stare at me and I looked up to find that he was. 'What does that mean?'

'He was getting old, and he got a lot older,' I said. 'Perhaps he still did not believe it himself – he certainly couldn't be sure – and it was all years and years before.'

Detective Sergeant Brown looked like a crouching dog. His chin was barely clearing the table. 'Or it could be he decided to extract vengeance *himself*,' he said.

I blinked carefully. 'Could it?'

'What you might call poetic,' he said. 'Annabel went over that same cliff, didn't she. A watery grave just like her sister.'

He leaned even further forward. He had an ordinary but pleasant face. 'I've had a bit of a look at it,' he said.

'At what?'

'The evidence or whatever you want to call it. The story. Apparently Lady Lucy – Lucy if I may call her that and I don't suppose she'll mind now after all this time. . . .'

He stopped and I prompted him. 'Lucy,' I said.

'Oh . . . oh yes. Sorry. Something else crossed my mind, no matter. Lucy was dressed for dinner. She was wearing a long velvet skirt. She liked long velvet skirts.'

I realised I was staring. 'You've been busy,' I said.

'I like to potter around a bit. Well, whatever she said at the inquest, Lady Annabel – Annabel we can call her – put around the story later that Lucy had actually *jumped*. And not just jumped but taken a running jump. Right over the cliff.'

'Does it matter now? They're all dead. It was years ago.'

'The records are still on file. Dorset police are good on records. They go back ages. I hate leaving loose ends around no matter how long ago it was.'

'So?'

'Well, that's it really,' he shrugged. 'Except that I don't know what Annabel could have been distracted by, looking the other way. There's bugger all to see – sorry – I mean nothing to see.'

'How do you know that?'

'I went and had a look. You can't even see much of the sea looking in that direction because there's some old ragged trees in the way, all bent over by the wind. They were there in those days, too, I've seen the pictures. Still, I suppose, something could have distracted her.'

He made a face and got up. 'I'd better be off. I'll come and see you again if you like – in my spare time, of course.'

I still could not believe him. 'All right.' He went towards the door. I could see the woman warder hanging about outside. 'You ought to be a detective,' I said.

'I might try it.'

As my solicitor, Mr Spelling, had promised the remand wing was not so bad; I even had an odd feeling of being safe in there. There were no men. My cell was at the end of the corridor so I had two barred windows. There was a bed, a locker and a wash-basin. I shared the toilet with six others, only one of whom was my age, a distracted woman who kept passing counterfeit cheques and did it so inexpertly that she was always caught. Four of the other five were on remand for theft or drugs, and Madonna was in, this time, for killing a man in a fit of rage. (She had run a kitchen knife through him. 'As far as it would go,' she said with gratification.) Two of the girls had babies and could go to the baby wing at certain hours to be with them. One of the babies was eighteen months old and, if the mother was convicted and sentenced to prison, it would be taken away. The girl used to cry half the night.

The oldest woman on remand was deaf and often got into trouble because she did not know what was going on. The young girls used to make fun, telling her things she could not hear. Her dog had been put down and she was worried because she thought her flat might be broken into while she was in prison. She was sixty if she was a day and she was awaiting sentence for non-payment of a fine for soliciting.

'It ain't no use thinking you're going to be out there, on the outside,' Madonna said to me with grim wisdom. 'Your 'ead's got to be in 'ere – right inside – because that's where you're going to be for years and fucking years. You've got to forget there's a place called out there.'

One day she brought me a present, a reward, as she put it, for teaching her to read as far as I had. 'I just found it,' she said. It was a bulky paperback with the covers missing back and front. 'It's too thick for me.' She laughed, her teeth suddenly flashing. 'Or I'm too thick for it, more like.'

When she had handed it to me almost shyly I saw what it was: *Gone with the Wind*. I let out a tight laugh. Madonna said: 'Don't say you've read it.' She looked at the title and said: '*Gone with the Wind*.' Her face lit again. 'There, now I can say I've read it.'

'Thanks,' I said giving her a kiss on her cheek. 'No, I haven't read it. I once knew somebody who tried, that's all. At least he said he had. You could never believe anything he said, even about a book.'

'The one that you got married to,' she guessed easily. She nodded at the book. 'Well, there's plenty of words there.'

'Even if I get life,' I said. I sat on the side of my bed and opened the first page. The warder came to lock us in and Madonna had to go. I began to read. If I took it slowly I might be able to fill up a year or so.

There was no garden where you could get air. Everything was inside, enclosed. Although I had two windows I could see nothing through them because they were high and murky. It was like living underwater. All I could look forward to were my journeys in the prison van to the magistrates' court, my outings I called them, and these would cease once I came to trial.

Only the girls who had the babies ever went out of the remand wing and into the main prison. They returned with terrible tales, about lesbian warders shouting and putting prisoners' names in books, strip searches and sudden compulsory showers and roll-calls. In the punishment block they took all your clothes away and made you wear a cotton smock while you were in solitary.

The warders in the remand wing were older and kinder. Mine told me she felt she was doing a sentence too. At least she went home at nine. They were nicknamed babysitters, not screws. They put on the lights in the morning and turned them off at night. There was nothing for us to do but everything had to be done by numbers, by rote, by routine.

We were allowed to wear our own clothes but only as many as we could hang in our lockers. The younger girls used to exchange clothes and tell each other how they looked. There was no full-length mirror for them to see.

There was a shower at the end of each corridor but we had to ask the babysitter in charge for shampoo and the use of a hairbrush. My old Mickey Mouse hairbrush was taken from me when I first arrived and I never saw it again.

In one of the tatty magazines in the association room I read that a woman is at her sexual best at forty. Somebody had written in the margin: 'What am I fucking doing in here then?'

10

I was forty-two when I began living in the cathedral close. Running the house, posting Lady Annabel's eccentric letters, listening obediently to her ramblings about Arabia, keeping Sir Benedict company on his tandem and in the evenings playing cards, did not afford many opportunities for romance.

Despite my almost daily loneliness I was grateful that there were no betrayals, disasters or heartaches to be faced; no need for tears. As the summer came on I used to sit in the garden for an hour or so in the afternoon under one of the blossomed apple trees, to read and run over things in my mind, often sadly wondering where my son Donny was. I wanted to find him, to see him, to talk to him, but I was afraid. Too much time had gone by. He would not want me now.

It was while I was lying back in the shady deck-chair one afternoon that Ivor Popple appeared around the side of the house and came across the grass on tiptoe like a daylight ghost. He was wearing a shiny black suit and a brimmed black hat with a crumpled open-necked shirt that had at some time been white but was now the same pasty hue as his face and neck. But he meant well. 'Is her ladyship in the vicinity?' he asked sliding against the tree for cover. It was angled to the ground and he had to hold his body at a strange position against the trunk.

'Did you want to see her?'

'No fear. On the contrary. I'd like to keep out of her sight. She doesn't like me, you know.'

He was quite pitiful. 'She keeps her curtains almost closed,' I said. 'She doesn't like the sun either.'

'No, she wouldn't,' he said looking relieved. 'I thought I would come to visit you, Chloe.'

'Here I am.' I smiled. I liked him because of his helplessness. The sun was glimmering from his shiny suit. 'Would you like a cup of tea?'

'As long as Lady Annabel doesn't spy me.'

'Why are you wearing that hat?'

'This . . .?' He touched the lopsided brim. 'Well, it keeps the sun off . . .' He regarded me with lame honesty. 'And I thought it lent me a certain . . . well, air of mystery.'

'Do you want to be mysterious?'

His hopeless hands flopped to his sides. 'I haven't got a lot else. I thought I might be able to manage some mystery.'

'So you give yourself an identity and hide it at the same time.'

'You're amazing, Chloe,' he mumbled unhappily. 'You seem to know me so well.'

It was at that moment that I set myself to make a man out of him. I had nothing better to do.

On the following Wednesday, my day off, Sir Benedict was complaining of what he called tandem tendons and decided to rest his legs.

'Ivor,' I said on the telephone, 'we are going to the place where you said your poet wrote.'

'Are we?' He became excited. 'When?'

'Today. Right now. In half an hour.'

'But ... oh, my goodness ... it's a little ...'

'It's not a *little* anything. We're *going*. There's a bus to Blandford, another to Bridport and another to Abbotsbury. I've got the timetable. I'll be at the close gate at ten. And don't wear that hat.'

He was there, waiting. I thought I could see him trembling even at a distance. I felt very good that day. Very sure and very happy. It was full English summer, sunny, the air warm, the clouds swollen yellow, the trees abundant, and I was wearing a pale blue dress that I could feel lying lightly against my skin. He had left his hat at home.

I would have kissed him on the cheek but before I could do so he pumped my hand as though I had just saved his life. 'This *is* exciting,' he enthused. He repeated it as we boarded the bus in town and he kept repeating it, sometimes below his breath, to himself, during our journey. 'The sun has caught your face already,' I said examining him sideways. 'It's light brown.'

'Since you advised me to lose the hat,' he admitted in a low voice, 'I have been practising. I sat in the garden for almost an hour yesterday in intermittent sunshine. I noticed last night that my forehead was quite tinged.'

'And your cheeks and neck,' I observed. 'They've got the odd splodge here and there.'

His face broadened with a beam. 'The new outdoor Ivor,' he said. 'It's a pity that so much of the Church is indoors.'

We were travelling through the crumpled countryside, past the modest Wiltshire hills and into the silence of Dorset. There were villages with the shadows of cottage roofs lolling across empty streets, and sheep on bright hillsides.

We had to change buses twice but by one o'clock we

were set down at the swannery at Abbotsbury and sat side by side on a seat facing the swans. I had brought sandwiches and a flask of tea and Ivor eyed the swans with his customary anxiety as he nibbled at the brown bread. There were several hundred swans gliding, preening, sleeping with their heads tucked below their wings, or walking, chests pushed out like drums. 'I do hope they're not hungry,' muttered Ivor viewing them over his crust. 'There are so many. But they'll probably ignore me.'

'It's time you stopped being ignored,' I suggested. There was chicken and tomato in the sandwiches, and the sky was blue and lofty above us as we munched.

'Even the visitors to the cathedral ignore me,' he said sadly. 'I guide them as best I can, but sometimes I feel like I'm ... well, soliciting. I move from one leg to another, trying to offer my services. Occasionally, somebody asks me the whereabouts of the toilet.'

Several earnest swans approached and Ivor, eyeing their every move, quickly ate his sandwich. They veered off. 'I feel almost claustrophobic in there,' he said. 'All those people. It's like a railway terminus.'

'What about your writing?'

'John Meade Falkner,' he murmured. 'Well, *he* probably gets a bit fed up with me sometimes, too. Perhaps today will help. Shall we walk to the chapel? It will take over an hour, but it's a lovely walk along the coast.'

It was a tiring walk in the warmth but we eventually reached the tiny chapel. It was all that was left of the original church apart from a pile of ruins. 'Washed away in a great tidal wave,' said Ivor as we made our way through the graveyard. 'The wave came over the pebble bank and flooded, drowned the villages. West Fleet and East Fleet. Everything.' In a moment, a change came over him; the way he spoke, even the way he moved. We became silent. Suddenly it was as though I were not there. When he spoke it was only to himself. 'The Mohuns,' he said. 'The family. This was their chapel.' There were two memorial stones and a faded plaque on the wall. 'And this is for John Meade Falkner,' he said, still without looking at me. 'His book *Moonfleet* was their story.'

He stood, his figure gaunt, and to my amazement began to recite in a fine voice:

> 'Friend, when the dews are falling,
> When the red sunset fades,
> When summer owls are calling
> Deep in the darkening glades.'

Slowly he turned to me. 'He composed that,' he said with a smile.

I felt a tremble inside me. In that instant he was a different man – his voice, the poem. I felt a thrill run down me. 'So sorry,' he said as we went outside again, and over to the ruins. 'It's embarrassing, isn't it.'

'It's not embarrassing.' I told him. 'Will you do it again?'

He blushed with real pleasure. I sat on a stone and he recited the poem right through. His voice had become strong, his face solid, his eyes cloudy. He seemed to have grown in front of me. When he had finished he stood in a bashful sort of way. I stepped forward and kissed him. He blushed and flapped his arms. 'I haven't had a lot of dealings . . .' he began. He backed off a few inches. 'I don't quite know how one positions oneself.'

'I'll show you,' I said.

I tenderly shifted him. We performed a shuffle, like a dance step, and I managed him into a position so that his legs were strongly astride and I was standing between them. His trousers felt hot. I fed his arms around me. 'The faces,' he muttered. 'I'm uncertain of the position of the faces.'

With an adjustable look into each other's eyes we closed and deeply kissed. I felt him go taut but he had the lips of a goldfish. 'Stay still,' I whispered. His hair was quite curly at the ends. 'Keep your lips ready.'

It was still not very good. He was apologetic to the point of tears. 'I knew I'd never get it right,' he sniffed. 'It's only lack of practice.'

I laughed outright and he cheered up. We walked back through the late afternoon the way we had come. We never saw another person nor even a car on the coastal road but the air was warm, and it was like walking through a rosy dream.

It was not difficult to smuggle Ivor into the house. It was scarcely dark by the time we returned, a close night, the top of the spire with its red warning light against the fading sky. We walked under the gate arch a little apart from each other. 'I'm very excited, Chloe,' he confided as we passed in front of the west door. 'I'm sure I'm going to like it.'

We had planned it quite blatantly because I wanted him to know exactly what would take place and I wanted no startled panic or fleeing on his part. My suggestion that we creep into his mother's house had filled him with terror. 'I couldn't, I really couldn't,' he confessed. 'The scene, if she discovered me – us – would be unimaginable.'

There would be no difficulty in getting him into Canon's House and into my room. It was Urchfont's night for the cinema and Lady Annabel would be enclosed in her room, the door locked, earmuffs clamped on. 'If burglars break in then I have no wish to disturb them, or they to disturb me,' she always said. Sir Benedict, even if he noticed Ivor's presence, would have thought little of it and would probably have forgotten by the next morning. I was looking forward to wearing the silk nightdress I had bought in the animal charities shop.

We went through the rear gate into the garden. Ducks mumbled under the river bank, an owl made itself known. 'One of your summer owls,' I whispered. 'Deep in the darkening glades,' he returned romantically. I led him by the hand.

There was scarcely a glow from the house, just the half-buried landing light that burned throughout night and day. No one could remember where the switch was; Urchfont swore it had been walled-in during alterations years before.

From the garden it looked so inviting, silent and dim. The kitchen door scraped open but without much noise. 'This way,' I croaked unnecessarily and I put my finger, just as unnecessarily, to my lips.

'It's all *so* exciting,' Ivor said, his timid eyes moving around the shadows. 'Are you *sure* it will be all right?'

'It will be,' I said navigating him between the pieces of furniture. His thin body went rigid when the hall clock boomed eleven; he stood frozen until the strikes had finished. I still held his hand as I led him up the stairs. Like children we carefully put our feet on the sides of each tread so that there were no creaks from the loose boards. All around us the house seemed to breathe warmly. I opened my bedroom door gently and, with a restrained eagerness, pushed him in. It was four and a half months since I had last made love.

When I switched on the bedside lamp he jumped at

the light. Then, as he surveyed the room, his eyes fell on the oval framed photograph by my bedside. 'Who is this?' he asked pointing his thin finger like an accusation.

'My son,' I said. 'Donny.'

He seemed nonplussed. 'But I didn't know.'

'He's twenty-two now. I don't know where he is. He sends me a pebble now and again.'

Even this unusual news did not divert him. 'I didn't know you had been married,' he said as if I owed him an explanation.

'I'm not married now,' I said.

'Divorced?'

'Divorced.'

'You must be very experienced, Chloe,' he said with a reluctant admiration. 'I wonder sometimes if I've been alive at all.'

He sat on the bed like an unhappy boy. I eased him back and leaned over and kissed him, my breasts lying mildly against his shirt. 'Tonight, Ivor,' I promised, 'you'll be alive.'

Quickly I undressed him. He covered his skinny nakedness by folding the duvet about him and sat and watched me with a sort of frightened interest while I began to take my clothes off. I turned my naked back to him. My silk nightdress was folded in the chest of drawers and when I was almost undressed, I took it out. Its sheen reflected the bedside lamplight. I turned again in the dim light. Ivor sat dumbstruck. I put the nightdress against my naked breasts and smiled reassuringly towards him. Next I eased the pearly garment over my head and let it drop around me. 'My mother has a nightie much like that,' he muttered.

I advanced on him, my expression serious, my eyes warm, my lips apart, my hands ready, everything I could do. Shimmering, I stood over him at the bedside. He pulled the duvet closer and up around his neck. 'This is *me*,' I told him. 'Me, Chloe Smith. *Not* your mother, Ivor.'

'No, no, of course you aren't, although I must confess I had forgotten that your surname is Smith. It was just . . .'

To halt his gabble I tilted forward and felt my breasts attempting to tumble from the front of the nightdress. I caught hold of his concealing bedcover with one hand and firmly whisked it away. He crouched, knees protectively bent, his eyes flooded with apprehension.

Easily I climbed above him, supporting myself on my hands. 'Ivor,' I ordered, 'take my straps down.'

'Your straps?'

'My shoulder straps.'

'Oh, the straps, yes. Of course.' He pulled himself out of his immobility and reached and fumbled. I balanced on one arm, poised above him, and tugged each strap away myself. My bosom dropped out more or less on top of him. With a low cry he fell back against the bed. I reached and caught his poor penis in my left hand, then changed to my right to get a better hold. Watching his face all the time, I tugged carefully at him. 'Recite something,' I said.

My breasts were lolling close to his chest and now he tentatively tapped them, one and then the other, as though carrying out a test. He began to recite, croakily at first:

> 'The mountains look on Marathon,
> And Marathon looks on the sea.
> And musing there an hour alone,
> I dreamed that Greece might still be free.'

It was better than nothing. His good voice, its cadences, and then the throb of his body as he lay below me, started me off. And once I had begun so did he. I spun him on top like a tumbler and pushed and manoeuvred his backside and coaxed him inside me. Once he had the hang of it he began to enjoy it. At his climax he gave a groan and mumbled something like a blessing. He lay like a boy against me while we cooled, then asked for a cup of tea.

On the following day he telephoned to tell me that he was deeply in love with me. Then he vanished, disappeared into the Salisbury air like a passing cloud. I made enquiries in the cathedral and anywhere else I could imagine he might go. But no one had seen him. Eventually I arranged for one of the younger, braver clergy to ask his mother but she merely said: 'He has left.'

Two weeks later I received a single sheet of notepaper headed 'St Ambrose, London, The Church for Men'. There was no message, only the signature 'Ivor'.

Then he telephoned. 'I have found my place, Chloe,' he said quite chattily. 'My work is here.'

'At St Ambrose,' I said flatly. 'The Church for Men.'

'Absolutely. St Ambrose, you know, according to St Augustine, was the first man to be able to read without moving his lips. He began a new way of life.'

'Really.'

'Yes. And he introduced hymns into worship.'

'Hymns,' I said.

'Yes. Hymns.'

'And you are continuing his work.'

'I am, Chloe.'

'So we are not going to meet again.'

'Oh, we may. But I shall always be grateful to you, Chloe. You showed me the way, the realisation, the *Truth*. Until I was with you, I didn't know.'

11

Teaching Madonna to read while we were in prison was
very hard. Because of our remand category, neither of us
was eligible for education and we had to get together
some simple books in a haphazard fashion. We had *Harry
Squirrel* which was useful, but beyond that we had to make
do with a 1991 seed catalogue, part of a manual for a
Ford Escort, and a copy of the *Highway Code* slightly but
ominously stained with blood.

'I been to school,' she assured me. We used to get a
couple of chairs and sit by the table-tennis table because
it was quiet in there although sometimes a suspicious
warder would come in to see what was going on because
she could not hear the click-clock of the ball. 'I been quite
a few times.'

She could manage *Harry Squirrel* quite well although she
had never seen a squirrel and thought that the creature
had just been made up for the purposes of the story. The
plot, unfortunately, failed to impress her. 'I can *tell* what's
going to 'appen,' she would exclaim sharply turning the
page. 'There, look.' Triumph would flood into her eyes
and her voice. 'All 'e does is post 'is letter and fuck off
'ome to 'is 'ole in the tree.'

God knows where the seed and plant catalogue
('Orders *must* be received by 20 March 1991') came from
but it proved very difficult. Why geraniums did not begin

with the letter 'j' angered her. What was the point of having a letter if you did not use it? Antirrhinums and mesembrianthemums were understandably beyond her although she had some fun with phlox and oddly she could manage some Latin names printed in italics because, she said, they were better to read when they were hanging to the side. The vegetable section was more satisfying; leek, parsnip, carrot, peas and potato were easy. She enjoyed reading them, syllable by syllable, over and over, and at mealtimes she would spell them out carefully to the dour serving women. I can see her now in the steam and clamour, holding out her plate and reciting: 'Ca-rrots and po-ta-toes and cour-g . . . cour . . . oh, fuck, give me some beans – b-e-a-n-s.' Poor Madonna.

It was the *Highway Code* which was her favourite, though (she had once driven a getaway car). 'I knowed 'ow to drive since I was eleven,' she claimed. 'I often used to 'elp out my old man when 'e was in an 'urry.' She took easily to all the motoring terms, although she had different names for them; the accelerator was the 'poke', the brake the 'drag' and the boot she called the 'loot'. It took no more than a few lessons to read it right through and she vowed that when she got her distant parole (she had no optimism about the outcome of her approaching trial) she was going to get a mean car. 'You'll have to save up,' I told her like a mother. But she smiled with her crafty black eyes and said: 'No way.' When we finished the reading lesson she pointed out in the torn Ford Escort manual the bits on the diagram which were the most easily removed and quickly sold. Madonna lived in that world.

Her enthusiasm for reading grew; she was bright and learned quickly. She soon conquered the motoring literature and it was the seed catalogue which occupied her most. She spent long lock-up hours in her cell attempting to recite the most difficult names of plants and flowers. One day she was going to buy a flower shop and live happily ever after. We talked of where it would be, what it was to be called, and she was really excited when I suggested 'Madonna's'. It was only a dream.

One night I heard the alarm bells and the rush of feet. Someone shouted that she had been found hanging in her cell but it was a false alarm; she was safe and well. There was a slant of light that came through her window from outside; it was an inch wide and filtered through, from some exterior lamp, at the very top of the bars. After lights out at nine thirty a duty warder passed outside and through the spyhole in the door saw her legs dangling. But Madonna was only reading. She had climbed on top of her iron locker and, head bent against the hard ceiling, was sitting studying her seed catalogue, her shiny legs drumming gently against the side of the locker.

'There's no way I'm goin' to top myself, not now I can read,' she promised me. 'I've got the flower shop to think about.'

Two weeks later she went for trial and knew it would be a great many years before she would be free to open her shop. She got the sentence she forecast and that night they spotted her legs dangling in the window again. But this time she had really done it. This time the drumming of her calves against the locker was not the happy captivation of words but the last movements of her poor body.

On the morning of my next remand I again passed the cake shop where I had worked and this time I saw Mr

Cooper himself. It had been years but I knew him unmistakably even though it was through the clouded window of the prison van taking me through Salisbury to the court. He was elderly by now, of course, but he still had his big moustache. He stood in front of his shop conversing in the sunshine with some passer-by, the cakes and pastries arrayed in the window behind him. Our vehicle stopped in the traffic and I could not resist it. I put my mouth against the glass and shouted: 'Mr Cooper!' I could see he had not heard but I tried again: 'Hilaire!' And by God he must have heard my cry faintly because he looked up and stared around as if he were hearing the calling of a ghost. The escorting security woman, sitting uniformed at the curious desk in the other portion of the van, beyond the grille which prevented her being attacked, said: 'Shush,' but only passively. 'You're not allowed to shout.'

Mr Cooper looked less agile now but there was a time when he could balance a tray of cakes on his head. In those days he was not yet forty and his wife had run away to the North. When I went to work in the pastry shop on Saturdays, when I was at school in Salisbury, he took a liking to me. He could make me laugh for he was an expert in all sorts of juggling tricks with doughnuts and even loaves of bread. He could catch a holed doughnut on his nose. I used to look forward to Saturdays. The shop was always busy and I wore a starched apron and a hat like a halo with 'Cooper's Bakery' embroidered across the front. After the shop closed for the day I would make a large pot of tea and Miss Fairchild, the full-time assistant, Mr Rollins, the pastry-cook, a fat boy called Dabs who was learning, Mr Cooper and I would all sit down and drink out of coloured mugs and eat whatever cakes we fancied from those that were left from the day's trading.

They were really nice times. In the winter we lowered the blinds and you could hear the people passing in the street waiting for a bus and talking, sometimes telling secrets or gossip and often making complimentary comments about Mr Cooper's confectionery and bread, making him smile in a pleased but faraway manner. The bus-stop was outside the window – from the prison van I could still see people waiting there – and while we drank our tea sitting on chairs or on the counter, we would listen like spies to what was being said. We would giggle as someone we knew was mentioned and Mr Rollins, who was a good comic, would imitate the voices of the country people waiting for their bus home. One evening, we heard a man and a woman talking loudly about Mr Cooper's wife going off. Being outside the shop must have reminded them. The woman said: 'It's no loss. She only made trouble.'

'A lot of wives will sleep sounder,' said the man. 'Mine for a start.'

Inside the shop we sat in deeply embarrassed silence. I was on the counter, my legs dangling, and at first I could not bring myself to look at Mr Cooper as the others were doing. When I did I saw the tears beginning to roll down his sugary cheeks (he had been juggling again). As if he thought we expected it of him, he got up and stamped to the door, lifted the blind and then turned the key. The bus had just arrived and the man and the woman were getting aboard. 'I'll have you know,' Mr Cooper said in a loud sob, 'that my wife is a decent woman and she's only gone on holiday.'

We did not hear anything they may have said in reply. They must have been shocked and probably said nothing, not until they got on the bus and it drove away. Fumbling, Mr Cooper relocked the door and, with the sugar on his cheeks damp, came back. He managed to say: 'Gossips,' and went into the rear of the shop to begin clearing up. One by one the others wordlessly went home. I was sweeping when he returned. 'I'm sorry, Mr Cooper,' I said.

'Call me Hilaire,' he pleaded. 'Please, Chloe.'

'I'm sorry, Hilaire.' It sounded such a funny name to me but he cheered up at once and did his trick of balancing the tray of cakes on his head. If they had tipped over it would not have mattered because it was Saturday night. He even began to do a dance. He held out his long pale hands to me and, not thinking twice, I joined with him and we danced around the shop with the tray still on his head, revolving slowly as he himself turned.

It all seemed very harmless to me. His eyes began to warm up and I was glad that his tears were done and his moustache did not look so downcast. I laughed at the easily spinning tray and we did a sort of waltz, both la-la-ing a tune. He held me only lightly and I felt happy and safe. Dancing with my father would have been like this. Then Hilaire did an especially big turn and when we came face to face again, he said earnestly: 'Chloe, will you marry me?'

It was such a shock. The tray slithered sideways and the maids of honour bounced on the floor. The tray fell on its edge and ended leaning against the counter. 'Oh, dear, now see what I've done,' said Mr Cooper.

Gratefully, I made flustered sounds and dropped to my knees to begin clearing the custard and cake-crumbs. 'It's all right,' I kept saying. 'I'll sweep it again. Don't worry, Mr Cooper.'

'Hilaire,' he repeated. He dropped to a kneeling

position in front of me, the knees of his trousers coated with icing sugar.

'Yes, I'll sweep it up, Hilaire,' I repeated wildly. I tried to look for the broom but he caught my hands in his and we remained kneeling. 'Not right *now*,' he said. 'I don't mean right away, Chloe. I don't expect you to marry me yet.'

'I'm only fifteen.'

'I know. And I'm . . .'

'Forty.'

'Well, not quite,' he said sombrely. 'But we're nowhere near. You can wait a few years. Three or four. Five at the most.'

'What difference will that make, Mr Cooper . . . Hilaire?'

'Ages have a habit of sort of closing up. By then people will hardly notice the difference.'

'What about Mrs Cooper?'

His moustache sagged. 'She's never coming back,' he said. 'She knows a man in Salford.'

'My knees are hurting,' I said.

'Yes, of course. Look at mine.' We got up. He had to hold the edge of the counter. He brushed his trousers off and I went towards the broom. As I got it I thought he was going to catch hold of me again but he compromised by grasping the handle. He was not a wicked man. 'I don't expect an answer now,' he said hoarsely. He still had sugar on his cheeks. 'I really look forward to Saturdays when you come in, Chloe.'

'I like it too,' I said.

'Do you honestly?'

'Yes, I like seeing all the fresh cakes in the morning and the sniff of the bread.'

'It could all be yours,' he said waving his hands around

the shop. 'All this.' He paused and said dramatically: 'And I'm planning to open in Stockbridge.'

He released the broom and I began to sweep while he stood helplessly as though searching for something else to say. 'There's a bit of a maid of honour over in the corner,' he pointed out.

Poor Mr Cooper, poor Hilaire. He later married a very businesslike woman who really set the shop working, and the other branches, eight in all in the end. They had two sons but she later left all three. He was the sort of man women do leave. We had stopped for the traffic lights and now we were moving off. Through the smoked glass I saw the lady he was talking with walk away. I decided against calling to him again. As we moved away he was looking up and down the street as though seeking someone. Anyone.

On this day there was no market and the town square was almost empty. But as the van turned in towards the Guildhall the escorting security woman glanced through her window and said: 'Looks like it's raining.' I knew what she meant. There were people waiting to see me. Hanging around, mothers with small children mostly, waiting to catch a glimpse of the woman charged with murder.

I put the grubby anorak which was offered over my head and she opened the door. It had been close inside the van and now the air came in. There were men's voices outside and I recognised Mr Victor, the court officer, giving instructions to make it quick, but above it I could hear the sound of the spectators, as frightening as a lynch mob. 'She's coming out now.' 'Look, there she is.' 'Look, Tracy, see the one with the coat on her head.'

Two pairs of hands guided me down the steps from the

van. I could only see my feet in my best shoes. I was shaking. I heard Mr Victor ordering people to move back. There was a scraping sound and I realised they must be behind a metal barrier which they were pushing forward. 'Get back,' Mr Victor told them angrily. 'Haven't you got anything better to do?'

I was led the few paces to the door and I felt the warmer air of the building close around me. The door was closed, then opened and Mr Victor came in. 'Peasants,' he said.

Pushing the anorak from my head I handed it to the escorting woman who was waiting with her hand outstretched. 'I'll keep it handy,' she said. 'You've got to go back.'

There were three other people in the small room, the driver of the prison van and two policemen, one of whom I recognised. 'I'm Phil,' he said. 'Remember?'

I smiled at him.

'Patty says to tell you she was glad you got second in the Grand National. You won fifty quid, didn't you?'

'It's going towards my defence,' I said and everyone laughed. 'I'll tell her,' said Phil. 'She'll like that.'

Mr Victor took me down to the cells, with Phil following. Mr Spelling was sitting there, reading over the top of his spectacles. He had a sheaf of papers in his hand. He stood in a pleased sort of way as if he had thought there was a chance that I might not turn up.

He shook my hand and said he had good news. 'We have managed to get you an excellent counsel,' he said. 'John Fellows QC. He's on a case in London at the moment but you'll meet him before your plea hearing.'

For the first time it came to me that this was just an episode, an incident, in the lives of these men, Mr Victor, Phil the policeman, the as yet unknown John Fellows and

Mr Spelling himself. The papers Mr Spelling had been reading, and which were exposed on the table, had nothing to do with me. I could read somebody else's name. And there was this John Fellows in court miles away defending, or prosecuting, someone else who I would never see. Tomorrow both men would be dealing with something different, a new crime, a new accused. I was just part of the general picture; the law and the lawless.

As if to emphasise this I had to wait for an hour while the magistrates were hearing a motoring case. 'Very complicated,' said Mr Victor on one of his return visits. 'All a matter of measuring brake marks to a zebra.' Mr Spelling had to go away, back to his office, on some urgent matter about somebody deciding to plead guilty to something. Policeman Phil ran out of conversation and lent me his *Daily Mail*. It was full of crime and health tips.

Eventually Mr Spelling returned and Mr Victor came back to call me into court. The public seats were crammed and I still could not believe they had come to see me. I thought they must be waiting for the next case or left over from the last. I had never had such attention in my life.

But it *was* me they wanted to see. As soon as I walked into the court there was a silence so complete I could hear my own heels on the floor, followed by a sudden buzz as though a motor had been switched on. I was still only taking my place facing the magistrates when Major Tully, who was the chairman again, told them to keep silence or he would clear them from the court. They obeyed in a moment.

There were four magistrates on the bench this time. The prosecution man asked for a further fourteen-day remand. Standing behind him was Detective Ron Brown and the lawyer turned and spoke to him briefly. It was strange to think, after our friendly chats, that he was really on their side.

They said that it would not be long before my committal, after which the case could go for trial at the Crown Court. I took this in but it did not seem to matter to me. I was convinced my life was set out for a good many years.

When I went out of the courtroom again with Mr Victor and policeman Phil I fell to the temptation to glance at the public eager in their seats. Suddenly a woman's hand waved. I never saw who it was. I did not want to see.

12

I was only twenty when Donny was born. His father, Alfred, was a burglar among other things. Once he told me that he would steal anything for me. He even stole a grand piano and brought it home for me to play.

Dishonesty was something he could not resist. Even if he had no reason to steal he would do it anyway. It was like a hobby.

When I was eighteen I had finally left my mother in Aldershot, in her flat, with its view of the parade-ground where she could see the men marching and sometimes hear a band playing. She liked to imagine that she was young again and that my father was striding out, his cheeks inflated, his tuba – his bombardon – reflecting the sun.

But by then it was two years since the evening on Salisbury Plain when we found him with the shot sheep. 'I realise he is never coming back,' she would say wiping one eye and going to make a cup of tea. 'But I can pretend he is. I can still hear him, Chloe.'

It was difficult to leave her. But I was eighteen and the marching squaddies meant nothing to me; they were just drab boys. I had worked hard and done well at school and they even talked of me going on to university. 'You can wear one of those nice flat hats with a tassel,' teased my mother hopefully.

But I wanted to be out on my own, if not too far out on my own. I wanted to go to Southampton and get a job. It was not London but it was a city and it was by the sea. In Aldershot, Southampton was reckoned to be exciting. Rosa was at her window sitting in a chair as she sometimes did if it was a long session of square-bashing. From the moment I had left school she had been hinting at possible local situations. 'It's not all soldiers,' she pointed out primly. 'There are building societies.'

'I want to go to Southampton.'

I could see she was shocked. 'It's a long way to go every day,' she said nervously. 'You have to change trains.' She regarded me with a bleak honesty, then returned to the view. I stood at her shoulder; I was all she had (you could not count Kneller, we never saw him) and I stared out of the window with her, my chin touching her hair. We could hear the sergeant bawling and the soldiers were halted in disarray, some facing one way, some another, with heads bowed as if they were ashamed or perhaps praying. 'You mean you want to go and *stay* there?' she asked without turning round. 'Southampton?'

I looped my arms about her, warm and chubby as she was. 'I'll always come back,' I said. 'I'll see you every weekend.'

'Let's have a cup of tea,' she suggested, her usual ploy for buying time. I made the tea while she continued sitting, the sun filtering through the glass. It was summer but Aldershot, to me, looked no different to the way it looked at any other time of the year. I was determined to head for freedom and the coast.

'It can be very chilly down there,' she said thoughtfully while we drank the tea. 'The wind blows cold off the sea around those shop corners.'

'I'll wrap up well,' I said. I was not going to cry because I knew it would set her off.

'Make sure you do.'

Welling with excitement and anticipation I left Aldershot. Rosa offered to come with me to find a job and somewhere to live but I managed to dissuade her. Nowhere would have been good enough.

For a girl of eighteen Southampton seemed like a city of adventures. In the docks there were two large liners and you could clearly see them, standing up like white buildings. Even glancing towards them from the station I imagined the places they had been, and would go again. It was a bright day with slaps of breezy air coming off the sea. After Aldershot it seemed like a place bulging with possibilities; there were people hurrying around the streets and shops, windows gleamed and there were flags flying from buildings and second-hand car sites. I walked around savouring it all, wondering but not worried. Everything, I was sure, would happen.

Nothing much did. No one spoke to me (I was used to passing chat from soldiers), the sun went in and the buildings grew grey. Eventually I bought a newspaper and sat in a café looking through the advertisements. I needed accommodation first. The tightly printed lines all seemed to cram against each other. There were phone numbers and brief recommendations for places to lodge and, in the Situations Vacant section, what appeared to be outstanding qualifications required for low salaries. There was a public telephone across the street but there always seemed to be someone occupying it and another three people circling it impatiently. I had a pot of tea and two cakes. Suddenly there were more people in the street and I realised it was five o'clock and they were going to their homes from their jobs and I had failed to find either. The evening was dull and the buildings darkened. Moodily, I faced the prospect of returning on the train to Aldershot with nothing accomplished. My mother would be confidently expecting me.

'You've got a nice figure.'

He was sitting two tables behind me. It was a wonder I had failed to notice him. He was handsome and broad, with fair hair and strong blue eyes. My future. 'I've been sitting here looking at you,' he said.

I had no idea what to say. Was this the sort of sophistication Southampton offered?

'Where do you come from?' he asked.

'Aldershot.' I was glad to find something I was sure of saying.

He nodded at the newspaper. 'Find anything?'

'Not much,' I admitted. 'They're all phone numbers and I haven't got a phone handy.'

'Run away, have you?'

'No. My mother knows where I am.'

'How about your father?'

'He's dead.'

'Oh, pity. A girl needs a father. I'll give you a job if you like.'

'Doing what?'

The waitress, not much older than me, was hovering protectively. 'Zane,' she said, 'she's not going to be a model for you.'

He looked only mildly annoyed. 'I only thought she would look nice in a showroom with some classy cars.'

'And wearing next to nothing,' she retorted.

'She could wear a bit.'

'I don't want to be a model.' I thought I was being left out of the argument.

'Well done,' said the waitress smiling at me. She was a streaky blonde and she looked kind but tired. Zane got up with a sigh. He looked even better standing. He wore a lovely corduroy jacket and a denim shirt and twill trousers. He drained his teacup as he stood and waved a dismissive goodbye. Both of us watched him go. 'He's all right,' said the waitress. 'Just dodgy.'

'What does he do?'

'Anything.' She wrinkled her nose. 'Anything that comes along.' She indicated the newspaper and repeated Zane's question: 'Find anything?'

Now I made a face. 'Nothing. It's difficult to know where to start.'

'Job or accommodation?'

'Both, really.'

She nodded understandingly. 'You're starting out on your own, are you? Making a new go of it.' I glanced around. The café was almost empty. She straightened some chairs and brushed some crumbs onto the floor, grumbling: 'How they get so many bits on the chairs I'll never understand.'

Looking at her watch she called over her shoulder to the man at the cash desk: 'All right, Lol?'

'All right,' answered Lol. He flicked the till with the side of his hand and said: 'Another golden day.' Then he walked around to the door and locked it. As he did so two old women appeared outside glaring challengingly through the glass. 'Closed,' he said opening the door a fraction. One pointed accusingly at the clock on the wall inside the café. It was barely five thirty. They turned away grousing.

'They'll have to go to the Ritz,' he said.

Swaying his large hips, he came through the chairs towards us. The girl handed him the cloth she had been holding and he wiped his hands in the way of someone who was glad the day was over. 'She's looking for work and lodgings,' said the waitress.

'What's your name, love?'

'Chloe,' I said. 'Smith.'

'That's unusual,' nodded Lol. 'Not Smith, I mean Chloe.'

'My name's Penny,' said the waitress. 'Lol owns this place.' She giggled. 'He's called Lol because he's always leaning on the counter.'

He smiled patiently and said: 'This is the social centre of Southampton.' He was unfit and olive-skinned with hair so thick and flat it might have been a cap. 'Where everybody meets everybody.'

'Nobody,' corrected the girl. Lol did not seem upset. He began casually flicking crumbs from the tables. 'That Zane Tomkins was trying to pick her up,' said Penny.

'He would,' said Lol. 'I wonder what he's up to now. You never know with him.'

'Zane,' I said. 'What a name.'

'It's not real,' said Lol. 'Not a lot is about Zane.'

'Chloe's looking for a roof,' repeated Penny. 'What about the back bedroom? There's only orange boxes. She'll have a job to get anywhere reasonable tonight, safe or anything. She's only young. Otherwise she'll have to go back to Aldershot.'

'You don't want to do that,' said Lol to me. 'We'll have to move those boxes.'

'You can have a proper look around then,' said Penny. 'Get settled.' She sat down confidingly. Lol went away still flicking at the tables and chairs. 'Crumbs,' he muttered. 'A world of crumbs.'

'Thanks very much,' I said to Penny. 'Are you sure?'

'It will be fine,' she assured patting my hand. 'There's

not that many orange boxes. And Lol won't charge you a fortune. He's very good-hearted. That's his trouble. I was like you, coming here to make a new start, and this is as far as I got. I've been here two years now.'

I was grateful and relieved. 'I'll start looking for a job tomorrow.'

'Get up early and do it,' she advised seriously. Her concern made her seem older. 'Put yourself about. Whatever you do, don't come and work *here*. Lol will ask you. He's good. But don't do it, it's too comfortable. It's not the way to see the world. Or even Southampton.'

I settled easily in Southampton, happy and ordinary, although I was soon to embark on the first of the misadventures which have plagued my life ever since, each one leading unerringly to the next.

Lol from the café had carried all the orange boxes from the small room in his house. He got support from the door jamb while he found his breath. He always found somewhere to lean. Penny had made up the single divan and put a bulb in the bedside lamp. By the time I had returned from getting some take-away for all of us I had a cosy place to stay. I stood in the doorway and looked at the tight bed and the warm lamplight and I felt myself break into a smile. Penny came up the stairs and said: 'Is it all right?' I nodded – I could hardly speak – and hugged her.

I stayed in that confined and contented place for a month. It would have been longer; indeed if I had stayed who knows what paths my life might have followed, but meeting with Dolores and Bet of the Sweet and Low Ensemble changed all that.

They were playing at a pub by the sea, on a summery evening; music in the garden while the waves sounded

and the lights of boats passed by slowly in the plushy
night. Further out a liner sailed, lit up like a city. There
were a lot of people in the garden, drinking and listening.
Lol was leaning against a tree holding a pint as if it were
heavy, and there were others ranged about. I was with
Brian, a nice and handsome fellow, who was in love with
me, but was dull and decent. He probably knows now, if
he's alive and reads the papers, what a lucky escape he
had.

Everything seemed right with my life at that time, if a
touch quiet. My job as a receptionist at Fayler's, Estate
Agents and Auctioneers, suited me well. It was a
comfortable office and it looked over the Solent which
could sparkle like a tropical sea or be hung with rain and
mist and spooky ships. But my work was never enclosed.
Every time the glass door opened I felt there was a
chance that a new story would start. All kinds of people
came in, the buyers and sellers of houses, flats and
businesses, people heading for the auctions department
with Chinese vases and ancient carpets and hopeful
paintings. Brian had come in that way too. He was
square and straight-looking and he wore a decent suit
and had a clean smile. He took me to the cinema and to
Chinese restaurants. He was a draughtsman and was
good at sport, a reliable goalkeeper. Poor Brian.

On the evening while we were listening to Sweet and
Low by the Southampton shore, I feared he was
gathering himself to propose. We had never had sex
although we had rolled about in his front room. He had
not protested, even called me a taxi, when I said I really
ought to go. We would have had a genuine honeymoon
night.

As the music played he shifted his half-pint tankard in
his left hand and held my right after some searching

around in the dark. The night was deep and close, the sailing liner passing across the front of the Isle of Wight, and the trio more or less in tune. I think that if he had asked me to marry him at that moment I might have accepted, paving the way for a life of normality and possible regret. Not that I have been short of regret.

It was the music that interrupted the moment. The three girls in their lace gowns were languidly playing, one on the harp, one on the viola and Brigit on the piano. I knew her name before I ever knew the names of Dolores and Bet. They were playing something from a dreamy film score when abruptly Brigit bashed her hands down on the keyboard with a thump and a discord. It stopped the talk and the tinkling of glasses. Every face turned to her. 'Sod it!' Brigit bellowed. 'I'm not playing this shit any more!'

There was a general moan of disapproval. She whirled stark-eyed, ashen-cheeked towards the audience in the romantic garden. Dolores tried to grab her shouting: 'Brigit!' but let go of the harp and it crashed like a golden tree. Bet kept on gamely scraping the viola.

Brigit was wearing a large, long dress. As she stood up furiously from the piano the hem snagged under the pedal and there was a resounding rip followed by a bellow from Brigit. She tugged at the dress and there was a second rip. It came away pathetically, like a long bandage. 'Now look what you've bloody well done!' she screamed at the entranced audience. 'Look!' She held up the ragged hem and turning only to poke a massive tongue at her fellow musicians she half-fell from the platform and rushed towards the gate of the garden. Wisely, people parted to let her through. We could hear her wailing outside in the dark and, as though in answer, a hoot came from a ship.

Dolores and Bet regarded each other uncertainly, one holding her harp, the other her viola. 'That's buggered it,' I heard Dolores say.

Brian, who had been standing beside me engulfed in his customary dumb calm, his half-pint poised while the drama went on, turned and asked if I would like another drink. He would probably have done the same if there had been a double slaying. Silently I passed him my glass and he went ruminating through the crowd.

It takes more than an odd tantrum to concern the Southampton social scene. Many of the crowd in the garden appeared to have already dismissed Brigit's outburst but Dolores and Bet remained nonplussed on the platform plucking at their strings uselessly, tunelessly.

'Do you need a pianist?' I was close to the edge of the platform and hardly needed to raise my voice. Dolores looked up as though a spirit had spoken. 'Like the earth needs rain,' she said.

'I'll say we bloody do,' said Bet.

It was not high so I easily stepped up. As I did so I was conscious of Brian bearing my drink like a chalice through the crowd. He stopped when he saw what I was doing and paused as if things were getting beyond him. The two girls were thick with smiles. 'You can play all this stuff?' asked Dolores. I said I could. I could with my eyes closed. Bet said: 'You can have that deaf cow's share of the dosh.'

We introduced ourselves. Dolores said that hers was only a professional name but I always called her that. Bet scraped her instrument heavily. I sat at the piano and ran my fingers over the notes. 'Lovely,' breathed Dolores.

'Better than her,' said Bet, repeating: 'Deaf cow.' They were leafing through their music sheets. 'The Barbra Streisand number,' whispered Dolores. We played 'The

Way We Were'. I did not need the music. Dolores had a big bosom and she heaved it happily. Bet wagged her head as we performed. At the first flourish the sounds dropped in the garden. At the second the audience began to applaud. Dolores and Bet went pink in the lights.

'You played really beautiful,' said Bet when we were sorting out the eighty pounds, a difficult division three ways, involving manoeuvres with small change. 'I'll say you did,' confirmed Dolores. 'Brigit's got wooden fingers.'

They had a flat in which the walls of the living-room and their bedrooms were covered to the last square inch with photographs of men. 'We like them,' said Bet. She called towards the kitchen. 'Don't we, Dol?'

'What's that?'

'Men. We like them.'

'Love 'em,' said Dolores. 'All shapes and sizes.'

'Sizes,' agreed Bet.

With one survey of the walls I picked out half a dozen glossy pop singers, the Southampton football team, and a nude of the Duke of Edinburgh. 'It's not really,' sniffed Dolores carrying in the coffee.

'His head, some other bloke's balls,' said Bet.

'Bet,' admonished Dolores.

'Sorry,' said Bet taking her coffee. She turned to me. 'Most of it is *not* His Royal Highness.'

'Much better,' said Dolores. She tapped the picture. 'I do fancy him, though. He looks like a man who knows more than he lets on. Not that I'll ever get the chance to find out.' She giggled as she sipped her coffee. She was on the edge of the jazzy settee and had hoisted up her long professional skirt over her fat knees. 'Come and see Rod Stewart.' She indicated the kitchen and lumbered to her feet carrying her cup in that direction. 'Want a refill, Bet?'

'No thanks. Keeps me awake. I'm seeing Kevin tomorrow.'

'You'll wear him out.'

I had followed her into the kitchen. She moved into the narrow galley and indicated a cut-out figure in a kilt over the kettle. 'Watch,' she invited.

She switched on the kettle and in a moment steam began to issue from it and rise below Rod Stewart's kilt, lifting it magically and revealing hairy naked thighs and a three-dimensional penis. 'It's plasticine,' revealed Dolores unnecessarily. 'We've tried to make it stand up but it won't.'

We returned to the erratically furnished living-room. 'Will you play with us again?' said Bet. Dolores looked put out as though she should have been the one to ask. 'There's no way that Brigit's coming back,' she said. 'That's a plus for music.'

'Even if she wants to,' nodded Bet.

'How often do you play?' I asked.

Dolores said: 'Weekends usually.'

'The money's not great,' said Bet.

'We're not the Amadeus String Quartet.'

'For a start there's only three of us,' pointed out Bet. 'Only two now. Unless you join.'

'All right,' I said. 'We could give it a try. I'd enjoy it.'

'What will your boyfriend say?'

'Not much,' I said.

'He looked a bit quiet,' said Dolores.

'The sort that likes to go home and play,' suggested Bet. 'With his train set.'

Dolores gave her another glare and asked where I lived.

Bet said: 'You can come and live here if you like. We've got a spare room. It's never boring.'

I said I would think about it and at the end of that week I moved in. A cavalcade of men passed through the flat. Even Monday, the traditional rest day of the raver, was rarely quiet and the place was littered with underwear and corks. What the girls lacked in appearance they made up in vivacity, enthusiasm and availability. We would sometimes drag in at midnight, Dolores with her harp and Bet with her viola, to find a man sitting dumbly on the doorstep. On entering the flat, you would occasionally find one squatting in his vest, someone you had never seen before. But Dolores and Bet always warned their guests that I was not part of the activities.

I had soundproofing material inserted around my bedroom door and I learned to sleep with the situation. Brian had left me to concentrate on his goalkeeping and I was alone by choice, waiting, I assured myself, for Mr Right.

He turned out to be Mr Wrong.

13

Each week I spent one dutiful day with my mother. She had greeted my first return with such ringed and downcast eyes and tight-lipped conversation that I had had to briskly assure her I was not walking Southampton Docks by night. 'You look tired,' she said. 'You just watch out for those Lascars.'

I told her I had met two jolly and chaste young women who were musicians. 'It's an ensemble. Harp, viola and piano.'

'Kneller is living with two musicians as well,' she sniffed. Her blackened eyes lifted. 'He has left the military.' I was shocked.

'But what about Dad?'

'He promised,' she agreed. 'Kneller promised your father he would play in a regimental band. But he's gone back on that. Thrown his life away. I went down the road to the kiosk and telephoned him. The one outside the Happy Gunner. One of his friends replied. He sounded odd. He called your brother Nelly.'

I returned to Southampton thinking sadly about her. She had given me Kneller's telephone number and I rang him the following day. A lemon-voiced man answered and asked me why I would be wanting Kneller. 'Because he's my brother,' I said as quietly as I could.

'Oh, I see,' he said. 'Well, he's at his modelling class.'

I tried to think that Kneller might be making wooden aeroplanes but I knew he was not. Without saying anything else I put the phone down.

Sometimes I would go to Fayler's country house sales to help with the paperwork and the accounting and it was at one of these that Mr Pyecraft, an antique dealer, and a bright and busy man, loitered late while other buyers were settling their bills and carrying away their lots. I wondered why he was doing this because he had little to detain him.

'Chloe,' he said. We were in the empty hall of what had been a grand house, now full of a sense of loss; not a chair nor a table left, a gallery of bleached oblongs on the walls where large pictures had been. 'Chloe, are you content in your present situation?' His expression was diffident.

'Yes. Yes, Mr Pyecraft, I'm very happy.'

'Yes, well, I suppose you would be.' He was such a pleasant little parsnip of a man who wore tweedy suits and gold glasses. As we spoke I saw someone loitering in the doorway.

'It's only that I am looking for a reliable person. Someone to live over my business and keep an eye on the shop and my dog, my Fluff, when I'm away.' He spread hopeful hands. 'To help me generally.'

I was tempted. Dolores and Bet had been particularly active that week and one night the police had been called and a man led away. I felt drained at work the next day. 'If you would like to think about it,' said Mr Pyecraft – he was very perceptive and had caught onto my briefest hesitation – 'perhaps we could talk again.'

As he went Zane Tomkins moved like a bad actor into the hallway. My life was closing in.

He had been hanging about outside like a suggestion. I knew he had recognised me, as I had recognised him, but he pretended that he had never seen me before. He was one of those people who would rather tell a lie than the truth, even when there was no need. He had an instinctive dishonesty.

He moved like a shifty shadow. 'Not much left here,' he said taking in the hall and inclining his head to examine an empty corridor. He smiled as though he were doing me a favour.

'We've sold everything,' I told him stiffly. 'We're auctioneers. That's what we do.'

'Great, good, excellent,' he answered. He was wearing a light grey flannel suit, a cream shirt and a club tie. His face was smoothly tanned, his smile cheeky and if the teeth were not quite regular it was an added attraction.

He only gave me a moment of his time and a smattering of smile before taking several strides towards the corridor. He was almost there, across the echoing floor of the hall, before I called and caught up with him as he halted. 'The sale's over,' I told him. 'We were just about to lock up.'

'No use locking it now,' he said. His head flicked about like a snake's. 'Not now everything's gone.'

'The sale's over.'

'Now look at that.' He had ignored my tone and taken a pace towards a leaded window. 'Just *look*.' I did. The catch and one of the diamond panes were broken. 'Never repaired,' he went on, shaking his head. 'Careless.'

Strangely I felt angry that he had so unerringly found something amiss. 'We're going to lock up,' I repeated.

'All right, darl, I'll be on my way,' he said doling out his smile again. He held out a hard, browned hand and, against my better judgement, I took it. He turned towards the main door but then paused and stepped back towards me, deeply serious. 'You didn't sell *everything*. Look what I found on the grass outside.'

I still recall the horror when he produced the pendant earring. I remembered it; there had been a small emerald at its centre. 'It was on the grass,' he repeated. 'Lying.'

'Lying,' I said thinking it was the appropriate word. 'Where's the other?'

He handed me the earring. 'There wasn't another.'

'And the emerald from this one?'

'Search me,' he invited spreading his hands. 'It was on the grass.'

'It was sold this afternoon,' I said.

'Well, they must have dropped it. You'd be surprised how careless people get.' That slightly inaccurate grin appeared again. 'Perhaps that lady only had one ear.'

It was six months before I saw Zane Tomkins again (even after it had all happened, and I was carrying his child, I found it difficult to call him by his true name, Alfred). Winter had come on and I was working at Pyecraft's Antiques and living over the shop with Fluff the Rottweiler. Two or three times a week I still played with Sweet and Low, taking Fluff along with me and tethering her to the leg of the piano. She was a gentle creature and enjoyed the music, lying chin down so it seemed that she was wearing a smile, and letting people pat and scratch her.

Often, late at night, particularly after we had been playing somewhere and Dolores and Bet had gone home to their energetic frolics, I would don a tracksuit and put the lead on Fluff and go for a long run through the almost empty city. It was wonderful out in the quiet, dark air with only a few car beams and perhaps some midnight rain. I liked to run where I had a moving view of the liners in the port, with their bright decks, their coloured funnels like illuminated banners.

Fluff enjoyed the running and could go as far as I could without puffing. There were people who regularly exercised on the midnight route and we got to know each other by nodding in passing, but I had never seen Zane jogging before the night when he came out of the lights lining the dual carriageway. He was clanking as he approached. I knew him at fifty yards and despite his physique, it was apparent that he was not fit for he was blowing hard. He was wearing a knapsack and the strange clanking was coming from that. When he saw the Rottweiler he did an instinctive jump over a low picket fence, coming to earth with a resounding clang. He straightened the knapsack, turned his head briefly towards me then, without a word, pounded and puffed off into the Southampton darkness. But I knew who he was.

Also I knew he had recognised me because a week later he spied through the window at Pyecraft's Antiques and then came into the shop. While I was attending to a customer my eyes followed him around the shelves and cabinets. He was carrying the knapsack which he placed on the floor. When the other man had gone Zane picked it up and once again I heard the clang of the contents.

'I never realised you worked here,' he lied. 'Fancy that.'

'Yes, fancy that.'

'You've got some nice stuff,' he said, his glance skimming around the shop. He was quite close. I was just up to his jaw. 'Really old stuff.'

'It's an antique shop.'

For a moment there was a glint like a needle in his eyes

but it quickly dimmed and he said: 'That's why I came. What do you think of these?'

He opened the bag and took out a pair of brass candlesticks, a candle snuffer and a pretty pair of grape scissors. 'Nice, eh?' he said. The candlesticks clanked together as he put them on the counter. Carefully I said: 'Where do they come from?'

'South Africa,' he replied. His voice always solidified when he was attempting to sound honest. 'My old auntie sent them. Her name is Flo. Auntie Flo.' I ran my finger over the shapes of the candlesticks, looked at the snuffer, then opened and squeezed the grape scissors.

'Mr Pyecraft does the buying,' I said. 'He doesn't allow me to buy anything.'

'Doesn't he trust you?'

I was trying to avoid staring into his handsome face. 'I don't have the experience.'

'These are good. I'll sell them cheap.'

'I saw you the other night,' I told him. 'Jogging. With your knapsack on your back.'

For a moment I thought he was going to cut and run but he controlled the urge. 'Right,' he conceded. 'So I was.' He picked up the articles and put them back into the knapsack with a blatant clang. 'I'll come back when the expert is in.' He turned and was making for the door with me watching his broad back when he asked. 'Was that your dog? The Rotter?'

'Rottweiler,' I corrected. 'No. But I look after her.'

'It's a she? I never thought about she-Rotters.' He stood as though thinking of making further enquiries but then with a grunt and a wave of his hand he went from the door, the candlesticks still clanking.

Three nights later he was back. Breaking in.

It was the sound I had feared ever since I had moved

into the close and comfortable flat over Mr Pyecraft's shop: the soft movements of someone outside, a shuffling, a trying of the rear door. There was a burglar alarm but this time it did not sound. Fearfully I sat up in bed and remained transfixed. Even then I did not put my hand to the telephone. Somehow, I suppose I have to admit, I knew it was him. From then on I was always making allowances for him. What a fool.

I had Fluff, of course, but Fluff was, in fact, one of a little-known sub-breed, a cowardly Rottweiler. Still listening I put my foot out of the bed and stirred her. She opened a nervous eye and rolled onto her other flank. 'Get up,' I whispered. 'Someone's trying to get in.'

Getting out of bed I had to haul her to her feet. With a half-puzzled, half-annoyed expression, which asked what time of night this was, she began to scratch herself. 'For Christ's sake,' I pleaded. '*Be fierce.*'

The sounds had ceased and I sat on the edge of the bed thinking that whoever it was had gone away but then I heard something shudder in the showroom below. He was in the shop. Trembling I moved to the bedroom door. There was an African spear in one corner of the room. Somebody had brought it to the shop. It was long, slim and black with a wicked point. I picked it up and Fluff, at last realising, whined and tried to hide behind her paws. I prodded her with the blunt end of the spear and pulled on my woollen dressing-gown and my slippers. Tentatively I went down the narrow stairs.

At the bottom was a light switch and bravely I leaned the spear against the wall and turned it on. I was dragging the moaning Fluff behind me with my other hand. The light only filled the showroom with shadows. I did not see him until he moved. He was sitting in a corner alongside a Regency cabinet. 'Hello, there,' he said. 'No need to worry. It's only me.'

'I know who it is,' I said hardly able to steady my voice. 'I've got this spear and this Rottweiler.'

Fluff was attempting to get back up the stairs. 'Looks like she doesn't want to know,' remarked Zane standing up and emerging from his concealing shadow. 'Where's she off to? To get her teeth?'

'You've frightened her.'

That grin appeared lighting the dimness. 'Do I frighten *you*?'

'Not much.' I waggled the spear. Its narrow shadow spread around the walls.

'You've got the point the wrong way.'

I had too. I turned the ugly end towards him but laid it carefully against a Victorian love-seat that Mr Pyecraft had bought only that day.

Zane said: 'That's a funny settee.'

'It's a love-seat.' My voice was steady now.

'How does it work?' He had his gaze fixed on me.

'You have to sit one each side,' I said scarcely believing I was talking with him in this way.

'Like this?' He sat himself in one of the curved seats. 'Now you,' he invited.

I must have been mad. I moved the spear, propped it in a corner, and sat in the other curly seat, so that we were side by side but facing opposite directions. My nightdressed knees poked from the dressing-gown. Zane wriggled to face me. Even the shadows on his features were flattering. 'It must have been hard work making love in one of these.'

'It was meant for talking ... for conversation ...'

'Chatting up.'

'Yes.'

He leaned, eased his head back and, mesmerised by the bastard, I did the same until our noses were side by side. Another inch and we kissed, my insides turning to jelly. He did it again and again and, to my shame, I would have gone on and on. Only I could have ended up in a passionate clinch with a burglar.

His arms were thick and strong; he eased them around my neck. He could have held on for as long as he cared. But then the bloody dog began to bark. Fluff had pulled herself together. She posed at the top of the stairs and howled. 'I think I'd better be off,' said Zane.

'Don't you want to steal anything?'

He would not have been Zane if he had not considered it but he desisted. 'I'll come back some other time,' he promised. He took his arms from me and I fell in a hot bundle half onto the floor. 'I only slipped the lock,' he said, 'and sorted the alarm. No damage done.'

Only to me. He slid out of the shop like the fucking Scarlet Pimpernel leaving me to stare out of the door into the black night.

Many months passed before I saw him again. He had been travelling 'at some distance' as he put it, having cheaply purloined the phrase from some song. He could even steal other people's sentiments. If he heard something, or caught sight of it in an occasional glance at a newspaper, and thought it might be useful in theft or seduction, he would learn it. Once he swotted a few lines from the Bible to impress some halfwit evangelist he was conning at the time. Years later I heard him trundle out the same verses to an impressionable magistrate. Considering he was by no means intelligent, excepting in the criminal sense, he remembered well and wasted nothing. He spent half his life vowing to read *Gone with the Wind*.

Whenever he promised to go straight he told me he was going to read it, cover to cover, but I know he never got beyond the first few pages. 'I'll finish it if it kills me,' he would say holding out the paperback and staring at it.

It took me several weeks to put the midnight encounter in the shop out of my mind. I kept wondering where he was, if he would arrive by darkness again. Lying awake above the shop I listened for, hoped for, the sounds of a felon.

When Zane said he had been travelling 'at some distance' you could, like most of his statements, take it as untrue. His version of doing time behind bars was 'travelling' and 'at some distance' probably meant Wormwood Scrubs. But he influenced, infected almost, people with his easy lies; people like me. Women wanted to, fell over themselves to, believe his every falsehood. Raffish looks and a fraudulent, racy charm covered all.

Stoutly I tried looking out for ordinary men; men who got up in the morning and went out to a job. Surely there were interesting and loving ordinary men. I nagged myself that I wanted a man who dug an allotment and proudly brought home shallots, or who (I was even regretting Brian) played hard and honestly at sports and then relished a well-earned pint, who would sit close by me and watch rubbishy television, who would kiss me fondly at night and make love at weekends. Now I was lying too.

The trouble with being selective and living alone was that before I was twenty I was in danger of becoming a recluse. A sort of stubborn laziness came over me. I was aware of this, lying across my bed on airy summer evenings and hearing the sounds of life going by below the window. I still played a couple of times a week with Sweet and Low and Dolores and Bet kept urging me to meet some of their more acceptable friends. My job in the antique shop was often solitary although I enjoyed it and I learned quickly. At the end of the day I would lock up and go to my flat under the eaves. There was the unusual arrangement of a kitchen–bathroom (you had to fold the little cooker away before you could have a bath) and I would usually cook myself something, then read or watch television. It was a comfortable existence, easy and lazy, without adventure or surprises. I began to worry about myself.

On some days when Mr Pyecraft was not searching the country for treasures or bygones he would fuss around the shop and would tell me to take the afternoon off. Sometimes I would go to Aldershot, getting my duty to my mother out of the way for another week. Although I still loved her dearly I found these visits had become wearing. We would go out and have tea in the Happy Gunner Café. We sat with our cups and cakes, both of us aware that we were merely using up a few more heavy minutes. The truth was neither of us led very interesting lives. I know she had a suspicion that my reticence veiled some sort of guilt. When I left gratefully for the station in the early evening ('I have to see the shop is properly locked') it was with her hooded eyes following me.

On other free afternoons I would wander about rather aimlessly, taking anonymous bus rides or going to the cinema and sitting solitary in the big darkness. One day I met a big, decent man called Caspar, and after we had been out a few times and he had told me his dull stories of working on a lighthouse, I made the decision to sleep with him before we ran out of conversation. He was almost forty but handsome in a sizeable sort of way. If I could not fall in love with someone then Caspar would have to do for the time being. He lived in a hostel by the sea with other lighthouse men. Very often their wives decamped while they were away. Caspar's wife had left. 'She must have wanted to,' he said. 'The night she went adrift there was a force eight and the glass was falling.'

It appeared that she had gone not because of his absences, on the light for four weeks at a stretch, but because of the two weeks he was ashore, at home.

He was shy to the point of speechlessness. On the night I invited him into the flat he looked nonplussed but then gave a shaky smile and said: 'Just for a cup of coffee then.'

I put the light on in the shop and led him carefully up the dim spiral stair although I realised that if there was anything in the world he could manage it was a spiral stair. We had coffee and talked about the film we had seen. 'I liked the scene where they were kissing,' he ventured, his eyes slowly rising to mine. 'In the laundry.'

'In the steam,' I said. I got up. He was on the settee (he looked very wide sitting down, his big knees in front of his chest) and I took his cup from him and fixing him with my eyes, I pushed him with one hand. He looked surprised but toppled easily.

He was powerful but polite and I enjoyed his company. I have never seen a huskier naked man. I was like a waif lying beside him. 'Thank you, Chloe,' he said, 'that was really enjoyable,' as though I had cooked him egg and chips. Then he yawned.

An hour later I realised why he had no wife. We had gone to sleep against each other after we had kissed in what was almost a formal good-night. I drifted, aware of his sturdy, steady heaving. Then he began to *shout*. 'BELOW!' he bellowed. 'BELAY BELOW!'

It was incredible. He had a huge voice. 'GET ASHORE! FOR GOD'S SAKE!' From next door Mrs

Penticost banged on the wall with her walking stick. I panicked. I pushed him, shoved him, punched him, cried to him to wake up. He rolled powerfully. 'ASHORE! ASHORE!' He began to swim in the bed.

Mrs Penticost's banging became furious. Lights went on in upstairs windows across the street. I was weeping and pummelling him. He howled: 'BEN, BEN! WHERE ARE YOU, BEN?'

'Never mind bloody Ben!' I bawled into his staring face. 'Shut up, will you, Caspar! Shut up!'

His eyes opened. 'It's my bane,' he moaned. 'I've been to the doctor.'

'You've woken half Southampton.'

'I'm sorry,' he mumbled putting his thick pale legs over the side of the bed. 'The men on the light are all deaf. It's the foghorns.'

14

I never saw Caspar or, more to the point, heard him again. But I discovered that even he, decent and honest as he seemed, had kept something from me. He was being posted the following day to a different lighthouse on an island off western Scotland, out of earshot I imagine of the mainland.

So my loneliness remained intact. Dolores and Bet kept telling me that I should not be so particular, that, in their experience, there were the odd good points to be found in nearly all men. But I became even more reclusive, living above the musty shop, looking at life through my window.

August is a difficult month for being by yourself. Mr Pyecraft went on holiday to Hunstanton and I was left alone with the antiques. Each day he would telephone and enquire politely what, if anything, I had sold, and for how much. Selling relics is not like selling sweets and there were always long times of inactivity, even more so in August, and I sometimes felt that I would be grateful to *anyone* who came through the door. Even Zane Tomkins.

But he did not appear either by day or in the dead of the night. He was probably away on one of his periodic visits to a distant cell. Once, after we came together, he let slip that word 'cell' and then tried to wriggle out of the error by saying he had been living in a monastery. Even I did not believe that although I could not help admiring the lie.

Southampton seemed empty as a moor at weekends. It was a hot month and everywhere was boring and dusty, the city buses groaning alongside the dull and unpopulated park where I used to walk the dog when my room became too close and unbearable. The ceiling seemed to get lower every afternoon. Fluff the Rottweiler hated the heat and would have preferred to lie under the Davenport in the shaded corner of the shop or below my Edwardian dressing-table upstairs. She groused when I fixed her lead to her collar and she plodded glumly through the park. I felt much that way myself, although I used to make a point of having a shower and dressing up in light clothes before I went out.

Sometimes as I walked I saw some distant cricketers in white, moving slowly as angels as they played; other times a tetchy, snot-smeared toddler, lugged by its worn mother, would come from the opposite direction. If the child made a beeline for the dog, the mother would tug it away with a snarl and Fluff would look hurt and miserable. In the playground some disenchanted father would wait at the foot of the slide for his descending infant. What a way to spend Saturday afternoon.

Halfway through our walk I usually sat on a bench for ten minutes. It was shaded by a great cloudy chestnut and the dog liked to arrange herself in the crumbled dust around the root. From there the empty grass fell away so that, if you shut your ears to the sound of the buses and managed not to breathe the wafted city fumes, you could imagine yourself in the country. (I would have gone to the country, to the New Forest or somewhere near, perhaps a beach or a river bank, which is where everyone else went at weekends, but the dog was always spectacu-larly sick on a bus or a train and was frightened when left alone.) Then I would return from the park and see pictures on the television news of crammed beaches and blocked roads and feel a perverse sort of jealousy for those thousands who were so much together, part of each other whether or not they liked it, sharing a summer's day.

From the bench looking downhill I also had a distant view of the ships in the port. They looked as if they were floating on the park trees. Massive container ships and liners, their coloured funnels against the dusty August sky. I felt envious of them for all the places they had been. I was getting older by the day and I had not been anywhere.

It was then that Olaf walked by. I did not know he was called Olaf then, of course (nor did he, for that matter), but in the vacant park it was like two strangers coming across each other in the middle of nowhere. He was young with fair hair and a light brown face, and walked with a nautical swagger. Because there was no one else around we half-smiled at each other and then he sauntered on and sat on a bench twenty yards along on the opposite side of the path. Nothing passed between us and it was almost to break this silence that I eventually got up, unwound Fluff from the tree root, and began to go in his direction.

'This is a nice dog.' The accent was just noticeable. 'I have dogs.'

'What sort?' I asked.

'Sled dogs. They pull the sled.' He made a tugging movement with his broad arm.

'Oh, that's different.'

'Not different in Norway.'

He shuffled along the bench and I sat down by him but with a space between us. Fluff gave me her spoilsport look. She wanted to go home. 'This park is very big, but no people,' he said after he had told me his name was Olaf and I had told him mine. 'Where are all these people?'

'Gone off for the weekend,' I said. 'They only come to the park in the week. Mostly to eat their sandwiches. Today they will all be at the seaside or in the country, the forest.'

'The forest? You mean with trees? There is a forest near to this park?'

'Not far. Is it your first time in Southampton?'

'I come and I go,' he shrugged. He had a fair forelock that I imagined would have been blowing had there been any breeze. 'Sometimes when my ship is in the dock I come here. Then I go with my ship, far off you know, and I do not come here again for many months.'

'Don't you know anyone here? No friends?' For some reason I was speaking in his foreign way. He looked downcast and my chest tightened. Even then I could have put my arms around him and before long I would. 'Never am I in port long enough for friends,' he told me fixing me with those pale eyes. 'I only come to the park to walk.'

'How long are you ashore?'

'Three hours for today only. Tonight the ship, she sails.'

'For where?'

'Long way,' he said sorrowfully but as though he were not quite sure. 'East. East is a long way.'

'Ever so,' I agreed. The sultry air and my own need closed about me. I felt myself moving closer to him. 'I will be your friend,' I whispered.

It was not all that far from there to my bed. The dog was tugging and I said I had to go home but that he could come for a soft drink if he liked. He did. In five minutes, seven at the outside, we were straddled across my patterned counterpane, hot as hell, going like a couple of young animals. I do not know who needed whom the most. Well, not then.

His muscles were sailor-hard, his neck strong as rope, and his breath was like the sea, like all the seas I thought he had smelt on his long voyages. He was hungry for me too. He had his shirt peeled off almost as soon as we were indoors and only just after he had mentioned what a nice place it was. He was stripped to the waist as we went into my bedroom. Fluff started trotting with us but I pushed her with my foot and shut the door against her nose. His jeans were held up with a thick leather belt and I looped my fingers under it. 'From Java,' he said. 'My belt is from Java.' By then I did not care where it came from. I know where it went: on the floor with his jeans and his bright underpants. It was the first time I could ever remember a lover undressed before I was. He stood sturdily on Mr Pyecraft's Turkish carpet, lightly tanned and confidently smiling; his dick like a ship's bowsprit.

He reached forward and, standing stark naked with his penis actually propped against my dress, he undid my front buttons. Trying to help I wriggled to ease it away from my shoulders but he made a quiet tutting noise and reached out and pulled it away himself. 'It is a nice dress,' he said flinging it over a chair back. Olaf tapped me between the legs while I was still wearing my pants and then leaned forward and kissed my bra. 'We do this in my country,' he said solemnly, doing it again.

When we were both naked we crammed against each other, kissed without needing much height adjustment and then he more or less shunted me across the bedroom and onto the bed. It was close and hot, the sun coming in bands through the lattice window. 'Good, so good,' he said checking over the accommodation and then me. 'At sea there is no space, everything is small.'

'Except Olaf,' I said pulling tenderly at him. God help me.

'Except Olaf,' he agreed.

We rolled and loved and rolled and loved again. It was a wonderful way to spend what had begun as another boring and solitary afternoon. Fluff managed to push the door, came into the room and lay disgruntled on the rug at the bottom of the bed. Olaf and I were running with sweat and we pulled away muckily and lay trying to get cool, trying to recover our breaths. Then we tried different ways; ways which I, with limited experience and unadventurous lovers, found strange and rousing.

'Do you all do these things in Norway?' I whispered from the floor.

'Always, we do this kind of fucken in Norway,' he answered from the side of the bed. He adjusted my legs below his arms. 'In wintertime the nights are very long.'

After he had gone I stood at the window straining to hear the sound of his ship's siren as it set out on its voyage east, and I stood on my toes to look across the housetops opposite, watching for its pattern of lights moving down the Solent.

I need not have bothered. I saw him the following Thursday in Lol's café. It was some time since I had been there but I was passing in the afternoon and I spotted Penny as ever serving teas in the window. She waved and I stopped and went in. Lol was still lolling on the counter and Penny came forward smiling. It was over her shoulder, while we hugged briefly, that I saw Olaf sitting with some other young men at the back of the café. I felt a stab of joyful surprise. Like a fool I thought he had somehow missed his ship, that he was still there in Southampton. For me.

He was involved in an argument about football and his voice sounded above the others, but it was not the Scandinavian voice of my Olaf. He looked up and saw me and stopped. His face dropped but then he recovered, grinned and said something to the others who looked at me and began to snigger. They knew.

15

One night in the winter when Sir Benedict and I were playing cards, when we could sense the wind stirring beyond the curtains and the room was dim and comforting, he said in his calm, conversational way: 'Chloe, have you ever been in love?'

I frowned at the cards and the question and said I had.

'With someone who also loved you?'

'It's ... it's always been a disappointment,' I said.

'Who was the father of your son? I have seen his photograph on your bedside.' He glanced up but still slowly. 'I went there once just after you first came to see that you had a comfortable place to sleep. Mrs Trebet took me up. I saw the photograph. It is your son, isn't it?'

'Donny,' I said feeling the guilt and the sadness I always felt when I mentioned him. 'Zane ... Alfred that is ... was his father.'

'Where is Donny now?'

When I had received the latest pebble, he had been in Spain, the nearest to home a pebble had been posted in years. Perhaps he was looking for his father. Donny might come in useful. I felt full of shame that he had gone.

'Donny travels,' I said inadequately. 'He went when he was eighteen.' I never knew how to discuss him. It had been so long. 'I ... don't see a lot of him. In fact I don't see him at all. I haven't seen him for eight years. He was going to be in the army. He was training as a boy soldier but when he was eighteen he wrote and said he'd changed his mind. He left and said he was going to travel. He would keep in touch.'

'But he didn't.'

'He sends me pebbles from places,' I said. 'But no letters, no address. Just pebbles. He sends them to the antiques shop where I used to work.'

Then, still dealing the cards, he said: 'We make mistakes, all of us. I slept with Lady Annabel once, you know.' He raised his blank eye. 'By mistake, you understand.'

We played a few hands in a silence only broken by the sounds of the night outside. Then Sir Benedict said: 'It was while I was wed to Lady Lucy, my true love. Annabel tricked me.'

'How did she do that?'

'There had been a merry party. It was on the Dorset coast, where poor Lucy eventually was shoved off the cliff by Annabel.'

I sat silent, sifting without aim through the cards.

'It had been very merry and I had drunk a little too much brandy,' he continued. I was glad I had said nothing. 'When I was a little tipsy like that Lucy would go and sleep in another room. It was not that she was affronted but she said brandy made me snore.'

It was my turn to deal and he fell to silence while I did. At times like this he could wander off in his fading mind. But he continued. I wondered why he was telling me. Perhaps he had to tell someone. Perhaps that is why he had asked me about Donny. It was so that we could share our pasts. There was no one else. 'In the very middle of the night, while I was asleep,' he said, 'Annabel came to my room and inserted herself between the sheets. I only half-awoke and thinking it was my Lucy I made room in the bed and then embraced her to me. There was only a year or so in age between the two and they were much the same size and shape. Only their dispositions differed. There was no wiliness in Lucy, no bad intent . . . no evil.'

Now he did stop and I thought that was the end. I even boxed the cards and made as if to go and prepare his bedtime drink. But he touched my wrist and motioned me to remain in the chair. 'Sometimes Lucy *did* come back into our room. If her substitute bed was uncomfortable or perhaps if she was kept awake by a tree brushing the window. I *really* thought it was her. Truly I did, Chloe.' I could see that it was important to him that I believed what he told me. I nodded acceptance and he continued. 'I was about forty at the time, at my very prime, not like now. Annabel kissed me in the darkness and I didn't realise.'

His eyes, the bad one just as expressive as the good one, lifted mournfully.

'Afterwards she went from the room and it was not until some time later, the next day at least, perhaps the day following, that I realised I had been tricked.'

'Lady Lucy never found out?'

'No, but Annabel remembered. She claimed it was the most wonderful night of her life.'

So carefully did Sir Benedict and Lady Annabel arrange their respective solitudes that, although they lived under the same roof, weeks would go by before they came into even remote contact and much longer before they were obliged to speak to each other. At Christmas he wrapped a little parcel and asked me to place it at the end of her counterpane. She sent nothing to him and it was weeks before she mentioned his present which she pretended she had just discovered under the bed. 'He's truly mad,' she said. 'Thinks it's Christmas.'

She would sometimes ask me slyly what he was doing. One morning when I took in her egg she said: 'You must be wary of Sir Benedict, Chloe. He is very carnal.'

'He's eighty-three,' I said providing what I thought was a complete answer. She beheaded the egg with a single blow from the spoon. 'He's carnal,' she mumbled through her first helping of yolk. 'Highly carnal. Always was, always will be.'

She called me by my name although to Urchfont she never offered more than a grunt. Her great fear was that I would leave her in the bath. Every morning I went into the museum of a bathroom with its peeling pipes and glowering geyser, and saw her sitting there, an irritable old bag of bones, wearing nothing but a shower cap like a plastic parcel and a barely concealed expression of desperation. It was not a straightforward job. She slipped and moaned and cried out and sometimes panicked. Her bones crackled and her skin flapped. She was always relieved to be on dry land again. 'You're not bad, Chloe,' she would pant. 'Not too bad at all.'

She rarely left the house except for funerals which gave her special delight. She prepared for them with the consciousness of an undertaker. 'Hah!' she would exclaim from her chair with *The Times* spread like a skirt over her knees, '*she's* gone then,' or '*he's* finished.' It was like a game of survival and one of the rare things in which she took any joy. She would get her mourning wardrobe together and sally happily out with a black feather in her hat and a face filled with sorrow and satisfaction.

'Lucy, my sister,' she remarked one day adding

disdainfully: '– the *first* Lady Bowling – she jumped, you know. Over a cliff.'

She had never mentioned Lady Lucy to me before. 'Really, Lady Annabel,' I said as mildly as I could.

'Forty years ago today,' she said with a little prim puff of her cheeks. 'Took a running jump. Like an athlete. I saw her, half a dozen strides, a quick acceleration and over she went. Whoosh. But I was never permitted to say it at the inquest, of course. The family and Sir Benedict and everything. As far as everyone was concerned she merely fell. I had to tell them I had turned away only for a moment on the edge of the cliff and – whoosh – she was gone. I had to lie. I had to tell them that she fell and that I looked far below and there she was floating in the sea. Well, her skirt was, that was all you could see. The rest of her was underwater.'

She had preserved a frail old copy of *The Times* which reported the tragedy and she brought it out to show me. It was too long to read at that moment so I watched where she kept it, intending to look at it later, but when I went to the drawer she had hidden it somewhere else. In that first moment when she showed it to me, however, I saw there was a photograph of a young, handsome Sir Benedict with separate shots of Lady Lucy and Lady Annabel.

'He was *always* in love with me, of course,' she said tapping the paper as brown as wrapping. 'He came to my room once and climbed into my bed. My husband, Peregrine, was in Worcester at the time. Or was it Turkey? He was well-named, always travelling. Benedict was as bold as you please. I tried to resist but he was too strong and ardent.'

'I see,' I said helplessly.

'But in society,' she said sniffily, 'one never complains.'

It was the anniversary of this happening, which she so carefully observed, that made her talk so much. Usually I worked to a background of grunts and sniffs. But I knew she liked me and what is more she depended on me. No one else would have put up with her.

This thought prompted me to ask for an increase in wages and, without too much hedging, I was given another ten pounds a week, making sixty. With my keep and accommodation provided and a daily round of duties that were not arduous, I was suddenly enjoying a pleasant life. When it was spring and the first good weather arrived Sir Benedict proudly wheeled out the tandem from the barn and announced that we were to take our first pedal of the season down into the New Forest. 'It has survived another winter,' he said patting the handlebars. So had he. 'It's flatter than the country to the north, Chloe,' he said as though he had been planning it in the off-season.

We bicycled on the main road, heads down alongside cars and lorries and then, with relief on my part, although Sir Benedict showed no sign of having noticed the other vehicles, to the rolling moorland. The forest is not a forest at all. There are wooded parts but it is really a huge open space, covered with gorse and ferns and split by little streams and rivers – a chase, a hunting ground once for William the Conqueror. We took to those breezy roads, up and down, through archways of new leaves trembling green in the sun, by ponds with swans and rivers with ducks, cycling around donkeys, forest ponies, cows, pigs and half-interested deer. Sir Benedict pedalled as well as he had ever done.

We went towards the coast, and as we did so I began to realise that we would be going through Cutcross, the village where I had lived with Zane when Donny was born. Pedalling behind Sir Benedict I kept my head down almost afraid I would recognise the landmarks. I had not been back there for more than twenty years.

We might have gone through without it being any more painful but when we arrived outside the Yew Tree Inn Sir Benedict called over his shoulder: 'Whoaah, Chloe! Time for refreshment.' I would have given anything to ride on, or at least part of me would, but as he applied the brake the unchanged scene was there before me, the paved yard in front of the pub, the apple trees billowing with blossom in the garden, the old Yew Tree sign swaying and creaking in the breeze coming from the coast. Suddenly I could see Zane there again, sitting with his pint at the long wooden table under the window with little Donny standing at his knee. What a lovely rural sight. What a shit.

The inn had changed hands in the twenty years, probably more than once, but when Sir Benedict and I were sitting in the empty bar with the landlord flicking a duster around, a man came in whom I knew at once and who, I could see by his narrowing eyes, recognised me: an old forester who carried a bundle of staves on his back and had a dead rabbit hung from his belt. He had always carried the staves around; it could even have been the same bundle. I remember that he was also the local snake catcher.

'How's things, Adder?' asked the landlord filling a pewter tankard. The man detached himself from the staves and placed them carefully against the bar.

'Aw, be about the same,' said Adder. I remembered when he had arrived in the yard outside with a snake three feet long, dead and dead-eyed, and he had held it out for Donny to touch. Strangely Zane refused to put his hand on the scaly back. Now the ancient forester unhurriedly turned and called across the room: "Aven't seed you for a bit.'

'I've been away,' I said lamely.

"Ow be that liddle one o' yours? 'Im that likes the vipers?'

My laugh was uncertain. 'He's quite grown up now,' I said. 'He's away.' He seemed lost for words. I said: 'This place doesn't seem to have changed much?'

'There's some that die and some's born,' he said apparently after thinking about it. 'Otherwise not much, 'tis true.' Drinking his beer brought on a new silence. When we lived in our cottage there I had fooled myself into believing that we were a real little family, that Zane was a decent man (or that the arrival of a son had miraculously transformed him into one) and that Donny would grow up happy and well in the forest.

Sir Benedict was sipping his customary slow half of cider. 'How long have you lived here?' he eventually asked the man.

'All the time,' responded Adder. He must have thought that the conversation had gone far enough for he put the empty tankard down, picked up his bundle of staves, hitched up his belt and the dangling rabbit and with no more than a nod headed for the door. The man behind the bar said: 'Catches snakes with his bare hands. Like his father, they say.'

We went out. The spring day had become cloudy and that is how I felt also. 'Can we go down this lane, Sir Benedict?' I had to take a look. Just one look. I had to hurt myself with the memory. His wise glance told me he understood and we rode the tandem a hundred yards down the lane. The cottage had gone.

For some reason I was shocked. I thought we must have passed it or not ridden far enough but then I knew there was no mistake. It was not there. The oak tree, bending low, was there, and that had been at the edge of the cottage garden. Zane used to climb it, bare chested, pretending to himself that he was Tarzan.

'It *was* here,' I said eventually to Sir Benedict. 'Behind the tree, over the hedge.' I dismounted from the back of the tandem and he stood holding it in the lane, looking very sorry for me. Walking to the unkempt hedge I looked over. Only the lowest walls of the cottage were left, the stones and bricks blackened and fallen. 'There's been a fire,' I said almost to myself. I thought I was going to cry. There were charred piles of damp debris in the overgrown garden, a window frame stood on edge, its glass shattered into a star. I faltered to the wooden gate. That at least was intact, although one hinge had cracked. Zane had been going to oil it. I remember Donny once looking out at the lane through the spaces between the wooden staves. 'He thinks he's inside,' Zane had said.

'He *is* inside,' I said.

He gave me his devilish grin. 'In the nick, I mean.'

I remember how shocked I was. 'He'll never be,' I said lifting Donny up and taking him away from the gate.

Zane laughed and said: 'He'd probably get probation.'

Now I opened the gate carefully. Sir Benedict was still holding the tandem and observing me silently. The gate creaked familiarly and scraped through piled, crackling leaves and other rubbish. I walked along the path: seven small paces. I knew exactly how far it was because when Donny was first walking we used to count his steps. The day we reached the front door from the gate was a triumph. I wanted to give the news to his father but it was one of those periods when we did not know where he was.

Although years had gone I recognised the outline of

the cottage, the doorstep and the old metal foot scrape, almost the only things left in place, the shape of the bay window and the opening in the blackened bricks where the kitchen door had been. Foolishly I looked towards the piles of rubble, mashed by rain and wind. But there was nothing to remember. Apart from the foot scrape all I could see that I knew were two overgrown shrubs spreading over the corner of the back garden and I remembered planting them. I never did discover what they were although gardeners in the village thought they were rare. Zane had brought them home one night after he had been jogging.

I heard Sir Benedict greet someone and at the gate I saw old Adder appear, his bundle of staves over his shoulder. He saw me standing with a sort of silly helplessness in the ruin and said: 'Burned down afore Christmas. Old Ma Jenkins lost her life. Only moved in there a year.'

'It looks very sad,' was all I could say.

'Aye,' he replied. He hitched his bundle on his shoulder. 'It were never a lucky house.'

He walked on, vanishing from view behind the hedge and the big tree. 'You can say that again,' I thought.

16

It was a few months after my afternoon encounter with Olaf the Norwegian sailor, trainer of sled dogs, more generally known as Terry from Gosport, crewman of the Isle of Wight Ferry, that I met Zane Tomkins again. There had been others in between, futile attempts on my part to settle my single and often solitary life into a proper shape. My job in the antique shop and my home above it were good and constant, but all my sincere efforts at making a decent relationship with a decent man were thwarted. Unsuitable suitors were always lurking unseen.

One man only wanted me to tug his golf cart around the hilly courses of Hampshire and Wiltshire. I trudged muddy miles, often in terrible weather, before, soaked and bone chilled, I told him through my cold tears one January afternoon that he had to choose either golf or me. With scarcely a goodbye he took his cart, counted his clubs, and in the fading daylight walked towards the clubhouse.

Another candidate used to abandon me with his old and bitchy aunt while he spent convivial evenings in the pub and a third kept his money in a little wedge of a purse which had been his mother's and insisted that we split the cost of keeping company. After he asked me for my bus fare I stood up and got off at the next stop. He rushed to the door as the bus was leaving shouting: 'I love you! I'll pay!' But I kept my head down and went in the other direction.

So I was ripe for something extravagant when Zane came into view again. I knew the risks, or some of them – nobody who is up to any good clanks around at night with candlesticks in their knapsack – but his looks and his Southampton charm captured me in the end.

Sweet and Low continued to play its limited repertoire at functions within a twenty-mile radius. Bet did not trust her car further than that so some tentative talk of conquering London remained just talk. Dolores and Bet actually only knew a certain number of tunes and did not learn others quickly or willingly. Often we played the entire repertoire from end to end and then started at the beginning again. Eventually I found myself performing a couple of solo pieces to break the monotony. We could have practised more but they did not want to give up their men.

It was while we were playing in the garden of a house in the New Forest that I set eyes on Zane again. It was June and it was a big gabled place with a splendidly sloping green garden, a small lake and a swimming-pool. We played under a dainty pink and white striped canopy, while a hundred people in summery clothes ate lunch at tables spread over the lawn.

At first I did not spot him because he was sitting at one of the outer tables (he instinctively preferred to be on the edge of events). But he had spotted me. I was wearing a light dress and a lovely hat. I remember him running his finger around the wide brim.

Sweet and Low played for about an hour during lunch and then they gave us drinks and sandwiches. That was when he appeared from the shadows inside the French windows and came over and kissed me casually on the cheek, while keeping both hands on my shoulders. Bet spluttered into her white wine and Dolores choked on her cucumber sandwich. 'How great to see you again,' said Zane in his deepest voice as he released me. He had, I grew to know, a range of voices, from an angry small squeak to this profoundly sexual drone. It was then that he touched my hat and it toppled. He caught it at my waist and held it there next to my dress. I flushed from my shoes up.

'I haven't seen you around,' I said hardly daring to look at him. I thanked him for catching my hat. Nobody else had seen him around either since he had been serving one of his shorter sentences.

He returned the hat with an old-fashioned Hollywood flourish. I promptly dropped it again, this time to the floor. Dolores and Bet giggled but their jaws dropped as he retrieved it a second time and, placing it gently on my head, said: 'It looks much better up there.'

My companions looked at me and then towards each other and then faltered away, as though they had experienced a major shock. I smiled into his handsome eyes. 'You've had quite an effect on my friends,' I said.

'It's always the wrong women. Are you going to play some more music?'

'In a few minutes.'

He started backing away and whispered: 'I'll be listening.'

As the hot afternoon went on everyone in the garden became very drunk. Old flames were relit, new ones were kindled. There were small fights and bickerings, especially among the women. Wine and tears mixed freely. Some guests went down to the pool and stripped naked before going in. There was a girl with swinging breasts sitting on the edge swigging from a wine bottle held to her lips by a thin nude man standing like a water-pixie in the shallow end.

Bet found a bottle of champagne and we shared it. Then another of white wine. The keyboard fell over with a twang that resounded across the forest but no one noticed or cared. The hostess, dress hoisted up to her waist, was sitting weeping furiously on the terrace while her husband frolicked in the pool, his backside floating like a rubber dinghy. Our music became meaningless as more wine appeared. Bet was sick in a flower-bed, Dolores showed some men how she could play the harp with her feet. Eventually, her face like a well-used paint palette, the hostess staggered to us and said, with a sort of final hopelessness, that we could go home. We were supposed to play for another hour but nobody was listening. Pop music was screeching from the house anyway. Still sobbing she paid us on the spot, drunkenly wiping her eyes with a twenty-pound note. We packed up our instruments and piled into Bet's little car with the harp projecting through the sun-roof.

I had been trying unsuccessfully to catch a glimpse of Zane. He was probably swimming naked skin to naked skin with some easy, lucky girl, I thought. Then, as we were going from the gate, I saw him sitting alone in a shadow on the terrace, his legs crossed like a gentleman, and with a modest glass of wine, still full, on the wicker table beside him. He waved languidly towards me but it was neither a summons nor an invitation, so I only waved in return.

'You ought to go and grab 'im,' suggested Bet as she skidded through the country lanes. Dolores had the harp clasped between her legs, and I was in the rear seat with the keyboard, the viola and our sheet music.

'I would,' confirmed Dolores giving the gilded pedestal a squeeze with her thighs. 'He wouldn't get away either.'

'Not in one piece,' muttered Bet.

They dropped me outside the antique shop. 'What you going to do now?' asked Dolores from the car window. 'Dream?'

'About that Zane,' sighed Bet. 'He'd keep me busy in dreams for a month.'

'Maybe,' I said. They waved as the car clattered off and I waved back. They left the evening street deserted and streaked with bored sunshine. I felt deflated. Then I realised that I had left my hat behind.

At first I was only annoyed. I tried to think where I had left it and called myself a fool for drinking so much. I had a shower and then lay with a dry towel across me on the bed. My eyes fell and I slept for more than an hour. When I woke there was muted sun outside the window. I decided to go and fetch my hat.

Although the house in the forest was quite isolated I knew that the country bus from Southampton to Lymington passed close by. I dressed and walked around to the bus station. A bus with 'Lymington' on the front was standing with its engine vibrating and I climbed aboard. It left only five minutes later. The driver straightened up from his slump across the steering wheel, rolled me out a ticket and said it was the last bus that day. 'Coming back?' he asked. He was young and hopeless. A half-note of optimism came into his voice. 'I am.'

'What time is the last bus back?'

'Nine o'clock. You have to walk after nine.'

I sat at the back of the bus as it went through the sallow countryside. A couple got on, loaded with fruit and flowers, and then got off three stops later without speaking to each other or anyone else but with a grunt to the driver for their tickets. It only took half an hour and I recognised the top of the house over the trees. 'This'll do,' I called to the driver. Jerkily he pulled up. The bus engine throbbed. 'See you at nine then,' he said.

'Probably. But don't wait.'

I gave a sideways wave with my hand and then the bus set off with a snort. I went down the lane towards the house.

The gate was open, flung open by the look of it, and the extensive garden was in disarray as if it had been the scene of a violent battle. Many of the chairs and two of the tables had been overturned, there were bottles and scattered food on the grass, the canopy under which we had played had collapsed like a flag and there were several crows strutting among the scattered cakes and sandwiches.

But I could not see any people. It was as if some magic had spirited everyone away.

It was getting towards dusk. I went to the terrace, for some reason on tiptoe. I thought I might have left the hat behind the lavatory door. Stepping up to the patio I almost tripped over a prostrate couple, embraced like the babes in the wood. There were two more people under the table, equally still, the woman in a crumpled red dress and the man clutching a bottle by the neck. Through the open French windows I saw several pairs of feet, soles up.

A few more steps and I turned the corner of the terrace. Zane was sitting soberly upright in a chair wearing my hat and grinning that swaggering grin I came to know so well. 'I found your bonnet,' he said. 'I thought you'd be back for it.'

Silently we drank some wine. No one else seemed alive.

'Have you just been sitting here?' I asked eventually. 'You were here when I went.'

'No, no,' Zane said casually. 'I've been round and about. But everybody's either smashed or gone.'

'You came with someone, though. You weren't by yourself at lunch.'

'I've had enough of her,' he shrugged. He picked up a worn paperback book from the terrace table. 'I found this,' he said. '*Gone with the Wind*. I've been reading it. I'm up to page three.'

'It's a long book.'

'One thousand and eleven pages,' he said weighing it in one hand. 'I've always wanted to try and read it.'

He took me by the fingers and we walked down the long lawn almost to the edge of the forest, where (as if by appointment) he calmly undressed me. I stood remarkably still while he was about this, upright, and somewhat surprised with myself, and wearing my recovered hat. Just under my skin I could feel a trembling. He went about it like the dab hand he was, scarcely touching me.

Because I so much wanted him to do it, I remained unmoving while he unbuttoned the summer dress, dropped it gently to the grass and then peeled away my underthings. He took his time as if he knew no one would interrupt. I was not afraid either although normally I would most certainly have been, being stripped naked in the open air. But I wanted him to have me. It's not every June evening you stand in the middle of the New Forest while a man divests you of your clothes. All the time he kept his practised eyes on me. I found it difficult to look him directly in the face; I kept gazing away as if I were studying the fuzzy horizon or a group of donkeys chewing on a rise beyond the garden hedge.

He should have been a film star for God knows he had

the looks and God knows he could act like fury. And learn lines. And recite them. And from the Bible.

'Whatsoever things are lovely,' he said touching my bare breasts. My legs were tight together, in a sort of military stance which I may have inherited, but he then reached down and like someone opening a cupboard he prised them apart. At this point I wondered if he was trying to remember my name. Not that I cared.

Now, thinking of it, I could cringe when I remember what I let him do; what I *wanted* him to do; what I would have missed so much if he had not done it. First he took his shirt off, revealing another worthwhile part: his fine shoulders, a grand spread of a chest, creamy, broad and undulating with a small, fair and curly copse of hair between his nipples and a long run of toned skin and muscle descending into his trousers.

His every movement was sure, accomplished. None of the fiddling and faddling and embarrassed apologies of other men. Holding my hands and then my warm hips (I could feel they were glowing) he dropped to his knees like a pilgrim in front of me and kissed me everywhere within sight and out of it. His tongue was strong and thrilling. Not wet, only damp. God, if only he had been a half-decent man.

My hands ruffled his thick blond hair. While he was kneeling in front of me I held onto his cheeks and felt the toughness of the skin. I tried to look at the donkeys, trying to delay. I had rarely known an orgasm and I did not want to waste this one. His tongue travelled up my right groin like an express snail, and then the left and then, like a man leaving part of a job to be completed later, he climbed to his feet, considerately wiped his mouth with the back of his hand and kissed me on my lips. Over the top of the hedge I saw the travelling roof of the last bus going towards Southampton.

'My turn,' I said. I undid the buckle of his belt, a silver rodeo horse. It fell open so noisily that I glanced around afraid that someone might hear the clunk. But we were still alone. From their raised ground the donkeys were beginning to take an interest, as if they suspected what might be coming, but we had the garden hedge for concealment. He was brilliant at getting rid of his trousers, a moment when men are generally at their most comic and vulnerable. But not Zane Tomkins. I did nothing but watch as he kicked them aside with a snort of arrogance, as though they had offended him and he never wanted to see them again. His multi-patterned underpants were revealed, poking out like a proffered bouquet. Blissfully my hands went to him and I manoeuvred the pants away and down his thighs. There it was, there *he* was.

'Let's swim,' he said.

'Swim?' I asked stupidly. 'Now?'

He pulled me close to his warmth, his penis prodding me like a promise. 'Now,' he muttered deeply. 'In the lake.'

'The lake?'

'It will make us smell good for each other.'

So into the bloody lake we went. Christ, it was terrible. Murky and manky with creepy, bug-eyed fish. Meanwhile Zane went crashing through the brown water, all arms and muscles.

As I was coldly thrashing about among the ornamental carp and lily leaves, trying to spit out the gravy-coloured water, he cruised over on those powerful arm muscles and, pulling up next to me, flung the water from his hair and caught me around the naked waist. 'Now is our time,' he grunted.

He did not even splutter but simply trawled me to the edge of the lake and pulled me up like a fish onto the grass. He stood, streaming wet, his dick in front of my eyes in the dusk.

I am ashamed to say that I sat on the bank of the lake like some daft water maiden waiting to see what he wanted to do. His feet, with their heavy toes, strode away. I looked up to see him holding his shirt. 'Now I dry you,' he said.

He kept on in this strange accent, a version of Tarzan's jungle speech. But I had no time to dwell on it for he lifted me upright and, after smiling so close into my face that I felt his warm breath, he began to dry my body which was starting to shiver, or tremble, with his shirt. Jesus, that was wonderful. He rubbed me all over like a mother. Everything within me began humming again.

When he had dried me I offered to do the same for him but the shirt was soaked and he whirled it aside like a matador. It fell into the lake and I saw it floating away over my shoulder as he faced me. 'You've just thrown your shirt in the lake,' I whispered. My breasts were squashed into his chest, and my hands were stroking his leg muscles. 'Fish can have shirt,' he said. He gave a jungle laugh. 'Now fish can eat.'

From the distant house came a hollow cry like the call of a survivor. Zane looked up but only briefly, before turning his loaded face towards me again. 'Fuck them,' he said in his Southampton voice.

The loss of the shirt, however, had upset his plans to lay me on it. He became distracted as he carried me up the bank towards the sheltering hedge. 'You wait,' he eventually grunted and turned and loped naked towards the swimming-pool. It was almost dark but I could see his buttocks gleaming. He returned with a towel and the grin of a hunter. He spread the towel. 'Now,' he grated, 'we will be together.' A moon like a plate had appeared.

He was the strongest lover I had ever known, or would ever know again. That night in the garden by the forest I relished every moment, the feel of him massed above me, shutting out the moon, and then below me, his presence inside my body, the water running from his ears and the slightly putrid, pondy smell. I was so hungry; there had been so many let-downs and no-shows and now I was grappling with this dumb but dreadnought lover. We had a terrific time and then we had another terrific time and then another. Eventually we lay under the moon and arriving stars and saw that two of the donkeys were gazing over the hedge at us. What they had seen I did not know. But I did not care either. And Donny was already on the way.

17

When I was in prison, awaiting trial, some well-meaning ladies from the outside used to come and give talks and demonstrations to the locked-up women. One of the lectures was 'How to Give an Intimate Dinner Party' and there was another person who came along to demonstrate how to make your own clothes-horse.

Because they were so bored (there was not even table tennis now; the ball had vanished with Madonna's death) quite a lot of the remand prisoners used to turn up for these lectures although few of them would ever need to be hostess at an intimate dinner party. There was a newly arrived, aristocratic-sounding lady, white and lofty with unmarked hands, who seemed to understand what the lecturer was talking about and contributed some experienced suggestions. She was in for forgery, which she refused to accept as a crime, and it took her a long time to learn to fold her own blankets and empty her night potty. Because you could be on report, and lose privileges, for taking a long time over your housework, one of the younger girls would go and help her. Only one person became deeply involved in the demonstration for making your own clothes-horse, a minute Chinese girl who intended one day to open her own laundry. They all had dreams.

It was during one of these lectures, 'How to Trace

Your Family', another subject which was beyond the reach or, indeed, ambition of most prisoners, including me, that a warder came and told me that Detective Sergeant Ron Brown had come to see me again. I pulled myself away from drawing a family tree and followed her back to the same small room where we had talked before.

He looked much better than when I had last seen him. 'The wife walked out,' he said as if he owed me an explanation. 'So I took myself off to the Costa. Met a few villains I've known down there. Had quite a good time. You got married once, didn't you. Alf Tomkins, wasn't it?'

'Zane,' I said.

He seemed pleased, as if a puzzle had been solved. 'Zane. That's what they still call him.' He nodded. 'I wondered why they did. On his criminal record he's called Alfred. They don't deal in pet names.'

'You saw him?'

'Just saw him. We didn't talk. It doesn't do to talk to them.' He looked up at me with a squint of sympathy. 'How long ago was that?'

'What, being married? Oh, years ago. We had a son, Donny.'

'Where's Donny?'

Miserably I returned his look. 'I don't know. He sends me a pebble now and then.'

He looked as though it was all getting beyond him. 'Funny, sending a pebble.'

'It's what he sends.'

'Well, Alf – Zane – is doing all right. Got a nice place down there. Proceeds, I expect.' He took my arm considerately and motioned me to the chair. 'And you're in here.'

'A lot of the women are in here because of men.'

'Life's not fair, is it,' he said thoughtfully as though wondering if he might be able to change it. 'Anyway, I've just come to clear up a few details. Oddments.' He gave me a look. 'Off the record of course.'

'What's going to happen to me?' I asked bluntly.

'Can't exactly say,' he shrugged. 'Depends on your defence and what the prosecution can drum up.' He leaned towards me confidingly. 'You *might* be all right. You didn't assist in the death of Lady What's-her-name ...' He glanced at some gradually unfolding papers which he had placed on the table. 'Lady Annabel Bowling, that's it. And the old boy was a sort of mercy job on your part. Helping him. You might just be lucky. If you get a half-decent jury.'

'I'd be acquitted?'

'Oh, I didn't say that.' It was as if the word, official as it sounded, had pulled him back to reality. 'I couldn't say at all, Chloe. It's not my job to say.'

He looked embarrassed that he had unwound too much. Changing the subject he looked around, beyond the open door. The voice of the lecturer echoed distortedly from the association area. 'What's she going on about?' he asked.

'Tracing your family.'

'Blimey, who'd want to?'

'Not that many, I shouldn't think. Not the women in here. What's *now* is bad enough without dredging up the past. They only go for someone else to listen to. There's not a lot on otherwise. I've almost read *Gone with the Wind*.'

'That's a long one, isn't it? I've never tried it.'

'One thousand and eleven pages,' I said. 'I've only got two to read. I'm up to where he says to her: 'Frankly, my dear, I don't give a damn.'

'Yes. Even I've heard of that. I might have seen the film. No table tennis?'

'The ball got lost.'

He nodded deeply and I thought he was going to go into another bit of philosophy. Now his wife had gone perhaps he had no one to talk with. But he thought the better of it and said: 'Well, while we're on the subject of the past I thought I'd show you something I've dug up.' His eyebrows appeared to thicken. 'This is not official, by the way. It's only out of interest.'

'Right,' I said. He was rummaging through the papers on the table. 'What is it?'

He found the paper but scraped his chair away so that I would not be able to focus on it. 'It's about the first Lady What's-her-name ... Lady Lucy Bowling, going over that cliff.'

'What about it?'

'Well, suicide's quite big in Dorset, you know. It's one of those places, a bit moody, out of the way, nowhere to go and lots of high cliffs.'

'She didn't commit suicide,' I said. 'Lady Annabel pushed her over.'

'Right,' he said. 'Like Sir What's-his-name said ...'

'Sir Benedict.'

'Yes, like he said in that statement we got from his solicitors. The one he'd written yonks ago. Spriggs and Spriggs it was. Well, there's a report in here. Folded up among the papers of the inquest ... 1956. Some bloke, Professor Pandarus Clements ... He repeated: 'Pandarus,' and smiled, apparently with pleasure that he had captured the name intact. 'This Professor Pandarus Clements had made a study of people jumping from cliffs.' He shook his head. 'You'd hardly believe that, would you. A special study.' He glanced at me and I agreed that you would not.

'Well, according to Lady Annabel – privately anyway, she didn't tell the inquest – she saw Lady Lucy, her sister, actually taking a running jump over the cliff. Going back a good distance, like a fast bowler, and then taking a run at it.'

'That's what she said to me.'

'Well, not to be too gruesome about it, Chloe, but if you fall over a cliff, or slip, or get pushed from the edge you sustain very nasty-looking injuries because, in most cases, you sort of bounce down the cliff face, the rocks or what have you. Especially a cliff like that which slopes outwards. It shows. You don't have to be a pathologist to know that. But ... but, Chloe ... if you take a *running* jump, like Lady Lucy is reckoned to have done, you actually *fly*. Especially a lady in a long skirt like she had apparently. A long evening skirt. She'd fly like Batwoman. You float through the air, over the cliff and the air currents keep you flying until you hit the water. You don't get any lacerations or bruises or dents of any kind. People have been known to get away with a nasty soaking even.'

'And Lady Lucy had dents?'

'Lots of them according to the pathologist's report.' He frowned at the document. 'Lots.'

'So you don't believe Lady Annabel's story that Lady Lucy took a long run and went over.'

'Not according to this,' he said tapping the papers and folding them. 'But it didn't come out before the coroner. Some things never do. Some quite important things.'

'Well, well,' I said. 'Thank you for telling me.'

'That's all right, Chloe. I thought you'd be interested to know, that's all.'

Not many of the women in prison had been properly married, although in their minds they had been and they lied fiercely about it. All the wrongdoing, the misery, the lousy luck of their lives and their hopeless hopes for the future were contained in their stories. The ones who vowed before God that they would never find themselves behind bars again were always the ones who returned.

They enjoyed anybody new because there was more to talk about. They say women in prison talk a lot more than men. Men sulk. Every woman vowed she would die for her children. On Sunday the children could come and visit their mothers and there were toys and even a bouncy castle. The warders all wore ordinary clothes instead of uniforms so the smaller children would not realise it was a prison, although they must have wondered why their mothers did not go home with them. Our own stories, those we cared to reveal, were soon worn out, threadbare with repetition, and somebody fresh to listen to them, and to tell their fantasies in return, was something to which we looked forward.

Some of the younger girls, for all their insolence, their tattoos, their babies, their tales of drugs, were themselves childlike. The bravado which led to snarling cat fights easily collapsed into anguished tears. Regulations only allowed eight personal photographs fixed inside the doors of each locker, but they loved these pictures, mostly of infants and very few of men, gazed at them, talked to them and displayed them to their friends. One timid girl had snapshots of four different babies, two white and two brown, inside her locker door.

'Why ain't you got any photos?' she asked. I was more than twice her age and she thought I should have a whole gallery pinned up.

'I don't, that's all,' I said. 'I'll put some of yours up if you like.'

She thought about it, then refused as if she would be lending me some of her loved ones.

'I feel sorry for you, not having nobody,' she said.

Almost without exception, they hated men as much as they loved the children which men had given them, children who they vowed were never going to have squalid lives like their mothers – or their fathers, wherever they were.

They loved weddings, and the talk of weddings. They dreamed of wearing white to marry some fabled man who would make them, and their babies, happy and safe for ever.

From eight to nine each evening we had the last association of the day. In some prisons the remand women could mix with selected prisoners from the already-sentenced wing but we could not. Most of the girls were glad because they felt they might became tainted while others knew they would soon be in that company anyway and for quite long enough.

Every evening, I went to the association room, which was a bare place with the ball-less table-tennis table in one corner and various broken or incomplete pastimes, including a dart board with one dart (which had a rubber sucker instead of a steel point) always planted firmly in the bull's-eye. The Scrabble was missing half its letters, playing cards were not allowed and there was no snakes and ladders because of the dice. Gambling was totally forbidden.

We were permitted to make cocoa on an electric ring and there was a toaster and a pile of fairly old bread. In a strange way these hours were among the most companionable I could ever recall. Not since I was in the army school had I felt such closeness. The others looked up to me too, for despite being on a murder charge, I was a first offender, I was older and I was more sensible. They came to me with their problems as if I did not have enough of my own, sought solutions and told their stories. They used to sit around, and often on, the heavy tables, smoking their roll-ups sometimes made from the outside wrappings of Tampax, and listening and arguing and pathetically trying to be wise.

One evening, when almost twenty of us in the remand wing were there, one eighteen-year-old, Sherrie, brought in a copy of *Brides* magazine and everyone gathered around exclaiming over the white gowns and handsome husbands and advice on presents, champagne receptions, and where to live in expensive bliss, none of which they would ever know. They became excited and started laughing. Everyone enjoyed themselves, everyone enjoyed being part of it. A black girl called Martine and a white girl from Wolverhampton, Bickie, decided to act out the parts of bride and groom. Everyone had something to say, to laugh about. The blonde Bickie was the bride, a tea towel for wiping the cocoa cups draped over her head, and Martine was the groom, her dark features comically straight. Everyone hummed the wedding march, someone was best man ('There ain't no *best* men!') and I was handed the bridal magazine so I could be the priest.

I held it before me like a prayer book and we mimicked our way through what we could collectively remember of the marriage service. It was only a childish game but a strange thing happened. The laughter and the catcalls died and a sort of sadness took over, a half-silence; the joke dried up. Someone began to cry in the background and was told to shut up. She climbed from the table, went from the room and back to her cell still snivelling. 'My husband was a *trainee*,' she called behind her.

'She thinks she's better than us,' said someone.

Although the jocular feeling had gone it was replaced by an odd expectancy, like a nervousness, and we went on with the charade. At the end I pronounced them 'woman and wife' and everybody giggled at that, with a sort of relief, except Martine and Bickie. Before my astonished eyes they clasped in a tight and tender embrace and kissed, the white lips and the black lips sticking together, half-parting and then joining again. Everyone else cheered. Then we saw that the warder was at the door. 'Nine o'clock,' she said with weary stoniness. 'All back.'

My cell was the furthest along the corridor. The warder, who was a grandmother and a decent woman, walked tiredly along with me. She had to check every cell was secure. 'Did you see that?' I asked knowing she had. 'The wedding.'

'Yes.'

'It seemed real,' I said.

'You have to love someone in this place.'

I went into the cell.

'Or outside,' she finished. 'I wish I did.'

18

On the evening of our wedding day Zane took me back
to our cottage at Cutcross and carried me through the
gate and up the garden path. It was only seven o'clock
and it was all done very suddenly. We were still at the
reception in the hotel when he came through the guests,
held my waist and whispered close to my ear, over the
music and voices, that we ought to be leaving. This came
as a surprise but he confided that there had been a
change of plan.

It had been a furtive sort of wedding. A police car was
stationed on the opposite side of the road outside the
church. The best man, whom I had never seen before but
who was said to have been overseas, kept glancing
towards the church door as if he expected somebody
unwelcome, and he disappeared almost before the
ceremony was over. I never saw him again. Several of the
guests refused to be in the wedding pictures and, as my
mother pointed out when we were compiling the album,
some of the others were either looking away from the
camera or half-hiding their faces. The wedding cars went
off at speed as soon as they had roared us to the hotel for
the reception. It was very odd. Still, I was pleased when
Zane said we ought to leave.

Even on that evening when he carried me through the
gate and along the path, he had a preoccupied air. He

almost overlooked carrying me across the threshold. There were three keys to three locks recently fitted to the front door and by the time he had undone them he seemed to have forgotten me. He walked in and nervously looked around leaving me standing outside.

'Zane,' I reminded him quietly.

'Darl,' he apologised. 'My brain's full, that's the trouble.'

I did not appreciate how full until we were sitting with our champagne in front of our first roaring log fire. I was in my dressing-gown but he had changed into a dark jersey and dark trousers. The flames lit his film-star face. He had looked wonderful that day in his morning suit with his cravat only a little more yellow than his hair. I swear even the vicar blinked.

We kissed before the fire. A big antique clock, which had appeared suddenly, was ticking on the oak mantel-shelf. Zane said it was a present but he could not remember who had given it. I was sitting at his feet, my head on his lap and aware of my baby inside me, when he stirred uneasily and stood. I thought he was going to the lavatory but he said: 'Darl, I've got to go out.'

'Out?' I know I only whispered.

'Just for half an hour. An hour at the most.' I heard a car pull up in the lane outside. He was already tripping towards the door. 'Zane, it's our wedding night,' I pleaded.

'I'll be back for that,' he said. 'Promise.'

He darted back to kiss me. I held onto him, already beginning to cry, but he was going. 'It's a favour,' he said.

Five hours later, when he came back, I was asleep in the chair with the fire reduced to red and grey ash. 'How was the favour?' I asked drowsily.

'A big one,' he answered. 'But it's done now. Let's go to bed, darl.'

What could I say? What could I do? It was a long time before I would be able to find any answers. We went to our deep bed under the eaves. He fell asleep at once leaving me staring into the dark.

The next day he said: 'Your mother's very religious, isn't she?'

'Not very.'

'All through the service she never got up from her knees. All she did was pray. Praying and praying.'

Rosa was praying for me. She had seen Zane a mile off. When I first took him to meet her in Aldershot, after we had decided to get married but before I told her I was expecting, we had gone for a meal at the El Alamein bistro and Zane began to describe some completely imaginary time when he had been a soldier. He even stood at the table and gave a salute.

'We don't salute like that,' pointed out Rosa. 'Not us.'

I felt myself blush and Zane said: 'Like what?'

'Like you did,' she said. She repeated the salute as he had done it, edge of the hand against the forehead. 'The British Army salutes with the hand flat.' She showed him. 'You did an American salute. Like in the films.'

'I spent a lot of time with the Americans,' he said. 'Great guys.'

It was the strangest thing, but when Zane knew I was pregnant he had right away asked me to marry him. He made a performance of it, of course, dropping onto his knee and doffing an imaginary cap. I laughed because I thought he was joking but he had a new copy of his favourite book from the library, and he put his hand on it, as though it were the Bible, and said: 'I swear on *Gone with the Wind* that I want you to marry me.' He was still only up to page eight.

Now I know, of course, that, no matter how lovely he looked on his knees, hand on the book, I should have refused him right then, blown him out, but I hesitated and I was lost. I did not know him then as I grew to know him later, although I had my suspicions.

Every day up to the wedding and after it, for that matter, I kept expecting him to change his mind. But instead a boyish enthusiasm took him over that was astonishing to see. When, a month before, he suddenly insisted that we should make no further love until we had taken our marriage vows, I could hardly believe what he was telling me. He wanted us to make a truly fresh start, even though I was already pregnant. In one way I felt flattered, almost as if he was returning at least part of my long-lost chastity; in another I knew I would miss him where he was best, in the dark between the sheets.

Then he announced that he had obtained the cottage at Cutcross. The first afternoon we went there I was in a dream, a few months gone and him driving a new car (stolen, as it turned out, although he had only borrowed it from the original thief and the police took no action). Even as we stopped outside the fence, as he opened the gate with a comic opera flourish, and as we walked together down the narrow, weedy path between the overgrown roses and the other straggling plants in the garden, even then I thought it was probably only one of his fancy games. But he produced a key, opened the door and invited me into our home.

There was a bit of poor furniture in there and a square of faded carpet, although not enough to stop my shoes sounding on the grubby stone floors. The windows were low and glowering, the walls felt damp but it seemed like a piece of paradise to me. 'But how ... why ... how ... ?' I asked clutching his arm.

'A favour,' said Zane descending to his mystery voice. 'I was owed.'

'That was a big favour,' I said.

'It was,' he grunted. 'We don't pay any rent. Not for ages.'

Even when we moved in I could hardly believe it. It was a fairy cottage in the forest, a gingerbread house that would be vanished next time I went down the lane. But, like a miracle, it stayed. Every time I went to Cutcross that autumn it remained beautifully where it was under the large oak tree with only the country colours around it changing.

Zane was amazing. All at once he became straight. He helped me to decorate the interior and one day turned up with a trailer loaded with very acceptable second-hand furniture which he said had cost him next to nothing. There was also a television which he had been able to borrow. Rapidly our lives were becoming complete. We had a little car with a logbook and he obtained some garden tools, including a mechanical cultivator which had 'Southampton Parks' faintly painted on the side. Through the warm but closing autumn days he tore through the wildly overgrown garden, uprooting plants and shrubs and putting others in their places. When I asked him where the bushes had come from he said he had found them growing wild and I had to take that for an answer. I was learning to compromise.

He swept the chimney by pointing a shotgun up it and pulling both triggers. Birds and old nests flew out of the top and clouds of soot cascaded into the room which I had just painted. We rolled in the soot laughing and hysterical. Suddenly I felt happy.

Then, two weeks before we were married, we moved permanently into the cottage. We slept in the large bed below the eaves where, because of our recent promise, we only held each other, rolled and kissed. It was so tempting under that warm roof, in that cosy bed, but although I told him I was happy, even eager, to abandon our chaste arrangement, and although we sweated sexily and gasped and sighed, he always pulled away at the last moment. 'I am going to keep my vow,' he said.

I said his vow did not matter but he would tug himself away and rush from the room. He had become amazing. He even went out and got a job.

When he told me I hooted with disbelief and he pursued me around the room and out into the garden jabbering about it being true. It was too. He had gone to work as a salesman in a car showroom in Southampton. He showed me his first week's wages. He had never appeared to be short of money (although he often obtained goods second-hand) and in fact we paid our bills on the dot in cash because he said it was better not to upset people. Where the money came from I could never understand. One day he announced that he thought insurance was the greatest boon to mankind. There was a youth of about fifteen who used to come to the house, often with parcels. Zane said he wanted to help him. He was called Smiley and he had dirty fingers and sticky eyes. I changed his name to Slimey.

'Insurance,' Zane explained to the boy while I watched, 'is good for everybody. It's the world's greatest invention. If somebody lifts some nooky . . .' He glanced at me: '. . . takes something that don't strictly belong to them, then the owner gets on to the insurance and reckons it's worth twice as much as it was really and the insurance company pays up. The insurance companies are rotten rich because they collect from people who never have anything nicked or never even make out they have. So everybody's happy: the villain what helped himself, the people he helped himself from and the insurance.' He spread his hands. 'Everybody.'

When Zane proudly showed me his letter of appointment from Opportunity Motors who promised to pay him two hundred pounds a week plus commission, I looked for signs of forgery because lying came so naturally to him. Once he even owned up to something he had not done – he could not have done it because he had not been within miles. Eventually the police realised he was lying again. But Opportunity Motors was genuine. I telephoned them and the owner said so. On his first pay day he and Slimey came to the cottage with a baby grand piano for me. They said they had found it, that nobody owned it, but I caught Slimey as he was creeping out of our lavatory and pushed him back inside putting both hands around his skinny throat and fixing him to the pipe on the wall, his windpipe and the cistern pipe in my grip. He soon owned up that the piano had been removed from a house at Beaulieu, wheeled through some French windows carelessly left open at night.

I shouted at both and somehow they returned it before the owners noticed it had gone. The following week Zane came back with a nice, old, upright piano, battered and scratched, in a trailer behind one of his cars. Smugly he showed me a receipt for eighty pounds and between us we wheeled it into our room and put it across the wall near the big fireplace. I used to sit at it, sitting there stuffed full of baby, playing songs all alone on winter nights when he was somewhere else.

One night there was a rough banging on the door. I

waddled to it and opened it a cautious two inches. Slimey was there. 'Zane sent me,' he said. His sticky eyes twitched. It was to be one of his longer speeches and he took a breath: 'He says you've got to get out. They're coming.' He disappeared into the forest night, not even going through the gate but turning sharply and vanishing somewhere to the side.

Who was coming? Where would I go if I went? I had no means of transport and I was six months' pregnant. I decided to stay and let the questions answer themselves. After bolting the door I went to the piano and played something restful. Among some sheet music I had found on a stall at a school fête in Lyndhurst was a piano arrangement called 'In an Eighteenth-century Drawing-Room'. I was playing that when they arrived.

There were only two of them but they were big and angry and I had to unbolt the door because they would soon have smashed their way in. One of them had a sledgehammer. They stayed outside and said their names were Daniel and Clarence. Daniel's eyes glittered in the night. There was a car out in the lane with the engine still running.

'Where is he?' demanded Clarence.

'Tomkins,' said Daniel.

'Zane?' I answered as if I knew him only slightly. I was hoping somebody would turn up, even the police. Perhaps Slimey had gone for the police. He knew where to find them.

'Him,' said Clarence.

My belly was projecting around the door. Clarence said roughly: 'Excuse us,' and less roughly pushed his way in. There were not many rooms to search and they went through them quickly. Eventually they stood in front of the fire downstairs and Daniel, with a wisp of an apologetic smile, began warming his hands behind his back. 'He's out,' I said, adding truthfully: 'I don't know where.'

'Right,' said Clarence nastily. 'Right. Get that axe, Dan.'

I did not like the way they were looking at me. I said: 'I'm pregnant. If you chop me up there's going to be a hell of a mess.'

Daniel still went for the axe. Clarence, less apologetically than Daniel, was now warming his backside against the fire. 'That Zane does himself all right, don't he,' he said looking around the room. 'The bastard.'

'What's he done?' I asked. I nearly added: 'Now?'

'Well, for starters, apart from nicking a lot of stuff, and a hundred quid that was being saved up for Christmas ... apart from that he's given my missus ...' I was amazed to hear a sob in his voice. '... my missus ... given her a dose ...'

I thought Donny was going to fall out. 'A dose?'

'A dose,' he repeated. 'You know what a dose is ... VD ... that's what ... Sillyfis ... you know ...'

'Syphilis,' I whispered. My hands went to my face. Now I realised why Zane had suggested the celibacy before our wedding night. Until after the treatment. But even with the shock, even then, mentally I found excuses for him. *Someone* must have given it to *him*, some wicked woman ... and he had protected me ... and Donny. I go limp now when I think of it, the swine.

'I've got the axe,' said Daniel arriving and brandishing it as if we could not see it. 'Here it is.' Clarence glanced my way. 'We're not chopping up you,' he said. He glared towards his companion: 'Start with the joanna.'

'No!' I flung myself across the piano keyboard, hanging

onto the top, spreading myself across it as though it were my old mother.

'All right,' said Clarence. He nodded at Daniel: 'Sort out the rest first.'

He eased me away from the piano and, selecting a lucky chair, politely placed it in the far corner of the room. There I sat, huge and hunched, while they axed and sledgehammered their way through all the furniture in the room, even our bit of carpet which, I was pleased to see, caused them more trouble than anything else. Daniel really enjoyed it, you could see. He seemed to be used to handling the axe and perhaps that is what he did for a living. At first Clarence appeared hesitant to join in but then he remembered his wife's pox and with a cry of: 'Mandy!' he bashed the sledgehammer onto our table. The television exploded as Daniel smashed it, giving us all a fright.

It took about ten minutes including the bed upstairs. All that survived was the chair upon which I sat and the piano standing heroically back to the wall. 'Don't break the piano,' I begged. 'It's all I've got.'

'It's not all *I've* got!' retorted Clarence adding to the Mandy drama. He went into a new frenzy lunging the hammer down on the keyboard, letting off the greatest discord ever heard. It was like pouring a concerto down a drain. He raised the hammer and smashed it down again. Daniel, apparently eager for something that did not submit dumbly like a chair, got to work with the axe and in no time my piano was scattered and piled on the floor like a jigsaw.

They were sweating by the time they had finished. Daniel, who had a nasty streak, went into the kitchen and returned with a bucket of water which he threw on the fire. It expired with a gush of steam. I sat sobbing on my corner chair.

They went. At the door Clarence said a formal: 'Good evening,' and Daniel laughed and said: 'Love to Zane.'

I sat there in the wrecked silence of the room. Steam was still struggling from the fire. I had another cry and then went almost on tiptoe to the pieces of the piano. It was sliced up, oddly like pieces of meat in a butcher's shop, but without the blood. There was one long section of keyboard, hung desperately together like a set of broken teeth and I picked this up and took it back to the chair with me. Fat, helpless and getting cold, I sat there with the broken keys on my lap amid the wreckage of our home and picked out a silent rendition of 'In an Eighteenth-century Drawing-Room'.

Although he could take a car apart (very quickly when necessary) and sometimes put it back together Zane was not very adept at most practical things. When he returned to the cottage that night and found me slumped, wet-faced and freezing among the chopped-up furniture by the doused fire, and still clutching the lump of keyboard, he said: 'Don't worry. I'll soon mend it.'

There was no question of that, of course, and in fact the remnants of our cosy home made a notable contribution to the Cutcross village bonfire that November. No one asked about this devastated furniture heaved onto the branches and other forest stuff that made up the rest of the pile. The villagers had soon realised that Zane was unusual and unorthodox and no one asked questions although the vicar did say that it seemed a pity to have dismembered such a nice Regency side-table, which Zane told me an old lady had given him for helping her.

The texture of the mattress had defeated Daniel's axe

and I had managed to restuff it and sew together the gashes, and we still had one chair. But we were not down to these for long. A van appeared in the lane two afternoons later and another set of furniture was unloaded including a very delicate, if impractical, washstand. There was no piano, however, and I was very sorry about that. I missed it. 'We couldn't find a piano,' said Zane.

Although I had described to Zane the two men who had burst in and done the damage, he did not seem deeply interested. Nor did I discuss Clarence's allegations about his wife's embarrassing ailment. Zane would never have admitted to anything like that; our sexual relations had resumed as soon as we were married and I wanted to keep him, cured as he doubtless was by then, so I said nothing. Accidents will happen.

I did my best to become part of village life, gossiping in the shop, waiting for the afternoon bus, planning and cooking meals, meeting the mobile library under the trees and even playing the piano at the Sunday school, resting my belly against the keyboard and singing lustily with the children. Christmas was approaching and I was looking forward to this almost as much as if Donny had already been born, instead of weighing me down like a bag of washing. My mother was to visit us at Christmas and Zane was looking out for a camp bed (which he found). The fire would fly up the chimney, there would be plenty to eat and drink and on Christmas Day we would go for a walk through the naked forest. Everything would be silent except for the few Christmas birds and our footfalls on the leaves and bracken. I settled contentedly into the country life, watching the wild skies and wild animals and truly believing that happiness, and even stability, were approaching. I would never learn.

Zane used to return home in a different car every day. He said he could take his pick from the Opportunity Motors forecourt. Sometimes the car would be some poor old thing that coughed along the lane and at others it would be a dashing sports job that came through the village red as a flying berry. Sometimes men would be waiting for him, loitering, chary-looking men who would circle the car, sniff under the bonnet and take it away. He did a lot of business from home.

His handsome face would fall to seriousness, his jaw jutting, on these occasions and he would become wise and cagey although I am sure most of the men knew him very well. With me he would put on this silent power act but I knew it for what it was, just another sort of bullshit. But I never tried to cut him down. He would become childishly fierce when exposed and, in any case, I suppose I liked to play the game too. I was always the victim.

19

Even years before in the army house in Singapore we had tried to pretend Christmas was cold and rosy and when my father was in the military prison we made a special effort among ourselves and the others in the army street where the head of the family was unavoidably absent. Once my brother Kneller dressed up as an angel, all in white with a golden halo and a touch of lipstick and holding a small trumpet on which he played 'While Shepherds Watched'.

Christmas in the forest with Zane and the unborn Donny and my mother was to have been the cosiest I could make it. Zane was out much of the time, even late in the evening and at times into early morning because the car business, he said, never stopped. So it fell to me to put up the seasonal decorations although my husband did appear breathlessly with an excellent Christmas tree, newly cut, which he said he had spotted growing unwanted in the woods.

It was left to me, swollen as I was, to put up the tree and ensure it would not topple and to load it with coloured bits and pieces, lights and slivers of silver tinsel. Holly and mistletoe I gathered from the forest on a solitary, thrilling expedition one afternoon with chiselled air and a rough sunset. It was wonderful to make myself a cup of tea at five, feeling my face glowing, to wonder if

Zane would be home for his meal, and to sit in front of the snapping logs in the open fireplace. Naturally I had planned everybody's presents, Zane's, my mother's and a soft toy dog for Donny, although he wasn't ready for it just yet.

Then, three days before Christmas Eve, while I was humming carols I had promised to play at the Sunday school, my husband braked noisily outside in a growling sports car, white, with the top down despite the season. My heart jumped. This time, I thought, he had really done something to make us rich.

He strutted up the path and came in through the door as I was opening it. Excitement crammed his face and he could hardly get the words out. 'Darl,' he managed to say eventually when he had hugged me and kissed me. 'I've got a fantastic job. It's going to make us rotten bloody rich.'

'Wonderful ! Where? When?'

'Abroad,' he said. 'But I've got to go *now*. I won't be here for Christmas.'

My mother came up the lane from the bus-stop through the Christmas Eve downpour. Standing distended and alone I watched her from the cottage window. The ragged trees swirled about and the wind stretched her white plastic mac like a sail, but she strode on indomitably. I wanted to cry.

By the time she had reached the wooden gate I was at the door. 'He's not here,' I said as soon as I had kissed her. She struggled from the plastic mac and crinkled hat. They were stiff and rain ran from their creases. Without answering she carried them into the scullery and dropped them like cardboard onto the stone floor. She looked around the room as if to make sure. 'Where's he gone?' she said.

'Abroad.' I really started to cry now. She put her arms out and smothered me in them as though I were still a girl. 'Never mind, Chloe,' she said. 'We'll have a good time together. Where's he gone?'

'I don't know. But it was a big opportunity, he said.' I was only snivelling now. 'It will make us rich. It's just that . . . well, it's Christmas.'

'Perhaps this opportunity, as you call it, only came up because it's Christmas,' she suggested shrewdly. 'Never mind. I've brought a couple of bottles of port. Let's have a drink.'

A vehicle pulled up in the lane as we were drinking our first glass. 'It might be my present,' I said. 'He promised my present would be coming.'

'Too big for the post,' she suggested. 'But there, he always does things in a big way, your Zane.'

The knocker sounded. A man stood in the rain, trying to smile, and hugging a big parcel in his hands. 'You'd better not lift it,' he said seeing my condition. 'I'll put it on the floor, just here.'

Rosa came up behind me. 'I bet I know what it is,' she said. 'It's the right size.'

'Have a look,' suggested the man strangely eager. 'I'd like to see as well, if you don't mind. We never see what's in the parcels, you know. We collect them at the store loading bay and we take them to houses and the people never ever show us what's inside. They just take them in and off we go. We never see what happens in the end.'

'Come in,' prompted my mother. 'Have a glass of port.'

'All right,' said the delivery man immediately jovial. 'Thanks very much.' He guffawed. 'Any port in a storm.'

'That's very good,' my mother told him gravely. She handed him the glass. 'You ought to go in for it.'

'I do,' he said in a pleased way. 'Just amateur. Charity shows and that. But people seem to like it.' He raised his glass and wished us the season's best. I was pulling the wrapping from the package and lifting the lid of the box.

'I knew it,' said Rosa. 'I knew ... I bet I'm right.'

'A keyboard,' said the man. He looked embarrassed for giving it away and said: 'Sorry.'

I pulled the keyboard from the box. 'Oh, that's wonderful.' I smiled. He had remembered. 'Now we'll be able to have a singsong.'

'I don't sing,' said the delivery man nervously. 'Just jokes and that.'

He leaned over and took hold of a document which was stuck to the outside of the package. 'Nothing to pay,' he said.

I looked at Rose and she said: 'I should hope not either.'

'Not till next month,' he continued. 'It's the special no-deposit offer.'

He lifted his glass in a final toast before going out into the windy rain. 'Well, at least he thought of you,' sighed my mother sitting down heavily.

'He said I can have anything I like,' I said. I regarded her defensively. 'As soon as he gets back.'

'I think we'd better drink to that,' she said grimly.

'All right, Mum,' I said. With a little defiance I raised my glass. 'To Zane Tomkins,' I said.

'Alias Alf,' mumbled my mother.

Even now I like to think of our cottage, low and little, its lights shining on that Christmas Eve in the ragged darkness of the forest. I like to think of the songs I sang with my mother and the sounds of the thumping keyboard going out through the trees where perhaps wet animals listened.

Rosa prepared the supper. She would not let me get up from the flowered armchair. I remained there, steadily getting through the port, staring into the blazing of the open fire and trying to pretend I did not need him. My mother made sausage and onions with bubble and squeak, whole frying pans full of it. I could hear it sizzling and sniff its friendly smell. We had a small television (the one destroyed so noisily by Clarence and Daniel had been vastly superior) and this flickered fitfully on its table hardly noticed by either of us.

Rosa kept coming in and out or calling from the kitchen as though in an effort to keep my spirits up, and hers, and when we sat down at the table we began talking about some of the funny things that had happened in the past, laughing at the memories. I even told her about Mr Gul the Indian schoolteacher in Singapore who had rolled with me down the grass bank all those years ago.

She fell silent at this and then said: 'It's funny you should say that, because he came around not all that long ago asking for you.' I felt my eyes widen.

'He turned up at the flat,' she said. 'Goodness knows how he found me, through the army I suppose. He was a wily one. Anyway he knocked on the door and said that he was very well off these days, newsagents and sweetshops, in the north somewhere, but that he had often dreamed about you since he came to England and wanted to see you again.'

I began to laugh into my hands. 'But . . . you never told me . . .'

'No, I certainly didn't. I probably thought you might

take up with him. You were daft enough for anything. You still are, Chloe. Look at us sitting here and that pillock Alf, Zane, or whatever he calls himself, off somewhere having a good time.'

'He's not,' I argued seriously. 'I'm sure he's working, Mum. We're going to be rich.'

'When Mr Gul turned up I thought he was one of the Lascars you'd got mixed up with . . .'

'I never did get mixed up with any Lascars,' I said primly. 'I don't know any.'

'No, but I was afraid you might. Anyway I nearly threw him out into the street before he'd had a chance to tell me who he was. In the end we had a cup of tea and I lied to him that you'd gone off to Australia to marry a sheep shearer. Whether he believed me or not, I don't know.'

'But he was nice.'

'Very nice and polite. And he remembered so much about Singapore. Do you know he even knew the name of that cat they had next door. Remember the big tom?'

'Persimmon,' I said. I felt myself blush in the firelight.

We had drained the port before the meal but I had some red wine and we began on that. I did not care about being pregnant. We got into a terrible state. Rosa slid off her chair and we laughed so much I thought I would have Donny right there in front of the fire. 'We'd have to call him Jesus!' hooted my mother as I tried to haul her up. 'What next!'

What next was a heavy banging on the door. We both had difficulty in standing up and getting there. We held onto each other as we staggered but it seemed a long way across the room. 'It might be Mary and Joseph,' giggled my mother.

She was half right. The bent and wrinkled person who

stood on the threshold in the dark rain said his name was Joe and that he was Irish. Having announced himself and his nationality he went into the worst fit of coughing I have ever heard. He almost fell onto the path with it, heaving, clutching his chest and spraying Rosa and me. Somehow we dragged him over the doorstep, three rolling figures. He had a sagging suitcase on wheels which he had abandoned halfway along the path. Rosa stumbled out into the rain to get it.

We got him into the house. His whole body was shaking as though with the echo of the coughing, and his face was wet with rain and perspiration. We pulled his old coat from his back. 'It's a long way from the station,' he complained.

There was no station within four miles. 'Brocken-hurst?' I said. Now he was sitting and demanding cough mixture. Rosa poured the dregs of the wine down his throat and he spluttered and choked. She went to the kitchen and got a tea towel to wipe his face. 'This place ought to be nearer,' he moaned. 'A lot nearer.'

With a limp and trembling hand he took the tea towel from Rosa and wiped his forehead. A scrap of wet hair which had been clinging to his pate came away with the movement. He studied it, caught like a big spider on the towel. 'Look at that,' he said. 'Supposed to be a disguise.'

Rosa took it away from him but remained standing over him. He began to cough achingly again, holding his ribs. Ominously she and I looked at each other. 'You ought to have the doctor,' said my mother.

He looked so alarmed he stopped coughing. 'Doctor? Doctor? I can't have a doctor, missus. It's bad enough with the police.'

It was getting beyond us. 'The police?' was all I could say.

'Them,' he said. 'I got to that station, that place you just mentioned . . .'

'Brockenhurst.'

'That's it. But I didn't know how to get here so I started walking. Walking and hoping, you know. Somebody always comes along who knows the way and they might give you a lift.'

'There's a bus,' said my mother a bit helplessly. 'I came on the bus.'

He almost glared at her, quite fiercely even though he was so small and wrinkled. 'But I didn't know that, did I? I was given very poor information.'

'Who gave you . . . ?' I began.

'. . . a lift?' he mistakenly completed. 'Wouldn't you know, it was the police. Of all people, the blinding police. I was walking along the road and it was raining and dark, pulling my luggage there, and they stopped and asked me where I was going. Well, for Jesus' sake. Of all the people I didn't want to tell it was the officers now, wasn't it. So I just said Cutcross, which was on the piece of paper, and they told me to get in and they brought me to about half a mile away. They had to go off then to some riot at a carol service or something. So I had to walk the rest, and what with that suitcase and getting soaking and this cough of mine . . .'

'Who are you?' I managed to say.

He appeared aghast, looking at me and then at Rosa and back again. 'We don't know,' explained my mother. She swayed as if the room were getting heavy.

'You don't? You didn't get the message then? I do have the right address . . .' He fumbled in his pocket and found a damp piece of paper which tore as he tried to open it. 'Drat it,' he muttered.

'It's Oak Cottage, Cutcross Lane, Cutcross,' I told him.

'Hampshire,' added my mother.

His eyes continued to swing. 'That's the address,' he insisted. 'That's what I was given. And I take it I have the pleasure of speaking to Mrs Zane Tomkins.'

Just the mention of the name went a long way to explaining everything. My mother was first with the question: 'Zane sent you?'

'Not him, not himself, personally. One of the others.'

'What others?'

'Oh, you know. I forget all the names. But they said it had been all fixed. The safe house where I could lie low for . . .'

'A safe house?' Now it was falling into place.

'Sure, sure. Somewhere for when you're on the run.'

'And Zane Tomkins has put it about that this is a safe house? Am I right?' My mother without thinking put the tea towel to her face and the man's scrap of wig adhered to her cheek. With a snort she pushed it away and threw it and the towel into the kitchen.

'You're right,' he said. 'Everybody knows. I heard in Ireland.'

'Who are you on the run from?' asked my mother in a low but firm voice. 'Nothing to do with the IRA?'

'IRA!' He almost spat the initials. 'No, much worse than that. It's the Shinty Gang.'

'Oh,' we said together as though we knew them well.

'I've got to keep low for a few days,' he said. 'I'll get to Southampton after Christmas and get a ferry from there. I'll have to get abroad.'

I had been standing and now I was finding it was too much. I sat down heavily. 'And what's your name?' I asked.

He seemed surprised. 'Joe,' he said. 'Short for Joseph. I thought I told you.'

'I'm Chloe Tomkins,' I said weakly. 'And this is my mother Rosa.'

'Delighted I'm sure,' he said holding out a crooked hand and smiling gummily. 'Would you have available a drop of the hard stuff?'

After our unexpected guest had eaten and warmed himself and drunk nearly all of the half-bottle of brandy we had intended to pour on the next day's Christmas pudding, he crumpled down to a deep and apparently comfortable sleep in front of the fire. My mother got a blanket and put it around his legs before we went to bed.

It had been planned that she would sleep in a camp-bed in the small room under the eaves, next to our bedroom. But with Zane being somewhere else, and Joe being downstairs, she crept in with me.

'What are we going to do with him?' she whispered.

'God knows. There's nowhere we can send him, not now it's Christmas, and he seems half-dead.'

'It's a shocking rattle he's got,' she said. As if to confirm it the old man downstairs was abruptly gripped by the most racking coughing fit. It was almost a seizure. We could hear him cursing, heaving and throwing himself about. We cowered below the bedclothes.

'Missus,' he eventually croaked up the stairs. Another spasm seized him and I had to answer three times before he heard. 'Missus,' he repeated. 'Have you got a drop more of that brandy?'

We only slept when he did after that. We crept down and found him snoring so powerfully that the flames in the hearth wavered. Then he would cough and throw himself about and slide from the chair to the floor in front of the fire. I had to stop him banging his fist on the wall because it was bringing the plaster down like an avalanche in the Alps. We were up and down the narrow staircase all night. Eventually we got the camp-bed downstairs and rolled him into that. He grumbled that we had not produced it before.

Christmas Day was hell. We thought he was dead a couple of times, although he recovered to eat and drink heartily at our delayed dinner. By the time we sat at the table it was dark outside and he said how grateful he was that we were looking after him and what a lucky man this Zane Tomkins must be to have such a wife and mother-in-law. He lay back like a corpse on the camp-bed while Rosa, determined to get something out of the day, thumped out some defiant carols on the keyboard that Zane had sent. Joe said he liked the old hymns best and sat up pitifully trying to sing them over the crackling of his chest while tears streamed down his creased cheeks. He drank everything in sight and enjoyed his supper. He even got my mother to rub his chest.

He slept better that night, which meant we all did. I was hoping that Zane would come back on Boxing Day so that we could confront him with the results of his general generosity. But by now it had begun to dawn on me where the money had come from for renting and refurbishing the house and installing two lots of furniture. A *safe house*, a hideaway for criminals on the run. I shivered. Who could we expect as our next guest?

On Boxing Day Joe seemed better but in the afternoon he vanished. It is difficult to imagine our concern, our panic, our terror. We went charging through the soaking forest calling him, frightening dozing ponies and damp donkeys. We found him sprawled in the village bus shelter eventually and somehow between us got him back to the house. I almost collapsed and I was sure that Donny was about to arrive early. It was terrible.

'Oh, missus,' Joe moaned when we had got him back in front of the fire. My mother rubbed his chest again. 'It's been too much trouble for you. And it's my intrusion ... I know it ... it's all because of me.'

Desperately we tried to reassure him that he was a welcome guest and we gave him some whisky of Zane's which I had discovered hidden away. But he was trembling now and sweating. 'He's going to die,' whispered my mother drawing me out to the kitchen. 'We'll have to get somebody.'

'What about the Shinty Gang? I said sourly.

'Sod the Shinty Gang.' Her voice was so forthright that he heard and croaked: 'Don't let the Shinty Gang get me! Don't let them, I beg you, missus!'

At nine o'clock he went off into what looked like a coma. 'We've got to do something,' I agreed. 'He'll be dead by morning.'

She ran like a flapping ghost along the dark lane to the telephone box at the crossroads. The ambulance arrived in twenty minutes. 'Surprising how busy we are,' said one of the men. He took one look at Joe prostrate on the camp-bed. 'Well, I'll be buggered, Bill,' he laughed to his fellow attendant. 'It's old Codger.'

'Up to his tricks,' nodded the other man staring down.

'What tricks?' I asked hollowly. My mother's face revolved slowly towards me.

'Board and lodging,' the man said. 'He'll always find somewhere to be comfortable. They call him Codger the Lodger. Last Christmas he spent with the Bishop of Salisbury, if I remember.'

Weakly I sat down. 'You all right?' the first ambulance man asked. His mate had gone for the stretcher. 'You look as if you ought to be coming too. When's the baby due?'

'Not just yet, I hope.' I said dully. 'He's not from Ireland then?'

'Never been nearer Ireland than a bottle of Guinness. He's well known in Brockenhurst. Been around there years. He used to be some sort of actor.'

'He still is.'

'He just turned up, did he?' The second man had now appeared and they manoeuvred Joe, or Codger, now deathly silent, perhaps to keep out of things, onto the stretcher.

'He came in and . . .' I needed to choose my words. 'He said he was a friend of my husband.'

'And your husband isn't here?'

'No. He's away on business. But he seemed to know him and about this house and he said he had been invited here. It was Christmas Eve, late, and it was pouring, and we couldn't send him away. I mean he's really ill, isn't he?'

'He always is,' sniffed the second ambulance man looking at the prostrate Codger on the stretcher. 'You should have called earlier. We never close for Christmas.'

'We know that,' put in my mother sharply. 'But this . . . this person begged us not to. He said something about the police wanting to interview him.'

'That's probably right too.' They heaved up the stretcher and made for the door. Their passenger suddenly appeared to know what was going on. 'Thank you so much, missus,' he whispered waving a ghostly arm.

'He got me to rub his chest,' my mother snorted as they went out.

'You're lucky,' said the rear man over his shoulder.
'He got the bishop's wife to hold the chamber-pot.'

20

'A criminal?' snarled Zane when he eventually came back. 'You mean you entertained a common criminal here over Christmas?'

'He said he knew you,' I pointed out. 'He said you had arranged it. He said this was a "safe house" as he called it.'

'And *you* believed him. *You'd* believe anyone, you would.'

'Yes, I would,' I said a bit quietly. 'That's my trouble.' Then I challenged him. We were in our bed, me a great lump projecting over the bedclothes, him naked with a light tan. '*Is* this a safe house?' I said bluntly.

'Safe as houses,' he answered and sniggered. That was quite witty for him and I laughed as well, God help me. He looked smug. I was glad to have him home. We could not make love from the front because of my protuberance but I rolled away from him and lifted my nightdress at the back. I felt him flexing his arms about me and he took my breasts one in each hand and we made love like two large and loving dogs. I meant it, every moment, and I know he meant it too. Then, he did. I am sure.

It was odd doing it that way because I could not see him, only feel him revolving against me. My bottom was in his lap and within me I could feel him probing and moving. 'Don't wake the baby,' I whispered.

He never failed to bring me to my moment, a lush feeling that always filled me, and I loved it because he was such a fine-looking husband. If only the fine looks could have been continued into his soul and character. If only he had not been such a crook.

'Where did you go?' I asked him.

By then he was stretched out beside me. Spent as it was, his penis still made a bump under the bedclothes. I was lying beside him looking, feeling, like a mountain. Even then he had to lie.

'Turkey,' he said.

'Turkey for Christmas.'

He laughed. 'You *can* be funny, you know, Chloe. And you've got some good ways of saying words, if you get what I mean. Yes, I was in Turkey.'

'Why?'

'Business.' He sighed as if it had been a sacrifice and something he could not share either because he did not want to involve me or because I would not understand. 'We wanted to do this deal and get in ahead of the others. They don't have Christmas in Turkey, see. They're not the same. They have these mosques and stuff. It's just like a normal day so we went over and did the business.' He turned to me and gave me his sincere-promise look. 'It's only to make us rich,' he said. 'One day.'

'What part of Turkey?'

'What d'you mean?'

'Which town?'

'Oh God, I don't know. You know me. Ignorant. I just got on the plane with the others. They knew where we was off to. Well, some of them.'

'Who are these others?'

'All these questions. You're like a copper sometimes. I

can't tell you, because everything is under wraps, see. Secret.'

He turned and tried to divert me. 'Want to do it again?'

I could wait for the answers. Heaving away from him I manoeuvred my buttocks into his lap. He was ready for me again. 'Our baby will be wondering what's going on,' I said. This time, afterwards, I remained where I was. I knew he was worried because solicitously he crept to get a towel and he offered to make tea. 'There's time,' I murmured pretending to be sleepy. 'Come back into bed.'

Now I turned like a steamroller and held him against my belly. We could both hear Donny's heart. Zane's eyes began to droop. 'Your passport says you went to Spain,' I mentioned.

He flicked open his eyes, loaded with hurt. 'Spain? I never. I went to Turkey. I know I went to Turkey. I know where I've bloody been.'

'Spain's a shorter flight,' I said helpfully. 'Turkey's much further.'

'I don't need a school lesson,' he said. He was angry now and got out of the bed. He went into the bathroom and I could hear him splashing and muttering. His head came around the door. 'And who said you can stick your nose into my passport?'

I reached under the pillow. My mother had seen it first. In the *Daily Mail* the day after Boxing Day. The headline said: 'London Gang Sought after Big Costa Raid.' When he came out of the bathroom, I said: 'I thought you might be something to do with this.'

'In the paper?' he said with a touch of excitement. It took him a moment to realise. Then he took it from me. 'Can't be anything to do with me,' he said lamely. 'It says

"London Gang" and I'm from Southampton and Harry's from somewhere north. Plymouth.'

'It was *you* though, wasn't it?'

He sat on the side of the bed, a real domestic moment. Crestfallen as a child he pushed his face into my breasts, his thick hair in my face. 'Look Chloe, we're never going to get anywhere otherwise. This was a sitting duck. Reckoned to be anyway. We went for the safe deposits. Half the buggers down there are villains anyway. They're not letting anybody know what was in those safe deposits. They wouldn't. Nobody's ever going to own up. It was a great idea. Clean them out over Christmas.' His face, which had recovered during the story, fell again. 'We only forgot one thing. The alarms, the gear, everything was no trouble. But we forgot the sodding Spanish don't have a day off on Boxing Day. So the time was cut. It was a long job as it was. It's hard work breaking open safe deposits, no matter how you do it. And the in the end we only had half the time. All the Spaniards turned up for work. We only just got away. We had to lie low for a couple of days. That's why I was late home.'

He said it as if he had been working overtime in a factory.

As I turned away from him I was crying. 'Is this how it's always going to be? Are we going to bring up a child like this?' I hauled myself around in the bed so that I could face him again. There were tears on his cheeks too. I did not know then that he could cry to order.

'Listen, Chloe,' he said. 'I'm never going to be any good. Don't you realise this is all I can bloody well do – be a villain?' He stood up and looked into the full-length mirror and smiled at himself through his tears. 'All I've got, all I've ever had, is *me* – see, what you can see now.'

'Your looks,' I said helpfully.

'Right. That's all. I can't *do* anything, see. I might be able to sell a dodgy car now and again but that's never going to make us rich.' He said goodbye to his reflection in the mirror and came back towards me. He was slipping into his Tarzan mode. His hands went on my shoulders. 'I want good things for us.'

I should have gone *then*, gone back to my mother and had my baby there, and got away from him. But I could not do it. Zane was all I had for myself.

So from then on it was a matter of pretending I did not notice. Sometimes he went off with a woman but he always came back and sometimes he would not appear for days or, as twice happened in the first year, for weeks. But I knew he was generally committing crime, not adultery. He would come home laughing and flush but then things would go wrong. He used to rage at the treachery of his accomplices. 'You can never trust those bastards,' he would snarl, blind to the fact that he was stating the obvious.

Even the Christmas raid on the safe deposits in Spain gained him nothing. 'They've got to sort it all out,' he had boasted. 'Big Tommy and Shellduck. We'll all get our bit. It might take weeks. Shellduck knows all the ways.'

Whoever Shellduck was he certainly knew ways of disappearing with the loot leaving Big Tommy looking small and the rest of the gang bad-tempered and unrewarded. 'We even had to pay our own air fares,' moaned Zane with his head in his hands.

When I had Donny in Southampton hospital he came to see us privately, handcuffed to a policeman. But there was not enough evidence, or possibly because he had just become a father, no charges were made. I had to tell the nurses and the ward sister it was all a joke, done for a bet, father in handcuffs going to see new-born boy, and they said strange things often happened in maternity wards.

There were long times when I think he really tried. He would go off to the car salesroom and work and come home in the evening with the paper under his arm and have his meal, tickle the baby and watch television, like any other man.

One afternoon, when I had been shopping in Southampton, I got off the bus and walked towards our cottage and I saw that Zane had climbed the oak at the corner of the garden and was amusing Donny, sitting below in his pushchair, by swinging on a branch and yodelling like Tarzan. It made me so happy to see it. Then the branch broke and Zane crashed to the ground. Dropping the shopping I ran to him. He was only winded. Donny was laughing. 'Just amusing him,' Zane said. Somehow he even kept a promise of providing a car for the Ambulance Service charity draw. It was in the summer and I took Donny. He was then fifteen months old. He beamed at the sun as it was beaming at him. Zane proudly introduced me and the baby to the Mayor and Mayoress and the Member of Parliament, and the same two ambulance men who had come to collect the old rogue I still called Joe, that Christmas, were there. There were stalls and bunting and a squeaky little band.

Zane looked marvellous on the stage, with his tanned face and his fawn suit and crimson tie and the sun glistening like a halo on his fair hair. There were a lot of people there, a couple of hundred, and a number of police. One of the plain-clothes men had a good look at the car, a shining new Ford, but said nothing and I afterwards saw him shaking hands with Zane as though he were congratulating him on doing something straight.

Zane made a speech. He could talk even if he was lacking in other areas and everyone clapped. He distributed his business cards like free money.

I could not believe everything had gone so well. Even the police had gone home. Donny was chuckling, held in his father's arms and, with a little help, encouraged to select the winning ticket from the revolving barrel on the stage.

The man who won the lovely and expensive car looked a touch familiar (he had been at our wedding) but it was not until later that I realised he was a relative of Zane's mother's neighbour. When Zane's mother died I saw this man at the funeral and there, in the cemetery, I realised what had happened on that bright, flag-flapping day in Southampton.

And Donny, our bright, decent baby, had been used. At the age of fifteen months he had become the innocent accomplice of his crooked father.

21

What I liked to think of as my married life with Zane Tomkins really came to an end when Donny was two. There was not much left after that. His lies and deceits trapped me all the time. I knew but I accepted. And he was so *quick* with them. Once I found him clutching a girl of about seventeen behind the inn in Cutcross. It was getting dark but I could see her dress was open down to her waist and the pale flesh below it. When he saw me he half-released her and said: 'Julie's father's just died.'

He was sent to prison for four years not long after that. Robbery at a small bank. Slimey, the boy he had been training, his witless accomplice, confessed to the police, but *before* the raid so that the law was waiting when they walked in wearing their balaclavas. I used to see him riding around on a new red motorbike, the reward for betraying Zane.

Three years, counting remission, is a long time to make conversation with somebody in prison. Nothing much happened in there on a week-by-week basis, only the quiz league and cigarette smuggling, and Zane, when he was not fantasising, had never been a conversationalist. But I loyally and regularly went to Winchester, which was fortunately very convenient, merely a bus and a short train ride from our cottage in the forest where Donny and I lived for another six months.

I never took Donny to the prison and Zane never asked to see him. I was worried enough about our son's future without showing him his father in there. Sometimes Donny would ask: 'How long is he going to be?' and I would say: 'Not long now.' But he never enquired further. It was as though he knew and realised that, at his age, there was not a lot he could do about the situation. Zane never mentioned him until I did. I would tell him all my accumulated trivial news, written minutely in a diary every day in case I forgot something even more trivial, and show him photographs of his son but he never put out his hand to see them twice and I might as well have been talking about a small stranger.

But even three years eventually goes. During the last six months, from Christmas onwards, I used a red crayon to mark off the calendar. Donny asked me why I was doing it but when I explained that I was crossing away the days until his father came out, or home as I always put it, he seemed to have only as much interest in seeing Zane as Zane apparently had in seeing him. By that time we were living in Southampton again, over Mr Pyecraft's antique shop, and Donny would be going to school for the first time on the Monday before his father's release. He began crossing off the days as well, using blue crayon to my red.

As the number of days shortened I even found it difficult to communicate my enthusiasm to Zane. As the years had gone by our talk had dwindled – sometimes we conversed separately with other visitors or prisoners or even with the occasionally talkative warder. There was a tiny woman with a big mouth, all bones and lipstick, whose husband was in for grievous bodily harm. 'Not on me,' she took pains to inform me. We used to talk as we walked away from the prison and down to the station.

'There's no way he'd touch me. He knows I'd floor him, big as he is.' Her grin was worn out but she said: 'Anyway, he loves me. Dearly.'

Zane seemed to find no joy, no anticipation, in his forthcoming freedom. It was almost as though he had become cosy in his confinement. 'In here,' he said, 'they call three years B and B.'

'What's B and B?'

'Bed and Breakfast. I'm reading *Gone with the Wind*.'

'You always have been.'

'I've read quite a few chapters.'

For the final year of his sentence he had been working in the kitchen, a choice place, and he vaguely talked about opening a restaurant on his release. I desperately encouraged him in this and even got some details from my former employers at the estate agents of restaurant premises for sale. But his old bombast and eye-on-the-main-chance had waned and he foresaw obstacles. 'It's a job to get people to wash up,' he grumbled. 'Even in here.' I persuaded myself that my enthusiasm would infect him. 'This is the last time I'll be doing this,' I said clutching his hand on my final visit.

'So it is,' he said as though it had not occurred to him before. 'I've enjoyed our little chats.'

For him that was a tender sentiment, and for me, an encouraging one, and I began to hope and prepare for the day. I got a new bedspread and had my hair done twice in the final week and bought a lovely summer dress and new shoes to greet him. I had gone over the scene in my mind so much (it could not be shared because my mother was openly cynical and Donny uninterested). How we would embrace, delicately because of passers-by, outside the gates; I would have a taxi waiting and we would go at once to a hotel down by the marina at

Southampton where my mother would be waiting with Donny. He would have the day off from school even though he had only started the day before, but he would bring his colouring book and show the colourings to his father when we arrived.

I had dreamed it and schemed it and when the morning came, I knew it by heart. The first thing that went wrong was that the day which, according to my plan anyway, was supposed to be as sunny as June can be, turned out to be grim and rainy. The television weather man had forecast it the night before, just as I was trying on my new nightdress again, but I refused to believe him, even laughed and said what fools they were. The nightdress lay softly against my skin, all the way down, and I knew that the sun would rise in a clear sky the next morning, like a fresh start.

I scarcely slept. The eight deep hours that were to make me clear-eyed and lively were whittled down through the night. Donny kept stirring and once I went in, fully woke him and told him his daddy would be back in the morning. His blue eyes opened but then he turned away into the warmth of the bedclothes muttering: 'So what?'

He was more of a realist than me. In the growing light I lay imagining that everything would be changed, that the long months, years, of confinement would have altered Zane in more ways than merely making him dull. Perhaps he would even become the forgotten Alf again, be transformed into a decent man, working and enjoying his life with his son and me. Perhaps he would even rent an allotment, the strong back curved over the busy spade, parsnips and shallots growing while we waited, potatoes dug white and fresh, straight rows of peas and champion marrows. We would never want for love or vegetables.

At four thirty in the morning on that June day the light was slicing through my curtains. I had only just drifted to sleep and when I focused on the clock, my ticking and reliable companion who had kept me company in my solitariness, I tried to squeeze my eyes and get another couple of hours' rest. But instead I lay there wondering what it would be like, hoping against hope really. It would be strange for him, living above the antique shop he had once tried to burgle; this thought had lurked with me for the year since Donny and I had moved from the cottage at Cutcross (after the arrival of a man with a knowing sneer and an eviction order). Zane seemed to think we still lived there. When our conversation dried, sometimes after only five minutes, he would suddenly ask: 'Are you keeping the garden tidy?' or 'Is Smiley allowed in the pub yet?' even though I had told him that we now lived over Mr Pyecraft's shop in Southampton. It did not seem to sink in, not permanently, and after a few weeks he would ask the same sort of questions again.

The thought, even on that last long, tossing night before his release, was a disturbing one. How would he settle down above the shop, would he feel caged (although he should have been used to that by then), would he need more air and a wider scope? Where would he store the vegetables he grew?

There were no answers, of course, only minutes moving on the clock while the daylight broadened outside the window. I had set the alarm for six thirty and it went off just as I was descending into a genuine sleep. The clock itself jumped up and down as if alive and agitated. Forcing myself out of bed and staggering around like a spider while cursing my luck and my appearance, I managed to get most things done, giving Donny his almost silent breakfast and trundling him around the corner to school. My mother was coming from Aldershot to pick him up and take him to the hotel where he would see his father. In my hurry and anxiety I put on odd shoes and stumbled all the way to the school gate and back again. Some of the other mothers (who naturally knew all about my troubles) looked at me in a pitying way as if they knew what I was in for.

There was just time for me to have a second bath and reapply at least some of my make-up, trying to disguise my swollen eyes, and to climb carefully into my new dress. It had looked more or less right the day before, lime green and summery with a shortish skirt and a deep round neckline, but now it shouted back at me from the mirror. With a real cry I threw it off and put on something that would have a more gentle appeal to a man who had been away from women for three years.

After all that time we were down to seconds. I only just caught the bus and the train. The sun had gone after its glancing first hour and rain was sheeting down the windows. A man sitting opposite told me that it would ruin the cricket but it would be good for the garden. 'My husband said exactly the same,' I said.

From my early days of visiting the gaol I had often had the same taxi-driver from Winchester station, although I had always walked the return. He was a thin fellow with a moustache almost stuffed up his nose but he was kind. From the beginning we had kept up a pretence that I was visiting my husband in the hospital which is directly opposite the prison. I would get out of the cab at the hospital entrance and wait until he had gone around the corner before joining the glum and faithful queue, mainly of women, at the prison gates.

'How long is your husband going to be in there?' this driver had asked on one of the earliest journeys. Without thinking I said sadly: 'Three years with remission,' and he shook his head and said: 'That's a long time to be in hospital.'

On this, the final day, he was waiting in his taxi outside the station, just as though he knew. 'My wife's in remission now,' he said. 'She's been ill nearly three years as well. Just like your husband.'

Even on that morning I waited for him to drive from view. From outside the hospital I stood rooted, staring at the prison gates, afraid to cross the road, afraid of what might happen. Very little did. The city clock sounded eleven which was the usual time they released them. In the past I had seen them coming out, some glad to be greeted, others looking shiftily up and down the road with nowhere to go. Not all the clocks struck at the same time and I waited until the last of the chimes sounded before my heart began to sink. The gate remained closed. I stayed on the other side of the road, willing it to open, willing Zane to appear and sniff the air of freedom. The rain had stopped but while I waited it began again and I put up the plastic umbrella I had picked up at the last dashing moment. Then it stopped and I put the umbrella down; then it began again and I raised it again. The man with a peaked cap in the gatehouse of the hospital smiled at me encouragingly, as though urging me to go to the other side. In the end I did.

The clocks sounded again from down in the cloudy city, staggering their chiming of the quarter hour. By now I had convinced myself that I had made a mistake, that release time was eleven thirty. Hardly able to take the steps I went along the wall to the window where a warder sat looking directly across the road to the uniformed chap in the hospital gatehouse. I had once had a dream in which these two men were waving their stiff caps at each other.

Nervously I tapped on the window and with what looked like a sigh the man opened it. I asked him what time the releases would be. 'It's always eleven o'clock,' he said quite kindly. He knew something, I could tell. 'But there's none today.'

I told him I had come for Zane (or actually Alf, because of course they used proper names and numbers in there) and he looked at a piece of paper on a clipboard. 'He went out yesterday,' he said.

I thought I would drop on the pavement. 'But . . . no . . . it's today,' I managed to say.

He checked his clipboard paper again. 'Yesterday,' he confirmed. 'Monday.'

It began to dawn on me. 'But he told me . . . Tuesday,' was all I could say.

'Monday,' he repeated.

As I began to cry he said: 'Sorry about that. He's not come home then.'

Sniffling I shook my head. 'Are you sure?'

'Well, unless he's hiding . . .' he began. 'I'd show you the cell but I can't because there's another bloke in it now.'

22

I only told Sir Benedict about my former life and misadventures if he expressly asked me but he rarely did and so he heard my story in fragments. He would ask a single question, apparently from nowhere, while we were at our evening cards or I was playing the piano to him or even sometimes when we were riding on the tandem and he would shout the question over his shoulder as he pedalled, quite often startling people on pavements.

One evening I told him how I had waited outside Winchester prison. 'It must have been most uncomfortable standing like that, being rained upon,' he mentioned quietly. 'Leaving you in the lurch like that.'

'It wasn't the first time.' I shrugged. We were sitting at the card table with the late fire moving in the big grate. Lady Annabel had been in bed for hours. I had been meaning to take a holiday that summer; I had some vague idea of searching for Donny but in the end I did not go. Perhaps I was still afraid. 'At least that day he didn't lie to me,' I said. 'He was always lying. This time he didn't tell me anything.'

'A lot of lies are told,' he said still watching his cards. 'Half the world tells lies. To the other half. And the other half tells them back.' His sound eye slowly came up. He could keep his blank one closed. It was strange but not frightening when he fixed you like that. 'Have you ever told any lies, Chloe?'

In my surprise at the question I showed him my cards and he politely turned his eye away and reaching out lifted the hand in front of my face. 'I suppose I must have done,' I said. Then: 'But not for a long time. Not since I've been here. In fact, I think the last time I lied was the day I came.'

He chuckled. 'To Lady Annabel,' he nodded. 'Well, they were worthwhile lies, whatever they were. You are here.'

I always felt so comfortable with him, particularly in that room on those evenings. It was so strange that the man I liked and trusted most, almost *loved* most, was over eighty and, apart from the occasional pat, had never needed to touch me. 'I was thinking that we might make a trip to Dorset,' he announced. He glanced up, this time with his blank eye as well. 'Do you think the machine would be up to it?'

It was not the tandem I doubted. 'Where?' I asked. 'Where in Dorset?'

'I want to go to the cliff,' he said, a small piece of hardness coming into his voice. 'At St Bride's Head. The place where Lucy went over.' It was still on his mind.

'It's too far, isn't it, Sir Benedict?' I suggested. 'On the tandem. It would take up three days, there and back.'

'Then we'll take three days,' he decided. We had finished playing. He had won but he habitually said nothing when he did. If I won he usually murmured: 'Well done, Chloe.'

'What about Lady Annabel?' I asked.

He looked startled. '*She's* not coming,' he said. 'There's not enough room on the bike.'

I laughed. 'But who will get her out of the bath? Somebody has to.'

'What about Urchfont? He hardly seems to do anything these days.'

The thought of Urchfont hauling her ladyship from the bath made me snigger again. 'I was thinking of having a holiday,' I said. He looked at me oddly, as if he suspected I might be planning an escape. 'But I haven't done anything about it,' I said quickly. 'Someone would have to stand in for me.'

His sigh broke into a dry cackle. 'We could always wait until she was dead.' He said it with a strange seriousness. 'And then go.'

I turned the conversation. 'We could get there and back in a day easily. But it would have to be by car. Bus would be too difficult.'

'Pity,' he said closing first his good eye and then the other. 'It's years since I've been on a bus.' He became resolute. 'We'll *get* a car,' he said giving the table a light decisive slap. 'And a man to drive it. We'll go down there and have lunch.' He leaned over the table, the dying light of the fire warming his skin, and his voice dropped. 'I'll show you the place where she plunged to her end.'

Although he progressed through life as sedately as any other man of his age, once Sir Benedict had made up his mind about something he liked to put it into action quickly. A few mornings later as I came down from drying Lady Annabel and helping her to her sitting-room, he was waiting in the hall, dressed in his out-of-doors sporting clothes, and the car was waiting.

That morning is crystallised in my mind because it marked the very beginning of the events which led me to be awaiting my fate in a prison cell. I can see clearly the big door of the house, Urchfont, the butler, trying to appear busy by holding it open (by his expression he looked as if he might be holding it up) and outside the comfortably dark car which was to take us on our adventure. I was so surprised that the trip was to take place that day, right then, that I scarcely had time to get myself changed and run down the stairs. Sir Benedict was already in the car. Urchfont was returning from having helped him into it and now hovered by the door again. 'Where's he off to then?' he enquired as though displeased by the sudden flurry of action and because I was going and he was not.

I said we were going for lunch but I did not say where.

'That's funny, he's got the radio on.' Urchfont nodded towards the car. 'See, he's got his head bobbing.'

When I reached the car and the capped chauffeur opened the door for me he said quickly: 'Sir Benedict told me *not* to turn the music off.'

'In that case leave it on.'

The man straightened his tie and opened the door. The music blasted out. 'I thought we'd have a few tunes,' shouted Sir Benedict happily. 'I don't seem to hear any tunes these days.'

I persuaded him to let the driver turn the volume down. We began to drive from the cathedral close. 'It never changes very much,' said the old man. 'It always seems to be the same. For centuries it has been.'

Then on the radio came a song which I knew from my not-too-distant past. I had danced to it with Zane.

'You . . . you make me feel brand new . . .
I sing this song for you . . .'

'That's very nice,' nodded Sir Benedict. 'A good tune, don't you think, Chloe?'

I agreed it was.

'Who is the performer?'

The driver half-glanced over his shoulder. 'The Stylistics,' he said smugly.

I glared at him in his driving mirror. Know-all. 'It's the Stylistics, Sir Benedict,' I said.

'They're *very* famous?'

'It was a big hit,' said the driver.

'You almost hit the arch then,' I pointed out leaning forward as we went under the old gate and out into the city street.

The driver sniffed. 'Nineteen seventies . . . seventy-four . . .'

Sir Benedict murmured: 'The Stylistics,' then glanced at me with his wild eye. 'Could you write down the words, Chloe. Perhaps we could sing it when you play the piano.'

The driver's ears straightened. 'The chauffeur will write them down,' I said. 'I'm sure he knows them.'

'I do,' boasted the driver to my annoyance. 'What's more I can sing it. I used to have a group once. Before I did this.' He thumped the steering wheel unhappily. 'I've thought of starting up again.'

'You can sing it, did you say?' Sir Benedict pushed his head eagerly forward. I was looking daggers into the man's mirror. 'Only after a fashion,' I suggested.

The driver turned the radio off just as the song was ending and the disc jockey was saying: 'A great oldie, that one. The Stylistics and "You Make Me Feel Brand New".'

It was quite a shock when the driver began to sing. I was annoyed because he had quite a decent voice. 'You . . . you make me feel brand new . . .'

'Wait! Wait!' Sir Benedict held up his long thin hand. 'You sing as well, Chloe. You know the words.'

'Yes, I do, Sir Benedict,' I said defiantly. I could see the driver's challenge in the mirror. 'One, two, three,' the old man counted. And we sang.

> 'You ... you make me feel brand new ...
> La, la ... la, la, la ...'

Even now when I try to sing it, my sadness reduces it to a whisper. I cannot sing much of it without crying. I can still hear Sir Benedict trying to join in. He had a terrible voice, cracked and gurgling, but he went for it loudly and bravely. All three of us sang as we drove from Salisbury and out into the morning countryside.

> 'You ... you make me feel brand new ...
> I sing this song for you ...'

I had never before been in a car with Sir Benedict, in fact, until that day, I could never remember him being in a car at all. Even when he had to visit the dentist we went there on the tandem – he sat on the rear saddle on the return because he was still groggy from the gas. Lady Annabel travelled by car when she made one of her occasional excursions beyond the house and the cathedral close, usually to some tasty funeral she had spotted in *The Times*. They always sent the same car for her journeys: a car with extra decorum which had room for her big black hat.

Travelling west that morning, we eventually exhausted the singing (the driver, despite his brag, did *not* know all the words) and progressed in slightly breathless but pleasant silence. The old man sat upright in the seat, looking like the Tsar of Russia, head a little back, his fine old hands on the silver knob of his cane. He needed this when he had to walk any distance but, since he scarcely left the house except on the tandem, he used it rarely. When we went on a tandem excursion and we expected to have to walk a little, to inspect some ruin or view some scenery, he sometimes took the cane and fixed it along part of the frame with sticky tape.

Although he was occasionally vague and confused, and sometimes deeply silent, he could plot things – plans that might even stretch over weeks or months – very deeply and carefully (as, that day, I was on the verge of learning).

He sat on the side of the car that gave him a view, with his good eye. The driver, to my relief, had now retreated from his familiarity, closed his window and straightened his cap. Sir Benedict quietly watched and sometimes tapped my knee as he drew my attention to something he had seen. He rarely touched me but I was pleased when he did. He only ever embraced me once in all the time I knew him and that was at the end.

On this airy day we trundled west towards Blandford Forum and then made for the coast. The first part of the route was the same as I had taken on the bus with the Reverend Ivor Pottle, another who had told me lies, although he did not know he was lying until I discovered the truth for him. Privately I smiled as I thought that if things – muddled nature for one – had been different, I might even now be a vicar's wife.

We drove by a folly, its towers standing up dark against the broad Wessex sky. The statues and memorials in that countryside often stand on the tops of hills so they can be seen, and the people remembered, for miles. Sir Benedict said: 'Henry Herring put that up.'

'Did you know him?' I asked.

He laughed drily. 'That would make me about two hundred years old, my dear. No, I just know it's called

Herring's Folly. I've seen it before, several times, years ago, and Lady Lucy read about it in her handbook. When we travelled this way she always read the places out of her handbook from the back of the tandem. She had a lovely voice, you know, even on the tandem. Quite beautiful.' We were almost below the tower. 'Well,' he said, 'if that was Herring's only folly then he did not do too badly.'

'Did you always come on the tandem?' I asked.

'At first we used to. We were younger then,' he remembered wistfully. 'And Lucy would read the guide-book over my shoulder. But later, when Annabel materialised out of Arabia we had to come down by motor.'

'How long was her ladyship in Arabia?' I asked.

'For several years,' he said with an unusually touchy grunt. 'Her husband rode a camel or something. British consul or some such thing. Then he vanished. Died, I imagine. Fell off the camel probably.' He gave a small, satisfied snort and repeated: 'Probably.'

'There's a lot of history about your family, Sir Benedict,' I said.

'Most of it hushed up,' he replied.

'Lady Annabel always says that she wants to return,' I said. 'She asked me if I spoke Arabic.'

'Do you?'

I laughed. 'No.'

'Arabic is no good to you. But she'd like to go back there, would she? Well, she could ... still do some travelling.'

At that time, of course, I thought this was just car talk. Although we were always comfortable in each other's company, there were few protracted conversations. It is difficult to talk for long on a tandem and in the evenings our games of cards were for the most part played in contented silence. Later, when Lady Annabel had gone, we conversed much more, as though her absence from the house had freed us, but even then I never felt we *had* to converse. Sometimes all I did was sing to him at the piano, something I had done only occasionally while Lady Annabel was around, and then only soft songs because her room was directly above and she no longer wore her ear muffs. Afterwards we had much louder evenings. We joined in fractured duets, with me singing and thumping out the tune and him croaking the words when he could catch up with them although by that time he was ill. He knew the same songs as my father had done including 'The Boers Have Got My Daddy' and he was astonished that I knew them too. And often, before we went to our beds, we sang together:

'You . . . you make me feel brand new . . .
La, la . . . la, la, la . . .'

23

As we turned along the coast rough skies began to appear, moving quickly on the wind. There was a hard shower that speckled the windscreen and made the driver turn the wipers on to their swiftest. He slid his dividing window aside. 'Don't want to go over there, sir,' he called back with professional heartiness. We were running alongside the cliffs. 'It's a long way down.'

I bit my lip but Sir Benedict's response was mild. 'It is,' he said. 'It always was.'

At the end of the journey he began to show small signs of excitement, or, I thought, perhaps agitation, tapping his silver-headed cane lightly on the carpet of the car. 'First left now, please,' he instructed. 'Then along this lane and right. That takes you to the Cliff Edge Hotel.' He glanced sideways as though he needed to explain to me and said: 'It's a short cut we used to take.'

I had often wondered what she was like, his Lady Lucy. Beautiful, naturally, I thought, and lively; someone you could imagine laughing. I realised I had never seen a photograph of her in the house. It was forty years before – long enough, but when he spoke of her and the things they had done, and where they had been, and the people who had been their friends, it was almost as if it were from another century. I imagined the women in long, slim skirts and the men with beards and dashing moustaches. It was not as though he spoke of her and those times very often but when he did it was very deep and well remembered.

The driver thanked him prissily for the instructions and followed them. The shower had cleared the sky and there were only strings of windy clouds; over the sea there was blue fading to the horizon. 'Well judged,' approved Sir Benedict. 'Just in time for lunch.'

After asking Sir Benedict, I told the driver to return at three thirty. The man did not like me but I did not care. Today was our day out not his. Sir Benedict pushed his silver-topped cane under his arm like an officer and we went firmly towards the hotel. At first I looped his arm in mine but he halted and paused and put my arm in his. I realised he was remembering.

I was astonished that the waiter knew him at once. 'Sir Benedict, you've come to see us again,' he said with apparent delight. He had come into the bar for our drinks order. The place was empty. He was a big, oldish man whose smile took years off him. 'It's been a long time.'

'Ah, yes,' said Sir Benedict holding out his hand. 'It's ... Goodhew ... that's right, isn't it?'

'Nearly sir. Mayhew. But then it's been forty years. I was just starting here then. And when you came back once I was on my holidays. But they told me. You came to see Mrs Goodbody, the coastguard's wife ... well, widow.'

'Yes, I did,' said Sir Benedict thoughtfully. 'It was an interesting visit.' He suddenly apologised and introduced me. He said I was his companion.

The man left us with our drinks but he served us again at the table in the almost empty dining-room. 'Lady Annabel is well, sir?'

'As well as can be expected.'

'I keep up with the news,' said Mayhew. 'I've got relations in Salisbury.'

When we were eating lunch Sir Benedict said: 'We always had this table. Each time we came. I would sit here and Lucy would be where you are.'

'Why did you want to come today?' I asked.

'I want to see again where it occurred. I want us to walk up the garden there and along the cliff. I'd like to show you and ask you what you think.'

'How will I be able to help?'

'You won't very much,' he said gently. 'But you'll be with me when I'm there. I don't want to go to that place by myself.'

I patted the mottled back of his hand. 'I'll be glad to be with you.'

'This chap Mayhew,' said Sir Benedict. He leaned across the table a little and glanced around. 'He was the chap who ran to the top of the cliff after me. He was a bit more sprightly then, of course, and so was I. But he was there and he saw Annabel prancing around screaming. *Telling* everyone that Lucy had gone over the cliff. That was her word – *gone*. She told everyone who arrived on the scene. It was as if she wanted to establish it. It was only later, at the inquest, that she said that she did not actually see her go, that she had been looking the other way. And then, of course, she began the dreadful story that Lucy had jumped.'

'And you don't believe either,' I said looking straight at him. This was always disconcerting because of his blank but fierce eye. All his feeling, his emotion, now was in the other eye.

'No, I don't and I never have,' he said. Mayhew

returned with a tray of tureens for our main course and Sir Benedict said: 'We were talking about that day . . .'

'Yes, sir,' said the waiter. 'I'll never forget that day.'

'We are going to take a stroll on the cliff after lunch,' said Sir Benedict studying his plate. 'Perhaps you would like to stroll with us.'

I could see the man's quick concern. But he said: 'Yes, sir. I'm sure that will be in order. We're not busy, as you can see.' He looked enquiringly out of the window. 'And it's turned out quite nice.'

When he had gone I told Sir Benedict about the time that I had been along the coast at Chesil Beach with Ivor Pottle. 'We went to the little chapel – where that book about smuggling is set.'

'Ah, *Moonfleet*,' he nodded. 'The Mohuns. Who did you say you went with?'

'Ivor Pottle,' I said. 'He helped me when I first came down to Salisbury.'

'Hmm. I'm amazed that poor chap could help anyone,' he said. 'He must have improved from his earlier days. Everybody shouted at him. Annabel particularly. She seemed to think he was interfering with her rabbits.' He glanced up. 'She kept rabbits then. I don't know why, but she did. His mother's still around, the busybody. She's always in the *Journal* doing something. But is he still in Salisbury?'

'No,' I said. 'He went off to found his own church.'

'Good gracious. Pottle? Did he now?'

'In London. Saint something.'

The sun flooded suddenly through the window. Two more couples came into the dining-room and had champagne to celebrate something. 'Would you like a glass of champagne?' asked Sir Benedict. His manner had cheered as though he had made up his mind about something. 'We ought to have a glass on a day like this.'

We did. And a second. 'We'll have to be careful,' he said jovially. 'It's still breezy. Wine and champagne don't mix very well if you're on the edge of a cliff.'

I had a sudden ridiculous but terrible thought that he had decided to jump over after his Lady Lucy. That was what he had made up his mind about. I could just see him doing it. God – *perhaps he wanted me to go too*! I dismissed the thought. We were at the end of the meal. Mayhew arrived with an anorak over his arm and said: 'I'm ready when you are, Sir Benedict.'

We walked down the lawn towards the cliff. The sun had paled and the trees and shrubs in the garden were being breezed about like green hair. Gulls screamed and kicked on the rim of the cliff, diving and disappearing and then swiftly coming into view again. At the end of the grass there was a low white fence and gate. I walked apprehensively. I knew the old man had something on his mind. Mayhew had not put his anorak on but now he offered it to Sir Benedict and then courteously to me. We both declined but he did not wear it himself, only carried it under his arm.

The small gate was quite difficult to open. 'We don't encourage people to wander too close to the edge,' said Mayhew. 'Most of them stand and admire the view from here.' He looked reflective. 'They miss the best part.'

'We must go on,' insisted Sir Benedict but as if he were talking to himself. 'It's only a few yards.'

'And there's no children, of course,' said Mayhew as an afterthought. 'The hotel doesn't take children.'

Like an elderly explorer returning to some place he had discovered long ago, Sir Benedict led the way. We followed, first me, then Mayhew, like followers full of doubt. The old man now pushed his silver-topped stick firmly into the soft sandy soil of the path. You could almost see the breeze and far below, unseen, the waves sounded as they surged in and hit the cliff. 'It's not far,' he shouted against the gulls. It was a wild and noisy place. 'He's nearly there now,' said Mayhew firmly over my shoulder. 'You can see the place.'

There was nothing remarkable about it. A space among the short gorse and flattened grass with a few bent flowers and the sun rushing in spasms across it. At the end of the cliff the grass was worn away and the chalky rock showed through. A long way down, the moving sea was blue and black.

Sir Benedict halted. 'Here! It was here,' he called back loudly although we were only a few yards distant. 'This was the place.' He waited and his voice dropped and once more it was as if he spoke to himself: 'The exact place.'

Mayhew and I more or less shuffled forward. There was room for the waiter to pass me now and he did so and stood by Sir Benedict staring at the ground as though, after all these years, they might find some clue. With a curious bent shuffle Sir Benedict moved towards the edge. I felt myself wanting to warn him. But he stopped and looked as far as he could over it, like someone peering to find something in a book. 'Yes,' he said still quietly but making a slightly comic diving movement with his hand. 'Over there. That's where she went.'

Now he might have been alone because he did not even glance at us. He straightened up and went further along the cliff and, shielding his forehead with his hand, stared out to where a pair of small white houses, like sugar lumps, stood on a headland across the next bay.

'That's where Mr Goodbody lived,' he called back. 'The coastguard.'

'Yes, sir. He did. His wife only passed away last winter,' responded Mayhew. He turned to me quickly, anxiously and privately. 'Her ladyship was floating in the sea down there,' he said. 'She had a long skirt and she was spread out like a fan. I was the one who called the rescue services.' He said it with a hint of pride but then added: 'Not that they were any good.'

Sir Benedict showed no signs of returning to us. He remained studying the distant faces of the cottages. Mayhew, hurriedly and quietly again, said to me: 'See that bit of clear grass there.' I already knew what he meant. It went at right angles to the cliff. 'That's where she took a run from. Well, supposed to have done. So the story came out. But it wasn't said at the inquest.'

Eventually, making a slow revolving movement around his stick, Sir Benedict turned and came back to us. 'That's all there is,' he said directly to me as though he feared I might be disappointed. 'All there is to see.'

I thought we were going to walk away then but he suddenly held up his hand and said: 'Just wait. Just a moment.' Then, to our alarm, he paced out what could only be a run along the soft grass, away from the edge. Turning and with wild looks in his eyes, a different one in each eye, he ran anciently towards the cliff rim. I was rooted, my hands to my face, but Mayhew lunged clumsily and made to catch the arm of the old man's sports coat. Sir Benedict halted, too close to the edge for my liking, and turned with a slow, grim smile. 'I am perfectly all right,' he said to Mayhew. 'But thank you for your concern.' His expression turned on me. 'I was just trying it out.'

We returned in a silent single file to the garden of the

hotel in our same order: Sir Benedict, then me, with Mayhew at the rear. The waiter looked a relieved man and I could half-see, half-sense him using his hands to usher us towards the safety beyond the small fence. Once we were inside the hotel, out of the sun and the breeze again, the old man relaxed and almost fell into an armchair. 'Let's have some tea,' he suggested.

Tea was served by a girl with the attentive Mayhew hovering. He did not look sorry when we finally announced that we must leave. The driver had brought the car to the front drive and waited with the door open. 'Had a nice lunch?' he asked me privately as we helped the old man into the rear seat. Sir Benedict said he would sit on the opposite side on the return journey, the one I had occupied previously, because he was tired and he did not want to see anything.

'I found a nice place,' chattered the driver. He closed the door on us and went around to the front. 'Had some fish and chips and spent a few quid in the amusement arcade.'

'Good,' I muttered discouragingly. 'I hope you won.'

He sniffed. 'You can't win at arcades, you're not meant to. Same as life.'

Sir Benedict grunted and settled into the corner of the car, his eyes closing. He looked very serene once his eyes were covered. 'He's gone off,' I warned the driver.

'I'll be quiet then.'

'Please do.'

Only the feathery snoring of the old man sounded on the return journey. We reached Salisbury by five thirty. Sir Benedict woke and was pleased we had got back so quickly, almost miraculously he seemed to think. The driver went off, muttering behind his window.

The old man climbed to his room to rest and I thought

that would be the last I would see of him for the day. But he amazed me, and Urchfont, by announcing that he and Lady Annabel were going to have a glass of sherry together early that evening. 'They seem to be getting on all right,' reported Urchfont after he had served them. 'Like they'd been chatting for years.'

As it was my day off I went to the cinema. That night I had dreams of floating, but not falling, over a cliff edge with the sea frothing and the gulls shouting: 'Don't! Don't!' It seemed a long way down.

Morning chased away the spectres. It was bright and warm, the sky cleared of rain and wind. I went into Salisbury to do some shopping and to post Lady Annabel's letters, deftly extracting those addressed to Her Majesty, His Holiness and the Foreign Secretary.

When I returned I heard voices on the terrace. The French windows to Lady Annabel's sitting-room had been flung wide and the light streamed strangely into the room. Urchfont gave me a sideways look as he carried a tray out. I followed him cautiously. Sir Benedict and his wife were sitting having lunch together at a table set below the wistaria.

The flagstone terrace was warm and their voices were cheerful. When her ladyship turned I saw a transformation for her face was strong and alive. He seemed jovial and as I stood looking out he slightly raised a glass of wine in my direction. He had a look in his eye which I had never seen before.

It was at that moment that I realised he intended to kill her.

24

It was difficult for me to believe what was taking place.
Every day I told myself that I was making a mistake, it
was a fantasy. It was like a play being acted out in the
house, very slowly, simple to see but still very deep and
involved. I would lie wondering in my bed above the
whole ticking drama, late at night, with only the wind
moving around and the chiming of the early hours from
the cathedral. Everything was so changed. I knew
something secret must be going on.

Time and again I told myself that I should leave before
anything serious happened but I could not abandon him
now, whatever his intentions. All I could do was to hold
on and hope that he would change his mind, forget his
plan.

If the night hours were worrying then daytime was
even more so. Everywhere in what had once been a
dimmed house was now light; curtains which had not
been opened for years were tugged apart to great fallings
of dust, windows were cleaned and forced open. 'Even
the sun seems to blink when it comes in,' grumbled
Urchfont. There were more things for him to do, there
were even visitors, and he shuffled about the house
muttering: 'Shit, shit, shit.'

For so long I had been trying to let some light into the
house, particularly in Lady Annabel's sitting-room, but

she had resisted it with her usual dismissive temper. It was only because she depended on me to haul her out of the bath that she was even civil. And now while she was apparently content, for her own reasons, to co-operate in a new feeling with Sir Benedict, she became more frosty with me. 'I heard you playing the piano last night,' she remarked nastily one day. 'Not very well, either. Perhaps you will desist when I am resting.'

As for Sir Benedict, a sort of wicked serenity came over him. He roamed around the house and garden much more than he had done in the past and with a tiny, secret smile. We went on two or three tandem rides and when we stopped for a rest or some refreshment he several times announced that he felt their marriage was reaching a new milestone. I waited for him to perhaps explain what this might be but he said nothing more, only smiled.

In the evenings we still played cards but, after his wife's complaint, Sir Benedict suggested that it might be as well if I did not play the piano. One night, as I took him his drink, I pecked his reddened cheek and said good-night. 'Things are changing, Chloe,' he said with a decided sadness. 'They have already started to change.'

'In what way?' I asked.

He appeared to be searching for an answer but in the end he said: 'Whatever happens, Lady Annabel *has to be looked after.*'

Cautiously, I went into Lady Annabel, carrying her lunch tray. 'We are going to entertain,' she announced. 'My nephew and his wife have returned from the Orange Free State. You are familiar with the Orange Free State, I take it?'

'Not familiar,' I said. 'I've heard of it.'

'Yes, yes, of course.' She was put out.

'In South Africa.'

She turned her lined and sullen eyes away and when she looked back they had a glint. 'They are rather important, my nephew and his wife.' Her eyes went around the room suspiciously. 'My only surviving relatives. Apart from Sir Benedict of course.'

Two afternoons later I was in my room below the eaves. It was always warm up there, even with the window open. There were birds singing furiously among the branches. I went to the window and looked out through the leaves to the flat green surrounding the cathedral. People were sitting, legs stretched before them, on the grass. A young uncaring couple lay locked in each other at the very middle of the space, the west window peering over them. In these solitary situations I often thought of Donny, how I would love to find him.

As I stood framed in the window, a long car came along the road, tentatively as if the driver were a stranger. It stopped directly outside and the driver got out and opened both rear doors, first on the side nearest the gate and then, with an anxious scamper, the other one. A thick man with a dark face and wearing a heavy suit got out of the first door and was joined, as he stared up at the house, by a flowery sort of woman clutching her hat as though in a gale. I knew who they were.

As they opened the front gate I heard the man giving instructions to the driver. The man's voice was accented, harsh and impolite. The woman let out a squeak as if she had seen an apparition and pointed up towards my window. I shifted out of sight.

Hurriedly I rearranged my hair and got into a clean dress. The man had rung the bell with the loudness that only came with a fierce pull. I went out onto the landing and heard Urchfont faintly mumbling: 'Shit . . . shit . . .' as he advanced from the back of the house.

He opened the door and in no time they were inside. 'They just about pushed me out of the way,' Urchfont complained as we were preparing a tray of tea together.

I carried it into Lady Annabel's sitting-room just as the man was saying: 'We wanted to see everything as it is.' He had big lips and he barely parted them to speak. He was coarse looking, bull necked and puffy eyed. She looked a bit trifling beside him although I suspected otherwise. She could snap orders. I could see her secretly feeling the edge of the curtain.

They only stayed an hour that day, but they managed a swift survey, touring the house with a vaguely arm-waving Sir Benedict, who could only just remember who they were. They went from room to room, Sir Benedict conducting them in a puzzled sort of way as the husband squinted into cornices and inspected ceilings while his wife ran her skinny little fingers down the sides of vases and cabinets. Eventually they went into the garden. The old man tottered after them and Lady Annabel watched carefully from her window. They did not need a guide, in fact they seemed to have forgotten Sir Benedict and left him to trundle behind them, belatedly trying to point out things they had already examined.

'That ought to come down,' I heard Pieter Branche say as he indicated a crooked apple tree that Sir Benedict sometimes boasted was the oldest in the close and still gave fruit. Mrs Branche hung over the ornamental pond like a heron, screwing her eyes up to pinpoint the fish. I was standing by the French windows observing them and I thought they had either not seen me or were not at all interested in my presence but, without even looking, Mrs

Branche crooked her little finger and called me over. I went as reluctantly as I could. 'Can I help you?' I asked.

'I think you may possibly be able to,' she said, still without looking at me but keeping her narrow face pointed to the dim water. 'How many fish are in this . . . this . . . area?'

'The pond,' I said. 'I can't say that I've ever counted them.'

'You can't see them to count.'

'No. The gardener only comes in once a week and he doesn't have a lot of time for the pond. I don't think Sir Benedict sees the point in counting them anyway. We always know when there's one less because it floats to the top.'

Her head came up sharply; her expression said she was not going to tolerate insolence. She said: 'You really *ought* to know how many there are.' She took out a miniature notebook with a tiny gold pencil slotted into the spine and made a note.

Their limousine arrived precisely on the hour although as it did the Branche couple simultaneously checked their watches to make sure this was so. They departed, inspecting the state of the front stone stairs and the old urn in the garden as they went, and both Sir Benedict and Lady Annabel waved them goodbye from the door.

'Mr and Mrs Branche took a great interest in the house,' I suggested to Sir Benedict that night. He said he did not want to play cards because he had a lot to think about. I made the remark as I took him his drink.

'And the garden,' he added.

'And the pond,' I said.

He aimed his one good eye at me. 'They are Lady Annabel's sole surviving relatives,' he said. 'At least they seem to believe they are. I don't have any of course.' All

226

at once he did a strange thing, unusual for him: he laughed out loud. It was as if machinery, unused for years, had been turned on. His old body shook, his eyes (both of them) watered, and his teeth rattled in his head. 'They ...' he blurted, '... are part of Annabel's ... Annabel's family tree. They ... oh, my goodness ... they are the Branches!'

He sat down heavily, his tears blurring his eyes and wetting his cheeks. He held his ribs and said: 'Oh, my goodness,' again.

I had never known him even attempt to make an outright joke and this one poleaxed him. He sat gasping while I hovered anxiously, asking him if he were all right. Eventually he was. His laughter had brought him close to real tears, sad tears, but now he calmed. He motioned me to sit on the chair opposite. I perched on the edge. His face was composed now. 'They may well feel, that being the case, that they stand to benefit should I predecease her ladyship.' His voice had dropped but his eye still gleamed. 'They hope ...' He almost giggled again. '... to make a *killing*.' He took a long drink of his cocoa and Demerara. 'But I fear they may have miscalculated.'

I looked at him very straight. His eye came up briefly and returned the look but then he turned away and I left him.

Towards the end of October, with Sir Benedict's birthday approaching, it was Lady Annabel who announced that they were going to have a special dinner for him. 'It will be in Dorset,' she told me succinctly. 'At the Cliff Edge Hotel.'

I almost dropped the tray and she saw it at once. She was very sharp. 'You know the hotel, Chloe?' she asked. I righted the things on the tray. 'Or you know of it?'

'Yes, I know what happened there.'

She made a diving motion with her hand and said: 'Lucy.'

'And that is where you're going to have it, the dinner?' I said.

'Yes. Sir Benedict wanted it and I think it is a splendid idea. We used to have such *good* times there before.' The wrinkles around her eyes rearranged themselves and the eyes themselves became brighter. 'Before Lucy spoiled it all.'

I left the room to tell Urchfont but before I could get to the kitchen I heard Sir Benedict rumbling down the stairs. He revolved on the landing. 'Chloe,' he called softly. He crooked his finger and I put the tray on the third step and went up. There was something different about him. He was wearing a country suit and somehow it seemed to stiffen him; he looked taller, his head higher, his creases straightened out. 'I am to have a birthday dinner,' he whispered.

'I know,' I whispered back, wondering why. 'At the Cliff Edge.'

'Splendid idea,' he enthused. He gave a chortle like a boy planning a prank. 'And, best of all . . . best of all . . . I've persuaded Annabel that it was *her* idea.'

'She told me.' I felt I was entering something murky. 'Who will you invite?' I asked.

It seemed he had never thought of that: 'Oh, I don't know. Various, you know. She wants her relatives, those Africans.'

'Mr and Mrs Branche,' I said. 'From the Orange Free State.'

'Yes, that's them. And I want you to be present, Chloe.'

'Thank you, Sir Benedict.' He was making towards the

lavatory on the landing so I went back down the stairs and picked up the tray. Urchfont was in the kitchen contemplating polishing the cutlery. 'It never seems worth it,' he grumbled. 'Some of this gear hasn't been used for forty years. Since they used to entertain.' He looked at me. 'Lady Lucy's time.'

'They're going to have a dinner,' I said. 'For the old man's birthday.'

Urchfont stared at the cutlery in a new way. His concerned face slowly rose. 'Here?' he asked.

'No. At the hotel, you know. . . . *The* hotel – where it happened. The Cliff Edge.'

He stood unbelieving. 'Christ. That place.'

'Odd,' I agreed. 'But they both want it.'

'His birthday, it's October 31st,' he said sombrely. 'Hallowe'en.'

I had put the tray on the kitchen table. I went back out just as Sir Benedict was reaching the bottom of the stairs. The flush was sounding from the lavatory. He winked enormously with his good eye. 'Ah yes, Chloe,' he said. 'A birthday dinner.' He walked a few paces away from me, then turned and winked again. 'A fight to the death.'

25

Detective Sergeant Ron Brown sniffed amiably. 'That was a funny thing for him to say.' He habitually rubbed his nose with his thumb. 'A fight to the death.' We were sitting in the prison interview room. He had brought a packet of wine gums and we were sharing them. From some distance away a woman's screams echoed. 'Did you ever ask him what he meant?'

From my side of the table I studied him, a steady-looking man with a decent, tired face and sparse hair. His wife had not returned and had sent her cousin around for her tennis racquet. 'She's not played for years,' he complained without bitterness. 'But this bloke she's with does.'

It did not seem to matter now. They were all dead. 'He just said that,' I confirmed. 'Just: "A fight to the death." But he was probably joking.'

'Probably,' said Ron Brown. 'Odd sort of joke though.'

'He was an odd man. They were odd people.'

'They're not like us, are they,' he agreed. 'They wouldn't have you as a friend.'

I said: 'I was his friend. And he was mine.'

'Right. But it's still different. I bet it was. You still called him "Sir Benedict". It always is with high-class people. It's not like you and me being friends.'

'Are we?' I said cautiously.

'Why not? We're both in the same boat.'

'What boat is that?'

He appeared embarrassed. 'A bit hopeless.'

'Why do you say that?' I asked. 'You're all right, you can't be hopeless. You're a policeman.'

He smiled sheepishly. He was not a good-looking man, a bit round faced, but when he smiled there was no malice, no threat; it looked real. 'I think it was a funny thing to say, that's all,' he said. 'A fight to the death.'

I tried not to look at him. There was not much else to look at in the interview room so I turned towards the bars of the window. 'It's still sunny,' I said.

'There's been a fair bit of good weather. It's a pity you've been in here. I went fishing at the weekend, didn't catch anything.' He became thoughtful. 'It's what they call a serious charge, but you might have even got bail. I've known funnier things. But then you haven't got anywhere permanent, have you. No fixed abode.'

'Not really. That couple from South Africa, the Branche people. There's no way they'd have me near the house. They've been loitering like vultures hoping to get their hands on things.'

'I know,' he said, again to my surprise. 'I don't like them. Where are they from? Orange Free State. Sounds like Nuclear Free Zone.'

'You've met them?'

'I've had to go around there. Quite a few times. They're certainly not my sort, nor yours, I expect. They keep asking when the trial is.' He remembered something and began searching the inside pocket of his sports jacket. 'By the way . . . if I can find it . . . there's a chap has asked to visit you when you go to court next. He lives nearby and he's getting on. I suppose your solicitor will tell you but it's all right our end anyway. That's if you want to see him.' At last he found the piece of paper and unfolded it while I watched. 'A Mr Pyecraft . . . old boy . . . was in antiques.'

I always looked forward to my court appearances, if only for the pleasure of looking out through the smoked window of the prison van. This time, the day after Detective Ron Brown had come to see me, the weather turned and there were not many people about, but as always I tried to recognise someone or pretend I did. In prison you see the same faces all the time.

We were almost at the court when I saw him standing on the pavement. 'Mr Pyecraft!' I called even though I knew he couldn't hear me. The escorting woman, sitting at her little desk in the front compartment of the van, never took much notice of what I was doing. Sometimes she took out some knitting and got on with that. 'Mr Pyecraft!' I shouted again. The woman tutted as if I had disturbed her concentration. 'It's soundproof,' she said tapping the side near her head. Mr Pyecraft always had been old to me and now he did not seem any more so, with grey hair (smartly parted), a tweedy brown suit and a bow-tie. I could see his eyes through his glasses, he was that close. But before I could call again we had moved on through the traffic.

It was my last appearance on remand at Salisbury. The prosecution had said that they would be ready to proceed in two weeks and everyone had looked pleased and looked towards me as if I should have been pleased too.

Mr Pyecraft was shown into the small room afterwards. We embraced. 'Oh, Chloe, what a terrible thing this is,' he said glancing furtively around the room as if looking for loopholes. There was a thin white tidemark around the edges of his mouth. 'I didn't know,' he said helplessly. 'I live close by but I hardly see a newspaper except for the football pools page, and the spire of the cathedral interferes with my television reception, so I just give up on that.'

'What do you do?' I asked him. I held his hand as if he were the one who needed comforting.

'Oh, me, I just sit and go through old auction catalogues. Just seeing the different lots makes me remember my life.' He looked a touch embarrassed. 'Such as it has been.'

There were two chairs in the room and a table pushed into a corner. 'Look at that,' Mr Pyecraft said. 'Edwardian. Fancy it being in here.'

A woman in an overall came in with two mugs of tea. 'I thought you might like a drop,' she said kindly. 'Do you take sugar?'

We both did. She fumbled in her flowered pocket and produced four lumps. 'They don't like you taking them outside,' she said. 'It's to do with the European Community.'

When she had gone we sat opposite each other on the chairs like two people left at the end of a party game. 'Probably evidence in some case and somehow was left behind,' I said indicating the table. We had left it against the wall and we held our cups in our hands.

'This is a bad business,' he said solemnly. 'What do you think will happen?'

'I *could* get life.'

His face dropped even further. 'That's a long time, Chloe.'

I tried to laugh but it came out like a cackle. 'At least I'll have a permanent address.'

'But you *will* plead not guilty.'

'I'm not. Not of murder.'

He was not going to pursue it. Instead he put his cup on the floor and held my free hand in both of his. 'What a life you've had,' he said. 'When you were alone above the shop with your little boy ...' His dried saliva line wriggled uncertainly.

'Donny,' I said. 'You were very good to us.'

'I would have liked to marry you,' he said flatly and to my astonishment. 'After your divorce. But there was my wife to consider. She lived in Bournemouth and she had never done me any harm.' He regarded me with an elderly smile. 'I realise how difficult it would have been,' he said, 'but I would have looked after you. I always thought you needed someone to do that.'

'So did I,' I said although I had never thought it might be him. 'You're a very kind man.'

'Your son went to live with your mother eventually, didn't he?'

'Yes. When he was ten. After that trouble at the school.'

'The fire. Yes, I recall.'

'My mother handled him very well. Better than I ever did,' I confessed. 'He lived there until he was sixteen. In Aldershot. He went to be a boy soldier.' I did not know why I was telling him. 'But at eighteen he quit and just vanished.'

Mr Pyecraft's glasses slithered from his nose. He caught them just in time. 'Good heavens. Vanished? Don't you ...'

'... know where he is?' I finished lamely. 'No, I don't actually. He used to send me pebbles.'

'Oh, yes,' he remembered. He reached into his pocket and pulled out two envelopes. 'I knew there were pebbles in them. The new owners of the shop forwarded them to me.'

I took them and thanked him.

'But there's no address?' he asked.

'Nothing. Just the pebbles.'

'So you know he's still . . . safe.'

A silence dropped between us and I thought at that point he would leave. But instead he said: 'Your husband, your former husband I should say . . . now, what was his name?'

'His proper name was Alf,' I said. 'But he called himself Zane. Tomkins.'

'Yes, now I remember, your name was Tomkins when you came back to live over the shop.' I could see he had made up his mind to tell me something. 'He came to see me,' he said hesitantly. 'Not very long ago.'

My hands went to my mouth. 'Zane?' The name threaded through my fingers. 'Came to the shop?' Almost without a pause I said: 'What did he take?'

'A bracelet. He said he was buying it for you. He said you were reunited.'

'Oh, God. When? When was it?'

'About two years ago. He came in a big shiny car and he looked very respectable, prosperous, well dressed and charming.'

'And he paid with a cheque,' I guessed.

Mr Pyecraft nodded.

'Which bounced.'

He gave a second nod. I could see that he wished he had not mentioned it.

'How much?' I asked.

'It wasn't a great deal. Not a fortune.'

'How much?'

'Fifteen hundred pounds. He looked at another

bracelet that was four thousand and then decided to take the one for fifteen hundred.'

'That's his sort of trick.'

Mr Pyecraft nodded. 'Choosing the lesser price made me think it would be all right. He said . . . he said the stone matched your eyes.' He regarded me closely. 'I can see now that it didn't. It was a blue stone and you've got brown eyes. But I couldn't quite remember. It was some time since I had seen your eyes.'

'How could he do it?' I asked myself, although I knew the answer too well. Easily. Something made me say: 'Was he by himself?'

'At first I thought so,' Mr Pyecraft said unhappily. 'But when I saw him to the door with the bracelet wrapped up I saw there was someone else driving the car. A young man with fair hair.'

My hand went to my throat. 'Donny.'

'I thought it might be.'

Donny had been almost eleven when he got into bad company and attempted to burn down his school. I was so shocked; I could never fully believe it. There were others, older than Donny and much more experienced, who were the main arsonists. But it was he who had struck the match and it was he who was very nearly burned in the fire. The others ran away.

He was only saved because the school caretaker was coming back from an evening's drinking and saw an orange glow from the basement as he staggered across the playground. After deciding that this was no figment of his boozed imagination, he managed to find the nine-hole on the telephone three times in succession and called the fire brigade. Then he collapsed with whisky and excitement and was the first person taken away in the ambulance.

Donny was the second. He had stayed to make sure that the blaze was well started and he was trapped. The firemen got him out. He looked like a little African when they carried him to the ambulance, his blond hair frizzled and black (and still smoking), his eyes staring red from his sooty face.

Donny was not seriously injured, but there was a lot of trouble for both of us. He had to appear in the juvenile court with the others and after that I decided to take up my mother's offer to keep him in Aldershot where he might grow up to be a soldier like his grandfather. Amazingly, he changed and became good the moment he went to live with her. Every time I visited them he seemed to have become taller and quieter. He looked after her almost as much as she looked after him. 'He's never a moment's trouble,' Rosa said with a certain loftiness a few months after he had gone there. 'He likes to watch the squaddies drilling and I think he will be doing it with them before too long. He'll be a boy soldier.'

'He could be in a war in no time,' I said caustically although it was lost on her.

'They still have them,' she said looking on the bright side. 'There'll always be soldiers.'

When Donny came home from school he seemed pleased to see me but he kissed Rosa first. She fussed about getting his tea and saying she had washed his football kit. He was going to the army cadets that evening and he had pressed his own uniform under her guidance and cleaned his boots to brightness.

He put his uniform on for me and Rosa straightened the trouser creases. I rearranged his cap but she altered it again. He paraded up and down the room like a small soldier. Then he had his tea and he and Rosa talked about things and people I knew nothing of. I attempted to keep up with them but eventually I was reduced to nothing more than a vague smile. I was only a spectator; I felt like an occasionally visiting aunt.

When he went out to his cadets Rosa told him to be home by nine thirty. He promised he would be. By that time I would be gone.

I went back to Southampton with a heavy heart because I knew that again I had failed. The feeling was inside me like an empty space. With my son gone I felt both free and guilty. Since we had left our cottage at Cutcross in the forest I had tried to make him feel loved and wanted and to make up for the absence of his father but even in those childhood days I knew that there was much of his father in him. He could tell untruths with open-eyed ease and I once caught him counting out dinner money stolen from school. He lied that he had been given charge of it because he was the best in the class at arithmetic.

I missed him as I missed his father, for all the trouble they made, and I led a half-life above the antique shop as I had done in the days before I was married. By then, of course, I had learned a good deal from experience with antiques. I could spot a repair at shop's length and I could almost smell anything odd about a piece of furniture (if not about men) as well as keep my cool over a real find until it was firmly and finally in our hands. Mr Pyecraft displayed none of the feelings he later professed to have for me although I had noticed him on occasions looking me over in a careful way, rather as he would assess a commode. 'You're a fine-looking young woman, Chloe,' he said one day as he passed out of the premises but then he was gone on his busy way and never mentioned it again.

26

Zane came back into my life as I was considering a second marriage, this time to Claude Pinchot, another villain. Sometimes I used to think that they passed my name around between them.

I did not know half of what Claude was into but anyway I was never in love with him. He was long and languid (as was his moustache), more Spanish than French my mother used to say, and he was to all appearances very rich. He had charm and decent looks, although his hair was on the thin side, and he took me to pleasant places including his boat.

'I want to violate you, Chloe,' he said while we were lying off Havant. He did not always choose his English well but I knew what he meant. We had been to a grand sailing dinner and ball the previous evening and he said we would soon be going to Paris, Monte Carlo and Marseilles. Gently I pointed out that 'violate' was not the appropriate word but he did it anyway. He gallantly spread a large towel beneath us and we lay naked keeping our love-making in time with the moving of the sunny wooden deck.

It was far from the first time (although it was the first time on water). I had gone to bed with him not long after seeing him at an antiques auction where he bought some ancient coins which Mr Pyecraft and I had already looked over. He said he dealt in them. Now, on his boat, a creamy craft called *Alouette* – lark – we lay bare to the Channel sky and he came to me again, so dark eyed, so brown shouldered, so manfully that I gasped and rolled against the warm boards. I took in a mouthful of salt air and began to cough while we were coupled which he seemed to find enjoyably novel. While we lay there rolling easily with the incoming tide he asked me to marry him.

I can never understand men who ask women to marry them when they already have a wife. There was no reason for him to do so. He never mentioned Nicolette in Marseilles, Pansy in Paris or the woman on a pig farm somewhere in Kent.

Claude was a speculator, an entrepreneur as he preferred to call it, with property and businesses (and wives) in many European cities and contacts in America. His main interest in Britain was getting people to invest in buried treasure.

He showed me a map of Brittany, spreading it out romantically on the bedspread in the Marine Hotel at Southsea. He looked just like a pirate that morning, bronzed and naked, his moustache trembling. 'The treasure place is here.' He pointed with a brown finger. 'And this is the little chart that I bought five years ago.'

He reached to the side of the bed where he had laid the satchel he always carried with him. It was full of papers, important-looking, prospectus-type papers with seals and signatures which he would thrust into people's hands or pockets at the first flicker of interest. Most of the documents were related to faraway buildings and houses which he said he was selling. The treasure syndicate was something which he kept very private. 'Only the people I can trust,' he whispered although we were alone. 'There is not room for too many.'

I can picture the scene now, me in my thirties and little else, sitting up in the big bed, a cup of tea and a piece of toast in my hands and an eagerness in my expression. He brought out the small chart. He kissed me and courteously flicked a crumb from my bosom as if to reassure me that he had not forgotten why we were there. 'It is only a copy,' he confided. 'The real chart is in the vaults of my bank in Zurich.' His moustache waggled and he came out with a well-practised sentence. 'Where *any* person who is interested in the great treasure can inspect it.'

Outside the hotel window there was wind and splattering rain but his voice was warm and lulling. The chart was incomprehensible to me but he pointed to directional lines and instructions in French and figures scrawled sideways. It was a treasure, he explained, concealed during the French Revolution by refugee aristocrats who fled from Paris and arrived in Brittany with only time to bury it before they were caught and led back to the guillotine.

It was wealth beyond dreams but very difficult to dig out. The syndicate, which stretched to half a dozen countries and now had a growing number of British believers, had poured good money after bad in a series of attempts to locate and claim the treasure which was on the coast near Dinard. Digging had gone on for several years but the shaft kept flooding and each time everything had to be started again. There were many disappointments and days of despair for Claude (not to mention the syndicate) but he persevered, showed the map and documents to more gullible fortune hunters, and the money never stopped. Investors went to their beds hoping, sometimes even believing, that the next day the treasure would be found.

'Where did you get the chart?' I asked, reverently touching the edge of the copy.

Claude seemed shocked. 'Please, never ask me that, Chloe,' he said his eyes growing big with alarm. 'For I can *never* tell you. It is more than life is worth. All that you can know is that I have it.'

I lay back in the bed and he turned over on top of me and let the treasure map slide to the floor. He was quite a greedy lover. When we had finished he picked up the chart from the carpet and lay staring at it. 'Haven't you been able to find anything?' I asked. 'Ever?'

He rolled against me in the bed and said: 'Yes, of course. We have found some old weapons, pistols and swords. The investors can see them before their eyes.'

'But no treasure?'

He paused as if undecided whether to tell me. '*Oui*,' he said eventually with a sort of dreaminess. 'The syndicate members are always able to see what we have found.' He leaned across me to his satchel once more and took out a large leather purse. 'These,' he said spilling the contents into his hand. 'French coins from the time of the Age of Terror. Touch them, Chloe, touch them.'

He showed them to me. I recognised them at once as the coins he had bought at the auction on the day I first met him. Another rogue.

Even then I did not realise just how much of a criminal he was, and so widespread. It was while we were staying at the Marine Hotel, Southsea, that I could see things were starting to go wrong. There were urgent telephone calls and he kept sending me out of the room or into the bathroom while he answered them, although, listening at the keyhole, I heard that most of the conversations were in French. I spent a long time sitting on the toilet seat.

The bathroom door, however, was no shield from his raised and worried voice. Sitting on the wooden cover I could look directly and, on the final occasion nakedly, into a mirror and wonder once more what I was doing in a situation. Eventually I heard him begin to sob and I thought it was time I tried to help. I left the lid and tentatively returned to the room.

'All is gone wrong,' he said. He was sitting on the bed in his robe, his head clutched in his hands, tears running through his fingers. To comfort him I sat beside him and he immediately slid onto the carpet and knelt in front of me, weeping into my naked lap like a penitent. In no time we were on the bed and making love for the last, swift time, sobbing as we did so.

Afterwards we dried our tears and ourselves and I lay on the quilt while he made a number of desperate telephone calls, none of which seemed to be welcomed. He demanded that he speak to Monsieur or Signor or Señor but they did not want to speak to him.

'Traitor, bastard,' he moaned after the final call. He said the words in French but they were more or less the same. He looked pleadingly at me. 'I must leave, Chloe,' he sobbed. 'Now, I must go.'

'There's no treasure, is there,' I said in a dull way.

'Maybe, maybe. If they look long. Now all they find is water.'

'There never was any,' I said.

He broke down, sobbing again, then picked up his satchel. '*Cherie*, I must go. I will pay the bill as I leave.'

I was rather hoping he would. We kissed with a counterfeit passion, his trembling hand on my breast. My only consolation was that I did not actually marry the villain. When, months later, they caught up with him in some foreign corner and it was all in the papers I realised the treasure trove was only one of many rackets. But on that day all I wanted to do was to get out, get clear of the Marine Hotel, Southsea and Claude Pinchot.

I hurried out into the chilly sunshine and was called politely but firmly back by the receptionist coming to the door. Would I please settle the bill. Wearily I did so. The telephone calls alone cost more than a hundred pounds.

A lurking private detective saw me dragging my way to the car and followed me to my little home above the antique shop. I was in a trance as I opened the door. It was Sunday and there were no people about. Going upstairs I put the kettle on and watched it as if to make sure it boiled. I did not trust anything. I was trying to feel safe. Just as I was sitting down with a cup of tea there was a harsh knock at the door downstairs. I took the cup with me.

Outside were four bad-tempered men demanding to know where Claude had gone. I told them I did not know, only that he had gone. They had obviously sustained serious losses and I did not care for their demeanour. Two were quite small but the other two were large. I felt the cup trembling and spilling as I confronted them. One had his foot in the door. 'Where is he gone?' he demanded. 'You must know where the bastard is.'

'I don't know where the bastard is,' I said.

'We'll find out,' promised one of the smaller men with a leer. He looked me up and down.

A voice came from behind them. I could not see who it was because of their closeness. 'Space,' it ordered like a Hollywood script. 'Give that lady space, you born berks.'

Before my amazed eyes one of the small men abruptly took off into the air; his feet left the ground and he went in a loop backwards onto the pavement. One of the big men turned and was struck on the forehead by a lump of wood. He fell back against the wall but then managed to stagger away. The others hurried after him, the little chap picking himself up from the gutter and trotting off apologising.

And there was my saviour. Standing tall, broad, fair and handsome, a cheeky grin spreading over his tanned face. Zane Tomkins. My Zane. My bloody Zane.

27

Detective Sergeant Ron Brown came to see me in prison the day after my committal for trial at Winchester Crown Court. He said he just happened to be passing, going somewhere on another matter, and it was no trouble to come in. 'How did your visitor turn out?' he asked. 'The old boy who came to see you at the court.'

'He wanted to marry me,' I said.

Not a lot surprised him but his forehead rose. 'When?' he said.

'Years ago. When I worked for him and lived above his antique shop in Southampton. His name's Mr Pyecraft.'

'I know the shop. But he didn't mention it at the time?'

'No, he didn't. He said he had his wife to consider.'

'I suppose there's that to it.' He rubbed his face as if he felt tired. 'People have some funny reasons for getting married, or not.'

'Does your wife want to marry this chap she's gone off with?'

'A right dodgy one he is. I've had to look at his bits and bobs naturally, the records, and he's very definitely dodgy. Young girls and getting younger. Last time he was about two days on the right side of being nicked for under-age, never mind the other stuff. But the girl wouldn't help.'

'Your wife knows this?'

'She does now because I told her. And now she says that's why he needs her. She's forty and she reckons she's going to save him from fifteen-year-olds. Save them from him, really.' He was sitting at the interview-room table with me; we were oddly like a domestic couple having breakfast except that the table was empty. 'You could plead guilty,' he suggested quietly. He studied his heavy hands. He saw that I was looking at them too. 'Digging, that is,' he grumbled and showed me the raw bits on each hand.

'Have you got an allotment?'

'No. I wouldn't mind one but I don't get enough time. It's enough with my bit.' He held up his hands. 'We've been digging somebody's garden. Looking for a body. Not that we found one. Dug it right over for him. He could go out now and plant his greens. We did a lovely job.' He regarded me over the hands. 'Your chap ought to try for manslaughter,' he said.

'I'll tell him.'

'Don't you care?'

I did care but I said: 'Not all that much. At least being jammed in here stops my life getting screwed up again.'

'Your Alf Tomkins is in trouble.'

'Zane? What's new?'

'In Spain. He got shopped by someone down there.'

'He was born for double-crossing. Doing it and having it done to him. How do you know?'

Detective Ron Brown shrugged. 'I found out.'

'Can you find *anybody*?'

His face creased. 'Not *anybody*. If we could we'd have a ruddy field day. But some people we *can* find.'

'Could you find my Donny? My son?'

'I could have a look,' he said.

28

Sir Benedict's birthday, October 31st, was approaching and I remember how glowing autumn was in the cathedral close. There were days when the sky was thick as lead and yet somehow, often towards early evening, the sun would slide under the clouds and light the spire and the red and yellow trees and the warm houses. Windy days would scatter leaves, some of them big as cabbage leaves, and the boys from the school would shout as they ran about at rugby on the small playing field. Lying on my bed during my couple of hours off in the afternoon I tried to imagine one of those boys was Donny, miraculously taken back in years, giving me a second chance. He would be home at teatime and watch the television and everything would be different and all right.

I always went downstairs at four and made tea. Urchfont would be sitting in his chair glowering at the cutlery. When the doorbell infrequently rang or one of our employers summoned him from his corner of the kitchen it was like a personal affront and he would shuffle away to answer, cursing under his breath.

'Something's up,' he muttered one afternoon. 'I don't like the look of it at all.'

'Why don't you?'

'The old man.' He lifted his eyes ominously. 'He's practising unarmed combat.'

'Don't be so silly.'

He put down his cloth. He always had a cloth although he rarely appeared to do anything with it. 'He's got a book of instructions. Drawings about it and he practises. I've seen him in his bedroom. He crouches and growls and stuff like that.'

'Well, I haven't seen it,' I said.

'I tell you it's true. He scared the daylights out of the cleaning girl. He bared his teeth and held his arms out stiff.' He demonstrated. 'She's not coming back.'

I said nothing but I had noticed a change. With the passing of summer, Sir Benedict had become a little removed and silent as though he had a lot on his mind. Sometimes he did not want to play cards in the evenings. I used to go to the pictures in Salisbury once or twice a week. He still smiled at me and patted my arm fondly but I sensed, no, I *knew*, there was something going on inside him. He kept closing and opening his fists.

'Another thing,' said Urchfont. 'He's crossing days off on his calendar. The one in his bathroom. In red. He's got hold of one of her lipsticks and he's using that to cross them off.'

'To his birthday?'

'When they go to the Cliff Edge Hotel.' Urchfont's eyes drooped ominously.

'He can count the days to his birthday if he wants to,' I said defensively. 'He'll be eighty-five after all. That's some sort of achievement.'

Urchfont wiped his mouth with his cloth. 'He's never done it before,' he objected. 'He didn't on his eighty-fourth.'

I told him he was talking nonsense and went from the

kitchen. It was time for her ladyship's afternoon tea and I took the tray in to her. She was sitting in her customary chair in her stiff way, looking down at her hands. I placed the tray on the side-table and turned towards her. With a wicked smile Lady Annabel held up her hands. 'Look,' she said. 'Knuckledusters.'

It seems unreal now, I know, but if two batty people are soaked in old hatred, him convinced that she had pushed his wife over a cliff forty years before, what can you do? He was bent on revenge. She was determined she would live longer, if only long enough to claim all there was to claim, to be able to sit smugly in the house knowing he was gone. Mr and Mrs Branche from the Orange Free State came to visit her frequently and had, of course, been invited to the fateful birthday party at the Cliff Edge Hotel.

'What are we going to do?' I said to Urchfont.

He looked unreasonably surprised. 'Do?'

'Well, for God's sake, if the pair of them are squaring up to kill each other . . .'

'I was going anyway,' he mumbled. 'I can't stand much more of this.'

'Never mind about *you*,' I insisted. 'What about *them*?'

'They won't do it. They haven't got the bloody puff. They're just pretending. Playing games.'

But they were not playing games. I was certain of that. Until long into the early hours I worried. I thought how they had come together quite socially and suddenly after scarcely exchanging a civil word for years, how surprised I was that morning when I had seen them on the terrace, leaning and talking, each with an upheld glass. He was like an old circling lion going carefully for his last kill, while she watched him with her confident, crafty smile.

They each knew the score, they understood the game, playing each move, every day pushing it a fraction more. It probably gave them something to live for. Unhappily I thought of his unarmed combat; I thought of her knuckledusters; I thought of the Cliff Edge Hotel and Hallowe'en, and I had to hide my head below my blankets.

I told Urchfont we ought to go to the police.

'We? Who's we?' he answered. 'I told you, I'm leaving before anything happens. I'm going at the end of the month.'

'Hallowe'en is the thirty-first.'

'I've got a couple of days owing.'

There was nothing for it but to hope it would not happen, to pray that he was right and that the old couple were just going through a strange ritual, the rules of which only they acknowledged and which, in the end, was only a grim elderly pretence, each trying to frighten the other.

During the final week of October, Sir Benedict announced that he would like to take a tandem ride. He sometimes called it 'the machine' and he said: 'Let's get the machine operating.' We had not been on the tandem since the summer but he insisted. 'One never knows how long one can do this sort of thing.'

We pedalled off under heavy morning clouds. It was a long way to the coast but we took the route which we had come to know, the road with the easiest hills, and saw the sky clearing as it hurried towards us. We bought two cups of Oxo at a little café that was still open, but the woman said she was shutting up for the season that very afternoon.

We leaned the tandem against the wall of her stall.

'Last cups this year,' she said as if it were a cheerful threat. 'I'm going home to my fire.'

I thought Sir Benedict was going to say something because the edges of his mouth creased with the beginnings of a smile but he changed his mind. He took me by the elbow and we sat down in a shelter facing the sea but shielded from the slight wind by the refreshment stall. Now I *had* to say something.

'I don't think your birthday party is a good idea.'

He turned slowly to face me, all innocent and surprised. 'Why ever not, Chloe?'

'Not at the Cliff Edge,' I said thinking even then that I was being melodramatic. Surely nothing would happen. 'It's ... such a long way.'

'No, no,' he said soothingly. 'Not at all, Chloe.' He turned and faced out to sea again. The blue sky had swiftly flown over and the horizon had become cold. He said: 'It will probably be the last birthday I shall have.'

I was looking the same way and the scene dissolved in my tears. I laid my hand on his arm. He did not turn to look at me for some time. We simply sat together staring out to sea and seeing nothing. Then he did turn and with his old grin and his eye lit he said: 'But perhaps not.'

'We're not going to be able to cycle back,' I told him. 'We've come too far.'

'I'm sure you're right, Chloe.' He looked around, through the glass of the shelter where we sat, as if trying to see the distance involved. 'But I wanted to see the coast.'

There was a telephone box beside the stall. 'I'll get a taxi,' I said.

'What about the machine?' He regarded it with a distraught expression. 'We can't leave it.'

'Perhaps we can get it in the taxi,' I said measuring it with my eye.

He shook his head. 'It would project. It wouldn't be fair to it.'

The woman in the stall said: 'Leave it in here if you like. It's locked up.' She laughed. 'Mind, you'll have to do without it till next Easter. I open at Easter.'

To my surprise, Sir Benedict murmured: 'A shelter for it. Through the winter. Splendid.' He began to wheel it towards the stall. I took it from him and the woman opened a door at the back and we manoeuvred it in behind the counter. 'That's all right there,' said the woman. 'I'm shutting it up as soon as you've gone.'

Once the tandem was in position Sir Benedict patted it sadly and I did too, as though it were a horse. 'It'll be safe here,' he said. 'I wouldn't want it falling into the wrong hands.'

The woman gave me an odd look but I just smiled. 'I've got a taxi number,' she mentioned and handed me a card. 'He wouldn't have been able to take the tandem. It's only a smallish car.'

She had been clearing up and now she continued putting crockery away into cupboards which she carefully locked. We walked out to the shelter again to wait. It was turning chill. 'Eventually, Chloe,' he said, 'I want you to have the tandem.' All I could do was touch his sleeve. Down the track to the beach came the taxi, the pebbles making it rattle. I helped him to climb in. He gave ten pounds to the woman as, he said, rent in advance for the tandem and she seemed pleased. 'I'm going home to my fire,' she repeated and pulled down the shutter with a crash of finality.

On the journey home, Sir Benedict's veined eyelids

drooped and he began to snore quietly. The driver said in a confiding way: 'He's getting on, isn't he.'

'I suppose he is.'

He did not say any more. We reached the close. Then the old man stirred and tapped the driver on the shoulder. 'During the war,' he said, 'I was trained in silent killing.'

The taxi-man still had a startled expression when we helped the old man from the car. 'By stealth,' Sir Benedict confirmed. 'Often at night.'

'I'm sure you did, sir,' said the driver like a cornered man. 'We owe a lot to you.'

Once inside the house the old man said that he was going to rest and went painfully up the stairs. Urchfont came from the kitchen, leaving the door swinging. 'They're here,' he said inclining an ominous face in the direction of Lady Annabel's sitting-room. 'The Africans.'

He jerked his head towards the kitchen and I followed him. 'You came back in a cab,' he said. 'Is he all right?'

'We left the tandem. Until next Easter.'

Doubt filled his face. 'If there is a next Easter,' he muttered. 'I'm getting worried about this whole situation. I don't like those Branche people creeping about as if they already own the flaming place. She keeps asking questions.'

'The old man,' I said, 'says that he was trained for silent killing in the war.'

'Oh, Gawd.' Urchfont involuntarily clutched his own throat. 'I don't like the sound of that.' He stared so fiercely the wrinkles on his forehead flattened out. '*One of them's going to do the other one in*,' he said. '*I* know it and *you* know it. It's only a case of which one. Him or her. You're right. We ought to go to the police.'

'I've thought about it. I don't think we can do it.'

'What can't you do?' It was Mrs Branche with her thin face and thick accent. She pushed the door fully open and walked in. Urchfont's face trembled. He hated anyone coming into his part of the house without knocking. Sometimes he sat there without his shoes and, in summer, even his socks.

She was looking directly at me. 'The brass. We were talking about polishing the brass today or tomorrow. I said we can't do it. Not today.'

'It needs polishing,' she said. 'Have you discovered how many fish we have in the garden pond yet?' Her lips hardly parted. She looked like a fish herself.

To my surprise Urchfont said: 'Thirty-seven. Not counting the baby ones.'

She looked hard at him but his expression was bland. Then her eyes flicked at me but without saying anything she went out. We gave her time to get clear, then Urchfont cautiously pushed open the door and checked both ways. He returned with a sniff. 'I certainly don't like the look of her,' he said. 'You noticed she's using the word "we" already. "How many fish have *we* got in the pond?"'

'What about him?'

'Bullying bugger. He's had me going around the house with him today, wine cellar, everything. Well, you know how bigoted I am, but I've got sod all on him. He's telling me how he'd put the world to rights. He's heavily into castration.'

'Who for?'

'Almost everybody.'

'They're closing in,' I said.

'They're her relatives. The only ones.'

'Not while the old man's around.'

He knew what I meant. 'Do you really, honestly

reckon they're going to have a final go at each other, him and her?'

'I'm trying not to.'

'I think they are,' he said grimly.

'You can't leave yet,' I told him.

To my relief he shrugged. 'I won't. Not yet.'

'Sir Benedict wants me to be at the birthday party at the Cliff Edge Hotel,' I said. 'And I'm going to persuade him and her as well – that you have to be there too.'

His initial alarm fell to despondency. 'All right,' he said. 'I might as well.'

'I may need you.'

'It might be difficult to stop the slaughter.' He sighed. 'But I'll come. I'll help you out, Chloe.'

29

'Poisoning,' said Ron Brown. 'Old folks generally try poisoning.'

'Why's that?'

He had come in unexpectedly again (I was beginning to wonder if he suspected me of other crimes) and had taken from a scarred briefcase a whole veal and ham pie and two cans of Coke. We sat in the interview room and shared them. 'What's the grub like in here?' he asked.

'For a prison it's said to be all right.'

'I had to buy something anyway for myself. I usually do on the way home. It seemed a shame for the shop to cut the pie up.'

I took a bite. 'Is there much of it?'

'What you see.'

'I meant the poisoning. Among old people.'

'Quite a decent amount,' he said munching. 'They can't manage physical violence when they're getting on and they don't fancy the sight of blood, and in their minds, poisoning looks easy. A couple of spoonfuls of something in the tea. Warfarin's very popular – rat poison.'

'You'd taste that, wouldn't you?'

'I'll say. That's why most of them don't succeed. But it's rare for them to go in for unarmed combat or knuckledusters.'

We raised the tins of Coke as though they were glasses of champagne. I said: 'Thanks,' and he said: 'Cheers.'

'You wouldn't think that, when you get to that age, you'd want to kill someone,' I suggested. 'Death comes soon enough.'

'It builds up.' He held the can like a microphone. 'Hatred. When they get very old sometimes they really get into hatred. Little bits of it, and it builds up. It's like they blame the other one for them getting old, for spoiling their lives. It's then all the nasty secrets and things from the past come out.'

'Well, you and I have been spared that,' I said. 'I can't see me growing old with anybody.'

He sniffed. 'In a way that's why I'm glad she has gone. I could see us groping along for a few years but in the end it would have been no good. Better you break up when you've still got a dog's chance.'

He asked me about the night at the Cliff Edge Hotel. 'You're very nosey about that,' I said. 'What's it got to do with my case?'

'Not a lot,' he admitted. 'But I find it interesting. I read a lot of detective stories. It's just like one of them. "A fight to the death," that's what he said, didn't he? It sounds like a book. This job of work is never like that. I bet it caught the local nick on the hop.'

'They were all there, the police. And the papers, of course. One member of a titled family going over the cliff and then another – forty years after. And in the same place.'

'Great stuff,' he said finishing the last corner of his pie. 'It's like it's poetic, isn't it.'

'Poetic,' I agreed.

When we had arrived at the Cliff Edge Hotel that night

there were three witches and a ghoul in the lobby, all drinking.

'Jesus,' said Urchfont as we got out of our taxi. 'Sodding Hallowe'en.'

We had been sent in a smaller cab, a little ahead of the others, and these were almost the first words we had spoken on the way. We were so silent, staring ahead, that the taxi-driver thought we were married. 'Life's too short for quarrelling,' he advised as we got out.

'Mind your own bleeding business,' said Urchfont.

We went into the hotel and saw the people dressed up. The head waiter, Mayhew, whom I had seen there before, hurried out apologetically when he saw us. 'An unfortunate mix-up,' he said, 'but these people will be in another room.' He attempted a plausible excuse. 'They're the chamber of commerce.'

It was frightening seeing them, even though under the high hats, paint, broken teeth and crooked noses, they were just small shopkeepers. 'All we needed was a load of sodding spooks,' said Urchfont bitterly.

'It's all right,' I said trying to convince myself as well. 'Nothing is going to happen.'

'What if it does?' he asked again. 'What do we do?'

'Stop them,' I told him firmly. 'Make sure they don't get at each other.'

'Has she got her knuckledusters?' We were waiting for the headlights of the second taxi to appear. Some more people, assorted spectres and wizards, arrived and we moved aside to let them pass. 'Prats,' muttered Urchfont.

'She had them in her evening bag but I took them out,' I said.

'That's not fair.'

'She put them back in, though. I had no time to hide them and I know she put them back.'

'Even Stevens.'

I caught him by the dandruffed shoulder of his dinner jacket. 'Listen, don't let's be stupid about this. We're probably completely wrong.'

'He was doing karate chops,' he said grimly. 'Only this morning. And grunting. And she's got the knuckledusters. It don't look at all promising.'

'Here they come,' I said nodding into the dark. Two lights came like a prowling cat through the hotel gate and along the drive. We both moved forward but Mr and Mrs Branche got out first. 'Ah, the harbingers are here,' said Mrs Branche patronising and jovial. 'Well done.' A small bus pulled up on the distant side of the car park and more tradesmen in fancy dress got out. 'What the hell's going on?' demanded Branche.

Sir Benedict clambered from the cab helped by Urchfont; courteously he took Lady Annabel's elbow and with some fuss hauled her out also. He seemed suddenly tall and straight, almost powerful. Her eyes were glittering and I thought: 'Oh God.'

'It's Hallowe'en,' Urchfont said to Mr Branche. 'People dress up.'

'They're like witch-doctors,' complained Mrs Branche. 'We should have made it another night.'

'Today is Sir Benedict's birthday,' I pointed out. 'He wanted to have the dinner this evening.' Her thin nose pointed at me like a dagger.

'But hell . . .' objected Mr Branche.

'They're in another room, another part of the hotel,' I said. 'We have a special table in the dining-room.'

'Who are these people?' asked Lady Annabel peering through the half-light outside the hotel.

'Fancy dress, my lady,' said Urchfont. 'For Hallowe'en.' He muttered to himself: 'Bastards.'

Both the old people seemed to find the matter of only marginal concern. Sir Benedict took Lady Annabel's arm and they walked quite grandly, sombrely and potently into the lobby. She was wearing a red velvet dress with pearls around her wrinkled neck and he was in the same dinner jacket, so he had told me, he had worn for forty years, ever since the night his Lucy died. 'I don't like the look of this at all,' muttered Urchfont as they went into the lighted entrance followed by the attendant Branches.

'Neither do I,' I said.

It was Sir Benedict who had suggested, *insisted* that Urchfont and I should be at the table with them. Lady Annabel had made no objection and in fact had even shown a brief enthusiasm.

'They want us,' said the butler with foreboding, 'like referees.'

The table was the same as Sir Benedict had always had. He smiled when he saw it. We had sat there on that sunny lunch day. Now it had been lengthened to take ten people. The other four were ancient friends and all had been there on that first tragic night. Sir Benedict had written to them specially.

A small room had been reserved for drinks before dinner and the four arrived while we were there. Urchfont and I served the gins and whiskies from a sideboard. He sniffed at them disdainfully. 'We should have brought our own,' he whispered. When the new guests came in the embraces were frail and the remembrances mild. For the elderly, I thought, perhaps time was different, swift. The evening started so convivially that I began to feel reassured. They were all infirm and harmless. But then, as they left the room to go to the dining table, Sir Benedict winked at me hugely with his blind eye.

Urchfont and I sat in our proper places, at the end of the long table, trying to look as if we were pleased. Every now and then Urchfont would whisper some sharp instruction to the waiter and the man would shift away with a grimace. From their distant room we could hear the wizards and witches. They were getting rowdier and Urchfont summoned the manager and whispered that they should be told to shut up. The manager went away shaking his head.

Conversation at the table was surprisingly brisk. Sir Benedict and Lady Annabel seemed determined to keep everyone animated. Mr and Mrs Branche described their lives in the Orange Free State and how they were glad to leave and resettle in dear England. I bet they were.

Then it all started. The dining-room had been quite full when we first entered but it emptied early and by the time we had finished the meal there were only two other tables occupied. A private room had been reserved for our coffee and after-dinner drinks and the slow procession left, Mr and Mrs Branche, Urchfont and myself hovering as the old people went out. All had gone so well, so amiably. As we reached the lobby I whispered to the butler that I was going to the ladies' room and he said: 'Looks like it's going to be all right.'

I had to push open the door of the ladies'. It was crowded with noisy witches at the wash-basins, looking at their black make-up in the mirrors, and others occupying the cubicles. I would have to wait. I stood, feeling odd among the pointed hats, the crepe capes and the girlie chatter. It was my turn next when the door crashed open and Urchfont bundled in. All the witches screamed and a ghoul hit him with her handbag. 'Chloe!' he bellowed ignoring the blow. 'They've gone! They're going towards the bloody cliff!'

'Shit,' I said.

'Language, language,' said a skeleton. I pushed past and we rushed through the lobby knocking broomsticks and stuffed cats aside. My heart was banging and I was gasping before we reached the dining-room. 'They went this way!' shouted Urchfont. He ran out into the shadowy garden.

I overtook him and pounded down the lawn towards the sea. The night was light as summer. There was a moon. I glanced behind and saw the Branche couple framed in the French door. 'It's locked,' said Urchfont. 'They can't get out that way.'

'Make sure they don't,' I said.

He rushed towards them shouting: 'I'm coming!'

I reached the end of the lawn and went onto the cliff path. I ran a few yards along the soft ground, with the sea sounding below, and then – oh God – I saw them. It was terrible. *Sir Benedict and Lady Annabel were fighting wildly on the edge of the cliff.* I screamed and ran towards them shouting for them to stop. They were slugging it out, hitting at each other, grappling, in silence apart from their gasps. Then I tripped and landed on my face. The fall knocked out what remaining breath I had. I lay there, gasping, bringing up bile. Then I heard her awful cry.

Somehow I got to my knees. Straight ahead, his hands held above his head like a winning boxer, was Sir Benedict. He began howling in the moonlight. I felt myself go cold. Slowly, for now I knew there was no hurry, I got to my feet and staggered along the path towards him.

'Chloe, Chloe.' It was not a shout; he was merely

giving information. 'Chloe, I'm afraid Lady Annabel has jumped over the cliff.' I made a few more paces towards him. He stood, hung almost, his arms now held out like the drying wings of a large sea-bird, gasping, knees trying to buckle. I could see his good eye flashing in the moonlight. He gave another howl. 'She's gone after Lucy!'

'Remorse,' said Ron Brown knowledgeably, 'is a terrible thing.'

'It is. Was,' I replied.

'*Was* in her case, you mean – Lady Annabel?'

'That's what I meant.'

'What did you say at the time? At the inquest. What was it? When the coroner asked you if you knew any reason why she should take her own life by jumping over the cliff like that. Didn't you say it then?'

'I said I didn't know,' I said firmly. 'There was nothing about remorse. I don't know what made her do it.'

'Well, you didn't actually *see* her either, did you. You weren't a witness to the act. I had a look at the inquest report but it was a bit untidy. You said you fell over on the path, tripped over in the dark, and when you looked up there was Sir Benedict looking over the edge. And he said to you: "She's gone after Lucy" or words to that effect.'

'What's that got to do with now, with me going for trial?'

He shrugged. 'Nothing really. I told you. I'm just interested and I'm often passing. You don't mind, do you?'

I said I did not mind.

'It was Sir Benedict who afterwards mentioned remorse,' I pointed out. We were in the interview room again.

He had brought along a couple of custard tarts and we ate them from the paper.

'I read it,' he said. 'Sir Benedict's evidence from the coroner's inquest. It wasn't long ago. Big news in the papers, titled old chap alleging his wife had pushed his first missus over a cliff in Dorset and then, full of remorse, years later jumped off the same cliff herself. They don't get lucky headlines like that very often, do they. The Press have to make up half the stuff these days.'

He suddenly studied his hands. 'You've been digging again,' I said.

'They're sore. I've been trying to get the garden into shape,' he said. 'Maybe I ought to have done it before. Then she would have had something decent to look at from the kitchen.'

'That's not the reason she cleared off.'

'No, never,' he agreed. 'I know that if I'm honest. She wanted a different bloke, not a different garden. But I'm getting it right so I can sell the house.' There were not many crumbs left from his custard tart but he gathered them into the wrapping. 'Want to finish yours?' he asked politely. I said I had.

As he turned to go and the woman warder appeared at the door to take me back to my cell (they always watched at a distance), Ron Brown said: 'It's less than a week now.'

'I know. But I'm not pleading guilty. Manslaughter's only murder under another name.'

'It's a shorter stretch,' he said. For some reason he seemed anxious not to go. 'By the way, you know I told you that your Alf Tomkins . . .'

'Zane.'

'Yes. Good old Zane, that's him.' Briefly his voice hardened. 'You know I told you he was away for some bank robbery or other, well, it wasn't him. Interpol's never much good. He's actually inside for being married to two women at the same time. They don't reckon much on bigamy in Spain.'

'That sounds like him,' I said.

'In fact I think he was involved with more. Three. I wonder if there is such a thing as trigamy.' Finally he turned to go. 'I'll have to look it up.'

'Women always took advantage of him,' I said caustically. He grimaced at me and I looked down at the bare table. There was one crumb he had missed and I swept it over the edge. 'I'm not surprised about the bigamy. Not a bit.'

'When did you last see him?'

'Ten years ago. He turned up again. I very nearly married him twice myself.'

30

When Zane had come back that morning ten years before and rescued me from the heavies looking for Claude the fraud, my rapidly departed fiancé, I steeled myself to tell him to get lost. I made him a cup of coffee and as we sat down I said: 'It's the wrong day for you to turn up. I've just got rid of one arsehole.'

'Language, language,' he tutted. 'You didn't used to swear like that.'

'I've been driven to it.' I was almost weeping over the coffee cup. The fact that he was there again was enough to make me weep. He still looked good and handsome, his fair hair cut short and curly, any lines on his face only making him look fraudulently wise.

'What did those wankers outside your door want?'

'Who's going on about language.'

'Well, that's what I saw out there. Threatening you. Four willie wankers.'

'They came after a man called Claude, a Frenchman,' I said, 'who has just gone out of my life, I hope for good. He was a crook.'

'They are,' he said as if he knew them all. 'Don't ever trust them. Same as the Spanish. Crooks.'

'What are you doing back here? I hoped you had gone for ever. I was the fool who waited outside Winchester bloody prison for you, remember.'

His firm and consoling hand came out and touched my shoulder and gave it a familiar rub. I felt a tremble. 'You're such a bastard.' I began to really cry, my tears running into the cup and the coffee. 'You always were.'

'Chloe,' he murmured like someone trying to help me. 'Darl, listen. I *had* to get away for *your* sake. When I came out of Winchester there was a gang gunning for me. *You* were in danger. I had to put enough distance between *them* and *you* and ... and ... Donny, of course. Oh ... how is Donny?'

'Kind of you to ask. He's living in Aldershot with my mother. She means him to be a soldier like his grandfather. Well, not quite like his grandfather. He's in the Army Cadets. I couldn't handle him here. He set the school on fire.'

'Kids,' he sighed.

'And himself as well.'

'God. He didn't get out in time?'

'That's right. But he wasn't badly burned or anything.'

'You've got to know when to leave.'

'You've learned that.'

He detected the tone. 'Oh, come on. Don't give me a hard time, Chloe. I've just come to see you. How is he getting on with your mother?'

'He's fine,' I said. 'He's settled down and he never gives her any problems. Plays football, watches television, goes to school. Takes an interest in girls. The things boys do. He's sixteen now.'

'Jesus, where does the time go?'

I felt like saying in his case quite a lot of it was behind bars.

'I'll go and see him,' he said dutifully.

'Don't,' I said sternly. 'I don't want you to, Zane. And

my mother will throw something hard or horrible at you, I promise. Just give him a chance.'

'Okay,' he muttered. He made his brow wrinkle. 'I know you're right, Chloe. What sort of example am I? What sort of father?'

'None at all. You've never even paid a bean.'

'I haven't had many beans.'

We sat silently as if, after the years that had passed, we had no more conversation. Eventually, I briskly picked up the cups and took them back to the kitchen. 'You're still here then,' he said.

'It's my only safe place,' I replied coming back. 'I can close that door and know where I am.'

'And you still work downstairs in the shop.'

'I do. And you're not going down there to see what's in stock either. If you try it, I'll call the police.'

'Chloe, Chloe,' he pleaded. His expression was full of pretended concern. He grasped my hand and held it in both of his. They were warm and his blue eyes were damp. 'I've had enough. I'm tired of it all. I know how I've been, but it's how I was born.'

'Nobody's born like you.'

'I mean it. I know you'll think it's just another excuse. But I've really, honestly, come to the end of it. I can't go on. I've even wanted to top myself . . .'

'Killing the person you love most.'

'All right,' he sighed. My heart hung as he stood up, all six feet of him. 'All right. I just wanted to come and see you, just to see how you were getting on, if you were managing. How Donny was.'

'I'm managing. So is Donny. Even if we are separate.'

'That's fine. It's all I wanted to know. I've always loved you.'

He went towards the door leaving me hunched, my

thumbs against my nose, at the table. 'Cheers then,' he said in a defeated way.

I made the first mistake and I knew it even as I asked: 'Where are you living?'

'Where I can. It's not easy. But I've got a job lined up. Cars.'

'Straight cars?'

He sighed. 'Straight cars. So straight they won't turn off the motorway.'

I must have given a little laugh. He was in there like an ambush. In a moment he had his arms about me, he was kissing me. I just collapsed. I could not manage. As I was trying to push him off I wanted him to keep doing it. Then we fell together and he did not embrace me, he *hugged* me, and I cried because I tried to believe he meant at least some of it. He held me close, so close that I could feel him grinning.

I managed to keep him, and myself, away from the bedroom which was visible through the open door. If I had not just got rid of one charlatan I might have given in to this one, the one I loved.

He sat down carefully, like someone who has been taken ill, and I made some more coffee. I could see there were grey flecks in the back of his fair hair. The cups rattled as I took them to the table and I made the excuse that I was tired. He seemed to have forgotten the men who had been at my door when he arrived and only wanted to tell me of his plans for yet another new start to his life.

'It's a friend,' he said as though he had many. 'He's offered me this job. Someone I can trust, not like those bastards in Spain. You've never seen so many bastards in one country. It's like it collects them. You can't even trust the police like you can here.'

I wanted to get him out of the place as soon as he had finished his coffee but even then I felt a stab of guilty disappointment when he went without argument. Dejectedly I cleared the coffee cups once the door had closed on him. He went cheerfully, full of assurance. He knew he would be back and so did I.

It was not a long wait. He appeared at the shop the following afternoon, framed against the sunlight in the door. We went for a cup of tea at Lol's where I had first seen him all those years before. Lol was still there, still lolling against the counter, but Penny had gone to Portsmouth to get married. 'She'll be back,' forecast Lol with indolent spite. 'What's Portsmouth got, I ask you? And *married*, for God's sake. What's getting married?' He half-remembered Zane and nodded to him gingerly as he said it.

We sat drinking thick tea out of thick cups. There were girls from the offices and shops in there and as usual, they all looked at Zane. A girl came across the street from the door of Fayler's, the estate agent's where I had worked. She sat alone and regarded him moodily over her teacup, just as I had done years before.

His eyes were steadily blue over the off-white curve of the cup. 'I've got somewhere lined up to live,' he said. 'Big house. Next week probably.'

'How did you come by that?'

He appeared affronted. 'Contacts, darl. All legal. The owner's abroad. In Spain, in fact.'

He could regard you with frankness shimmering from his eyes and still be lying in his teeth. But I wanted to believe him, wanted to believe that he and his life had changed; no more cheating, no more crime, no more scams. I was ashamed, but I was glad he had returned and I wanted him back.

'I want to take you to show you the house, Chloe,' he said zooming in unerringly on my mood. 'There's a big field around it and a long drive and trees. We could be just like we used to be, but much better.'

'And older,' I said hopefully.

'Wiser,' he added on cue.

'Where is it?'

'Not far. It's near the sea. You can see the Solent if you climb on the roof.'

'What about the job?' I asked. I needed to get everything spelled out.

He leaned across the fake marble table and cupped my hands in his. The girls sitting around stared and the one from the estate agents let her tea dribble down her chin. Nothing like that was ever lost on him and I thought for a moment he was going to take a bow. But he said: 'Listen, if we can get together again we can settle down and . . . and Donny can come back.'

He had me pinned there and he knew it. 'He's been very settled with my mother,' I said inadequately. 'He's going away soon. He telephoned today. He's going to be what they call a boy soldier, a sort of apprentice.'

'Will he go in the band like your father?'

'He's learned to play the bugle, that's all,' I said.

'We'll have him back and be a real family again.'

'He won't want to come back. I told you, he's set on the army.'

'With your mother's encouragement.'

'Yes. He's been with her, remember.'

He appeared thoughtful. 'He could come on leave,' he said. His sincerity was reflected in Lol's table. 'We should never have been divorced, darl. You know that.'

'I couldn't find you,' I pointed out. 'You just vanished. What did you expect me to do? Wait until you reappeared in another puff of smoke? And you had a woman. Don't tell me that's not true because it is. I made as many enquiries as I could, as I could afford, and I found you'd gone off to Spain with her.' I felt my eyes getting damp again. The estate agent girl leaned so far over to listen that she half-fell from her chair. Zane caught her and helped her up. Pink-faced she headed for the door.

'It's not true about the woman,' said Zane solidly. 'I swear on my mother's life.'

'Your mother's dead.'

'On her grave, I mean. I swear it. The woman was just a way of getting out ahead of being sliced up by the gang who were after me. That's true, Chloe, it's the dead, honest truth.'

'And you're never going off again? Not to Spain or anywhere else?'

He knew he was winning. He said: 'Nowhere. I love England. And I love you.'

It is difficult to credit now but I was making myself believe this tripe. I wanted him to be mine again. I wanted the tree in the garden and the fire in the room. I kidded myself that this was the last chance for both of us. 'What about this job?' I repeated feebly.

'It's on,' he whispered and glanced around as though afraid somebody else might get it. 'It's what I know. Cars.'

'Not stealing them.'

His mouth tightened and his eyes became hard. 'All right, Chloe,' he said getting up. 'I'll pay for the teas. If you don't want me, I'm going.'

I caught his sleeve and, without much tugging, he sat down. 'What is it then, with cars?' I asked.

He sighed as though hanging onto his patience. 'Delivering them,' he said. 'All over the country. All sorts of vehicles, but mostly cars. He has a lot of smart stuff through his hands, this bloke, and he knows I can drive even if I can't do much else.'

I prevented myself from reassuring him that he could do anything. 'He's got some beautiful cars,' insisted Zane. 'And I get to drive them.' His eyes glistened. 'I can't wait to take you for a ride, Chloe.'

By that time he already had.

31

For more than a week I managed to keep Zane at a distance although he kept telephoning me, mostly with encouraging news about his future. And, according to him, mine.

Then one afternoon, late, just as I was about to shut the shop and go upstairs, he arrived in the street driving the most beautiful red sports car, hood down, its bits and pieces gleaming in the late sun. If a car could smirk, this did. Almost as much as the driver. He looked born to be behind the wheel, unreal as a television commercial. There he sat, music playing around him, tanned and handsomely assured, his eyes brimming with fun, his open shirt framing the thickness of his brown neck. He did not need an advertiser's backdrop of mountains or beaches; he looked splendid with only the street behind him. Oh shit, I thought, why not?

He said: 'Come on, Chloe, we've got to talk.'

'I'll lock up.' I did so and then, with a glance towards him lounging in the car, checked the locks and alarms a second time. Keeping a sober expression and pretending not to notice the car, I climbed in as he courteously opened the door for me. I settled back behind the windscreen taking in the glistening dials and dashboard. It was like a small aeroplane. He kissed me seriously on the cheek and asked: 'What do you think of it?'

'What?' I asked unsportingly. I wasn't going to make it easy.

'The car!' He sounded hurt and I was glad to hear it. 'Oh, come on darl, the *car*. Have you ever even *seen* – a car like this?'

'It's very pleasant,' I said deliberately. 'Why doesn't it have a roof?'

He exploded with laughter. 'All right, be difficult.' He pressed a button and the roof eased over us fixing itself with a sigh. 'There. Now are you happy?'

'It's a bit stuffy in here,' I said but he only laughed. It was no good; he leaned and kissed me on the lips and I let him do it. I could only keep up the act for so long. His face remained close and I half-expected a bright flash to come from his teeth as he smiled, as you sometimes see in jokey films. 'Where are we going?' I enquired.

'For drinks,' he said. 'Then dinner. Is that all right? You're not busy tonight, are you?'

'I was going out with Prince Charles.'

I could see he was getting annoyed so I stopped. 'Where did you come by the car?' I asked as if I did not care. We were going through Southampton, whirring rather than whizzing, people turning on the pavements to stare at us and point.

'I *told* you,' he said. 'It's what I'll be doing. I have to take this to Manchester tomorrow. But for tonight, it's mine. Ours, Chloe.'

I gave him the news that Donny had gone to the North that week to start his training as a boy soldier.

'Your mother's going to miss him,' he said.

'Like she once missed my father.'

'Maybe she could come and live with us.' His smile was broad.

'I don't think so. Anyway, who said there's going to be any "us"?'

'All right, maybe she could live with me.'

We both laughed.

At that point I more or less gave up. We went to dinner in a nice place that had not been open long but where they apparently knew him. 'Your table for two is this way, Mr Tomkins,' said the man leading us in. We had already been in the bar of the Burlington Hotel for an hour.

'You were sure I'd come, then?' I said as we sat in the restaurant and the waiter spread out the napkin on my lap.

'What makes you think that?'

'You booked for two,' I pointed out. 'Oh, don't tell me. You had someone in reserve.'

He just laughed and said: 'I was counting on you.'

It was a strange but lovely evening, one of the best we ever spent together (although that left a lot of scope). Afterwards, we walked through the subdued streets, his arm comfortably round my waist as I waited for him to say something that was going to ruin everything. But all he said was: 'Let's go in here.' It was a bar, mid-week empty at eleven o'clock. We had a drink and then he appeared to notice some coloured lights flashing rhythmically from below. 'They've got a disco,' he said in a surprised way. 'It's ages since we danced.'

I stopped myself from saying that it was ages since we had done anything and allowed him to usher me down the steps. The place was empty, the lights flashing eerily and, on cue, a romantic tune filled the reflecting room. His smirk was all over his face now and he led me onto the floor. We danced close and alone. I let the feeling, the music, the highly suspect closeness of him, roll over me. I remembered his aftershave. He kissed me and I kissed him.

But I was still watchful. Too much had happened before. I had trouble in even believing he was there, that it was not another illusion, another trick. The music drained away and we held each other in the moving pool of lights on the empty floor. All around were the shapes of unoccupied chairs and tables. The revolving discs played on Zane's face, yellow, green, red, like traffic signals. He moved as he sensed the colours did not suit him. 'I've got a present for you,' he whispered.

I thought he might have. The second thought was where had he got it. 'You haven't,' I breathed. 'What is it?'

If he had produced the Crown Jewels I would not have been all that amazed and, at least, I would have known where they had come from. But from the breast pocket of his smart jacket he took a square of tissue and from that a gold chain. 'It's got your name on it,' he said.

It had too, spelled correctly, on a flat, thin, gold oblong bevelled at the edges. I held my neck out like a chicken so that he could put it on because I knew he would want to. His hands slid slightly over my skin and he fastened it behind. 'Thank you, Zane,' I said managing a husky voice. 'It's very nice.'

I thought it was also probably legitimate. He would not have stolen or received something that small, unless it were part of a larger haul. And my name *was* engraved on it. He had gone to some trouble.

He held out his arms and we danced again, this time even slower and closer. It was like being on a sedate roundabout with the lights and the music swirling gently around us. I kissed him genuinely although I still had doubts. There was no risk in it, I told myself. I would never, ever, marry him again.

At the end of the music we kissed again and remained in the embrace, my face on his chest, until he eased himself away and led me like a prize from the floor. 'Would you like to see my house?' he asked.

'Is it far?' This was surrender.

'No distance.' His voice was still controlled, although eager as if he had not been sure all this was going to work. But I did not mind. I looked forward to it, to his arms and the rest of him which I had missed so much until they had faded into a distant memory. I wondered if it would still be the same.

We reached the stairs. There was a bulky man standing waiting at the exit. 'All right, Zane?' he enquired. Zane looked taken aback, found some money, gave it to him and nodded in the dimness. 'Can I put the lights out now?' asked the man.

'You're still up to your tricks,' I said, but easily, as we went out into the street. 'You fixed all that.'

The street lights lit the surprise on his face. 'Would I do something like that?'

His arm slipped around my waist. The pavement was dark and nobody was about. I could see the red Mercedes glistening under a lamp. 'I've known you do worse things,' I said pushing my head to his shoulder. 'A lot worse.'

'I've told you, I've changed,' he said with a long sigh. 'Now I only do nice things. Do you want to see my mansion? It looks wonderful in the moonlight.'

'There's no moon.'

'I'll soon fix that.'

He was acting again, playing the romantic, like in one of those old films that turn up on television with Cary

Grant in a tuxedo and a girl with bare shoulders. Cary Grant always said lines like Zane. 'How about it, baby?' he murmured.

'I'm with you.' I swear I whispered it with a Hollywood accent. A Southampton corporation bus trundled by and I saw the faces looking out as we got into the Mercedes. As we did so the moon came out.

He had almost told the truth. It was not far, west from the city into the odd no man's land between the Solent and the forest, with scruffy lanes, scrapyards, big neglected houses that had once been country estates, ragged trees and fields with caravans and scraggy ponies. I remembered it by daylight. Suspect car dealers took vehicles into lanes and back yards, there were gypsies and loud dogs.

'We could have been happy,' I said as we drove.

'I know. It was all my fault.'

I was not going to contradict him but I leaned over and kissed him on the cheek as we drove. He said: 'We've got to make up for lost time.'

At that moment I thought that there might be hope for us yet.

Some hope.

We turned off one of the lanes, tight as a trench with torn branches hanging over it, in through a gate which sagged as though blinded by our headlights, and along a dark, rutted and rising path.

'There it is,' said Zane.

On the summit of the ground the house stood big and ghostly, the moon faintly glowing on what had once been white walls. Even by night it looked in a poor way and as we neared my apprehension grew. A pony suddenly appeared on the path and jumped away, whinnying. The trees rustled heavily. There should have been an owl.

'It's better than it looks,' said Zane realising my thoughts. 'It won't take much getting right. And there's ten acres.'

'You're paying rent?'

'Sort of rent.' He attempted enthusiasm. 'But it's got possibilities, darl. Possibilities.'

'Possibilities cost money.'

He sounded a touch annoyed. 'I can get money,' he said. 'Money's no problem.'

My warning bells were jangling, if only softly, as I got out of the car and surveyed the sad wreck in the moonlight. 'Are you living in *all* of it?' I asked.

'In the housekeeper's flat at the moment. There's no housekeeper.'

'There's not much house.'

He muttered something. I could feel the romance evaporating. It was chilly standing there and he hurried to unlock the scarred front door, pushing it open with a grinding squeak. 'I'll have to oil that,' he said.

I remembered that he had never got around to oiling the cottage gate. 'Yes, it spoils it,' I said stepping into the yawning hall.

He suddenly turned on me. Even in the moonlight I could see his face flush. 'Listen, Chloe,' he said. 'If you want to keep taking the piss ... I'm only *showing* you. Can't you see, I'm *trying* ...'

He did not say what he was trying but at once I felt guilty. I said I was sorry. His arm went around my shoulder protectively and I was glad to feel it. A dead bird, legs in the air, lay in the shaft of moonlight that went before us through the door. Zane moved it with his foot. 'I usually come in the back way,' he explained.

I performed a circuit around the bird for he had not sent it very far. He eventually located a light switch and pushed it down, illuminating a solitary bulb which dangled pathetically from the ornate and deeply cracked ceiling. The light showed up ancient wallpaper on three walls and a crazily hanging staircase, like a scene in a film about a wrecked liner. Something nasty scurried in a corner.

He shrugged, the shadow of his shoulders enormous on the opposite wall. I waved to myself in silhouette. 'The owner's in Spain . . .' he said.

'In Spain, in gaol?'

'Possession of a firearm. Forgot he had it.'

'How much is the rent?'

I had caught him off guard. 'I haven't actually paid anything yet. He just said to come here and see what I thought.'

'It's got to be worth a couple of quid a week.'

'Stop it,' he said. 'Don't spoil everything.'

He took my hand and led me along a damp and damaged corridor, through what had once been a kitchen now lit only by shafts of dirty moonlight through its windows. Zane tripped over a kettle on the floor and cursed mildly. He was heading for a further door and took a key from his pocket to unlock it. He pushed it open without resistance. 'My quarters,' he said confidently.

I entered with a sort of fear, not of him, not of the house, but of what I might be getting myself into again. But the encouraging touch of his hand on my waist propelled me through the door and into a heavily furnished room with thick but open curtains and two carpets one on top of the other. 'He piled a lot of the furniture in here,' explained Zane. 'As much as he had time for.' The apologetic look appeared. 'Before he scarpered.'

He had turned the light on at the door but now he went around to an array of table lamps and activated two. There were four armchairs in the room and two settees plus no fewer than three handsome long-case clocks. 'Did he collect these?' I enquired.

Zane looked at them standing in a gleaming line as though he had never before noticed them. 'The grandfather clocks?' he said. 'Well, it looks a bit like it. Are they any good?'

'Lovely,' I said taking two paces across the room and running my fingertips down the burnished wood. I saw there was another, smaller, clock tucked behind them as though hiding. 'And this . . .' I said, 'is really beautiful. You don't see many Georgian *grandmother* clocks.'

'No,' he said sounding a little worried. 'Not grandmothers.' In an effort to change the subject he opened one of two identical cocktail cabinets and asked if I would like a drink. I had a vodka and tonic. There was a choice of four brands of vodka but no ice or lemon. The space was crammed with bottles. He had a drink himself and stood smiling. 'Home sweet home,' he said.

'The contents of several by the look of it.'

'Oh, give it a rest, darl. He collected clocks, that's all.'

'And vodka, and gin and whisky and a few other bits,' I pointed out. He stopped the conversation by moving close and kissing me with passion. I enjoyed it immediately and all the dubiousness of the place receded in my mind. I hung against him and deeply returned the kiss. His body felt fuller than it once had but just as strong and firm.

284

'You bastard,' I said. 'You're just as beautiful.'

'I know. So are you,' he said. 'Come and see the bedroom.'

It led directly off the living-room. There were two double beds (one on its end against the wall), pictures in frames piled on the top of three wardrobes and a long rail of male and female clothes. Without giving me time to ask questions, he sat on the main bed with a resounding creak of springs and firmly pulled me towards him. 'Remember how I used to undress you?' he said.

We must have made an unusual sight among all those piled belongings (there was even an empty parrot's cage in one corner), with me standing in front of him while he undid buttons and buckles and gradually took my clothes away. When he unhooked my bra he patted my breasts like twins. Then he kissed them busily and continued down to my navel. His hands went behind me and inserted themselves into my white pants. 'Put your hands on your head please, Chloe,' he said. I obeyed, stretching myself up while he pulled my pants down and continued kissing. He was very good at it, even better than I remembered.

'Are you going somewhere?' I asked the top of his head.

'That was the plan,' he said without looking up.

'I mean, you've still got your clothes on. You're not planning to clear off ... and leave me like this?'

His laugh was fruity. He could be good company at times. He got himself out of his clothes except for his shirt and sat me on the bed and stood in front of me. My fingers went below his shirt. 'Darl, your hands are cold,' he said. I blew on them and returned them to where they had been. He responded at once. I felt him growing to fill my palms. For tonight anyway, he was mine.

Gently, I pulled on him like a languid ringer on a bell rope. He writhed with pleasure, his hands rubbing my shoulders. Like that, still holding him, I towed him into the chilly bed. But we were stoked up enough by then. I could hardly wait to have him again after all those years.

It was just the same, just as good, no matter where he had been or what he had done in the meantime. It is fine now to say what a fool I was, and not for the first time, but for that moment it was all I wanted, *he* was all I wanted.

We roamed and rolled around the big bed, now engulfed in warmth and sex. At one time we were pumping up and down so violently that the second bed, the one propped against the wall, slid down with a sigh and a great shoot of dust.

In the morning strong sunshine woke me. It was striking through the window into one of the room's assorted mirrors. I felt for Zane but he was not there. I heard him in the bathroom, whistling happily among the spare toilet cabinets, ornamental jugs and Victorian chamber-pots and a box containing, so it claimed, a hundred heavy-duty lavatory rolls. 'I've got to get on the road, Chloe,' he answered when I called to him. 'I'll drop you home.'

We had a cup of tea with condensed milk. There was nothing else. The place appeared even more eerie in daylight than it had at night. 'We'll get it cleaned up, once we're settled,' he said.

'I'm not living with you, Zane. I've got my job and my place above the shop and I don't want to give that up.'

'No, no,' he replied with expansive reasonableness. 'Why should you? We've got plenty of time.'

We walked out, holding hands, into the dewy morning. I felt like Alice in Wonderland. Rabbits and pheasants were on the lawn and there were deer at the foot of the paddock. Birds sang crazily. The air was bright.

He took me to the shop and kissed me outside the door before driving impressively away on his long journey north. I smiled at the receding Mercedes and turned lightly as a girl to open the shop. There was a letter on the mat from my mother in which she confidently forecast that she would die very soon. She was right, too. Scarcely had I completed reading it, shaking my head and smiling, than the telephone rang; it was someone in Aldershot who said that she had been found dead. Sitting at her window, watching the soldiers.

32

Rosa's chair was still facing the Aldershot sunshine when I arrived, empty now and polished by her backside over the years. It was the bombardier who owned the Happy Gunner Café, where we had gossiped over teacups on many an afternoon, who had raised the alarm. He had seen her as she sat in the upper window at mid-morning when he was taking his dog for a walk. He was used to seeing her framed face there and they had waved to each other. At nine in the evening when he was walking his dog again she was still there. This time there was no answering wave even though he tried two or three times. Moving closer he saw that her eyes were closed. He went back to the Happy Gunner to call the police.

I found a number and telephoned the camp where Donny was. He called back an hour later. His voice sounded straight. 'We were on the firing range,' he said. 'They've given me compassionate leave. I'll be down tomorrow.'

'I'm sorry, Donny,' I said, not sure what I was saying.

'Me too,' he said. 'Very sorry.'

I went to see Rosa in the undertaker's, stretched out in an uncomfortable coffin but with a smile of achievement, as if she had come to the end of a long journey and was with my father again or at least looking forward to it. I could almost see him polishing his buttons as he waited.

That is what I tried to think, anyway. Then I found Kneller's number and told him.

I sat and had a soft cry in the chair that she had vacated, looking out over the parade-ground where a squad of young soldiers was stamping under the shouts of a drill sergeant. I wondered if she had really found my father again. There must have been a lot of soldiers where he was. It was not only for her and him, and Donny, that I cried, but for myself too. For my failure with my son and for my mother dying, sitting unattended in that chair, for the fact that I now had no one except Zane and, realistically, I knew that when you had no one but Zane, you were in a poor way indeed.

It was Zane, however, who rallied and the next day came to Aldershot and said he would organise the funeral. He mentioned mysteriously that he had gained experience in Spain. It was the sort of claim which he would come out with and which I had learned not to question. 'Your mother deserves to be buried with full military honours,' he asserted. 'She lived her life for the army, as good as any general.'

He went off to see what he could arrange. I let him go ahead while I stayed in the flat and occupied myself with the usual sad fascination of sorting through papers and belongings. I was weary. I had slept in Donny's bed the night before. I was not afraid of hers but it looked too neatly made to be disturbed. I did not sleep well and in the early hours I got up and made myself a shadowy cup of tea, which is what Rosa would have done.

She had kept bundles of letters from my father full of fairy-tales and faint with age, and photographs I had last seen years before. Taking my time I sorted them. There were pictures of me in Singapore in a long, frilled dress, sitting next to a large cat which I recognised, with a guilty start, was the promiscuous Persimmon. There was me with the school class, photographed under an awning sheltering us from the oriental sun, with the Indian Mr Gul standing close against me.

All these relics were in a scarred army trunk with my father's initials, florid but faded, displayed on top. There were sheets of music, songs we used to sing around the piano to cheer us during the times of his military misery. Beneath these was, to my astonishment, another unmistakable picture of Mr Gul, beaming and appearing important, rounder and older, taken with my mother. *With my mother!* Arms about each other, the sun glistening on his smooth, brown face and her happy smile. When I had blinked several times and even brought the photograph up to my nose under the room's middle light, I realised they were on holiday together. She was in a summery dress and he sported an open-necked shirt. Judging by her appearance it must have been within the past few years. In the fuzzy background was a steel tower and at first I thought it must have been in Paris but then I realised it was Blackpool. My mother had been to Blackpool with Mr Gul!

While I was still staring at the picture I heard the door. Donny had let himself in and was standing there in his new, stiff uniform. I fell suddenly weeping into his arms and he put them around me. They felt like the arms of a stranger and I realised how long it had been since we had embraced so closely.

He did not say much but laid his bag down, took off his cap and stood at the window overlooking the parade-ground. I went to make him a cup of tea and he was still standing there when I brought it into the room.

The doorbell rang. 'That's Zane,' I said.

Donny looked startled. He knew I had met with his

father again although he had not seemed very interested. Suddenly I realised how long it had been.

'It's ten years,' he said. 'More.'

Even Zane had trouble with this scene. The pair shook hands gravely and Zane made some lame comments about how the uniform suited Donny. He could scarcely have remembered seeing him out of it.

I escaped to make more tea. I was becoming like Rosa. I felt the warm pot and washed the cups as if they were an inheritance.

When I returned they were sitting in opposite chairs and Zane was saying how useless the Spanish army was. Donny was laughing.

Zane boasted that he was in advanced negotiations for a funeral with military honours, although he hinted that it might have to be slightly unofficial. 'She deserves a twenty-one-gun salute,' he said but even he considered this might be beyond him. His plan for rifle shots fired over the grave was thwarted by his inability to obtain enough off-duty soldiers who could bring along their rifles.

In the end he had to make do with the presence of some limping veteran soldiers he had managed to recruit from the ex-services club bar, with what promises I never heard, and these in their shabby pressed suits and medals paraded shakily on both sides of the grave; not one ever looked down into it as though for fear they might be next.

A surprising number of people were there. I had not realised my mother knew so many. Donny in uniform stood by me in the church with Zane on my other side. I looked slyly around for a round, brown face, but Mr Gul was not present. I also looked for Kneller and felt angry that he had allowed himself to be delayed or had not come at all.

But then, walking down the church with Zane, upright and smart in a new suit and gallantly holding my elbow, I raised my eyes as we reached the back pews. There sat two women, silent faced, wearing black coats and black hats. As we came abreast of them the nearest pair of eyes came up and met mine. What a terrible shock. It was my brother. My brother Nelly.

Zane cut a grand dash that sad day with his tall, broad good looks, his glinting fair hair, his dark suit and black tie. Women looked at him and I felt proud but guilty, too, that he was taking the limelight from my mother confined in her coffin. It seemed that Donny, by contrast, and despite his uniform, had in that same solemn morning become a young boy again. His face was pale and set, his eyes not far from tears. He scarcely muttered the hymns and the prayers.

In the cemetery one of the old ex-servicemen unfurled the flag of the Pay Corps. They had polished their medals so that they glowed a little even on that dull day.

Donny had been standing beside me. The two apparent ladies, one of whom was Kneller, stood on the other side. Kneller was crying beneath his veil. His companion blew loudly into an embroidered handker-chief. Then Donny moved towards Zane who gave him an encouraging wink and to my amazement handed him a bugle from behind his back.

Most people seemed to believe this was only to be expected but I stood astonished, then choked with tears, as Donny took the bugle and, at attention, blew the Last Post over the open grave. It echoed around the cemetery.

The vicar blinked. He, like me, had not been told. It was an unmistakable touch of Zane Tomkins.

Kneller and his friend were very taken with Zane and invited him to an exclusive club any time he happened to be in London. To my relief they then said that they had to hurry for the train and would not stay for drinks. In the small flat they would have attracted attention. People did not linger long, anyway, a glass of sherry and some stilted conversation and they were gone.

There were now the three of us again. Zane suggested that we should go out for a meal. We went to the El Alamein bistro where my mother had once shown him how the British Army salutes. The owner, who had known Rosa, remembered. He nodded at the uniformed Donny and said to Zane: 'I bet he doesn't salute like the Americans.'

We pretended to laugh but it was an awkward meal. At the end of it Donny said he would have to go back north tomorrow.

'I'll sleep at the flat,' he said.

'Won't you mind?' It was Zane who asked.

'Mind?' said Donny as he stood. 'Why should I? It's been my home.' He looked at us each in turn, me first, then Zane. 'She was like a mother to me,' he said. 'And a father.'

I was now on the frontier of a new relationship with Zane and old doubts rose like warning fingers. But he said gravely: 'I'll look after you, Chloe.' What could a woman in her middle thirties, who had lost her mother and as good as lost her son, say to that?

He stayed with me, or rather I stayed with him, for the following three days, before he went off on another car-delivering journey to the remote North. I had taken a week's holiday from the shop and we spent the time getting the accommodation in the big rough house in some sort of order. The weather was sunny and I loved those days. Despite what had gone before and, for God's sake, what followed, I still think of them as among my best of times.

There was not much we could do about the general state of the place but even that, for all its decayed emptiness, had a different aspect, a new smell, once the doors and windows were opened and the sun and fresh air flooded in. We moved all the surplus furniture and stuff like the heavy-duty toilet rolls from our own quarters to the driest rooms in the main house, and we rearranged what was left. The grandfather and grandmother clocks we shrouded in sheets. I still do not know if they were ever claimed. Too much happened. I brought flowers in from the overgrown garden and from the wild paddock. I felt my face and my neck and the top of my bosom glowing with the sun and he said I looked like the country girl on the front of the Ovaltine tin. Every day we had lunch in a space on the lawn which he had cut with a rusting scythe discovered in a shed. Stripped to the waist he looked a fine sight swinging it although he often perilously missed the grass. It reminded me of the days when he used to climb trees to amuse Donny.

We had wine with our daily picnics and in the afternoon we would go into the bedroom and for two hours lie naked against each other. Sometimes we would make love but not every afternoon. At four I would get up and make tea. It was a lovely time and I miss it even now. It is the 'if only' which women like me harbour in their innermost thoughts.

The night before he had to leave on his trip north we

went into Lymington and seated at a candlelit dinner overlooking the harbour he asked me to marry him again. 'We could sort everything out, our lives, everything,' he promised leaning sincerely to me and taking my hand. People around us paused with their forks halfway to their mouths and began listening.

A woman sitting with a much older man at the next table whispered to me: 'Go on.' When I glanced at her, as if she might really help, she turned away and spilled her wine. Mopping it up she muttered something about some people being so choosy.

We left the restaurant and walked in the wide moonlight down the sloping street to the harbour. The following day I was going to my own flat and resuming work in the antique shop. I had to have that job and I was determined to keep it. We kissed on the jetty like new lovers with the boats below us creaking as if they were hidden listeners. I asked him to give me time.

He was gone the next day. I returned to the shop and my little home above it. Mr Pyecraft came in and out with some find or other but mostly left me in charge. My mind was on one thing: should I marry Zane again?

Over the next five or six weeks we entered into an easy and promising domesticity. Zane's work was well paid and he was always arriving with yet another expensive car to be delivered the following day. The company had an extensive network and after the delivery he would sometimes be sent with another vehicle to another place. I was able to continue with my life, at least in part, as it had been. When he was with me we usually slept at the manor house. It was astonishing how happy and untroubled our relationship was. I could not believe what had happened to him. If he had asked me again to marry him I would have accepted but he seemed to have forgotten or was, I told myself, giving me time to consider, and I could not bring myself to prompt him. I decided to wait.

I even asked Donny what I should do. On his first leave I persuaded him to come and stay with me above the shop. He slept in his old bed although his feet projected at the bottom. 'Marry him again?' he said. We were walking in the park. 'Only you know the answer to that, Mum. He'll always be full of surprises.'

He only stayed three days. It was not the most comfortable time for either of us. Nor did it become easier. He met a girl in the North and found a new family where he took his leaves and weekends. He telephoned me and we wrote but I knew I had lost him forever.

With Zane, though, I could not help but expect something to go wrong. His smile was honest, his demeanour untroubled, his movements reliable, but one small fragment of me still did not trust him.

He arrived to pick me up one evening in a beautiful silver car, low and lovely, and I stood admiring it after locking the shop door. It even had a special number-plate, something with 'BEN' at the front. We went to the cinema in Southampton and when we came out people were gathered around the car, not attempting to touch it, merely looking. Men circled it and asked Zane questions about it; he boasted quietly that it was Italian and there was not another one like it in Britain. Women looked at the car, then at Zane and then at me with undisguised admiration. I could feel myself glowing. When we went back to the manor house that night, we buried ourselves in the deep bed and made love. Though I didn't know it then, it was for the last time.

He left early because it was raining and he faced a long drive to Inverness. I went to the shop and after an hour

Mr Pyecraft arrived and announced with his everyday enthusiasm that he had been very lucky, he had bought a bargain, a painting which was waiting to be picked up in Guildford. He asked me to go and fetch it.

It was about midday by the time I got there and found a place to park. The rain had stopped and I walked along the street towards the shop where the painting was waiting. I thought I would make myself known and then have some lunch before collecting it and returning to Southampton. It was then that I saw the car.

I looked twice and then again but there was no mistaking it. It was across the street, proudly parked, silver and beautiful and the only one in the country. My heart already falling (although even then I began assuring myself that there could be a dozen explanations), I crossed through the traffic and standing ten yards away saw the same number-plate.

Almost on tiptoe I approached. There was a movement in the back seat, a head outlined against the window. A small head. I went trembling along the pavement and, after glancing about once, looked into the back seat as I drew level. Kneeling there, playing with a toy aeroplane was a little boy, about three, with fair curly hair, a bright face and blue eyes. The image of my Donny.

I can still feel the awful shock that came over me in that busy street. People walked by unnoticing while I stood dumb, knowing all too well that what I saw, what I thought, was undoubtedly true.

Scarcely realising what I was about I stepped shakily towards the car window and tapped on it lightly. His assured little face came to the other side of the glass and he pressed his lips and impudent nose to it. I felt like opening the door and running away with him; running and running, anywhere. To my past, I suppose, but anywhere as long as it was out of the reach of Zane Tomkins. I waved an infant wave through the glass and he returned it gravely. Perhaps I was going mad; maybe this was an illusion, a throwback into our lives when Donny was a baby. The child had put his aeroplane on the seat behind him. Now he picked it up and demonstrated to me how it could fly and I imitated a plane with my hand, my smile nailed to my face.

Then he reached and pressed a button and the window slid down. With some instilled caution he moved it back up again and then opened it just enough for me to speak through the gap. Quickly and guiltily I looked behind and around. No one was noticing. 'Hello,' I croaked. 'What's your name?'

'I'm Zane,' he answered. He scrambled to a kneeling position and put his face confidently closer. 'My daddy's called Zane. Do you know my daddy?'

'Yes,' I somehow mumbled. 'I know him.'

At that moment his mother arrived. She was pretty in a fairly dumpy way, dark hair around a pleased face. Around her neck she had a gold chain just like mine. Hers said 'Marie'. I was close enough to read it before she spoke, putting down a white carrier bag and producing a set of keys. I pushed my name on the chain out of sight. 'Sorry,' I said having no trouble in looking embarrassed. 'I hope you don't mind. He's such a lovely little boy. We were having a chat.'

Her smile was meant to dismiss what she thought was the reason for my embarrassment. 'He'll talk to anyone,' she said. She assumed a guilty look. 'And I was only in the shop just behind. I'd forgotten something. Now I've got to wait for my husband.'

Hurriedly I said goodbye and gave a quick mini-wave to the small boy who was once more flying his aeroplane. Going down the hill because I thought it would be faster, I performed a swift about-turn when I saw Zane coming up the other way. Staring into a shop window I saw his reflection go past. My eyes turned to follow him, full of tears of anger and sorrow. How could he?

Easily. Zane Tomkins could lie his way into heaven.

33

On the morning before my first appearance at Winchester Crown Court, for my plea hearing, Mr Spelling, my solicitor, came into the cell. I was still so abject thinking about that day long ago in Guildford, that he mistook my mood. 'Don't look so bad, Chloe,' he said in his kind, stilted way. He sat down carefully. 'If you want to get it over you could plead guilty to manslaughter. They know the story. I'm sure that would be accepted.' He patted the back of my hand. I glanced down and noticed how old it looked.

'I don't want to plead guilty to anything, Mr Spelling,' I said wearily. 'I wouldn't kill anyone, least of all someone I loved so much.' I looked at him. 'It was because of loving him that I helped him on his way. He asked me to do it.' I felt my voice crack. 'I knew what I had to do.'

My solicitor sat there looking more helpless, if that were possible, than I felt. 'We'd been singing,' I remembered. 'We often used to sing after Lady Annabel went. Sometimes we'd sing two or three times a week, in the evenings before we played cards or sometimes after. I'd play the piano and we'd sing.'

I could see us, sitting at the concert grand, me thumping out a good tune or some old sentimental ballad, and both singing. Well, I sang and he tried although by that time he could hardly do anything. He would wheeze and choke and cough and then, in a sort of mad rush, almost a frenzy, shout the words, as though no mere song was going to defeat him. 'We sang all sorts,' I said. 'Music-hall songs and army songs. My father taught me them.'

I began to cry and he patted me. 'Don't,' he said. He seemed embarrassed and sad.

We were reduced to a silence broken by the door opening and a warder's face appearing. 'You have another visitor,' she said.

A fat, florid, middle-aged man was shown in, followed by an earnest-looking younger man carrying an armful of papers loosely tied with pink ribbon. Mr Spelling rose to welcome them. 'These are your barristers, Chloe,' he explained. 'Mr Fellows is your QC and Mr Franks will be assisting him.'

I stood and shook their hands. The younger barrister, dressed in a chalk-striped suit, stepped aside to give Mr Fellows room. He wore a dark courtroom sort of jacket and striped trousers; his white collar looked too tight for his neck and he had a grey tie. 'Had to have a quick lunch,' he said as if excusing himself. He looked as though he had eaten four lunches.

'I won't be able to pay you,' I said.

He put his hand over his mouth and pretended to be shocked. But then he and Mr Franks laughed pleasantly. I was entitled to legal aid.

Mr Fellows looked about the room apparently for a chair he thought would safely hold his weight. He picked one and tested it thoroughly before carefully sitting down. His barrister's trousers bulged over the sides.

He asked me kindly to tell them my story and I did so, as completely as I could. Sometimes, but not often, he asked a question and nodded his round head wisely when I replied. It took another hour. Mr Spelling and Mr Franks made notes. A prison officer came in with three cups of tea and I continued talking while I drank mine.

At the end of it Mr Fellows had his eyes closed as though I had sent him to sleep. Then he opened them, pale blue and intense. 'Miss Smith,' he said. 'How do you wish to plead to this charge of murder?'

I almost choked. 'Not guilty.'

'My advice,' he said after eyeing Mr Spelling, 'is to plead guilty to manslaughter. We can get a reduced sentence.'

I shook my head.

'Right. It's up to you to make the decision.' He weighed a wedge of papers in his hand and said: 'Mr Justice Jenkins.'

'Who is he?'

'The judge in your case.'

'Oh. Is he friendly?'

Mr Fellows looked thoughtful. 'I've seen him most unfriendly on occasions,' he said. 'But he'll be fair. As fair as he can be.'

He sorted the papers. For half an hour we went through the statement I had made to the police. After he had finished he said: 'Sir Benedict has left you fifty thousand pounds, you know.'

'I didn't,' I said. 'Will I be able to keep it?'

'It depends.'

Mr Fellows looked doubtfully at the solicitor who said: 'Yes, it does.'

He continued: 'There was a small annuity for the butler ... er, Mr Urchfont ... but the house was mortgaged twice over and the lease is all but finished.'

'How about Mr and Mrs Branche?' I asked.

'Ah, yes. Them. They got nothing as far as I can ascertain. They have returned to Africa.'

'Good.'

'You realise he *knew* he was dying several months before Lady Annabel had her fatal accident?'

'I didn't know at that time. It was later I knew. That was why he . . .'

'He what?'

'He made preparations for his death,' I stumbled.

'For Lady Annabel as well?' suggested Mr Fellows.

I said, not blinking: 'I wouldn't know.'

34

There had been plenty of time to think about the past (and there would be in the future, I suspected). My present situation was so grim, and what might happen after my trial probably worse, that I took refuge, poor though it was, in what had already gone. At least I knew what the past was like. My meagre consolation was that at least behind bars not a lot could happen to me, I would be safe from the dreads and realities of the outside.

When my solicitor and my counsel had gone away muttering as low as doctors and after each giving me an uncertain handshake and an unconvincing good-luck wish for the next day, I began to think again of the little boy who had looked so much like my Donny.

At a distance I had followed Zane up the hilly street and had watched sideways on among the Guildford shoppers, my breath held, tempted to run and shout a warning when Zane kissed the woman and the boy who had now climbed out of the car. Zane climbed into the flashy vehicle. For a moment I thought he had spotted me among the people but he was too busy posing behind the wheel and he drove away, and past me, with a flourish. The woman and the boy were left on the pavement, both waving until the car had vanished down the hill. They then went into a knitwear shop and remained there for half an hour. I thought it was a long time to keep a child occupied among balls of wool and, sitting in the coffee bar opposite, I wondered if they had gone out by another exit.

They eventually reappeared, however, and walked hand in hand up the hill to a bus-stop. I followed them on the opposite pavement, my heart full at just seeing them together like that. They were about halfway along the short queue and I waited until three or four other people had joined it before I went across the road and stood at the end, trying to keep my face away from her. The bus arrived; its destination board said 'Godalming'. The queue began to get aboard. I felt my breath tighten as I followed them.

As I got on the woman saw me and, after a double take, smiled pleasantly. The boy studied me quizzically as though he could not quite remember where we had met. Then he treated me to the familiar smile. I had always known it as Donny's smile; it was also his father's, but more sincere.

They rose to leave the bus just outside Godalming and I followed them. The woman turned, almost as though she had expected it, and said: 'Oh, it's your stop as well.'

We stood for a moment face to face, little Zane between us. 'Yes,' I said. 'I'd like to have a word with you, if you don't mind.'

'You'd better come in and have a cup of tea,' she said, strangely with no surprise or curiosity in her tone. The small boy said: 'I want an orange drink.'

'It's only along here,' she said. There was a sudden dullness in her attitude, her shoulders, even in her walk, as though she had been waiting for something like this. We were going towards a line of cottages. Almost without thinking I took the boy's other hand and we walked with him between us. 'It's nice here,' I said turning around at the countryside falling away on all sides.

'It gets windy in the winter,' she said looking straight ahead. 'It can be quite scary when my husband is away.' She put her free hand down to her wedding ring and turned it as if it were better displayed from that side.

'The bus is handy,' she went on. 'One way to Guildford and the other to Godalming. It runs every hour, right past the door. I used to work in a wool shop in Guildford. I still do some paperwork for them.' She swung the envelope that she had carried from the shop.

'I saw you,' I said.

It was almost as if it had been rehearsed, remembered, like a play we had both acted but at different times. We kept walking and she opened the garden gate which squeaked. 'It keeps doing that,' she said. 'He promised he'd fix it.'

'Yes,' I said. 'Mine used to do that ... my gate.'

She unlocked the front door. I could sense that he had been there; feel him, smell him almost. There was a coat I knew hanging on a hall stand. Behind it was a Chinese porcelain dish for which I had been searching in the shop. I would have recognised it anywhere. 'That's nice,' I said.

'It's pretty. I don't know where it came from. My husband knows people in the antique business.' Suddenly distraught she turned and said: 'I suppose you could be one of them.'

I could not help reaching out and touching her hand. The boy had gone into the front room and turned on the television. She went after him and I followed her. 'Go and watch upstairs please, Zane,' she said unhappily. 'This lady wants to tell me something.'

He went and shouted his way up the stairs. 'Noisy,' she

said. She looked at me straight. 'You know what they're like.'

'Yes.'

'Let's have a cup of tea, then we can have a chat.' She went to a cabinet and took out her best china. She arranged it on the table nervously. The cups rattled against the saucers. 'How long have you known Zane – my husband?' she asked bluntly.

I had not expected her to be so direct. 'A long time,' I said. 'Twenty years or so.'

The shock filled her face. 'But . . . how . . .'

'I was married to him once,' I told her. 'We had a little boy, Donny, just like your little boy.'

I thought she was going to faint. She fell back into the chair opposite me and stared as though I had brought news of a sudden death. 'You . . . you . . . were married? You and Zane?'

'Shall *I* get the tea?' I suggested.

She visibly made herself rally and rose from the chair. 'No, no, please. I know where everything is.' She almost staggered towards the kitchen. 'I'll put the kettle on. I'm going to need a cup of tea, I think.'

'Me too,' I said. 'And *I'm* used to him.'

We showed each other our gold chains engraved with our names. 'I thought you were his woman in Newcastle,' she muttered miserably. She looked up. 'He's got one, you know.'

'I didn't,' I said. 'But I'm not surprised.'

'I thought you'd come down to suss me out, see what I was like. You know what women are like.' She glanced up with embarrassment. 'Some women.'

We talked through two hours and three pots of tea. Her son came down at intervals to report something he had seen on television. He was so like Donny had been, not only his bright looks and fair hair but his mannerisms and the things he said. I told her almost everything. Her story was just as long. 'I met him when I was in Spain on holiday,' she said. 'He was at a beach bar laughing with some people. He looked wonderful. He had a book – *Gone with the Wind* – on the bar and we started talking about it.'

'How far had he got with it?' I asked. I felt odd because I was as upset as she was, and with every right, but I felt almost protective towards her, like someone senior listening and passing on experience to someone who was still learning the game. 'He hadn't got far with the book,' she went on, 'but he soon did with me. In no time I was pregnant, then married. He's hardly ever here. He kept going off to Spain, for weeks sometimes, and once he stopped that he started delivering cars.' Her face and her voice became reflective. 'Among other things.'

She was ten years younger than me. After the third pot of tea she opened a bottle of white wine. It seemed to revive her spirit. 'I know where she lives,' she confided. 'The one in Newcastle.'

I took it in over my tilted wine glass. 'We ought to go up there.'

'I know.' She gave a sly grin. 'I'd thought of it myself but I backed off. But if we *both* went . . .'

'We will. Do you know her name?'

'Sandra,' she said. 'She would be.'

She got up and went upstairs. I heard her talking to her son. He was going to his gran's house. He liked his gran, didn't he. 'She's not too bad,' I heard him say.

When she returned it was with a folded piece of paper. 'Sandra,' she read from it. 'Beyond Belief Fashions,

Gateshead.' When she looked up her eyes were glinting. 'Shall we go now? While the bugger is up there?'

'Yes. Let's catch him.'

I telephoned Mr Pyecraft and he gave me the rest of the week off. I said it was important. I would pick up his painting on the way back.

Marie could have been my sister. As we drove and talked it was as though we had known each other a long time before, but then were parted and were now catching up on all the family news. We both realised this. We stopped on the motorway and had a meal and spent so long about it that there was no chance of getting even halfway to Newcastle that night.

We talked of my son and her son and, of course, Zane. He took up some of the conversation but, as if we were both tired of discussing him, by no means all of it. She told me where she was born and what she had done and I told her my story. When we seemed to have exhausted our reminiscences we both became silent in the M1 service café, our chips gone cold on the plates. 'At least,' she said at last with a sign, 'he's given us plenty to talk about.'

'We've both had a life of excitement.' I sighed also. 'Never a dull bloody moment.'

That night we shared a room in a small hotel outside Coventry. Neither of us felt self-conscious as we climbed into our beds. Two salesmen had tried to pick us up in the bar and we giggled like girls in the dark discussing them. Eventually she said: 'Good-night, Chloe. I'm glad we met.'

'Good-night, Marie.' I smiled. 'I am too. We'll nail that Zane.'

'That Zane,' she mumbled. She went to sleep quickly,

breathing deeply in the next bed. I lay awake thinking and wondered if she were dreaming about him.

Marie knew about Sandra, the other woman (or the other-other woman), because of a chance discovery. One day Zane had left a car outside Marie's house and she had gone to the glove compartment where she thought she had left a pair of sunglasses. And there was a card with 'Beyond Belief Fashions' printed in curly letters with 'Gateshead Today, Tomorrow the World' and an address. 'Sandra' was written on the reverse in rounded letters in blue biro, with a telephone number.

'I was ashamed about being so nosey,' Marie said. 'After all, it could have been quite innocent. He might have gone there to buy me something.'

'It's a nice thought,' I said. 'But unlikely.'

'But it kept nagging me. I have a cousin, Barbara, who lives up near Newcastle and I gave her a call and she said she would check the place out. When she rang me back she was all excited, she'd done a real detective job. She went into the shop and found Sandra right away. It was no trouble because she was standing there looking a bit vacant, Barbara said, and with a *gold chain around her neck with her name on it.* Just like ours.'

She touched hers and I said: 'He must have got a job lot.'

As we continued our drive north the next day we talked over what we should do. 'I'm going right in there and ask her what it's all about,' said Marie. 'After all, *I'm* his wife.'

It made me feel oddly miserable to hear her say that. 'That's true,' I said.

We reached Newcastle at three in the afternoon and followed the signs to Gateshead. Beyond Belief Fashions was in the huge shopping mall there. We wandered around looking for the window. Then Marie nudged me. 'There she is.'

Sandra was standing outside the door of the boutique as if she had emerged for some fresh air although the whole enormous place was under one roof. 'Hide your chain,' I warned as I hid mine. The thin gold around the other woman's narrow neck was caught by the interior lights. With a dull certainty I saw that she was younger than either of us. She was commonly pretty with cold blonde hair and a chalky face made more so by crimson lipstick. She wore earrings which neither Marie nor I would have worn. I sensed the tension in Marie. I felt like a spectator, no longer part of the game.

'Hello,' said Sandra when she saw us advancing. She half-turned and ushered us into the shop. 'What can I do to help you?' She had the Geordie accent and she sounded tired.

'I need something special,' said Marie. She could act. I swear she was enjoying it.

'We only *have* special things,' said Sandra looking her up and down. 'What's it for?'

'A divorce,' said Marie.

The girl's pencilled eyebrows went up. We were standing in front of her now surrounded by clothes on racks. An older woman was attending to a fussy customer at the till. Marie leaned forward and tapped Sandra's chain. 'I've got one just like that,' she said showing it.

'So have I,' I said revealing mine.

'Mine says "Marie",' said my companion.

Sandra was staring at me. 'And yours says "Chloe",' she read with a mutter. You could tell that, like all Zane's women, she had always suspected something was wrong.

'Mrs Dampier,' she called. 'Why don't you go to tea now.'

The woman at the till, now free of the difficult customer, said: 'But I've already been.'

'Go again,' said Sandra. It was almost a snarl. I was beginning to like her too. We were going to get on well.

Mrs Dampier went out looking over her shoulder. Sandra confronted us, her face full, her eyes suddenly wet. 'From Zane?' she asked with two nods at the chains. 'You guessed,' said Marie not unkindly. 'I'm his wife.'

Sandra looked downwards. 'But ... you've got two legs,' she said. She looked up, her eyes aghast.

'Always have had,' said Marie. She waved her hand in my direction. 'And this is Chloe ... Tomkins.'

Shocked, Sandra said: 'You ... you're not his wife as well?'

'Very nearly for the *second* time,' I said.

'I think we had better sit down,' said Sandra practically. A middle-aged woman was coming in the door. The girl leaped up and pushed her out again, locking the door. 'Shut!' she almost bawled. 'Stocktaking.'

In a way it was.

'I was married to Zane once,' I said. We were sitting in a half-circle on three chairs like a sort of mothers' meeting. 'We have a son, Donny.'

'He's proposed,' she said defeatedly. 'We're supposed to be getting married when his divorce is ...' She turned frankly to Marie. 'He said you only had one leg and it made you bad-tempered and bitchy.'

'It's not the leg,' said Marie. 'It's him.'

Sandra looked so deflated that I had to feel sorry for her. I could see that Marie did too. 'We've got a little boy,' Marie said quite quickly, as if to get it out of the way. 'We're still married. It's the first I've heard about our divorce. He must have been keeping it as a surprise.'

'But ...' Sandra was trying to find words. 'But he *proposed*.'

'To me too,' I said as though it might be some comfort. 'A second time.'

'He does it a lot,' grunted Marie.

We became silent, hushed, crushed, sitting in our half-hoop of chairs. Two more expectant female faces appeared at the door but Sandra, with a testy fling of her hand, dismissed them. 'Piss off,' she sniffed. She was hunched forward but then she straightened. 'He's coming here,' she told us. 'Tonight. To pick me up.' We all looked at our watches. Mrs Dampier, the other woman from the shop, was pushing unavailingly at the door. Sandra ignored her.

'We've got to confront him,' I said.

'Stuff him more like it,' said Sandra. Her anger was overtaking her distress. She snivelled. 'He's too old for me anyway.'

Mrs Dampier was now telling a wandering security man that she was locked out of the shop.

'Silly old fart,' growled Sandra as she made for the door. She opened it with ill grace.

'Stuck,' she said to the security man.

Mrs Dampier took in the scene. Sandra swung round on her. 'This is Zane's wife,' she said pointing to Marie. And then to me. 'And this is his ex-wife who he's just proposed to again.'

'Oh,' said Mrs Dampier struggling. 'He *has* been busy.'

'Will you make us some tea, Mrs Dampier, and then you can clear off for the day.'

'He's coming to pick you up, isn't he,' said Mrs Dampier expectantly. She went into a curtained alcove and busied herself with the cups. 'He always looked to have too much experience, Sandra,' she called through the muslin.

'Shut up,' suggested Sandra but so the other woman did not hear. She brought the tea out on a tray. 'What are we going to do?' Sandra said.

'I think,' I said, 'that *you* ought to wear all three gold chains and make sure he notices. And we'll hide and jump out on him.'

'And all kick him in the fruit bowl,' said Sandra.

We drank the tea together. Now all three of us had become sisters, which in a way I suppose we were. Sandra told us how Zane had come into the shop the first time. 'He was lovely,' she said. 'The bastard.' Marie and I told our stories. Marie described how he would dutifully wait in a car outside the wool shop in Guildford where she worked. I told them how he had tried to burgle the antique business. Sandra began snivelling again. 'We're all in retail,' she said.

Mrs Dampier was sent home for the day but she did not go. There was a wine shop with a pyramid of bottles in the window across the way and I saw her slide in there.

At five to five we gave Sandra our gold chains and she put all three around her neck. 'How many more are there like these?' she wondered. She gestured to two of the three changing cubicles and Marie and I went in, drawing the curtains behind us. I sat on the tight chair suddenly trembling. I tapped on the partition. 'Are you all right, Marie?'

'Shaking,' she said. 'He'll see the curtain shaking.'

We did not have to wait long. The outer door was opened and his voice laughed across the premises. You could hear him walk to her. 'Darl,' he breathed. 'Darl, darl . . .' There was a pause. 'Where's the old girl?' My knuckles were grinding into each other. Small squeaking sounds came from Marie's hiding place and I feared he might hear. Commendably calm, Sandra said to Zane: 'I've sent her off early.'

I could just imagine him them. Folding his handsome arms about her. 'We could do it in here,' he said seriously. 'I've always wanted to make love in a . . .'

His voice trailed off. That was the moment. 'What's this?' he said instead.

'This?' repeated Sandra. 'It's the chain you gave me, remember, darling. With "Sandra" on it . . . And these . . .' I crouched hardly breathing. 'And these . . . Chloe and Marie . . . they're two new friends of mine.' You had to admire her. She kept her voice sweet and steady as an actress. 'They came in to see me today.'

'They . . .' was all he could manage.

'Surely you *must* know them. You married them both . . . Marie you're still married to.'

She was not afraid. I swear she was enjoying it. We heard her move towards the changing cubicles. 'Presenting . . .' she announced as she threw both curtains open, 'Chloe and Marie . . . the Tomkins girls!'

You have never seen a man's face like it. When we stepped out he stood transfixed, the blood rising in his neck, his eyes bulging. He looked *ugly*. 'You . . . you bloody . . .' he stammered.

With a splendid whoop Sandra advanced on him, putting her arms about him and bringing her thin knee up enthusiastically into the region with which we were all so familiar. He let out an amazingly boylike howl, clutching himself and stumbling back towards the door. Marie burst into anger, advanced on him and kicked him on the shin. He howled again and managed to open the

315

door. As he was facing away from the shop I put my hands on his back and pushed him the rest of the way. Sandra then locked the door and we stood behind the glass laughing and pointing at him out there, bent like a gnome, his face screwed up. We laughed and shouted and taunted him through the glass. Shoppers gathered. Bottles fell over in the window of the wine shop revealing Mrs Dampier.

Zane, with what appeared to be a huge manly effort, straightened himself and with a weak wave of his fist stumbled away. He shouted something like: 'I'll get you for this!'

Laughing and slapping each other on the back we went back to our three seats. People were now peering through the glass at us. Sandra said she had a bottle of wine and she opened it. We sat in a row, the glasses held before us. Sandra raised hers. 'A toast to Zane,' she said caustically. 'Zane,' we echoed. Then we all began to cry. Marie set me off and Sandra howled louder than either of us. Mrs Dampier and a dozen other spectators, hands shading their eyes, were ogling in the window. We sobbed and wept and held onto each other.

'My dad will kill him,' moaned Sandra.

Marie howled: 'It's time somebody did.'

35

After the wooden cosiness of the magistrates' court, going before the judge at Winchester Crown Court was a bigger ordeal than I had imagined. Mr Fellows had assured me that it was not much different to going into a quiet and formal office, a bit bigger, that's all, but then he was used to it.

The magistrates' court in the old Salisbury Guildhall had been the most comfortable place I had known for months. I had even got used to the spectators. You could smell the polish on the wood when you went in there and it was warm and people talked in everyday voices and smiled, even at me. Mr Victor, the court official, had said that it was often used for film and television scenes. 'That dock where you were standing today,' he had told me. 'Elizabeth Hurley stood there.'

In the remand wing in prison they paid you a certain deference when you were going up for trial on a murder charge. New women who came in had me pointed out to them and I was treated like somebody senior. As I got to know the staff, from the warders right up to the governor, who came to see me the day before I went to Winchester for my plea hearing, they offered me trifling pieces of advice. Not to blink too often, not to smile even if anything funny occurred (although I could not see for the life of me how this would happen) and the governor advised me not to wear too much make-up. 'It gives a bad impression,' she said kindly.

They made a special breakfast for me at six o'clock: bacon, eggs, beans, sausages, as much as I wanted which was not much. 'They used to give this sort of feed to women before they was hanged in the old days,' the woman who served it said morosely.

On the ride to the Crown Court I crouched and stared through the orange glass of the concealing window at the outer moving world until my body ached. The escorting security woman did nothing to stop me and indeed when I eventually sat facing into the vehicle she said: 'Not a lot to see, is there?'

Well, I thought there was quite a lot. It was all right for her; like Elizabeth Hurley, she would be going home that night. This, for me, might be one of my last views outside a tall wall for a long time. It was June and it was rainy and the colour of the trees and walls and fields were all like fresh paint; people hurrying under coloured umbrellas looked as if they might be going to a carnival. I saw a group of boys, swimming towels rolled under their arms, laughing outside a school and some girls catcalling at them. Everybody had somewhere they could go, someone they could go to, a person to gossip with about the day's ordinary things, about neighbours and work, late buses, the rain and what they had for lunch. For me this was to be one of the most important days of my life. My name and my picture would be in the newspapers, I might even be on television; thousands would know about me and what I had done but I would be all alone with no comfort.

I bent against the window again and watched the scenes go by. It was like going on a childhood coach trip to the seaside, but now silently and by yourself. In those days I enjoyed the journey there as much as the waves and the sands, trying to imagine who lived at the farms and who had built the haystacks while most of the others chattered or sang and played pranks. In the van now I tried to involve my travelling companion in what I was observing but it was all everyday stuff to her. Even when we drove slowly past a mishap, a car nosed into a tree, she did not accept my suggestion that she should look at it. Instead she said: 'My daughter's taking her driving test tomorrow.'

Eventually we were going downhill and the outside was grey with buildings so I knew we were almost there. 'It's quite new, Winchester Crown Court,' said the woman, as if they had just built it especially for me. 'Well, not very old anyway. I remember the Queen coming down to open it. It's very nice. For a court.'

When we drove into the special enclosed yard she said: 'You're going in the back door. It's more private.' And then, without meaning to hurt: 'They've had some famous murderers going in this way.'

Inside there were a lot of people. 'You're down for Court Number One,' my escort said. 'That shows they reckon it's an important case.'

I was glad when she went and I was left with a matronly lady and a harassed and embarrassed-looking policeman. The woman produced some decent cups and saucers and poured me tea from a pot shaped like a chicken. 'I had to bring this from home this morning,' she chatted. 'It's my spare. Somebody threw our teapot at the wall.' She pointed to the place where the stain and the dent in the plaster were visible. 'Blenkinsop,' said the policeman apparently glad to contribute. 'The master forger. Got six years.'

My solicitor, Mr Spelling, came in. He was wearing a new suit. Mr Fellows looked even fatter and pinker under his wig. 'Given it any more thought, Chloe?' he asked.

'About what?' I said.

'Your plea.'

'I'm not pleading guilty.'

'Right.' His intense blue eyes turned on Mr Spelling. 'If that's your final word then we must find some other way around this problem.'

An usher came in. 'Mr Fellows,' he said deferentially, 'your case is number one in Number One. You can go in now, sir.'

Mr Fellows gave me a tubby smile and Mr Spelling shook my hand less optimistically. They told me to wait. 'You've got time to finish your tea, love,' said the matronly lady. We sat silently until the policeman said: 'Brilliant, he was.'

'Who?' I asked.

'Blenkinsop, the forger. Brilliant.'

'He won't be if I get my hands on him,' said the tea lady wringing her cloth symbolically. 'Smashing a teapot like that. Nasty temper.'

That day in the Number One Court it all seemed to be going on around me but, strangely, I was apart from it. It was like being on an island in the middle of a busy whirlpool. They talked about Chloe Smith all the time but no one seemed to be taking any notice of me at all. I might as well have been a ghost. It was as if I was watching a drama concerning somebody else, someone remote, someone I did not even know, I had never heard mentioned until then. But it was me in the dock.

When I was first taken in there the Press, jammed together on two benches, one behind the other, all took a good look at me. The journalists scribbled down their descriptions, looking up in snatches like artists sketching, and then scribbling again. Once the judge arrived, however, and everyone had stood up and sat down again, they seemed to lose interest in me and I was left solitary in my place.

The dock was to the rear of the court and when I was told to sit down I felt like a dog in a box with its head just poking above the rim. I asked one of the court officials where the public gallery was and he pointed above my head to where it jutted out over the court. I could not see who was in it and they could not see me but the officer said: 'You've got a good crowd in.'

After the enclosed wooden courtroom at Salisbury this place looked enormously new. Its walls were smooth and dark as chocolate, and the windows were far too high to see anything but sky. Now and again a pigeon would flap across the panes and I found myself waiting for the next one, pretending that it would bring a message reprieving me. The judge, in his red robes and silvery wig, sat loftily, as if he were on a slightly unsafe shelf. Above him was a gold coat of arms, hanging like a massive angel, and below were the clerks, the solicitors and the four counsel – the prosecution QC and accompanying barrister, and Mr Fellows and Mr Franks. I had been glad and impressed that my leading barrister, Mr Fellows, was a Queen's Counsel. Now I realised the other side had one too.

While they ignored me, they were all talking about me and what they thought I had done. When I had to stand to say how I pleaded everyone turned and looked a bit surprised to see that I was still there. The charge was read out by the woman clerk. She had a young, piping voice that sounded unreal. At the end of the rigmarole the judge, peering out from below his grey curls, located me.

'Do you understand the charge?' asked the clerk.

'Yes, I do.'

'How do you plead? Guilty or not guilty?'

'Not guilty.'

There was a murmur all around. The reporters wrote briefly but feverishly.

That was all they did that day; the court had been assembled just to hear me plead not guilty. It would be a few weeks more before my trial actually began.

'You may sit down.'

I did. Gratefully.

36

The story so many people were eventually to hear and read about was continued when we returned to the house in the close at Salisbury after Lady Annabel's death. Sir Benedict seemed immediately to begin fading. It was almost as if he missed her. He rallied in December for the inquest at Dorchester, which he said he enjoyed, but a sombreness came over him that never fully went away again.

At the inquest he lied with contained bravado, so convincingly that even I began to wonder if I had been mistaken that night, six weeks before on the Dorset cliff top. Perhaps they were *not* struggling, perhaps she *had* jumped. Perhaps he was even trying to stop her. I was able to give evidence of what I had seen, how I had tripped and fallen and how Lady Annabel was gone when I next looked up, all of which was the truth. Urchfont eyed me unblinkingly during the time I was being questioned, as did Mr and Mrs Branche, sitting and seething. Lady Annabel's body was not washed up for months and by then not a great deal of her was left, although oddly enough her false teeth were still in position and it was by these and her wedding ring that she was finally identified. There was no sign of her knuckledusters.

On the way home from the coroner's court Sir

Benedict went to sleep in the car, a troubled sleep which went on troubling him for the remainder of his life. We called his doctor, Dr Hesketh, who had known him for twenty years, and he came into the kitchen and told Urchfont and me that he did not expect Sir Benedict to be with us by the spring. He said he had told Sir Benedict three months before that he had cancer and what his approximate life expectancy was. The doctor hesitated before telling us the next thing although we doubted if he knew, or suspected, as much as we did. 'Time enough,' the old man had said to him then, 'to do what I have to do.'

'He did too,' said Urchfont lugubriously when the doctor had gone. 'And that's why he did it, then, shoved her off the cliff. While he was strong enough. While he still *could*.'

'You must never say that,' I said. 'Never again. Not even to me.'

'I won't,' he said. 'I don't want to think about it.'

It would have been better if he had died sooner, more peacefully, and certainly more naturally. I would not have been standing in the Winchester dock for a start. But he battled on, rallying some days, even talking of going out on the tandem which he had forgotten was locked up in the refreshment kiosk, now facing the waves of winter. There were other times when he was in pain and some when he was in agony and suffering from all the indignities that elderly illness apparently reserves for those who are most proud. 'If I shit myself once more I'll go mad,' I heard him moan.

After some persuasion he agreed to a nurse coming in every morning. She would rescue and restore him from the night's embarrassments and discomforts and together we would get him to his chair in his room, half-looking out into the bleak garden. *The Times* and the activities of birds and squirrels occupied him until lunch. He left most of his food although he always finished three glasses of wine, and then went to sleep until the early evening news came on the television.

'But I've seen all this before,' he would grumble waving his hand at the screen. 'Are you sure it's not a repeat? It's the same people fighting and talking. How can it be *news* if it's all the same.'

Even when he was deep in his pain he was never anything but sweet with me and he was always kindly civil to Urchfont. I used to cut his toenails and his fingernails and trim his fine hair. But he would get into terrible rages with himself and his inabilities. One night I heard him fling the bedpan across his room.

He had a bell by his side and he could have called me if he had chosen but he rarely rang it. He struggled through the dark hours as though it was a task only for him. I would help him into bed, give him his late drink of cocoa and Demerara and leave him. Before I went to bed I would listen at his door. At times he would be silent but at others he would groan and curse. If I opened the door, no matter how softly, he would pretend to be snoring.

One night I had been to the cinema (as though I did not have enough drama) and, having put my ear to his door, I went to bed. As I often did, I lay sleepless, wondering and worrying, the pale green hands on my clock turning to half past one. Then I heard him cry out and I jumped up. Urchfont was outside his door when I reached the landing and we both went in together.

Sir Benedict was half in and half out of bed, clinging like a frail mountaineer. 'Help me,' he pleaded. 'Help me. I'm falling.'

We lifted him back into the bed and sorted him out. 'I dreamed I was falling after Lucy and Annabel,' he explained in a shamefaced way, his cheeks red and damp, his eye whirling as it did when he was upset. 'Down, down into the sea.' He was touchingly grateful to us for rescuing him. Urchfont went back to bed and I stayed sitting beside Sir Benedict until he went to sleep again. He began to groan and draw his breath in painful gasps. I did not want to leave him but my head was dropping. I stood up beside the bed and then made the decision. Going to the door and locking it, I returned and climbed into the other side of the bed with him, taking off my dressing-gown as I did so.

There I lay in the dark and he seemed to know because he began to breathe more easily. I found his skeletal hand under the sheet and held it. He stirred. 'Is that you, Lucy?' he almost whimpered. 'You're back at last. I hope that side of the bed is dry.'

I am not a person who would ever think of killing someone. But as his illness and the days went on I came to feel that I would do anything to help him to die. The doctor kept prescribing pills that gave him only a little respite. For ten days he went into hospital but he made such a fuss in there that they more or less expelled him, just like a difficult boy thrown out of school. They had other patients to think about, they said, and anyway there was nothing they could do for him.

Once back home he became more peaceful, happier. 'Couldn't stand all those invalids around me, Chloe,' he said.

I talked to him, sitting by his chair or by his bedside until he was tired. I learned more about him, and he about me I imagine, in those few weeks than we had ever known before. He was most pleased when he could make me laugh, telling me some adventure from his youth. He told me once that he and some other young men had removed a civic statue from its plinth in some country town. It was snowing and after they had carried it off they raked the snow over and impressed a single set of footprints going away from the plinth towards the river bank where they abruptly stopped. They then rolled the statue into the shallows at that point. 'It was all in the newspapers,' he giggled. 'The Statue that Walked, they called it.' He laughed and spluttered and ended with real tears dripping down his cheeks. 'The trouble with life, Chloe,' he said, 'is that as soon as you get the hang of it, it's too late.'

Sometimes in the evenings he would ask me to play the piano in the room below his bedroom. Urchfont and I manhandled it to the best position and I would play as loudly as I could and sing at the top of my voice so that he could hear. To my amazement, Urchfont announced that he had once been slightly known as a singer and what is more, knew all the words to 'The Road to Mandalay' and 'Boots, Boots, Boots, Marching Up and Down Again'. He had the reedy remnants of a tenor and we sang duets from *The Maid of the Mountains* and *Rose Marie* and other half-forgotten, half-remembered things. When we had finished one song we would wait, ourselves now listening to hear the feeble applause from upstairs.

On the afternoon of the day in question, as they kept saying in court, Sir Benedict had been in great pain. The doctor came but was helpless, and looked it. He came out of the room and stood wringing his hands on the landing. He looked just as ill as his patient. 'There are times, Chloe,' he said, 'when there is little of what they call job satisfaction.'

By evening, however, the old man seemed to have rallied. I played some tunes on the piano and I thought he had gone to sleep because everything was silent above the ceiling. I was just about to get up from the stool and go to him when to my astonishment he appeared at the doorway. He was like a spectre, skin white and creased, emaciated, nose running, holding himself up on the wall. Only his good eye was moving (the other, curiously, seemed to have progressively dimmed and died as the weeks of his sickness went on). 'Let's . . . have a singsong, Chloe,' he said.

He was in his pyjamas. Carefully I sat him on a chair close by the piano and went up to get his dressing-gown. When I returned he was leaning his head against the piano and making small noises. Tenderly I put his dressing-gown around his shoulders and we began to sing, or tried to.

He could barely manage but he was gallant as ever, propping himself on his stiffened hands, his skinny, tall body arched; bawling, howling, wheezing out the approximate words and something like the tune. My face running with tears I sang with him.

The songs were the same as we had always sung. He hung onto the side of the piano and in his cracked and ghostly voice did his best. I thumped on the notes and sang and sobbed at the same time. He did not seem to notice I was crying, only that I was singing. He tapped out the tune with a wasted hand. Then Urchfont appeared in the doorway. As he took in the scene I saw his face break up. Sir Benedict had not seen him. I rolled my tearful eyes at him indicating that he should leave us. He looked grateful and turned and went out.

At the end of every song, or the end of the bit we could manage, we had to rest. The old man leaned against the piano and I sat drained. Eventually he asked if I would get him a glass of whisky. I went into the other part of the room and poured a Black Label. 'A large one, Chloe,' he called in his quivering voice. 'And have one yourself.'

I poured two big glasses. They said that the fact that we had been drinking together could have been part of my defence but I would not allow it. We drank and then he said: 'I want that song. The one we both like.'

The Stylistics will never know what they did when they sang: 'You Make Me Feel Brand New'. We sang as best we could, with me conducting and playing at the same time, because he always liked to get the 'la, la . . . la, la, la' right. We did not know many of the words, so we repeated the ones we did again and again. Then we suddenly, finally as it happened, stopped. 'Very good,' he breathed eventually. 'I think we're singing better.' He attempted to rise. He could not do it and he said: 'Chloe, I would like you to help me to the settee over there.'

It was heartbreaking to get him only a few yards. His body seemed to be falling to pieces. I held him up but his legs went different ways and, if I had not known how greatly it would have offended him, I would have picked up the poor, shattered man and carried him in my arms.

Once I had stretched him on the settee a resigned sort of sigh came from him. 'This is it,' he said in a private way. 'This is where it will be.'

I stood helplessly. Urchfont had fled to the cinema although he had already seen the film once that week. Sir Benedict lay with closed eyes. Then he opened his good one and asked quite strongly and lucidly for another whisky. I went and poured it for him wondering if he would be able, if he would be alive, to drink it when I went back. I put it to his lips but his fingers came up, suddenly and temporarily strong, and took the glass. 'You have another, Chloe,' he said. 'You may need it.'

I knew I would. I poured myself half his measure and sat by him on the sofa holding his hand, as suddenly weak as it had been powerful minutes before. His eyes were only half-open; I was not sure if he was seeing me or not. Then he embraced me – the only time he ever did so – and, sobbing quietly, I returned the embrace. A thought visibly came to him as we parted and his grip tightened a little. 'I want you to have our tandem, Chloe,' he said. And almost in the same summoned breath: 'I hope *both* of them aren't waiting for me. Lucy, yes, I'd love to see Lucy again after all these years. But I don't want that Annabel there. Not her.'

It was no use lying to him, telling him that he was not dying. He was seized with a fit of coughing and trembling. I tried to hold onto him to stop him shaking. Eventually he did and when he had calmed he said in the same voice with which he had asked me to get him a whisky: 'Chloe, be a good girl and bring that cushion over here, will you. The blue one.'

I picked up the cushion and returned to the sofa. I stood with it, thinking that he wanted more support behind his head. As I moved towards placing it there, he tapped me with his finger and said: 'At the front of the head, please. Over my face.'

As I stood horrified stiffly clutching the cushion, he was suddenly creased with another spasm of pain. 'Please, please,' he said. His eye closed. 'Do it now, Chloe.'

It was as if I had gone into a trance. My hands moved the cushion forward and I placed it lightly on his face. 'Let's sing, Chloe,' he pleaded. 'That song we know.'

'Yes,' I whispered. 'Yes, let's sing it.'

'You must press the cushion,' he said. 'When I stop singing you'll know I've gone.'

The words and the tune staggered out. I was shaking and weeping and trying to sing through it. He gathered everything he had and we sang together.

'You . . . you make me feel brand new . . .
La, la . . . la, la, la . . .'

I pressed down on the cushion and his face, softly at first because I did not want to hurt him. Now I had stopped shaking and, although I still cried, I felt strangely strong. I could feel his gasping as he still tried to sing.

'You . . . you make me feel brand new . . .
La . . . la . . .'

He stopped and became still. Fearfully I took the cushion away. His eye opened. 'I'm not gone yet,' he murmured. 'Do it again, my dear.'

I did it again, pressed and pressed on his dear face, singing all the time, singing at the top of my voice. Then he *was* still, peace all over him. I took the blue cushion away and saw that I had done what he wanted. I cried like a little girl, my tears splashing on his old face as I kissed it for the last time.

37

It seemed a long time to wait before the first day of my trial. I wondered what everyone could be doing. All I wanted now was to get it over with, to get on with my life whatever it was to be.

Once more I occupied the dock, almost incidental it seemed to the action and activity, aside from what was going on around me like a solitary passenger waiting for a train on a station where everyone else was busy and preoccupied.

The jury was sworn in, a dozen men and women who looked as if they had been brought in at random from the street which, in a way, I suppose they had. After they had taken the oath they sat down and almost as one body they looked towards me in a slightly embarrassed way. But they settled quickly because, I imagine, they had seen juries on television and more or less knew what they were supposed to do. As time, and my trial, went on they stretched and scratched and a woman in horned glasses began to draw on a pad. She studied me closely but briefly at intervals and then returned to her sketch. Most of the others leaned back and several closed their eyes as though it were a chance to catch up on lost sleep. Nobody seemed to appreciate what a mess I was in.

Most of the people wearing wigs, including the judge, seemed to be writing. The judge put something in an envelope and handed it down to the clerk who took it from the room. This happened several times and I had the horrified thought that he might be writing letters or (since below his disguise he looked like a smallish, ordinary man) even doing his football pools.

The reporters whispered and sometimes smirked like members of an occasional club. There were two women, one very dark and pretty who regarded me with a sad face. I remembered when I was young like her.

When I was sitting only my hair and my forehead projected over the edge of the high-sided dock. I had to strain my neck to see the leading prosecution counsel, Mr Sankey QC, rise to open the case against me. He kept rising, it seemed, a long man with a long, thin voice. In my mind he became Mr Snakey.

'This, members of the jury,' he began, 'is a very tragic and, in its many aspects, mysterious story.' A court official leaned over the dock and offered to raise the seat so that I could see better. I declined and settled back, almost hidden, while the reedy voice continued.

'It is a sequence of events,' he said, 'which goes back more than forty years, culminating on the night of March 28th this year when, the prosecution say, Sir Benedict Bowling, a gentleman of eighty-five who lived in the close of Salisbury Cathedral, was murdered by the accused Chloe Smith.'

It was such a small, savage shock to hear it put like that. It made me feel hollow, a sharp, slight, icy draught blowing through me. Without stretching my neck very much I could see the reporters were busily scribbling, glancing at each other's notebooks in case they had missed something. The jurors were paying attention; the woman had stopped sketching and one older man had his mouth hanging open in some sort of astonishment.

I cannot remember how long it was, it seemed an age, until Mr Sankey came to a halt and said he would call his first witness. For a moment I wondered who it could be. That night there had only been the two of us in the room. The court official was standing near and I asked him if he would raise the seat of the dock after all. It took only a minute. Now I could see.

When the policeman went into the witness-box I again had difficulty in recognising him as the one who had arrived in the room that night. Then he had come on a motorcycle and was swathed and helmeted like some outlandish warrior. When he had lifted his helmet his face had been red with sweat and consternation.

Now he looked pink, almost boy-like, standing blinking in the light, licking his lips and glancing around nervously as if it were him, not me, in dire trouble. His uniform was pressed to sharp edges and the silver bits twinkled. His hair was sparse and dark, combed in streaks across his forehead so that it might easily have been worried wrinkles. He gave his name.

Sankey rose in his slow, long way and said in his reasonable voice: 'Constable, would you tell the court what happened when you arrived at the Canon's House, Salisbury, on the night of March 28th this year.'

The policeman opened his notebook. 'A call was received at eleven thirty-three and I proceeded to the address given. A Mr Urchfont came to the door and showed me into a room where a lady was sitting drinking tea and a gentleman was lying on the settee with his eyes closed. I ascertained he was Sir Benedict Bowling and I came to the conclusion that he was dead.'

'You tried his pulse?'

'Yes, sir. There wasn't any.'

'Do you see the lady in this court?'

334

He nodded towards me like a greeting and said: 'That lady, sir.'

'What did she say to you?'

Confusion immediately fell over the young man. He creased his eyes trying to read his notebook. 'She said: "Look what I have done." ' His face became more puckered. I could see he really did have deep lines across his brow. 'Or words to that effect.'

My counsel, Mr Fellows, sat suddenly upright. Mr Sankey blinked but recovered. His expression had hardened when he continued with his questions. The constable knew he was in trouble.

'Let us move on to what you saw in the room when you arrived.'

'Yes, sir,' said the policeman. He waited and Mr Sankey nodded at him brusquely.

'Who was present?'

The policeman now spoke with exaggerated slowness. 'There was this lady, Miss Chloe Smith.' He indicated me. 'And Mr Urchfont, the butler I understand. And Sir Benedict Bowling, although he was apparently dead.'

'Well done,' said Mr Sankey unpleasantly. 'And did you see a cushion, officer?'

'Yes, sir. It was under the old gentleman's head.'

'Is this the cushion?' From a plastic bag he produced a pink cushion and held it up. I was astonished.

'No, sir.'

I thought Sankey was going to fall down. 'No? Did you say "No"?'

'Yes, sir. No.'

Mr Sankey stared at the cushion in front of his face. 'This cushion . . . is not the cushion?'

'No, sir. That's a pink cushion. It was a blue cushion that was used to . . . er . . . that I saw and I was told was used . . .' He was on the verge of panic. '. . . in the case,' he finished helplessly.

The judge, who had been hanging over his bench apparently unable to believe what was going on, said: 'How, may I ask, did a blue cushion become pink?'

I was conscious of a movement at the side of my dock. It was Detective Sergeant Ron Brown. 'I think I can explain it, my Lord,' he said looking up to the small puzzled face under the wig and the golden coat of arms.

'Ah, good,' said the judge. 'Then please do so. I'm sure we will all be glad to hear it.'

'Yes, my Lord. The cushion which was a prosecution exhibit in this case was in its proper cupboard in the police station until the day before yesterday. Unfortunately, there was a clear-out of unwanted objects and it was . . . disposed of.'

Both QCs were sitting still and listening with obvious disbelief. 'Disposed of?' asked the judge. Ron Brown remained calm, it seemed, with difficulty. 'Given away, my Lord. They were giving away odds and ends for a charity jumble sale and somehow the wrong cushion was sent. The pink cushion should have been donated. Not the blue one. I can only offer my apologies to the court.'

'I think,' said the judge sharply, 'you had better get the blue cushion back.'

'Of course, my Lord. We have officers out now, searching for it.'

Mr Fellows rose fatly and turned to the young constable in the witness-box. The policeman's face coloured further as if he guessed what was coming.

' "Or words to that effect," ' began my counsel. 'When you were asked what the accused said to you on that night, officer, you told the jury: "Look what I have done – or words to that effect." '

'Yes, sir.' It was almost a mumble. I leaned forward in the dock. I did not understand what was taking place.

'What does that mean? Don't you have a proper note in your notebook?'

The policeman looked around like someone hoping to make a sharp getaway. 'I did, sir. But I haven't now.'

'Why not?'

'It's been . . . blotted.'

'But how? How did these important details come to be blotted from your notebook?'

At first there was no answer but then he said: 'Soup, sir.'

'Ah,' said my Mr Fellows as if that explained everything perfectly. 'Soup.'

'Yes, sir. I left the notebook with some other things on the table in the police canteen, sir. The book must have been open, I must have left it when I went to get another cup of tea. There was a bit of high-jinks going on among the other officers. They were throwing things.'

'Like soup.'

'Including that, sir. Mushroom soup. When I got back to my table after a few minutes there was a big blob of mushroom soup right on the page. When I managed to get it off, the page was all messed up and the writing just about wiped out.' I felt sorry for him.

'So you have no correct record of what the accused said at the time, on that evening?'

'No, sir. Except she said: "Look what I have done." ' He sagged with defeat. 'Or words to that effect, like I say.'

'No further questions,' said Mr Fellows and sat down softly.

38

On the morning that I was to begin my evidence there was a palpable feeling of excitement and anticipation about the court. Even in the prison van the woman escort only completed a few rows of her knitting. 'They're all waiting to hear what you've got to say,' she said.

'So am I,' I told her dismally. As usual, I was eyeing the streets through the iron mesh and windows of my moving cell. It might be my last chance to see people freely going about their ordinary day. It was dull with a smattering of rain on the shop windows. 'It will be all right,' she said as though she had secret informants. Carefully she picked up a dropped stitch. She did not seem to realise my predicament. Perhaps *I* had scarcely realised it until now, now that everything was closing in. But then why should she care? She was like the people in the streets outside the van, what did they care about it? They probably did not even *know* about it. They would have been astonished if the wall of the van had suddenly become transparent and they could see me staring out at them so enviously. When I was taken off to gaol for several years Mr Fellows and the nice other barrister, Mr Franks, Mr Spelling, the judge, the jury and everybody else would just carry on with their lives, turn to other things.

The van bumped a little, stopped at traffic lights, then

moved again. I could see two women who had paused while walking their dogs, the owners conversing, the dogs smelling each other. Music was coming from somewhere and three children looked in a shop front. Then the scene was changed and blank, grey walls filled the window.

'We're here,' my escort said brightly. She looked through her own window. 'Big crowd. And the Press. Lots of photographers. Do you want the coat over your head?'

'No, thanks. It makes me claustrophobic.'

'No,' she agreed. 'You don't want to feel like that. Not until you have to.'

When I walked the few feet from the dock to the witness-box that morning I felt and heard the atmosphere in the courtroom change. While before I had been isolated, hardly part of the proceedings, I was now stepping into the very centre of the stage. The single beam of light shone down like an accusation. The men who had been discussing me so deeply with hardly a glance in my direction now turned their eyes towards me. I felt Mr Sankey's face fix me every pace I walked, my QC smiled like a fat boy, and the other barristers beside each man studied me as if for further reference. The jury sat motionless, one stare between them, the journalists sucked their pens and pencils, and the public gallery which, since it was perched directly over the dock, I had not seen before, was crammed with faces like coins, leaning dangerously to get a better view. I knew this was my moment.

I stood in the witness-box, to the left of the judge and facing the jury. A woman had her fingers hooked over what I realised was a shorthand machine. I caught her eye and she seemed to be suppressing an encouraging smile. I took the oath in the best voice I could muster. Mr Fellows took me through my evidence so carefully it was like a girl being questioned by a kindly schoolteacher. It was slow, so slow the court seemed to be in suspense, the faces set, the eyes blank, movements deliberate. As I stood in the witness-box I noticed one of the jurors scratching his elbow. He did it every fifteen minutes or so as the long time went by.

It was a long time too. What had seemed to me a simple and tragic story had so many details which had never occurred to me before. Everything had to be spelled out, repeated, made clear; times and places, people, what they did, what they said, incidents that seemed to me to have no bearing on the serious matter before us.

After two hours I felt drained. They brought me a glass of water, so warm it was scarcely refreshing. Mr Fellows eyed me with quiet encouragement. He nodded towards Mr Sankey and secretly made a face. I suppressed a smile.

Mr Sankey uncoiled. For more than a minute he remained silent. Then he began, very carefully, very craftily, circling me. How long had I been employed by Sir Benedict and Lady Annabel? What were my duties? Why had I gone to work for them in the first place?

'I had nowhere else to go.'

'Nowhere?'

'I needed somewhere to live and I had no money.'

'So you turned up on their doorstep and they took you in.'

'I answered an advertisement and they gave me the job.' I saw my counsel's approving nod, but not looking at me, as if to himself.

'A domestic job?'

'Yes. As a housekeeper.'

'What sort of situation did you find yourself in, what sort of household was it?'

I told him. I described Sir Benedict and his tandem and his gentleness and then told him about Lady Annabel's spite and isolation.

'You did not like Lady Annabel?'

'She was difficult to like,' I said. 'But I did my best with her. I think she even liked me. She depended on me.'

'In what sorts of way?'

'There was nobody else to get her out of the bath.'

He looked as if he were not expecting that. A half-suppressed snigger came from somewhere and the judge looked up disapprovingly. Mr Sankey changed direction. 'But the old people did not get on together?'

'They lived separate lives. They even had Christmas dinner in separate rooms. But towards the end they seemed to make up in a way. They saw more of each other, started having lunch together and a glass of wine in the evenings.'

He sniffed, a sniff that travelled the length of his body. 'Towards the end, you say. What do you mean by that? Towards Lady Annabel's end, you mean?'

'Yes, sir.'

'Their relationship improved? Why do you think that was?'

'I don't know.'

He continued: 'Perhaps they both knew they had not long to live? They were elderly, and perhaps they were trying to get some pleasure out of what was left of their lives?' There was a pause. 'Or was there some other reason?'

My counsel got heavily to his feet. 'This is supposition,

my Lord,' he said. 'My client has said she does not know the reason.'

The judge nodded. He was keeping his nose pointing straight at me. His wig pushed out a little at the front and his eyes gleamed in the shadows.

'Right,' sighed Mr Sankey. 'You have no idea why the relationship between these two old people improved so noticeably and so suddenly, but it did. So much so that on October 31st last they arranged a birthday party for Sir Benedict at the Cliff Edge Hotel at St Bride's Head in Dorset. And they were both enthusiastic about this, looking forward to it.'

'They were, sir.'

'Who was in the party on that night?'

'Apart from Sir Benedict and Lady Annabel there was Mr and Mrs Branche, her ladyship's relatives from Africa, and several other people, old friends whose names I can't recall, and Mr Urchfont and myself.'

'You and Mr Urchfont – how did you feel about your employers?'

'I think we both felt, well, loyal to them. Very loyal. They would have been helpless without us. Towards the end especially.'

'Loyalty,' he mused. He was thoughtful as if trying to think what loyalty was.

During his questions his long body bent gradually forward until he had gone almost into a stoop but then he straightened himself. 'Which is presumably why, with Lady Annabel already gone, Sir Benedict left you both with a considerable legacy. In your case, fifty thousand pounds and in Mr Urchfont's case, a substantial pension.'

'I understand Sir Benedict did leave me a legacy of fifty thousand pounds.'

'That's a lot of money.'

'Yes. I think it is.'

'Right. Let us go back to the evening of October 31st last year at the Cliff Edge Hotel in Dorset. Why do you think Mr Urchfont and yourself were invited to his birthday dinner?'

'Sir Benedict wanted us to be there, and Lady Annabel apparently did too. It was partly in recognition, I suppose, of our service to them and partly so that we could assist them. It was difficult for them to manage by themselves.'

'And on that night of celebration, something very tragic occurred, did it not? Astonishingly, there had been another family tragedy many years before at the same hotel on the cliff top. On that occasion the first Lady Bowling, Lady Lucinda Bowling, died in a fall from the cliff. An open verdict was recorded at the inquest.' He suddenly turned on my counsel. 'None of that is in dispute, I take it.'

Mr Fellows acknowledged that none of it was. Like a bent stork, Mr Sankey revolved to me again. 'And on this October night the *very same tragedy was repeated*.' He studied me. 'Would you please describe what happened. What did you see?'

In the witness-box, under oath, I closed my eyes. 'I was in the ladies' room,' I said. 'And Urchfont came in and told me that the old couple were walking down the garden towards ... towards the cliff top.'

'Urchfont came into the ladies'?'

'Yes. He was very worried.'

'Why should he be worried? They were only going for a walk.'

'It was October and night-time.' I was aware my answer was hurried. 'And we knew the cliff top was in that direction.'

343

'But it was odd that they should do such a thing, wasn't it? It was very odd, bearing in mind the tragic memories of the place, that they had returned there *at all*, to the very hotel where Lady Lucinda Bowling had lost her life. Why did they go there?'

My counsel bounced up like a bright boy with the answer in class. 'This is asking my client things that she cannot know.'

The judge leaned from his perch. 'If Miss Smith wishes to answer she may do so.'

'I don't mind, my Lord,' I said. 'I believe the hotel had a lot of *happy* memories as well, family gatherings and suchlike.'

'Or perhaps a fatal fascination? Or a place for *justice*? For *revenge*?'

This time my man was on his feet angrily. Sankey backed down. 'Right, let us concentrate, in that case, on what you actually saw on the night. When Urchfont told you that these two old and eccentric people were off down the garden, what did you do?'

'I rushed down there.'

'Urchfont at your heels.'

'Well, no. Mr and Mrs Branche had somehow got behind a glass exit door that was locked and he went back to try and open it.' It was only a small lie. 'There were a lot of people crowding the place that night. It was Hallowe'en.'

'So you were alone going down the garden. Tell us what happened next.'

'I opened the gate at the bottom. There's a fence there to stop people straying too near the cliff and there's a gate in it. I went through that and saw Sir Benedict and Lady Annabel on the cliff top.'

'How far away would that be?'

'About a hundred yards, maybe a bit more.'

'And you could see them quite clearly?'

'Yes. It was a fine night and I could see them.'

'What were they doing?'

Now I had to tell lies.

'They were talking,' I said.

'Just talking. Conversing. On the cliff top. Weren't you worried, anxious?'

'Yes, sir. They were not all that rational, either of them, and I thought they might not realise where they were.'

'But ... this was the place – the very place – where Lady Lucinda, Lady Annabel's sister and Sir Benedict's first wife, had fallen to her death.'

'Forty years before,' I agreed. 'I know, but they were both slightly strange at times.'

'A bit gaga would you say?'

'I would say a bit strange.'

'Right. And then what happened?'

'I hurried towards them. I was very worried, not looking where I was going, and I tripped over something or other, a tuft of grass, and I fell forward onto my face. It knocked the breath out of me. When I was lying flat like that I heard a cry and then a shout.'

'Was it a female cry, Lady Annabel's perhaps, followed by Sir Benedict's shout?'

'Yes, sir. That's what I thought.'

'And then?'

'When I looked up Sir Benedict was alone on the cliff top. He shouted that Lady Annabel had gone over the cliff ... just like Lady Lucy.'

'Were those his words?'

The utter silence in the court was broken by some crows quarrelling outside the window. It was directly across the big room and I could see them flapping their black wings.

'Yes, sir,' I said. 'He said she'd gone over "just like Lucy".'

There was a long pause. He seemed to have bent lower as he questioned me. For a moment I hoped he had finished, but he had not. Eventually, he stretched his long body upwards again and peered towards me as if he were a bit surprised to see I was still waiting in the witness-box. Then he said: 'How would you describe your relationship with Sir Benedict Bowling?'

It took me off guard. 'My relationship? Well, I was his housekeeper.'

'You were fond of him?'

'I loved him,' I said bluntly. Why not tell them, I thought. 'He was the best man I have ever met.'

'This feeling extended beyond your duties as his house-keeper?'

'I cared for him very deeply. We used to play cards and I played the piano for him and sometimes we used to sing. And we used to go out on his tandem.'

'Sing? What did you sing?'

'We just used to have a singsong around the piano. I did most of the singing but he tried to join in. It cheered him up.'

'What did you call him? Sir Benedict?'

'Yes. Of course.'

'Never "Ben"?'

'Oh, no. I would never have done that. He was Sir Benedict to everyone.'

'Did you . . . did you, at any time, share his bed?'

I was so shocked I could scarcely get the answer out. I said eventually: 'I loved him dearly but it was not like that. He was an old man. He loved me too.'

'So you never entered his bed?'

Then I realised I had. 'Yes,' I said. 'I did once.'

Every eye in the court was on me. I could feel them stabbing me like points.

'When was that?' asked Mr Sankey slowly but eagerly. 'When did you enter his bed?'

I could feel my voice faltering. 'Not long before he died. He was in a terrible state. He was incontinent, he could hardly keep a mouthful of food down, hardly a sip of water. He was wasting away in front of my eyes. And he was in great pain.'

'When,' repeated Mr Sankey coldly, 'did you share his bed?'

'I was just telling you,' I replied looking straight at him. 'It was about a week before . . . he died. I had my door open so I could hear him and he was crying out. I heard him crying in the darkness.'

'For you?'

'He was just crying out. He'd fallen out of bed. Urchfont helped me put him back, then I cleaned him up a bit and tried to make him comfortable. He was crying with pain. I couldn't leave him, not like that. When Urchfont had gone I got into bed beside him and held his hand.'

Mr Sankey looked up at the ceiling. 'And that was the only time?'

'Yes, sir. The only time.'

'Did he say anything to you?'

'Not much. He thought I was his Lucy, Lady Lucinda.'

'Sir Benedict left you the bulk of his estate, did he not? It was only a small estate. Did you know that?'

'No, sir. I did not know how much he was worth.'

'Did you know that, with Lady Annabel gone, he was going to leave you the bulk of his money?'

'I did not know anything about that. I never discussed money with him.'

'Right.' I could not tell from his expression whether he thought he had won or lost. 'Now let us move to the events of the night of March 28th this year. The night Sir Benedict Bowling was ... met his death.'

It took more than another hour. He picked and probed. I told him what happened, he pulled it apart and kept asking questions, questions, questions. Just as I thought it would never end, it did. There was a long break and he said: 'Chloe Smith, now, this moment, tell the court why you murdered Sir Benedict Bowling that night.'

At last I broke. I began to cry. The court was swimming around me. He waited. Then he said: 'Will you answer the question.'

Everyone was watching me. I could see the judge leaning forward from above like an eagle in a tree. 'I did it because I *loved* him,' I said. My voice was wet and trembling. 'He asked me to do it and I did. I could not see someone I cared for so much go on suffering like that.'

'Thank you.'

39

Urchfont took my place in the witness-box. I was oddly surprised to see him, as though he had been produced by some trick, and he even looked different. He looked at me, back in my dock now, and gave me a hopeless smile. It seemed to say that everything had gone wrong, but that it was not his fault.

Mr Fellows led him through his evidence without any trouble or surprises, like someone leading an old obedient horse down a familiar way. In his best butler's voice Urchfont answered the questions.

Then Mr Sankey, slowly uncoiling, stood.

'Your name is James Henry Urchfont?'

'Yes, sir.'

'Is James Henry Urchfont your real ... your true name?'

'Yes ... no, sir.'

I stared at him from the dock. Another man, another liar.

'What is your true name?'

'James Henry Butler, sir.'

'Not Urchfont?'

'No, sir. Urchfont is just my professional name. I borrowed it from a village in Wiltshire, near Devizes.'

I still could scarcely believe what I was hearing. I had

known him two years. Everything in that court seemed to be altered, amended, stood on its head.

The prosecuting counsel seemed very pleased with himself.

Urchfont looked at the judge as though trying to get help but the judge was busily writing. 'Well, my name's really Butler, but I *am* a butler. It was embarrassing. You can't be a butler called Butler. It doesn't sound right, people would make jokes all the time.'

'I see. Was that the only reason you changed it?'

I could tell that Urchfont was gathering himself to lie. 'Yes, sir. There wasn't any other reason.'

'But you were also called Giles at one time, weren't you?'

Urchfont's eyelids dropped, concealing the bags under them. 'Yes, sir.'

'When was that?'

'About ten years ago.'

'Why did you change from Giles? Giles seems an appropriate name for a butler.'

'Yes, sir.' He had decided to come clean in the absence of any other course. 'It was because I worked for Sir Benedict and Lady Bowling once before.'

I felt my eyes widen.

'And when was that?'

'About twenty years ago. I was called Giles then.'

'Why did you leave on that first occasion?'

'There was a misunderstanding, sir. About a house-maid.'

'In what way was there a misunderstanding?'

By now I was leaning out of the dock as eager for the next word as anyone. I could hear people in the public gallery above me even if I could not see them. The judge and the clerks and my counsel and the Press were all writing like fury. Only one man in the jury – the older man who let his mouth sag – was not fixed on Urchfont and he seemed to have swallowed a sweet or something. His neighbour, still not taking his eyes away from the witness-box, patted him on the back while he coughed. Eventually he stopped and began quietly sucking the sweet again.

'The housemaid got pregnant, sir. I found myself in a difficult position. So did Florence. That was her name, Florence.'

'She was pregnant. And who was the father?'

'I was.'

The fact that Urchfont was capable of fathering a child had curiously never occurred to me before. He had always seemed such a one-man band.

'And you had to leave Sir Benedict.'

'Yes, sir. We went away together, Florence and I, but she left me in Shepherd's Bush.'

'I see. And some years after that parting in Shepherd's Bush you decided to try and get employment with Sir Benedict and Lady Bowling again. But you feared they would recognise you, or at least your name.'

'That's right, sir. That's why I changed it to Urchfont to get the job. It was about ten years after I left the first time with Flo. Our baby was stillborn.'

For the first time the prosecutor softened as though he had known the same loss. 'That was sad.'

'Very sad for me, sir. Everything ended.'

'So ten years after your first employment you went back under the name of Urchfont and were accepted for work with them again. And they did not recognise you.'

'They did not seem to, sir. Some upper-class people hardly ever recognise their servants, even when they're actually working for them. They wouldn't recognise them in the street, out of the house. And this was after years. I did think of going in disguise, like growing whiskers or something, but butlers don't have whiskers generally. They get in the way.'

'Of the work?'

'Yes.'

'But anyway you returned to work for the Bowlings under false pretences.'

Urchfont appeared embarrassed. His pale face coloured a touch under the light. 'Yes, I suppose you could put it like that.'

'I do. You went under false pretences. You were acting out a dishonesty. Why did you need to go back to this couple? Are there not plenty of jobs for butlers, even if they are called Butler?' There was a brief smirk around the court but the judge looked up like a warning and the lawyer put his wig straight and continued. 'Why did you go back to them?'

'I liked the old man, sir.'

'They were both getting elderly and they were both eccentric?'

'Yes, sir. There's no doubt about that.'

'Also they had poor memories. For a start they failed to recognise you.'

'Some things they remembered but not others.'

'And they had no relatives?'

'Not that I knew of. Then the people from Africa turned up, the Orange Tree people.'

'Ah, Mr and Mrs Branche, you mean. From Orange Free State, I think you intended to say.'

'That's them, sir.'

'Did you think, Mr Butler, Giles, Urchfont, that there might be an opportunity to gain something, by a legacy perhaps?'

My counsel stood up, his face flushed pink. 'I must object to this line of questioning, my Lord.' He sat down. I was pleased he was paying attention. The judge waved his pen at the prosecutor who bowed in his direction and then turned to the easier meat in the witness-box. 'Mr Urchfont. I think we will keep to that name although it is not strictly correct. Mr Urchfont, how were your feelings towards the lady accused in the dock here today, Chloe Smith?'

'I loved her, sir. I loved her very deeply.'

I started to stand and almost fell out of the dock. I tried to say something but my counsel half-waved a paper at me. Weakly I sat down on the hard seat.

'She was the second love you had harboured under that same roof? First there was the housemaid Florence, who had a baby, and then, years later, Chloe Smith.'

'Yes sir, I suppose so. But I never told Chloe, I never made my feelings plain to her. I was dreading her laughing at me. But I loved her every day. I used to think that eventually we might settle down together somewhere and have a happy life, what was left of it.'

By now I had my head in my hands.

'This,' said Mr Sankey, 'is a very touching picture you paint. Is it not closer to the truth that perhaps Chloe Smith was well aware of your feelings and indeed returned them . . .'

'No!' I shouted from the dock. 'No. That's not true!'

Everybody looked at me now, all at once, all together for the first time. The judge frowned. Mr Sankey looked venomously in my direction but then returned to Urchfont. 'I suggest, Mr Butler . . .'

'Urchfont, sir,' Urchfont reminded him. 'I understood we'd settled on Urchfont.'

I very nearly cheered.

'Yes, we did,' murmured the counsel in his nastiest tone. 'Eventually. All right, Mr Urchfont, I suggest that you were mutually aware of each other's feelings and that you hoped to provide for this future of your dreams by being the recipients of whatever money the Bowlings could be persuaded to leave to you, remembering they had no other relatives. You had talked about it, even plotted it perhaps . . .'

My counsel was on his feet again. Angrily this time. His pink cheeks quivered. He spluttered horribly and the judge peered over his glasses and said: 'This line of questioning must be discontinued Mr Sankey.'

The barrister bowed like a thin tree in the wind. He returned to Urchfont. 'Perhaps we could now move on to the night Sir Benedict passed away . . . rather suddenly,' he said. 'You recall that night?'

Urchfont seemed astonished at the question. 'Yes, sir. Of course I do. I'm not likely to forget it.'

'Where were you?'

'Out. I went to the pictures. I'd already seen the film but I went anyway.'

Mr Sankey gave a start like a fisherman with a bite. 'Oh? And why did you see the film twice? Were the two occasions close together?'

'The day before.'

'The day before? You enjoyed the film that much?'

'Hated it, sir. *Remains of the Day*. About a butler.'

'But you went a second time? Why was that?'

'Chloe suggested I went out,' said Urchfont. 'And I wanted to anyway.'

'She wanted you out of the house?'

'I wanted to go. I could see the old man, Sir Benedict, was in a terrible state. In agony. Dying.'

'So you left?'

'I would have stayed if she'd wanted but I was glad when Chloe told me to go.'

'Why do you think she wanted you out of the way?'

'Objection,' said my counsel. 'This witness cannot know the defendant's thoughts.'

'Upheld,' said the judge grumpily. But it sounded as if he wanted to hear the answer.

Mr Sankey said: 'She did not say why she wanted you to go from the house? What she had in mind to do that evening?'

'No, sir. But I could see what the situation was. They were sitting by the piano and he was in terrible pain. And despair. He didn't want to live, sir.'

'Now it's my turn to object,' said the prosecution sharply. 'You cannot know what Sir Benedict wanted or did not want.'

'I could see,' said Urchfont stoutly. I was glad to realise that he was really into it now, much firmer, less servile, less willing to accept the bullying.

'So you left the house. You went to see this film you hated so much and then you returned.'

'Yes. I went to the New Inn and had a drink before going back.'

'Was that your habit?'

'Yes, I'd usually go in for one.'

'You didn't go in there because you were reluctant to return to the house? In case of what you might find there?'

'I'd usually go in for one,' repeated Urchfont doggedly.

'And then you went back ... home. What time was that?'

Curiously, Urchfont looked at his watch. 'About eleven, eleven thirty, sir.'

'And you went into the house. You let yourself in with your own key.'

'Yes sir. At the back, the rear door.'

'And what did you find? Describe the scene.'

'Terrible,' said Urchfont.

'Describe it.'

'I went into the drawing-room and I saw Chloe sitting on the sofa holding Sir Benedict. His head was hung back. She had her arms around him. He was dead.' Briefly, Urchfont looked towards me. 'She was in a state,' he said. 'She had been crying. The old man's cheeks were still wet. When she saw me she burst out crying again and I joined in. It was a terrible moment. She told me to call the police.'

'Did she say anything else?'

'Yes, sir. She was crying and she called out: "Oh, Urchfont, what will I do?" And I said: "About ten years."' He looked around the court in a shamefaced way and then looked at me. His eyes were streaming. 'But I only meant it as a joke,' he said.

40

There were eight courts in that building. Mine was only one of the dramas. In the lunch interval I heard the staff gossiping. 'That was a juicy one. He didn't look the type, did he?' 'Poor woman, just led astray.' 'He'll go down for a long time.' Eight stories being wrangled out under one roof. There was pie and peas and chips for lunch. They said all the prisoners got the same.

'You did very well, Chloe,' said Mr Spelling. 'You didn't let him bully you.'

Mr Fellows came in with Mr Franks. 'Now it's our turn,' he said.

I found a smile for him. 'Did you have a good lunch?' I asked.

'Not very,' he said. His puffy face looked downcast. 'In fact, not any. I've been walking and thinking. We both have.' He glanced towards Mr Franks.

'It doesn't look good, does it?' I said.

'Not exceptionally good,' said Mr Fellows. We all sat despondently. Then he said slowly: 'When you sang with Sir Benedict – on that last night – describe the scene again to me.'

'Well . . .' I hesitated. 'It was more or less the same as the other times. We quite often sang, especially when Lady Annabel was gone. We would sit by the piano and I would play and sing and Sir Benedict would join in as best he could.'

'Just the two of you at the piano. Singing.'

'Yes.'

'You told me you sang some of the old songs with him,' put in Mr Spelling. 'The songs you had learned from your father.'

'What has this got to do with it?' I asked quietly. I thought they were clutching at straws.

Mr Fellows held up his fleshy hand. 'It gives an insight into your relationship,' he said. 'And it was just old songs you sang? I don't suppose a man of eighty-five would know anything in the Top Twenty.'

I said: 'We used to sing one song, a pop song he liked.'

He looked up carefully. 'And what was that?'

Mr Fellows stood in court. 'My Lord,' he said, 'members of the jury. There is one matter I propose to raise in re-examination of the defendant.'

The judge raised his eyebrow a little, then nodded. Mr Sankey looked concerned. I walked to the witness-box again and took the oath.

'You mentioned in your cross-examination, Miss Smith, that you and Sir Benedict quite often sang at the piano. You played and you both sang.'

'Yes, sir. We did.'

'What did you sing on that last tragic evening?'

'The same as usual, I suppose. He always asked for the same pieces, the same songs. Some of them were very old but I knew them because my father used to play them and we used to sing.'

'And on that last evening you played and Sir Benedict listened.'

'Mostly. He was too weak to do anything else. He sat

in the chair, white as a ghost, wasted, and listened. He did try to sing with me especially for one song. He liked it. It was his favourite. We used to sing it together when he could sing. He used to call it after me.'

'What did he call it?'

'Chloe's Song,' I whispered. I had to whisper because it was all getting too much for me. I could see him now, trying to sing, howling in his efforts. His old red mouth open, his bad eye blank, his good eye bulging, his skin dying on his face. Oh, God.

'Is that an old song?' asked Mr Fellows gently. 'Like the others?'

'No. It's quite modern. It's just a pop song. But he liked it. He liked to try and sing it with me.'

'And he sang it with you on this last evening.'

I thought I was going to burst into weeping. He nodded at me, telling me to be strong. 'Yes,' I said. 'As best he could.'

'Will you sing it to us now, Miss Smith?'

My hands went to my mouth. I heard the amazement go around the court. All those faces. All those eyes. The jury, the Press, the people in the public gallery all leaned forward. The judge started forward and I thought he was going to object.

Mr Fellows fixed him. 'This, my Lord, is highly unusual. I am aware of that. But it is a matter of unusual importance.'

The judge was still unsure. But then he said: 'Proceed.'

'Now?' I asked stupidly.

'Yes, now please. Sing Chloe's Song.'

I tried. Like poor howling Sir Benedict that night I could not get beyond the first two lines. But I tried. I had two false starts. 'You . . . you make me . . .' Mr Fellows was encouraging me, his hands waving slightly, like a vague conductor. 'You ... you make me ...' I tried again. I made myself stop crying; this time I did it.

'You ... you make me feel brand new ...
I sing this song for you ...'

It was impossible. I could not go on. In the witness-box I crumpled and broke down again. There was a deep silence. Then I heard a sob. I looked up to see startled faces and glistening eyes. The judge was apparently attracted by pigeons outside the window.

Mr Fellows said: 'Thank you, Miss Smith. That will be enough.'

In his summing-up the judge said that he had never before heard anyone sing in court. 'It was highly irregular but, as everyone who witnessed it will remember, a most emotivemoment and one which told us more about Chloe Smith and her relationship with this sad and dying old man than all the evidence in the world could have done.'

I was back in my enclosed place, the dock (well named too, I had begun to realise, for it was like a haven). This morning all the faces appeared new and shining. The end of the ordeal was in sight. Mr Fellows was rounder and rosier than ever, fresh, by the look of him, from a large breakfast; Mr Spelling and Mr Franks were cheerfully tidying up thick papers. Mr Sankey sat looking steadily at me as if he did not quite believe what he was seeing.

'But that moment notwithstanding,' the judge continued, 'it must be made plain that to take a human life, no matter what the situation and the circumstances, is outside the law. Whatever the motives, the killing of another deliberately, as this was, remains the most serious offence.'

It was difficult to know to whom he was speaking. He certainly never looked at me. 'I can only reject, and I hope the jury will reject, the prosecution's suggestion, and it was only a suggestion, that there might possibly have been another motive for the killing of Sir Benedict Bowling – that the accused had some financial gain in mind when she put that blue cushion over the old man's face.

'Nor was I impressed with the police handling of the case. The defacing of a constable's notebook in the police canteen and the fact that the wrong cushion, even the wrong *colour* cushion, was produced as an exhibit, indicates that there was much to be desired in the police work.'

He said a great many other things but I cannot remember them. The jury were only retired for an hour and ten minutes.

It was so odd because it was so familiar. Anyone in the court who had ever watched television knew the ritual.

'Members of the jury, have you reached a verdict on which you are all agreed?'

'Yes, my Lord.'

'Do you find the defendant guilty or not guilty of murder?'

'Not guilty of murder. Guilty of manslaughter.'

All around me there was pandemonium. People, unseen in the gallery above me, were sobbing and cheering. It was several minutes before order was restored.

My sentence – and the judge's voice sounded to me like angels singing – was three years suspended. I promised I would never do it again.

People started cheering again in the public gallery, the judge disappeared quite briskly as though he had to post his letters, the four counsel shook hands and I felt a hand on my elbow and was led from the dock. It was as much as I could do to leave it. I dragged myself out, shaking at the knees, and Mr Fellows, Mr Franks and Mr Spelling closed around me and hurried me, as if I were under arrest, to a side door.

Ten minutes later I was out in the open air. After the indoors, it felt fresh and strange. It was a pale summer afternoon and I could hear the city clocks chiming to welcome me back. We went out into an empty courtyard, the back way away from the crowds. There was a police car parked on the far side and in front of it another car. And standing by the second car was a figure I would have known anywhere in the world, although I had not seen him for so long. Donny.

41

I stood transfixed. I could see his smile even from a distance. A hand on my elbow brought me out of my trance. At first, I thought it was Mr Spelling but then I saw that the solicitor was hovering protectively a pace behind me. It was Ron Brown. We stood on the steps and Donny was at the far end of the courtyard just as though we had been arranged by a director on a stage. A tardy clock was chiming in the city but the only other sounds were the afternoon birds.

'The car is Donny's,' said Ron in his practical way. 'You ought to clear out of here now. We can close this yard off, but not the street. There'll be a crowd out there when they realise you're not going out of the front. And the Press.'

As I walked towards Donny, Ron said: 'We'll lead you out of town.'

Donny was walking slowly towards me as well. I went at the same pace to him. After all this time it seemed the best way to meet. But Ron Brown was moving sharply towards the police car and both Donny and I quickened our strides and ended up running towards each other. I pulled him into my arms. He felt like his father. He kissed me but then said: 'The man says we've got to move.' He took my hand and we hurried towards the car. It was like a getaway – I suppose it was in a way.

Falling into the seat beside him I more or less gasped: 'I can't believe all this is happening. I just can't.'

He started the engine as he turned and grinned at me. God, he looked just like Zane. Even in my excitement and the confusion I had a quick fear that he would be like Zane too.

I hung onto his arm as he drove. 'Oh, Donny, where have you been?'

'For the last three days I've been just over your head.' He laughed. 'In the public gallery.'

'Oh. And I couldn't see you.'

'I couldn't see you either. Except when you were giving evidence.' The police car was still behind us. It was like an unhurried chase. At the outskirts of the city it peeled away. Briefly I saw Ron Brown's face in the back. I waved and wondered if I would ever see him again.

'Where are we going, Donny?'

'Not far. Somewhere we can talk.' He paused. 'When you sang in the witness-box, that was terrific. Not a dry bloody eye. I thought: "That's my mum." '

'What would have happened if I'd been found guilty? With you, I mean.'

'I knew you wouldn't be,' he said simply.

There was so much to say, years of it, and yet we were suddenly caught by a silence. 'You always sent me a pebble,' I said eventually.

He turned the car into the drive of a stony country hotel. The garden was full of sunlight. 'The pebbles,' he said. 'Yes. That has to be explained.'

They were expecting us and we quickly found ourselves in a sitting-room with a vision of England outside its window, rounded fields and shadows, exploding summer trees and sedate clouds. Just to see it was joy enough. But to be there with *Donny* . . .

They knew who we were and why we were there and the manager had sent a bottle of champagne, but we had a tray of tea first. It was delicious. I was free.

'You got the pebbles then?' asked Donny.

'Yes. I used to look forward to them. I always hoped there would be a note.'

'Sorry,' he smiled.

'They always arrived at Mr Pyecraft's,' I said. 'And when I left for London he would send them on to me when he knew where I was. When he retired the new people used to keep them and I would pick them up when I went to Southampton. Sometimes I went specially for them.'

'Mr Pyecraft . . .' he smiled again.

'He came to see me before I went for trial, when I was in Salisbury Court, and he brought me some pebbles then, just a couple. He said he'd been to the shop and collected them.' I paused. 'He told me he'd always wanted to marry me.'

To my surprise Donny said: 'I knew. He asked me to ask you once. When I was a little kid. But I forgot.' He drank from his glass. 'I have to tell you, Mum, I did not send the pebbles myself. I knew people who were always travelling and I gave them the pebbles to post. It's amazing they all got there.'

Another of my dreams slid away. 'Where were you?' I asked.

'In Spain, mostly.'

'Why did you go off like that?'

'Rosa left me some money, you know.'

He could see I was astounded. 'She did?'

'One thousand and fifty pounds,' he said. 'It was in a deposit account in Birmingham of all places. A solicitor sent me the bank book and that's how much was left in it.'

'Left in it?' It was already dawning.

'There had been about five thousand quid but over the years she had been drawing on it. She said it had been left by my grandfather.'

'I wondered where the money went.'

'Well, there it was. Over a thousand. That's when I thought I would quit the army and travel.'

I still could scarcely believe it. I began to laugh.

He said: 'I went off first of all because I had big ideas of working with my dad. I thought he was terrific. *Then* I did. I changed my mind later. He got me into all sorts of things in Spain over the years and I even came back to this country. We went to the shop in Southampton where you used to work.'

'I know,' I said, suddenly dismal. 'He stole some jewellery from there. He bounced a cheque.'

'It wasn't the first or the last,' said Donny. 'I was going that way too. Then *he* saved me from it. He double-crossed me. Me, his son. He set me up and got away himself.'

'What were you up to?'

'It hardly matters, Mum. It was no good, I can tell you. He just cleared out and left me in it. Or that was his intention. But I had some luck and I got away. The police didn't sniff me.'

'You're on the run then, Donny.'

He seemed surprised by the truth. 'Yes, I suppose I am really. But it was a couple of years ago.'

'Where have you been since?'

'Living a new life, you'd call it. Up in the mountains in the south. It's the wettest place in Spain, the rain in Spain is right there. It's a wonderful wild place, great for growing vegetables.'

'You grow vegetables?'

'My father-in-law does. I help him.'

I was shocked. 'Donny, you're married?'

'Married. And I've got a baby, a daughter. My wife is called Pilar.'

'Oh God, I'm a granny!'

He laughed. A waiter put his head around the door and asked if we would like some more tea. Donny suggested he should open the champagne instead. While he did we sat silently holding hands. When the man had gone, Donny said: 'I live safe up there. I don't need to run. We've got eighty hectares, cabbages, sprouts, beans, everything.'

'I always wanted a man who had an allotment,' I said.

We talked until nine thirty. And then we stopped. It was amazing but, after all the years, we could find nothing more to say. There did not seem to be anything. As the light drifted from the fields and we finished the meal they had brought us, we ran out of conversation. It had all been covered. Donny stood and said he had to go. I was astonished. 'I've got to get the ferry,' he said. 'I'm driving back.'

'To Spain?' I sat gazing at the table. I picked up my glass but it was empty. He leaned across me and poured out the last of the wine. 'Yes,' he said. 'That's where I live.'

When he had kissed me and gone I stood alone against the window and watched the summer dusk across the countryside. He was right, of course. Things had moved on. Now, today, was not yesterday. I was free. So was he. The boy I knew and had lost was gone for ever. I had missed him, mislaid him more like. This was Donny as he really was.

I wondered what his wife was like, Pilar. I tried to picture my grandchild. But I knew now that when I had allowed him to go that time years before, when he was only a boy, when I let him slip through my fingers so carelessly, that was as final as anything could be. The same child would never come back. From now on we would each know where the other was. But that was as far as it went.

I stayed the night, waking and thinking and sleeping again, and left the following morning. Donny had settled the bill. His father would have left it for me.

It was not until I got into the taxi that clear blue morning that I realised I had nowhere to go. I had made no preparations, having confidently expected to be behind bars. Now, here I was, free to take myself anywhere (Mr Spelling had told me to call him when I felt ready) and thanks to Sir Benedict I even had the money to do it, but I could not think of anywhere I wanted to go; anywhere that would be right; anywhere that would accept me. Sitting in the back of the taxi I found myself shaking my head. 'Where was it?' asked the driver patiently.

Was it. That was the right phrase. My life was somewhere in the past. 'Salisbury,' I told him eventually. It was more like a suggestion. 'Take me to Salisbury.'

Even when we got there I did not know where to go, or whether it was the right place for me. I had a single overnight bag with me, the only thing I had brought from the prison. It was like the day I had arrived on the train. I walked through the old streets and eventually under the familiar arch and into the cathedral close. It had not occurred to me that anyone would notice me, that anyone would know my face, but it gradually dawned on me that I was a curiosity; I had been in the newspapers, on television, and people were staring. I turned away and hurried towards the house.

It looked the same although it was now empty, awaiting a new owner: the windows were blank, the door looked as though it had never been opened. There was no sign of anyone there so I pushed the gate and walked around the side wall and through the door into the garden.

It had always been a touch wild – Sir Benedict had enjoyed its mystery – but now it was rapidly overgrowing. The grass was knee high and wet, the trees bent almost to the grass as though under some sorrow, the flowers bright and brave but being choked by weeds. All the fish had gone from the pond. It was now just an oblong hole filled with grubby water. Wrily I wondered if Mr and Mrs Branche had taken them back to the Orange Free State.

I must have looked odd traipsing through the thick garden in that way, like some woman in one of those ghostly Victorian scenes. But no one could see me. I surveyed the dumb back of the house and remembered him, and indeed her, and felt myself give a sad smile. Again, as with Donny, things had changed and moved on. They were not there any more. Only I was.

Going up the stone steps at the back I pushed aside a rose bramble and looked with a sort of nervousness through the dusty glass. I rubbed some of the outside grit away and looked again. It was all empty, not a piece of furniture, not a lamp, not a picture on the wall, it was just a room. I wondered who, if anybody, had bought the sofa where it had happened.

It was no use remaining. All that was vanished now. I could feel the morning sunshine on the nape of my neck.

It was streaming through the apple branches. I went carefully, as I had always done, down the cracked steps and left the way I had gone in.

I closed the iron gate at the front deliberately so that it did not creak. In front of me the grass spread to the cathedral door. There were plenty of tourists that bright morning and once someone had spotted me, others began to. Some even pointed. I was the woman who had got away with murder. Everywhere I turned there seemed to be faces. I went into the cathedral and I heard a girl's piping voice shout: 'She's gone in to pray, Mum.'

In there at least nobody recognised me. It was shaded and quiet and in cathedrals few people look directly at anyone else. I sat in the middle of the ranks of chairs and looked at nothing in particular. Whether I was seeking inspiration or not, it suddenly arrived. A soft, friendly-looking woman came and sat almost beside me, one chair away. I tried not to look at her but she said: 'Do you mind if I call you Chloe? I can't remember your other name.'

'Smith,' I said.

She laughed quietly. 'Fancy forgetting that.' She looked faintly familiar and she asked me if I remembered her. 'We went to school together,' she said. 'You were in the class above me. I'm Mrs Faulkner now. Would you like to come and stay with us?'

Spire House was almost opposite the St Ann's Gate of the close. The Faulkners took paying guests and they let me have their first-floor front room with its bay window overlooking the street, the grey, high wall and beyond that the fine bulk of the cathedral itself. A vision of the tallest spire in England filled the window. 'Nobody will bother you here,' said Mrs Faulkner. 'You'll be quite safe.'

For a week I scarcely left that room, only sat in the window trying to think, trying not to think, doing neither. They brought my meals up to me but otherwise left me alone. I was grateful.

Then I decided to go and retrieve the tandem. I went down to the coast by bus, sitting in the back seat and gazing resolutely through the window. The woman we had left it with was busy in her refreshment kiosk. She had moved the tandem to a rough boat shed and a boy took me there and opened the door. 'That's a funny bike, missus,' he said as I wheeled it squeakily out into the sunshine, feeling its familiar frame again after all that had happened.

'It's for two people,' I explained. 'One at the front, one at the back.'

'Who's going to ride it with you then?'

'I don't know. Someone may turn up.'

At that moment he did. Detective Sergeant Ron Brown, strolling towards us from the kiosk. His face was tanned and he was wearing a short-sleeved shirt. I had never seen his arms before.

'On holiday,' he said before I had a chance to ask. 'Retirement leave really.' He made a grimace. 'Early retirement.'

'Do you always come here for your holidays?'

'Not as a regular thing. But I called in at Spire House and the lady said you had gone to fetch the tandem. I remembered you saying where you'd left it.' I was still holding the machine. He studied it. 'In quite good nick, really.'

'It squeaks,' I said. 'Who told you where I was living?'

'Your solicitor, Mr Spelling,' he said. 'Nice bloke. I

told him it was police business, just clearing up the bits and bobs.'

'What are they?' He took the tandem from me and we began to walk back towards the kiosk and the beach. The squeaking diminished as the wheels went around.

'The bits and bobs? Well, not much really. But I've got to do a final report. It *is* final too.'

'They've sacked you.'

He only repeated: 'Early retirement.' He asked if I wanted a cup of tea and he went to the kiosk leaving me sitting on the seat where Sir Benedict and I had sat. I kept my face towards the sea, just gazed at it. Something was happening to me again. He returned with the teas. 'You take sugar, don't you?' he said.

'One.'

He sat beside me. 'Yes, early retirement, they call it. You don't get the sack these days even for messing things up like I did.'

'The cushion and the constable's notebook?' I said. 'You didn't have anything to do with that, did you?'

'What?'

'The cushion and the notebook.'

'Tampering with evidence?' He whistled. 'Now would I?'

He turned towards the sea shaking his head. 'I can't understand how things like that happen. What a way to run a police force.' He paused. 'And it didn't help when my informal visits to you in prison came to light. But it doesn't matter now, I'm glad to be out. A bit like you, I should imagine.'

We finished the tea. He asked if I would like another cup and I offered to get it this time. The lady in the kiosk looked at the two cups, peered across to Ron, and said: 'The bike's all right, is it?' I thanked her and said it was.

372

When I paid for the tea I gave her another ten pounds for looking after it for longer than she had expected. She looked pleased and said: 'I thought you was never coming back.'

I returned to the bench. 'One sugar for you too,' I said. He put the lump in and stirred the tea. 'Donny's gone back, is he?' he said casually.

'He went that same night. It was you who found him, wasn't it.'

'It wasn't difficult. Not in Spain.'

'Was he wanted by the police?'

'No, no. They had nothing on him. But a foreigner's quite simple to find in Spain. It's getting them out is difficult. Anyway his wife's five brothers are all coppers.'

'He didn't tell me that.'

'He probably will next time.' He appeared to be wondering whether to say something further. He did. 'Your Zane is back.'

'Zane? He's not *my* Zane.'

'Well, he's back. He's in Winchester.'

'In the prison.' It was not a question.

'Yes. He's got ten years this time. I'll take you there tomorrow if you like. If you want to.'

I almost refused. But then I said: 'All right. We'll go tomorrow.'

He put his hands on the tandem. 'Always fancied riding one of these,' he said.

'Want to try?'

'Why not. Shall I get on the front?'

'You'd better.' I smiled. 'I'd like to keep an eye on you.'

42

I swear it was the same man in the prison gatehouse, the one who had been there when I waited for Zane all those years before only to find and he had already gone. Perhaps they kept the guards even longer than the inmates. Zane seemed only mildly glad to see me and only mildly surprised that I had turned up. But he soon began to mumble and cry. 'You're the only decent thing that ever happened to me, Chloe,' he said. 'My true, dear wife.'

He did not seem to know that I had been on a murder charge, or he had forgotten. I did not mention it. 'I want you to wait for me,' he said. 'Please, Chloe.'

'I waited for you before,' I pointed out. He looked a bit rusty at the edges now, his eyes dark ringed and furtive, his hair sparse and greying.

'That was all a mistake, I told you.' His head went into his hands and he began to sob. 'I'll be out of here in six years and forty-three days if I behave. We could start again. Have another cottage in the forest.' He looked up wet-faced, but as though an inspiration had struck him. 'Have another Donny.'

I left him and walked out into the reception area. There was a toilet there and I went into it to dab my eyes, then went out into the bare room again. There were rows of seats for waiting visitors. A blonde girl, in her twenties, was sitting there. In her hand she had a copy of *Gone with the Wind*.

'I'm a bit early,' she said to me. I sat next to her. There was no one else in the area except the security guard at his elevated desk. 'I don't like to miss a minute.'

'Is that for him?' I asked nodding at the book although I already knew.

'Yes, for Zane,' she said. 'My fiancé. He's always wanted to read it and now's his chance.'

I leaned over and took it from her. 'It's years since I read this,' I said. I ran my eyes over the first paragraph and then, after one thousand and eleven pages, the last.

'He'll be a long time,' she sighed. 'And all for something he didn't do. He swore to me on his mother's life that he didn't. He was set up. But everybody's against him, my Zane. See this.' She pointed to the end words of the book. 'I like the last bit. Where she says: "After all, tomorrow is another day." I reckon that's inspiring, that is.'

'He's your fiancé, you said?'

'Yes.' She showed me her ring. I wondered where he had got that. 'He loves me deeply and though he's older I love him. Some day we'll be together.' She opened her blouse at the neck. She had the usual gold chain, this one with the name 'Alison'. She said: 'I've got this as well.'

I stood up and patted the book. 'Good luck,' I said. 'With Zane.'

Outside the gaol it was a bright day and the hill was busy with cars. One went by with the driver singing like mad to the radio. His wife was singing too and so were three children in the back seat. On the roof was a red, white and blue inflatable dinghy. Ron saw me come out and pulled over to the pavement. 'All right?' he said as I got in.

'I'm fine,' I said truthfully.

'And how was Zane?'

I leaned across and kissed him on the cheek. 'Frankly, my dear, I don't give a damn,' I said.